KU-452-147

# SCARRED

A Never After Novel

## EMILY MCINTIRE

B*loom* books

Copyright © 2021, 2022 by Emily McIntire
Cover and internal design © 2022 by Sourcebooks
Cover design by Cat/TRC Designs
Cover images © AntonMatukha/DepositPhotos, Rastan/DepositPhotos,
rehanalisoomro10/DepositPhotos, tanantornanut/DepositPhotos,
Cassandra Madsen/Shutterstock, P Maxwell Photography/Shutterstock
Internal design by Ashley Holstrom/Sourcebooks

Sourcebooks and the colophon are registered trademarks of
Sourcebooks. Bloom Books is a trademark of Sourcebooks.

All rights reserved. No part of this book may be reproduced in any form or by
any electronic or mechanical means including information storage and retrieval
systems—except in the case of brief quotations embodied in critical articles or
reviews—without permission in writing from its publisher, Sourcebooks.

The characters and events portrayed in this book are fictitious or
are used fictitiously. Any similarity to real persons, living or dead,
is purely coincidental and not intended by the author.

All brand names and product names used in this book are trademarks,
registered trademarks, or trade names of their respective holders.
Sourcebooks is not associated with any product or vendor in this book.

Published by Bloom Books, an imprint of Sourcebooks
P.O. Box 4410, Naperville, Illinois 60567-4410
(630) 961-3900
sourcebooks.com

Originally self-published in 2021 by Emily McIntire.

Cataloging-in-Publication Data is on file with the Library of Congress.

Manufactured in the UK by Clays and distributed
by Dorling Kindersley Limited, London
10 9 8 7 6 5
005-336055-Nov/22

# *Playlist*

"you should see me in a crown"—Billie Eilish

"lovely"—Billie Eilish and Khalid

"Sucker for Pain"—Lil Wayne, Wiz Khalifa,
Imagine Dragons, X Ambassadors, Logic, Ty Dolla $ign

"Human"—Christina Perri

"Million Reasons"—Lady Gaga

"Take Me to Church"—Hozier

"Mad World"—Demi Lovato

"Everybody Wants to Rule the World"—Lorde

"Play with Fire"—Sam Tinnesz ft. Yacht Money

"This Is Me"—Keala Settle and *The Greatest Showman*
ensemble

*For the freaks.*
*The misfits.*
*The bullied.*
*The loners.*
*The insecure.*
*The damaged.*
*You are worthy. You are warriors.*

"Doubt thou the stars are fire; Doubt that the sun doth move; Doubt truth to be a liar; But never doubt I love."
—William Shakespeare, *Hamlet*

GLORIA TERRA

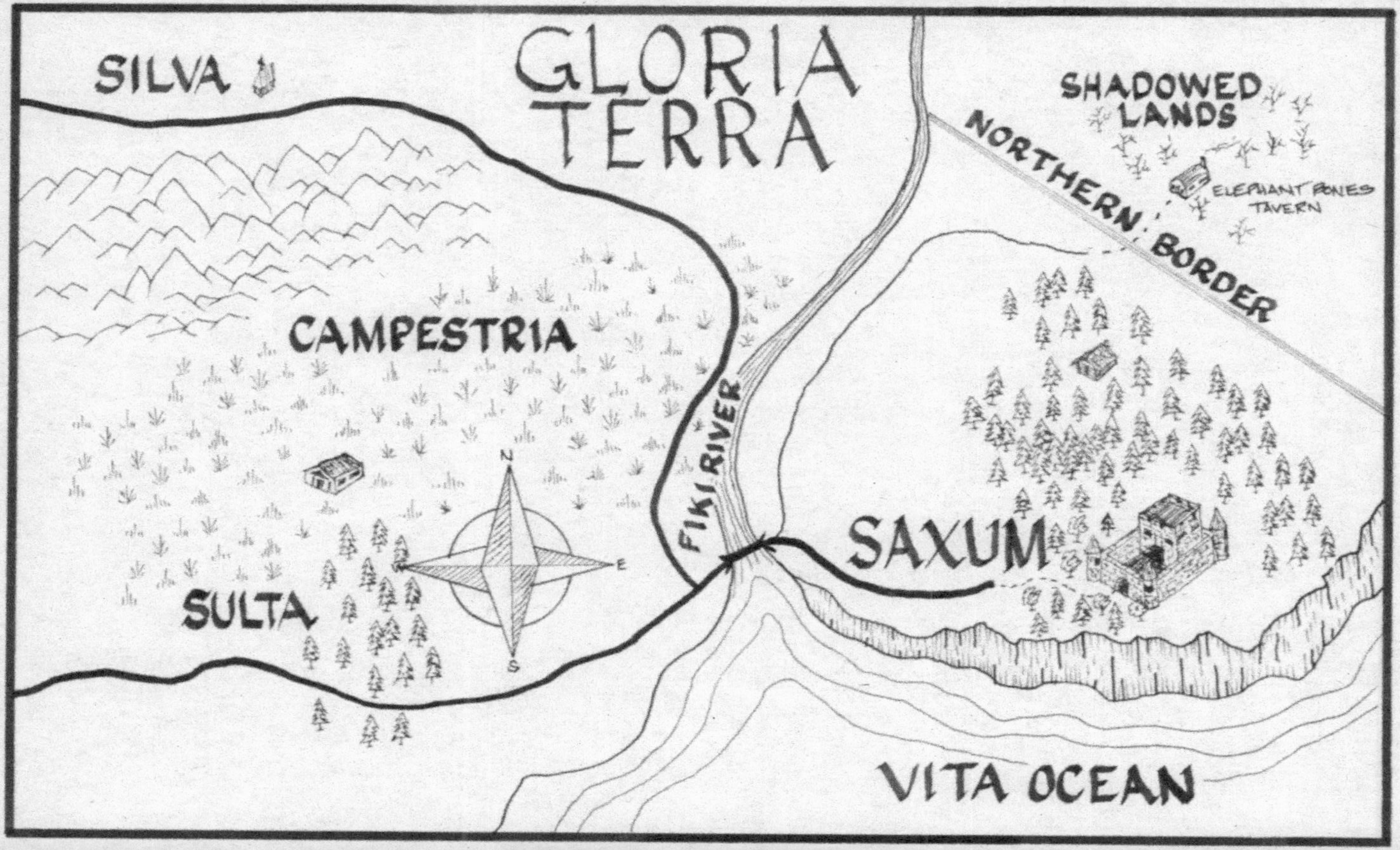

GLORIA TERRA
SILVA
SHADOWED LANDS
NORTHERN BORDER
ELEPHANT BONES TAVERN
CAMPESTRIA
FIKI RIVER
SAXUM
SULTA
N
E
S
W
VITA OCEAN

# *Author's Note*

*Scarred* is a dark royal romance.

It is a fractured fairy tale, not fantasy or a retelling.

The main character is a villain. If you're looking for a safe read, you will not find it in these pages.

———

*Scarred* contains mature and graphic content that is not suitable for all audiences. **Reader discretion is advised**. I highly prefer for you to go in blind, but if you would like a detailed trigger warning list, you can find it on EmilyMcIntire.com.

# PROLOGUE

## *Tristan*

LOYALTY.

One word. Three syllables. Seven letters.

Zero meaning.

Although if you listen to my brother's never-ending speeches, you'd think it runs through his veins thicker than the blood that binds us.

If you listened to gossip in the court, you'd believe the same.

*"Prince Michael will make a fine king."*

*"Carry on his father's legacy, that's to be sure."*

Something thick lodges its spiked edges in my throat, my gaze moving between the roaring flames of the fireplace at the other end of the room and the oil lamp placed in the center of the table, the one occupied by members of the privy council. Half a dozen faces and not one of them filled with grief.

My chest pulls.

"Life is about appearances, sire, and for appearance's sake, we must do what needs to be done," Xander, my father's— now my brother's—head adviser, states, his focus on where Michael sits. "Just as it's known your father passed peacefully in his bed, it's also known you have quite the…appetite."

"Xander, please," I cut in, pressing my back against the wood-paneled wall. "No need to convince *us* of where my father died."

My eyes move to my mother, the only woman in the room, as she dabs beneath her hollow brown eyes with a monogrammed handkerchief. Normally she wouldn't be here in Saxum at all, choosing to spend most of her days in the countryside estate, but seeing as how we're fresh off the funeral of her husband, Michael insisted she stay.

And his word is law.

"It's the peaceful part we have to lie about," I continue, my gaze settling on my brother.

A small smirk pulls at his lips, his amber eyes sparking. A fiery rage surges through my middle and up my throat, wrapping around my tongue, the taste bitter and tart.

My boot smacks the wood as I push off the wall and move toward the center of the room until I'm towering over the table, wedged between my mother and Xander. I take my time, soaking in every single face that sits here as if it's just another day, their statures stuffed full of pomp and importance.

As if we didn't just lose someone important.

Someone vital.

The only person left who cared.

"I'm sure I don't know what you mean,"Xander squawks, his voice pinched as he pushes up his horn-rimmed glasses.

I lift my chin as I stare down at him, noting the gray strands peppering his otherwise dark hair. He's been with the family for years—ever since I was a boy—and at first, he was a treasured person in my life. But life is ever changing, and Xander's warmth was doused quickly with the icy bitterness of greed.

Just like the rest of them.

"Mmm, of course not," I hum, tapping my finger against my temple. "Silly me."

"Can we get back to the subject?" Michael huffs, running his hand over his head, the light-brown strands ruffling under his fingers. "How father took his last breath is not what's important."

"Michael," my mother gasps, still dabbing away under her lids.

Spinning until I face her, I lean down, reaching out to wipe her face, the ridge of her cheek hard against my palm. She sucks in a breath as she looks up at me, her eyes shimmering, and I press my thumb into her skin before pulling away to glance at my hand.

My stomach burns when I realize the pads of my fingers are still dry as a bone.

Actors, all of them.

"Mother," I tsk. "Stop the dramatics. Any more fake tears and you'll wrinkle."

Winking, I pat her cheek and stand up straight, noticing every eye in the room is on us.

It's no secret there's no love lost between her and me.

I grin, allowing my lips to peel back from my teeth as I look from one person to the next. The air thins and Lord Reginald, one of the council members, shifts in his velvet-backed chair.

"Relax." I roll my eyes. "I won't do anything untoward." Lord Reginald scoffs, and my attention falls to him. "Something you'd like to share, Reginald?"

He clears his throat, his cheeks growing ruddy, showcasing the nerves he's trying so very hard to hide. "You'll forgive me for not believing you, Tristan."

I cock my head. "I think you mean Your Highness."

His mouth purses before he bows his head. "Of course, Your Highness."

My jaw ticks as I take him in. Reginald has always been one of the weakest members of the council, bitter and jealous of everyone else. He attached himself to my brother's side when they were young, and he stayed through every moment of torture inflicted on me through the years at Michael's—and his pack's—hands.

But I'm no longer a child, and they can't bully me like they used to.

Xander pinches the bridge of his nose. "Sire, please. You need a wife. Your people need a queen."

"They have one," Michael booms, his head nodding toward our mother. "I do not wish to marry."

"No one is asking you to stop your dalliances." Xander sighs. "But these laws have been in place for generations. To not take a wife, it will make you look weak."

"If you're not up to the duty, Brother, by all means, do us a favor and disappear." I wave my hand through the air.

Michael's eyes narrow as they snap to mine, the corner of his mouth twisting into a mocking grin. "And leave Gloria Terra to who, you?"

Chuckles burst from around the table, and my muscles tighten beneath the surface of my skin, the urge to show them all just how easily I could make them bow streaming through my insides.

The wooden clock snicks as its long hand moves, drawing my attention away.

It's nearing supper.

My fingers tense as they run through the disheveled black strands of my hair, and I back up a pace toward the large double oak doors. "Well, this has been a treat," I start. "But sadly, I've grown bored."

"You're not dismissed, Tristan," Michael snaps.

"You do not *dismiss* me, Brother," I sneer, anger snapping at my chest. "I could not care less about which unfortunate soul will have the torment of you rutting into them for eternity."

"So disrespectful," Xander spits, shaking his head. "Your brother is the king."

A grin spreads across my face, and I lock my gaze on Michael's, anticipation thrumming through my veins.

"Well then." I incline my head. "Long live the king."

# CHAPTER 1

## *Sara*

"YOU'LL LEAVE IN THE MORNING."

My uncle sips his wine, his dark eyes like arrows soaring across the table and filleting the flesh of my chest. He's never been an affectionate man, but he's my family all the same, and we have the same goal.

To seek vengeance on the Faasa family for the murder of my father.

We have slotted many moving pieces carefully into place, ensuring that when the crown prince was in need, I would be the one there to accept his hand. Finally, we've received word.

It's time.

Arranged betrothals, while not uncommon, have gone slightly out of fashion in recent years. After all, it's 1910, no longer the 1800s, and in all the storybooks and even here in the poverty-ridden streets of Silva, people marry for love.

Or their idea of it anyway.

But I've never been one with ideas of grandeur, thinking some white knight will ride in on his steed and save me like some helpless damsel in distress.

There may be distress, but I'm no helpless damsel.

Besides, sometimes the only way to enact genuine change is by becoming part of the machine and ripping out the broken pieces yourself. So if I have to smile, flirt, and seduce my way into the new king's good graces, that's what I intend to do.

It's my duty, after all.

To both my family *and* my people.

Silva, which was once known for its abundant lands and groundbreaking industrialization, has now become barren and lame. Cast to the side like an ugly redheaded stepchild, unworthy of the crown's time or attention. Now we're not known at all, drought and famine mixing with the despair that runs through the city streets like cracks in the pavement.

I suppose that's what happens when you're situated deep within a forest nestled high in the clouds. You become hard to see and easy to forget.

"You understand what's at stake?" Uncle Raf asks, bringing me out of my reverie.

Nodding, I wipe my mouth with a white cloth napkin, placing it back in my lap. "Yes, of course."

He grins, his skin crinkling as he taps his fingers on

the bulbous top of his wood cane. "You'll bring honor to our name."

The heady sense of his approval lights me up like a cannon, and I sit a little straighter in my chair, smiling back at him.

"And you'll trust no one except your cousin," he adds.

He glances at my mother, ever docile and quiet as she eats her meal, taking small bites, her unruly black hair so like mine creating a curtain around her face. She rarely makes eye contact, always choosing to keep her head down and her fingers busy with needlework and dusty books rather than forge a relationship with the daughter who's taken over everything since my father left her a widow.

I suspect she never wanted to be a mother and that she wanted to marry even less. She's never said the words, but there's no need when her actions speak so loudly. But my father wanted her, and that was all that mattered.

And when she grew with child, they expected it to be the next male heir to the Beatreaux line.

Instead, they got a wild raven-haired female with a sense of adventure and a mouth that speaks out of turn. And my father loved me all the same, even if my mother never showed a lick of affection.

The day I lost him, a piece of me was lost too, curdled like sour milk and left in the center of my chest to fester and rot.

He went to plead with the monarchy for aid. Took it upon himself to travel through our forests and over the plains until he made it to the Saxum castle. But the crown didn't listen to his plight, and my cousin Alexander sent word that they had him hung for treason. Because he dared to speak out and say they needed to do more.

Xander tried to save him, but there's only so much he can do when he's head adviser to the king.

My uncle Raf has been indispensable ever since, and while he's done nothing but support me, I still ache to be held in the arms of my father. Instead, all that's left is a family pendant that I wear around my neck like an oath, one that reminds me every single day of what I've lost.

And who's to blame for my sorrow.

So now, while other girls my age spend their time daydreaming about falling in love, I spend mine learning how to play into political warfare while still portraying the etiquette of nobility.

If you want to burn down hell, you must learn to play the devil's game.

The metaphorical crown being placed on my head is almost as heavy as the knowledge that everyone depends on me to see things through.

And the Faasa family's reign has been allowed to go on too long, their power and influence having decayed with time, becoming less about people and country and more about overindulgence and greed.

So I'll go to court. And I'll do what needs to be done to save my people and seek justice for those we've lost.

Still, it isn't until hours later that full realization hits.

*Tonight is my last night in Silva.*

My heart beats a staccato rhythm as I shove my feet into thick black boots and wrap my cloak around my shoulders, pinning my frizzy hair back until it's in a tight bun at the nape of my neck. Pulling the hood over my head, I look in the mirror, ensuring it's hiding my features. Glancing at the door to my bedroom, I eye the lock, making sure it's in place, before spinning back around and heading to my window.

My room is on the second floor, but I'm no stranger to the height, having made my way down the jagged stone wall dozens of times before. My lungs cramp from my shallow breaths, and adrenaline whips through my veins as I make my descent, my feet plopping onto the grass.

It's always a risk sneaking out, but one that I'd take a thousand times over.

I stand stock-still for a few moments, making sure no one heard me leave before I head around the side of our run-down estate, keeping to the shadowed areas until I reach the cobblestone drive and stare up at the rusted ten-foot gate. My fingers ache as they press into the metal and my muscles burn as I hoist myself up, climbing the jagged iron until I swing my leg over and hop down to the other side.

My chest heaves once my foot meets solid ground, and then I'm off, dashing down the pavement, pulling my hooded cloak tighter, hoping I don't run into anyone on my way.

I take twenty minutes to make it to the orphanage on the outskirts of town. It's a small, dilapidated building with zero funding and not enough beds, but Daria, the woman who runs it, is one of my key contacts, and I know that anything I slip her way will make it into the right hands.

"There should be enough here to get you by until I can send more." I press my fingers into the backs of Daria's as she holds the bundle of money and the small basket of bread that I've thrust into her palms.

She sniffles, the glossy sheen of her eyes sparkling against the dim candlelight of the small kitchen. "Thank you, Sara. I can't—" Her whisper cuts off as a sound from outside the room slices through the air.

My heart spasms in my chest and I suck in a breath, my eyes snapping to the darkened hallway, hoping it's not a child loitering outside their bed.

No one can know I'm here.

"I have to leave," I say, withdrawing my hands and lifting my hood. "I'll try to get word to you when I'm able, make sure things are safe."

Daria shakes her head. "You've done so much already."

"Please," I scoff. "I've hardly done enough."

The clock chimes and I note the time. Soon the sun will press against the horizon until its light bathes the ground, erasing the darkness and with it, my cover.

"I have to go," I repeat in a hushed tone, reaching out to drag her in for a hug. My stomach flips as her arms wind around me, squeezing tight. "Don't forget me, Daria."

"Never." She laughs, although it's a hollow sound.

Pulling away, I make my way to the door off the side of the kitchen, my hand wrapping around the cool brass handle.

"Be safe, my queen," Daria whispers to my back.

My heart stutters. "I'm no one's queen. I'm just the one who will burn the crown."

# CHAPTER 2

## *Tristan*

"TRISTAN!" THE CHILDLIKE VOICE SOARS across the courtyard, and I glance up from where I'm lounging against the trunk of the weeping willow, charcoal lining my palms and sketchbook splayed open in my lap. I rub my fingertips on my pant leg, flicking my head to move the strands of hair from my face.

The small boy skips over, stopping when he's in front of me, his clothing loose and dirty, like he's been running through the secret underground passages all day.

The ones I've shown him.

"Hello, little tiger," I say, amusement tiptoeing its way through my insides.

His face splits into a grin, his amber eyes sparkling, a sheen of sweat causing his light-brown skin to glisten. "Hi. What're you doing?" He peers down into my lap.

I straighten, closing the book. "Drawing."

"For your arms?" He nods toward my tattoos, hidden beneath my long-sleeve tunic, the dark ink peeking through the cream fabric.

The corner of my lips tilts up. "Perhaps."

"Mama says those things make you a disgrace." He lowers his voice and leans in so close his nose almost brushes against my forearm.

Disgust rolls through me at the fact that a scullery maid assumes she has any right to speak my name.

I tilt my head. "And what do you think?"

"Me?" He straightens, his teeth sinking into his lower lip.

"You can tell me." I lean forward. "I'm very good at keeping secrets."

His eyes sparkle. "I think I want some too."

My brow quirks. "Only the bravest little tigers can have them."

"I'm brave." His chest puffs out.

"Well then." I nod. "When you get a little older, if you still feel the same, you come see me."

"Simon!" a woman's voice hisses as she runs forward, her gaze growing wide as she looks between us. She stops short when she approaches, her black skirt dusting the ground as she drops into a deep curtsy. "Your Highness, I apologize if he's bothering you."

My jaw ticks, irritation bubbling in the center of my gut. "I wasn't bothered until just now."

"See, Mama? Tristan likes me," Simon says.

She gasps, reaching out while still in a curtsy and gripping her son's arm tight. "Address him appropriately, Simon."

"Why? You never do." His forehead scrunches.

Her shoulders grow taut.

My stomach burns, my hand trailing along my brow bone, feeling the thin line of raised flesh that runs from my hairline to just above my cheek.

She needn't worry about voicing what we both know she calls me. It's what everyone calls me, although never to my face. They're all far too cowardly for that. Instead, they speak it in secret, their whispers soaking into the stone walls until even the silence suffocates me with its judgment.

"Tristan is fine, little tiger." I stand, brushing off my pants as I do. "But only in private. Wouldn't want the others to get any ideas."

"Simon," his mother snaps. "Go back to our quarters. Now."

He glances at her and then at me. I give a slight nod and he smirks. "Bye, Your Highness."

Spinning around, he runs off.

His mother stays in her crouched position, head bowed, until a loud commotion at the front gates has her rising and turning toward the noise. I step in close, my hand reaching out to cup her cheek and turn her face back, the small slivers of muted sun peeking through the clouds and glinting off the silver of my rings.

"Kara," I purr, my fingertips stroking against her silky, dark skin.

She sucks in a breath as our gazes lock.

My grip tightens until she winces. "I didn't give you permission to rise."

Her breathing stutters as she drops back into a curtsy, once again bowing her head. I stare down at her, her son's earlier words churning like a storm inside my mind.

"Your son says you love to speak of me." I step forward, the tips of my shoes hitting the hem of her skirt. "You should be careful about the things you say, Kara. Not everyone is as forgiving. Wouldn't want word to get around that you seem to have forgotten your place. *Again.*" I crouch down in front of her. "Is it true you believe I'm a disgrace?"

She shakes her head. "He's a child. He loves to make up stories."

"Children have such incredible imaginations, don't they? Although…" My hand reaches out, my fingers skimming across the back of her neck. I revel in the way her body trembles beneath my touch. "If anyone knows about disgraceful acts, it would be his mother."

My hand grips the knot of tight ringlets on the back of her head and pulls, satisfaction burning through my chest as she gasps in pain. I lean forward as her back bows, my nose brushing against the side of her face.

"Do you think I don't know?" I hiss.

She whimpers, and it makes my stomach tense in delight.

"That I'm as stupid as every other person who walks these castle halls? That I don't see the resemblance?"

"Pl-please..." she stutters, her hands pushing at my chest.

"Mmm," I hum. "Did you plead for *him* like this?" I whisper in her ear, my free hand grasping her throat. My eyes glance at the royal guards lining the entrance gates and the bystanders gathering around them. A few people's gazes skim over us but just as quickly leave.

They all know better than to interfere.

"Do not make the mistake of confusing me with my brother," I continue, my fingers flexing in her strands. "And don't forget your place again, or I'll take great pleasure in reminding you." I release her, pushing her head until she collapses onto the ground, her hands reaching out to catch her fall. "And unlike him, I won't care how much you beg."

Standing straight, I pick up my sketchbook and stare down at her, enjoying the view of her cowering at my feet.

"You may rise."

She sniffles as she stands, brushing the dirt from her clothing and keeping her eyes pointed toward the ground.

"Go." I flick my hand. "Don't let me see you out here again."

"Sir," she whispers.

I turn before she finishes speaking, walking to the shade of the weeping willow and leaning against its trunk, the bark scratching against my back. Xander, my brother, and his personal guard, Timothy, walk out the castle doors and into the courtyard, making their way to where an automobile is rolling through the gates.

Curiosity holds me in place like my feet are encased in lead, and I watch from the shadows, my grip tightening on my notebook as Xander moves toward the auto and opens the door. A thin woman with blond hair peeking from under a purple hat exits first, smiling, before moving to the side.

And then a dainty hand reaches out, and another woman places her palm in Xander's.

My stomach rises and falls like an avalanche, knowing that I should take my leave but not being able to move away.

Because there she is.

The new queen consort has arrived.

# CHAPTER 3

## *Sara*

I'VE SEEN PAINTINGS OF THE SAXUM KINGDOM my entire life. There's one hanging above the mantle in my uncle's great room back home: a dreary picture, with thunderous clouds looming over a darkened castle, one that was built in the sixteenth century and has blackened with age. I've always assumed the sight was exaggerated for the artwork. Turns out the paintings don't come anywhere near the reality.

The king's driver winds the automobile through the Saxum city streets, passing by women as they laugh in the arms of men as if there isn't a care in the world. Blissfully unaware that five minutes down the road, the cobblestone turns into dirt, and the wide-brimmed hats turn into dirty bonnets and torn clothing over skin and bone.

Or maybe they are aware, and they simply don't care.

"Nothing does justice to the real thing, does it?" Sheina,

my closest friend turned lady-in-waiting, sighs as she gazes out the window, her blond hair peeking from beneath the brim of her hat. "You spend your whole life hearing tales, but it *is* an eerie sight."

Her head nods toward the castle, perched on a cliff at the end of a long winding road, lush green forestry surrounding either side.

*Paintings don't do it justice, indeed.*

This part of the country seems to lend itself to more of an overcast gloom—a stark difference to the sunshine that used to help grow the crops in Silva—and an anxious energy eats its way through my middle as the buildings that line the streets give way to sycamore and pine, the smell of evergreen permeating the automobile and stinging my nostrils.

The road narrows and my anxiety grows, my stomach rising and falling with the quickened beats of my heart as I realize the castle backs up to the angry Vita Ocean and this is the only way in. *And the only way out.*

"Do you think what they say is true?" Sheina asks, twisting her body toward me.

I lift a brow. "Depends on what part you're referring to."

"That the ghosts of the fallen kings haunt the castle corridors." She wiggles her fingers in front of her face.

I laugh, even though truthfully, I've wondered the same thing. "Sheina, you're too old to still believe in ghost stories."

Her head tilts. "So you're saying you don't?"

A shiver notches its way down my spine. "I believe

in superstition," I say. "But I'd also like to imagine that when someone leaves us, their soul moves on to rest in the kingdom of heaven."

She nods.

"Or hell," I add, the corner of my mouth tilting. "If they deserve it."

A giggle escapes, her hand coming up to smother the sound. "Sara, you shouldn't say such things."

"It's just us, Sheina." My grin spreads as I shrug, leaning into her. "Can't you keep a secret?"

She scoffs. "Please. I've kept every single one of your wicked deeds to myself since we were little girls."

I adjust against the back of the seat, the steel bones of my corset digging into my ribs. "Would they make a wicked girl a queen?"

Her lips purse, her blue eyes sparkling. "With you, Sara, anything is possible."

Warm contentment settles in my chest, happy that my uncle allowed me to bring her along. Having a familiar face helps to ease the tension knotting its way through my shoulders.

I've known Sheina since I was a little girl, us having grown up together on my family's estate. Her mother is a maid, and Sheina and I used to spend our summer days sneaking into the fields and picking fresh berries, making up stories about how we'd find the poisonous ones and bring them back to the boys who gave us trouble.

But one of the first things my father taught me was to keep your friends close and your secrets even closer. So while I love Sheina, I don't trust her with the heavy burden of my truths.

Even to her, I play the part, and she's none the wiser.

Slowly, the landscape stops whizzing by as our automobile stalls, my gaze snapping to the dual towers housing the entrance to the castle's courtyard. The stone itself is a dark gray, wet from the earlier rain—or maybe just stained from years of wear—deep ivy winding up the sides until it reaches the steepled tops and disappears into the small, glassless windows.

A lookout area, I'm sure.

I wonder if my father had the same view when he arrived, his mind full of hope and his heart filled with courage.

The hole in my chest aches.

"We've arrived, milady," the driver announces.

"Yes, I can see that, thank you," I reply, my spine straightening as I run my hands over the lap of my light-green travel dress.

The metal from the iron gates creaks as they open wide, royal guards lining both sides of the yard, their forms draped in black and gold, the crest of a roaring lion on their breast. It's the same image that adorns every flag in Gloria Terra.

*The Faasa family coat of arms.*

I swallow down the nerves, staring at their rigid faces as

the automobile moves again, stopping once we're just inside the gates. There are a dozen bystanders staring our way, but other than that, there isn't any type of grand fanfare.

A small group of men stand in front of us, and I recognize the shorter one immediately, relief flooding through my system at the sight of my cousin Xander making his way over.

The door opens, and Sheina is helped first, and then Xander's hand reaches for mine. The lace of my sleeve rustles against my wrist as I place my palm on his and step down to the ground.

"Xander," I say as he bows, bringing my hand to his lips for a kiss.

"Cousin, it's been too long," he replies as he straightens. "Your travels went well?"

I smile. "Long and uncomfortable, I'm afraid. But happy to be here all the same."

He clucks his tongue. "And my father? He's well?"

"As well as he can be. He sends his regrets he couldn't make the trip."

"Of course." He inclines his head. "Come. Let me introduce you to His Majesty."

He pulls my hand until it loops into the crook of his arm and leads me to a man standing in a tan country suit, a smile growing on his handsome face as he trails his gaze over my form.

I've learned so much about the royal family over the

years that I could point them out with a single glance despite never having seen them before. And from this man's coiffed brown hair to his broad chest and giant frame, coupled with the unusual amber shade of his eyes, I immediately recognize him.

King Michael Faasa III of Gloria Terra.

Fire consumes my chest, hatred dripping down my insides as I dip into a curtsy, the lace hem of my skirt swishing against the ground. "Your Majesty."

"Lady Beatreaux." His voice is a deep rumble, booming through the courtyard. "You're much better looking than I imagined."

I straighten and incline my head to hide the flash of irritation that crosses my face. "You're too kind, sir."

He tilts his chin, his hands resting in his pockets. "I've met your father, you know."

I let my smile widen, even though his mention of my father sends a ball of anguish tearing through my center. "What a pleasure for him to have held your company."

King Michael's eyes spark, his posture straightening as a grin blooms on his face. "Yes, well…it would seem that pleasure's being paid forward, since now I'll have yours."

Satisfaction spreads through my chest, warming the blood in my veins as my uncle's voice whispers through my head.

*The faster you gain his favor, the quicker you also gain his trust.*

Michael steps forward until he's in front of me, so close I can smell the starch of his clothes, and he leans down, pressing a lingering kiss to my cheek. My stomach jolts at how forward he is, and my eyes scan across the courtyard to see people's reactions, curious to know if this is common demeanor or something special, just for me. But other than a few people scattered through the massive yard, no one seems to pay us much mind, although I feel their lingering stares.

His hand grazes my waist.

I allow his touch, knowing I have no other choice. You can't deny the king, and I have no interest in coming across as difficult. Continuing my perusal of the area, my gaze snags on a beautiful weeping willow in the far corner, a shadowy figure perched beneath its crying branches, his eyes locked on me.

My stomach tightens.

King Michael whispers something in my ear, and I hum in agreement, although I couldn't tell you what he said. I'm too busy being sucked into this stranger's stare, knowing I should look away but unable to force myself to follow through. There's a challenge in his gaze that keeps me glued in place, one that stiffens my spine and irritates my nerves, wishing he would be the first to surrender. He doesn't, of course. He simply smirks as he leans against the trunk of the tree, running his hand through the messy locks of his jet-black hair, pushing the wayward strands from his forehead.

My breathing grows unsteady as I track along the harsh lines of his pale face, his fingers adorned in silver as they brush against his chiseled jaw and his forearms dark with ink. And then my heart stutters when I notice the scar running through his brow bone and ending just above his cheek, barely visible from this distance and dull compared to the piercing jade green of his eyes.

My middle clamps down tight as I realize who he is.

Even if I hadn't spent years studying the Faasa family, his reputation precedes him, rumors of his temper and tales of his extracurricular activities reaching even the farthest corners of Gloria Terra.

They say he's as dangerous as he is unhinged, and I've been firmly instructed to keep my distance.

Tristan Faasa.

The younger brother of the king.

*The scarred prince.*

# CHAPTER 4

## *Tristan*

"WHAT'S SHE LIKE?"

My gaze cuts to Edward, whom most people would think of as my closest friend, my only friend. The truth is that I *have* no friends, because friendships are fickle and often a waste of time. However, he is my closest confidant and the only one I trust enough to be at my side. That he's a general in the king's military is a bonus because it allows him access to whatever I may need without drawing attention to the fact that *I'm* the one who needs it.

His lean frame lounges in the chair across the room, his blond hair falling over his brows. I glance down at the heavy wooden table, my touch smoothing along the rice paper in my hands, making sure the contents are wrapped nice and tight before I apply the gum edges.

"She was…" I pause, rubbing my fingers together to remove the sticky residue of the ganja, small bits of green buds still lingering on my skin. "Mediocre."

I sit back, grasping a match and striking it against the rough edge of the tan Lucifer box, my gaze soaking in the bright orange glow of the flame. It transfixes my mind as I watch it burn down the wood stick, the heat becoming intense as it licks against my skin. I move the fire to the end of the cigarette, inhaling before allowing the light to extinguish.

"Michael Faasa's bride is 'mediocre'?" Edward laughs.

I hum, my mind picturing the girl who came through the castle gates earlier today, wide-eyed and wild-haired, looking so eager to please. She irritated me with her sweet smile and the way she batted her lashes Michael's way.

But it wasn't my brother who stained her cheeks pink.

"The word in court is she's quite the beauty," Edward continues.

"My standards are much higher than that of the court," I reply. Lifting my legs, I prop my feet up, my black boots chunking down on the table as I cross my ankles. "She's pleasing to stare at but as useless as the rest of them."

"What more do you need than beauty?" Edward shrugs. "Studious conversation?"

My chair tilts on its back legs until I'm staring at the textured ceiling, feeling cold even though there's a fire roaring in the room's corner. Or maybe that's just my insides—where my heart used to be—now empty and lacking, a hollow ache that craves chaos just to see it burn.

Moving the joint to my lips, I inhale, the smoke pouring down my throat and into my lungs, providing a calm my nerves never feel without it. "Edward, it's extremely unsettling to me you underestimate the wiles of a woman. They're snakes in sheep's clothing. Remember that, always."

He purses his lips, his brows lifting and spine straightening, almost as if I've offended him. "You've always been dramatic."

I blow a plume in the air. "I've always been right."

Irritation sours my stomach at his loose tongue but reprimanding him will take energy that I don't have, so I'll file it away and remind him of it later when the mood strikes. Right now, I'd rather make him leave.

I've never been one to crave the company of others. Perhaps that's because when I was a child, everyone could tell that I was just a little *different*, no matter how badly I tried to fit in.

And even if they couldn't tell, my brother made sure they knew.

I snap my chair forward, the impact of the legs hitting the floor vibrating through my body. "Leave me."

Suddenly I'm craving retribution, needing to rid myself of the memories from when I was powerless and at the mercy of Michael and his *pack*.

---

There's an unofficial gathering to welcome Lady Beatreaux to court.

Unofficial because I'm not required to be in attendance.

Although, even if I were, I'm not known for adhering to the rules of nobility, and I doubt they'd expect me to show up. Which is exactly why I've come.

The who's who of the kingdom are all here. High-ranking officials, dukes and viscounts from nearby areas, and all the ladies and gentlemen of the court. Laughter and small chatter echo off the high ceilings and stone columns of the great hall, crystal glasses clutched in bejeweled fingers, and rosy cheeks that belie the truth of their intoxication levels.

My brother sits at the front on a raised dais, two empty chairs on either side of him, sipping wine and gazing at his people.

He's always been this way, even when we were children, always needing to be above it all, flashy and glamorized, admired by everyone regardless of who he has to push down to do it.

The disgust rolls through my stomach, clawing up my throat as he flirts with a servant girl who fills his flute with more to drink.

I stick to the shadows, making sure not to draw attention to myself, wanting to see little doe-eyed Lady Beatreaux when she makes her way into the lion's den. And I don't need to wait long, because the double oak doors creak open and in she walks, her head held high and black hair pinned back, perfect ringlets framing her face.

Her dress shimmers as she moves, the green

complementing the pale cream of her skin, and it would be a lie for me to pretend she doesn't steal the show. She draws every single person, like moths to a flame, as she makes her way through the crowd and toward my brother.

Behind her is that same wisp of a girl with sandy-blond hair she showed up with. Suddenly, the girl stumbles, her foot sticking in the hem of my new sister-in-law's dress, making them both falter in their steps.

Lady Beatreaux's face twists as she cuts her a quick glare.

It's quick—the slip in her mask—before she smooths the irritation and replaces it once again with a soft, appealing look, but awareness tingles down my spine, and my interest piques.

That interest grows when she stops in front of my brother and curtsies low before taking the spot next to him, his eyes sparkling and lips curving upward as he takes her in.

*He likes her.*

Straightening off the darkened wall, I move into the light, the crowd parting for me just as it did for her, only this time, it's accompanied by stuttered breaths and whispers.

People give me a wide berth because they worry about what will happen if they don't.

Rumors about the scarred prince run rampant around the kingdom, and while most are fabrication, some start with at least a hint of truth, and I've found the more they fear me, the less they look.

And at least for the moment, that's the way I like it.

When I near the dais, my brother's face draws down, and I know with every fiber of my being it's because he didn't expect me to be here. Because even though people warily gaze my way, it's still *my* way instead of his.

I sit down in the high-back velvet chair next to him, sinking into the seat and crossing my ankle on my knee, adopting an air of boredom.

"Tristan, I didn't expect to see you here. Come to meet your future queen?" Michael says, gesturing toward Lady Beatreaux on his opposite side.

I glance over, something tightening in my gut when I lock eyes with her. Reaching across the lap of my brother, I hold out my palm, the left side of my mouth curling up. It's improper to lean across the lap of the king to hold conversation, and part of me is surprised Michael doesn't put a stop to it. But of course, that would draw the wrong attention his way. Can't have outbursts in public. That wouldn't mesh well with his *charisma*.

She stares at my outstretched hand for long moments before placing her fingers in mine. A twinge of surprise flickers in my chest as I bring her palm to my lips, pressing a soft kiss to the back. "Hello, dear sister."

Michael scoffs. "Don't scare the girl off before she's even been here for a fortnight."

"Sara," she whispers, ignoring my brother's words.

I quirk a brow.

"Call me Sara. We're about to be family, after all." A pleasant smile breaks across her face, but it doesn't reach her eyes, and it does nothing except heighten my curiosity.

"Don't waste your breath on being cordial with Tristan, sweetheart," Michael says. "He'll disappear into whatever gutter he likes to play in soon enough and won't even remember he's met you."

My jaw clenches, anger bubbling as it spreads through my blood and singes my veins.

Sara leans in, the upper half of her body almost entirely in Michael's lap now as her muddy brown gaze sears into mine. "You're hurting me."

Glancing down, I realize I'm still holding her hand, my fingers having tightened around hers until my knuckles are blanching white. I drop her palm.

"Am I?" I smirk. "So easily?"

Her eyes narrow.

"That's enough," Michael hisses.

I chuckle, leaning back in my chair and turning my attention to the soiree. Resting my elbow on the arm of my seat, I rub my jaw with my fingers, the days-old stubble rough against my skin.

Lady Beatreaux starts a conversation with my brother, droning on about the most boring of subjects: the weather in Silva compared to here, how she enjoyed riding in an automobile, and if she should plan to attend mass on Sunday morning on his arm or come with her ladies.

I'm only half paying attention, and my heart kicks in my chest when I spot a dark figure in the back corner of the hall.

Edward stands proud a few meters away, his hand on his belt, his attire decked in the black and gold of our country, a gold-woven rope decorating his left shoulder and my family crest roaring on his chest.

Our eyes meet, and I nod toward the shadowed stranger.

He follows the movement before understanding dawns on his face, and he makes his way toward them. And then, suddenly, there's a piercing scream that wails through the air, so curdling it makes the ends of my hair rise.

"By God!" someone else yells.

Edward rushes through the crowd then, all pretense having disappeared, tackling the figure and wrestling them to the ground. The stranger drops to their knees, and the hood of their cloak falls with them, long, dirty hair spilling down the intruder's shoulders.

It's a woman.

Something heavy thuds, and it's followed by shocked gasps and squeals. People jump backward, looks of horror overcoming their features.

As if in slow motion, the object rolls toward the dais and comes to a stop almost perfectly in front of Michael's throne.

He shoots up from the seat, his gaze widening as he

stares down at Lord Reginald's severed head, his gaping eyes and lolling tongue blue, severed neck tendons dangling, having left a trail of blood behind it.

"What is the meaning of this?" Michael demands.

Edward jerks the woman to stand, wrenching her bony wrists behind her back with one hand and gripping her hair in the other, forcing her to meet Michael's gaze.

My heart rate speeds up, fingers steepling as I watch the scene unfold.

She smiles wickedly, her eyes glazed and crazy. "This is your warning, Michael Faasa III."

"Warning from whom?" Michael booms.

Her grin widens.

Michael's fists clench, his jaw muscles working back and forth. My eyes move from him to his bride-to-be, expecting her to stare in terror and selfishly wanting to revel in her fear, to soak it in like sunshine and let it fuel me through the night.

But she sits in silence instead, her head tilted, a curious sheen coasting across her eyes. She's perfectly poised and seems unaffected.

*Interesting.*

"I am your king," Michael snaps.

The woman bends at the waist, a high-pitched cackle pouring from her mouth and bleeding into the tense and silent air. Edward pulls her upright, tightening his grip on her skull.

She spits on the ground. "You are no king of mine."

Xander appears out of the crowd, storming his way to stand in front of the maniacal woman. "Who did this to Lord Reginald? Was it you?"

She grins, her head tilting so far to the side, her neck looks as though it may snap in half. "I'd do anything to please His Majesty."

Xander's palm is quick as it whips through the air, the crack reverberating off the walls as the woman's face is thrown to the side.

"That's enough. Let her speak." Michael's hand flies up, his gaze falling on her. "You've already committed treason. Surely you know death awaits you. So finish your message, filth, and then rot in the dungeons."

"He's coming for you," she singsongs, her body seeming to vibrate in place.

"Who?" Michael demands.

She stills. Her head lowers the tiniest amount, and her mouth breaks into a smile so wide, you can see every single rotten tooth.

"The rebel king."

# CHAPTER 5

## *Sara*

THE KING'S PRIVATE OFFICE IS AS BEAUTIFUL as the rest of the rooms in the castle. Deep-purple velvet covers almost every inch of the dark mahogany furniture, and intricate paintwork lines the ceiling, money bleeding from the walls.

The room itself is spacious, almost as large as my personal quarters, but even with its size, it feels stifling.

A tall, thin royal guard stands to attention behind Michael's desk, and Michael perches in front of it, leaning against the lip. His eyes move back and forth, tracking Xander as he paces a hole in the carpet.

The queen mother is nowhere to be found—I haven't even met her—and Prince Tristan disappeared after the decapitated head rolled to our feet. Honestly, I was surprised to see him there at all, having been told he rarely makes appearances in court. But I've been here for two days and have seen him twice already.

My stomach tightens and I shift in my seat, thankful he isn't here right now. He's unsettling. He stares at me as though he can see into the darkest corners of my soul. Or maybe that's just *his* darkness reaching out and trying to find the blackest parts of mine.

"Xander, you worry too much. Have a cigar and calm down," Michael says, flipping open a cedar box on the corner of the desk.

He puts one into his own mouth before passing the other off to Xander, who takes it with a sharp look.

My cousin is worried. It's clear in the crow's-feet that crinkle the corners of his eyes and in the frown lines that deepen with every passing second. His bony fingers run through his thinning salt-and-pepper hair, and when they aren't busy pulling on the strands, they're adjusting his circular glasses that slip down the bridge of his nose from his jerky movements.

"I'd like to speak with Uncle Raf," I interject.

It's all I've been able to think of since the scene in the great hall. I hadn't expected there to be an uprising on the outskirts, a mystery man wanting to take the throne for himself, and I'm desperate to find out more. I'm fascinated by the blind loyalty that bled from the treasonous woman's soul, her willingness to sacrifice so much for her leader, making curiosity bite at my insides.

And I need to figure out if this is a wrench in my plans.

The worst type of ignorance is one that can be avoided yet isn't. I won't allow myself to fall into that trap.

And my uncle, he'll know what to do.

Xander turns to me, although his words are for the king. "Sire, I don't think it's safe to allow communication on such sensitive terms."

Something hot spikes through my chest at his disagreement.

"I'll tell my father," he continues, deciding to speak to me instead of around me.

"Cousin, I'd prefer to speak with him myself. He'll worry once he hears news."

Xander frowns. "Sara, you aren't here to tell us about your preferences. You're here to be the king's bride. All you need to do is sit down, look pretty, and let me handle things. He'd want to know you're safe, and I'll ensure he does."

My stomach twists, but I settle back in my seat, my hands folding together on my lap.

Michael's eyes are watching me, their glassy sheen peeking through the cloud of smoke that curls around his face.

"Xander, don't be so harsh on the girl," he says.

Xander spins toward him, his hand whipping through the air. "Are you not concerned, sire? Reginald is dead. And a filthy *jackal* has made it into court and tossed his severed head at your feet, screaming about 'the rebel king.'"

Michael straightens, his jaw tightening. "Yes. We were all there."

My eyes flick back and forth between them. Did he just call that woman a jackal? My jaw tightens at the derogatory name. It's no secret that's what the have-nots are called in this country, but to hear it being spoken so plainly, as if they aren't worthy of names or respect just because of their circumstance, slaps against my insides and makes me seethe with anger.

"Regardless, this isn't proper conversation for a beautiful woman." Michael winks at me.

Xander nods, running a hand through his hair again. "Yes, of course not. Timothy," he snaps, spinning to the royal guard in the room's corner. "Escort Lady Beatreaux back to her quarters."

Disappointment plops in the middle of my gut, but I'm not surprised they're sending me away. I'm not stupid. They won't say anything of importance in front of me, especially before we're wed, and if I'm honest, most likely even after. Women aren't granted the same respect as a man, as if what's between my legs has anything to do with the way my brain works or my ability to process information.

I was about to pluck my eyeballs out from listening to these two morons drone on anyway.

I rise from my seat and move toward King Michael, curtsying. "Your Majesty."

His hand tips up my chin, bringing me to a stand. "Sara, sweetheart. I'm sorry we haven't been able to become better acquainted. But you know what they say...good things come to those who wait."

I force a small grin. "I've always been told patience is rewarded."

His eyes flare, and that's my cue.

My skirts rustle around my ankles as I walk to the heavy wood door. Timothy, the royal guard, moves behind me, the black and gold of his uniform highlighting the deep tan of his skin, so different from the pale creams I've seen so far in this region.

"Timothy, right?" My voice echoes off the cold stone walls of the castle halls.

He glances at me out of his peripheral but stays silent.

"Are you from here?"

Still, he stays silent.

"Saxum, I mean."

After a few long moments of no response, I sigh. "All right then. Not a conversationalist. Xander was speaking of that woman. That...jackal?" The word is rough on my tongue, and I watch his reaction, not expecting a verbal response but hoping he gives away clues on his face.

He doesn't. He's trained well.

"Are you mute?" I purse my lips. "Or just not allowed to speak."

The corners of his lips twitch.

"Honestly, that sounds terrible," I continue. "Doesn't it bother you? Being told that you can't even talk?"

He side-eyes me again as we approach the wing of my personal quarters, stopping once we reach my room.

I reach out, the metal knob rough against my fingertips. Timothy moves to the side of my door, his back straight and his eyes scanning the area. I pause, my stomach tightening. "Are you planning to stand out here all night?"

He quirks a brow.

"Right, right. No speaking." I grin. "Got it."

He inclines his head in a half bow, and I slip inside my bedroom, shutting the door behind me, the grin dropping from my face as I make my way across the sitting area, looking for Sheina.

I don't find her, so I assume she's already turned in for the night.

Good.

There's a woman in the dungeons, and if no one will give me answers, I'll find them for myself.

# CHAPTER 6

## *Sara*

I'VE MADE IT TO THE SERVANTS' QUARTERS—
without meaning to—but this castle is large and a little
eerie, and it's difficult to navigate the corridors in secret
without knowing where you're going. Anxiety teases my
middle, and I hope I don't forget my way back.

Muffled voices filter through the darkened hall, the
only light coming from small sconces placed between the
arched windows. My steps falter, heart stuttering. I hadn't
expected anyone at this time of night, but I shouldn't have
been so stupid. There are always people roaming halls.

I continue forward, leaning against the stone, my
breathing choppy as I glance both ways, making sure
nobody is here to see me.

*This was foolish.*

The voices become louder as I inch my way closer to
the room, and my brows draw in as I strain to hear.

The door is ajar, and I move from the wall and spin toward it, crouching, my fingers gripping the wooden frame as I press my face to the crack. My breathing is shaky and my heart kicks against my chest cavity as adrenaline floods my system.

The three thin silver daggers slipped between my leather garter are cold as they press against my thigh, but I'm not stupid enough to sneak through the castle halls at night alone and unprotected.

Besides, there's something thrilling about the rush of being caught. Of doing something I'm not supposed to.

Squinting, I try to make out the details, but other than a long wooden table and a bookshelf in the far corner, it seems barren. A tall man stands in the center, his shadow looming over another person, who's on their knees at his feet.

It's difficult to see who it is at first, but the longer I stare, the more my vision clears.

Prince Tristan.

My heart jumps to my throat. *What is he doing down here in the servants' quarters?*

"Do you understand?"

My stomach twists at his voice, just like it did the first time I heard it: velvet words while his hand was wrapped around mine and his brother was between us.

His tone is deep. As if it was made in hell, then woven through silk. A gentle caress that singes your senses.

Although it's too dark to make out heavy detail, I can see the person at his feet is a woman.

*Is Prince Tristan with a servant?*

Her head drops, the subservience bleeding from her pores. "M—"

Tristan's spine stiffens, his head cocking to the side. "That's quite enough," he cuts her off. "Leave."

She moves to stand and nods. My insides seize, worried she'll come my way, but she twists the opposite direction, her hand pressing against the wall until the small bookshelf spins in place, revealing a small opening that she slips into.

My eyes grow wide as she disappears.

The prince stands in the center of the room, completely still, like a lion hunting prey, waiting to attack. I bite my lip, afraid to even breathe with how silent the air becomes.

My hands grow clammy, fingers gripping the chipping wood of the doorframe until it splinters. I should have waited until I learned the lay of the land. As it is, I'm lucky this is all I've run into, instead of a soldier or worse. Gossip spreads like wildfire, and the wrong eyes and lips can have disastrous consequences.

I won't make the same mistake again.

"Are you planning to come into the room?"

My stomach somersaults, my eyes scanning the area to look for another person. There is none.

Quick as lightning, he turns, his gaze locking on me.

"Or we can continue to pretend you're not here if you'd like?" His boots clap on the floor as he makes his way toward me, his stride long and sure.

My heart throws itself into my ribs, panic welling like a flooding dam about to burst, but there's nowhere for me to run. Nowhere to hide.

So instead, I straighten from where I'm crouched, my legs screaming in relief from the change in position, and I smooth my hands down the front of my skirt. Weakness is never a strong suit, and no matter how much I may feel it trying to wrap around my middle and break apart my shield, I'll never let it show.

Reaching out, I push open the door before he can, coming face-to-face with him for the third time in less than twenty-four hours.

"I didn't want to interrupt." I smile.

His green eyes are calculating as they move from the top of my head down to the hem of my thin skirt and back, every millisecond pumping more blood through my veins, my heart working overtime as I try to control my reaction.

"Lost?" he asks.

I lift a shoulder. "Taking a leisurely stroll."

"Hmm." He nods. "Is that something you do often?"

"What, walking?" I reply, holding his stare, even though it makes my chest pull tight.

He steps in closer. He's dressed down, dark pants with suspenders hanging off his waist and a light tunic rolled up to his elbows, the black ink that's etched into his skin on full display.

I swallow around the sudden dryness in my mouth. I've never seen a tattoo in person, but he's covered. Intricate designs weave their way from his forearms and disappear beneath the fabric of his clothes. I've heard the whispers, even in Silva, of the scarred prince having drawings on his flesh, but I had thought they were only rumors.

It surprises me how much I like them.

His brother, King Michael, is attractive. But Prince Tristan is hauntingly beautiful.

He tsks. "I meant eavesdropping, little doe."

"I'm no doe."

"No?" His head tilts. "Then what are you?"

My chin lifts as I hold his gaze.

He's so close now I can see the jagged flesh clearly on his face, and I bite back the urge to reach out and touch it, to ask him what the true story is of how he got his scars. It doesn't disfigure him the way you'd expect. Instead, it makes him even more striking, adding to his already intimidating stature.

But I don't falter. I don't retreat.

My nostrils flare as I move in even closer until I can taste his breath as if it were my own.

"I'm your future queen," I whisper. "Maybe you should show some respect."

His eyes spark at this, his hand reaching out and

touching one of the spiral curls that's fallen from my hairpin. He winds it around his finger, the corner of his mouth lifting into a mocking grin. "Well then, I'll be sure to work on my bow."

Anxiety stomps through my center like a stampede of wildebeests, but I keep my face neutral so he doesn't realize how strongly he's affecting me.

"Do you think you've earned it? Respect." His voice is soft as it slices against my skin.

I keep my breathing shallow, not wanting to suck in the lungfuls of air my body is craving, afraid that if I do, my chest will brush against his torso.

My teeth grind together, my mind whirling with a warning to tread carefully.

"I do," I reply.

His brows lift, and he steps back a space, the strands of my hair bouncing as he releases the curl. His fingers rub across the front of his mouth. My eyes catch on the glint of diamonds in one of his silver rings, realizing they're the eyes of a lion, mouth wide as if in the middle of a roar.

His family crest.

My stomach flips when my gaze comes back to his, and the air grows thick, wrapping around us both with an unspoken challenge.

A loud slam echoes off the walls, making my gut fall to the floor.

Quick as a flash, Tristan's large hand wraps around my

wrist, pulling me fully into the room, my fingers grabbing for his chest so I don't topple over from the sudden movement. His arm winds around my waist to steady me, pulling me flush against him.

"What are you—"

His other palm smacks against my mouth, his rings cutting into my lips.

"Quiet," he demands. "Unless you think being caught alone in a dark hallway with your betrothed's brother is good for your reputation."

That shuts me up.

He doesn't remove his hand, and my stomach squeezes tight, my heart pumping blood so hard it whooshes through my ears. Glancing down at me, his fingers tighten around my waist. My body heats in response.

His jaw muscles tighten, and he releases me, shoving until I stumble, my hand reaching behind to catch myself from falling.

"Don't let me find you down here again, or I won't be so kind."

I huff. "Don't presume to tell me what to do and think I'll listen like your little servant girls."

His eyes narrow and he moves forward, pressing into me until my back hits the cold stone of the wall. "Jealous?"

"Hardly," I bite out.

"Careful, little doe. Keep running into places you don't belong, and someone may mistake you for prey."

"I'm not afraid of being prey."

"No?" He quirks a brow, leaning in until his nose skims along the side of my face. "You should be."

And then as fast as he came, he's gone, spinning around and striding out the door as if he was never here.

# CHAPTER 7

## *Tristan*

LADY BEATREAUX IS NOT WHO SHE SEEMS TO be.

When you live your life having to look over your shoulder, you learn to sense shifts in the air long before you ever see the change. And I felt her outside the door the moment she arrived, although I didn't know it was her until she stood in front of me.

My fingers flex as I remember the way her curly strands of hair spun around my finger, her eyes like ice picks as she glared at me in her simple gown and pinned-back hair. She looked nothing like the regal lady who sat next to my brother.

I prefer her this way.

Leaning back against the observatory tower at the castle gates, I pull a matchbox from my pocket and strike a flame, allowing the orange heat to tease my skin as I reflect on her intrusion.

*Is she spying for my brother? Is he watching me?*

Possible but improbable. Although I don't put it past her to do his bidding, I do put it past him to think that highly of her. He's not known for his respect for women.

Still, she's different than I expected. More sinister, perhaps.

If it wasn't *me* she was spying on, I'd be able to find admiration in her falsities. But since it is, it does nothing but leave a bitter tang in the back of my throat, one I choose to let linger, so I'm always reminded of the taste.

That's the difference between me and other people. They run away from the bad things, and I become them.

Reaching up, I pluck the rolled blunt from behind my ear and place it in my mouth, waiting until the fire has almost completely engulfed the match before lighting the end, the smell of hash curling up in the air, making my tightened insides unravel into a buzzing sort of calm.

My boot kicks against the wall, my head leaning against the cool stone as I gaze out over the streets of Saxum. The castle sits on a cliff, an easy vantage point to see everything, even beyond the dense trees.

When I was a young boy, my father would bring me here, whispering words of grandeur and teaching me the ways of the land.

*"This is my legacy. And one day it will be yours."*

*"You mean Michael's," I correct, glancing up at my father.*

*His dark hair blows in the nighttime breeze as he looks*

over at me. "You and your brother need to set aside your differences. Faasa blood runs through your veins as surely as it does his. Together we rule, divided we fall. Remember that."

I scoff, rubbing my swollen wrist, remembering how just a few hours earlier, Michael shoved me into the dirt and called me a freak. "Tell him that."

He chuckles. "Michael is still trying to find his place in this world."

"And I'm not?" I ask, my voice rising in defense.

"From the moment you were born, you've been different." He reaches out, tapping the center of my chest. "In here."

Different.

My chest twists. I don't want to be different. I just want to be left alone.

"You learned to talk faster," he continues. "Walked sooner. And you were drawing as soon as you could hold charcoal in your little hands."

I glance down at my fingers, flexing them in my lap, hissing as sharp pain shoots through the tendons of my throbbing wrist. Anger at Michael and his friends bubbles like a simmering pot in the pit of my stomach.

"It's an admirable trait—to be so sure of yourself in a world without answers. An enviable one."

My brows dip in confusion. "Why would Michael be envious of me? He gets all this." I wave my arm over the forest and the darkened city streets just beyond, lit only by the full moon hanging above us in the sky.

*My father sighs, wrapping his arm around me and pulling me in tighter to his side. "Sometimes, it's hard to know who you are when there's pressure to be something else. Your brother will be king one day."*

*Pride coasts through the tone of his voice, and my heart dives deep into my stomach, something heavy and green whipping through my insides.*

*"And you, my little tiger, are free to roam."*

But I'm not free. I never have been—not really. Years later, and I'm still here in Gloria Terra. *Glory of the earth.*

Flicking the ash from my smoke, I raise the tips of my fingers to my scar, running them along the raised edge, something sour tightening my gut.

The moon is full, and it casts a glow on the darkened forest, the groans of wind the only sound other than the occasional howl from feral wolves and the hoots from owls that frequent the observatory windows at night.

Pushing myself off the wall, I drop the burned paper and herb to the ground and crush it between my boot before walking into the trees and away from the safety of the castle.

---

I scan the dilapidated room, taking in several dozen faces crammed together at the long tables and benches, all eyes focused on me. The air smells dank, as if the frequent rainstorms have weakened the foundation and sank their way through the interior, growing and rotting the wood from the inside out.

But the Elephant Bones Tavern isn't a place known for its prosperity or its upstanding patrons.

It's dangerous and exists amid the shadowed lands, a place they warn even the strongest soldiers to keep far away from. And until recently, it's where I've spent most of my time, cultivating the watering hole as the home base for the rebels. Its owners are Belinda and her husband, Earl, both of them faithful followers of my cause.

If you spend time within the inner circles of Saxum, however, you'll hear the shadowed lands referred to by a different name.

*The jackal battlegrounds. Where the rebels roam.*

Although it's said in jest by those with gold lining their pockets. The ones who have never had to suffer under the cruel hands of fate. People who allow ego to be their crutch, never taking the less fortunate seriously. Whispers of "rebels" mean nothing to them. And why would they? No one is stupid enough to go against the crown.

The Faasa family has reigned for centuries. We're too strong. Too powerful. Too bold.

But with greed and power come boastful ignorance and blind eyes to threats. Chinks in the armor that erode until a chasm forms, big enough for someone to slip through and fracture the core from within.

Which isn't a bad thing. I'd rather live in chaos, ruling

over the rubble, than spend a second longer watching my brother sit on the throne.

He doesn't deserve it.

"Sire," a trembling voice breaks through the crowd, Belinda rushing through and throwing herself at my feet. Her bony hands snake out, her body bowing forward as her lips meet the top of my boot.

"You may rise."

She moves to her knees, her dark eyes glimmering with unshed tears. I reach out to tip up her chin, and her palms wrap around my wrist. I swallow back the disgust at having her touch me, focusing on the fact that I gave her Reginald's head, and she delivered, just the way I asked.

"You've pleased me," I say.

"Anything for you, sire," she whispers, staring up at me with clear adoration.

My hand moves from her face up to the top of her head, petting her hair and gazing out at the crowd.

"Let this be a lesson for all of you. While the roads ahead will be difficult and treacherous, they will also be paved with success. There will be great sacrifice, and I will accept nothing less than absolute obedience. I know the gravity of the situation—of what I'm asking. But if you do for me, I swear." I pause, moving my palm to rest over my heart, attempting to show sincerity through my movements and hoping it bleeds through my tone. "I will do for you." I wave my free hand toward the woman at my feet. "This beautiful soldier—this *warrior*—trusted in me." I gaze down at her, my touch moving back to her jaw and stroking her pallid skin as my eyes meet hers. "Loyalty. The highest kind. The type that is rewarded." My focus goes back to the people. "Aren't we tired of growing hungry while the noble gorge and feast?"

Angry murmurs whisper through the air, their grievances music to my ears.

"Aren't we exhausted of being spit on and forgotten, as if we aren't the ones keeping Gloria Terra afloat?" I slam my free hand into my chest. "Isn't it time for us to rise up and rise against?"

Cheers erupt, fists banging on the worn tables.

"Down with the king!" someone yells.

A laugh escapes from my throat, and I raise a palm in the air, quieting them, their attention rapt once again.

"Trust in *me*, friends, and I promise…I'll lead you home."

Belinda cries, dropping into a bow so deep her arms splay in front of her and her nose skims the floor.

Everyone else in the crowd follows suit, lowering their bodies to the ground, their heads dipped in subservience.

Satisfaction sneaks through my veins, and a smirk tips the corner of my lips. My eyes meet Edward's as he kneels in the back corner. I nod, pleased at the way he freed our messenger from the dungeons and brought her back.

This was important. A statement. One that shows

everyone I keep my word and will keep them safe. This is but a small portion of the support I've garnered, but it's enough for the message to spread.

It's hardly the truth, but perception is reality, and not *everything* is a lie.

I'm the one who will storm the castle and burn it all to the ground, along with my brother, his queen, and anyone else who gets in my way.

I'm the one who will rebuild Gloria Terra. The way it should be.

And if these peons are casualties in the war?

I search for a modicum of empathy to their plight but come up blank. They're simply tools. Plain and crude outcasts who have found safety within me.

Their lord. Their savior.

And the leader of the rebellion against the king.

# CHAPTER 8

## *Sara*

I HAVE SEEN NO ONE OF IMPORTANCE IN three days. Sighing, I shuffle the playing cards, my eyes glancing around the table at my brand-new ladies-in-waiting.

Ophelia, a young girl with rosy cheeks and bright red hair, and Marisol, a woman who is here to help train me for the king. Both of them sit in front of me, whispering words of adoration any time I so much as blink.

Part of me is disgusted because I know their loyalty is false, but the other part is enjoying their attention. There's something nice about being treated so well, even if it comes from a place of wanting to climb a social ladder.

Still, I wonder which of them is here on behalf of their families, hoping to bed my future husband and become his mistress.

I wonder how many already have.

Not that it bothers me either way. It's well known that

kings take pleasure from many sources, and it's even more well known that King Michael prefers a buffet and isn't particular about his tastes.

The more he gets it from somewhere else, the less he'll have need of me.

He'll be after my purity, of course, and he'll wish to produce an heir. I don't intend to let things get that far.

"This is quite boring, isn't it?" I say, placing down the cards and tapping my nails on the table.

Sheina stands behind me, brushing through my hair as she laughs. "Milady likes to go on adventures. When we were girls, you couldn't bribe her to stay still for a second."

I huff out a breath, rolling my eyes as I lock my gaze on the youngest girl in the room. "Don't listen to her, dear Ophelia. I'm perfectly fit to sit here and…drink tea all day and eat crumpets."

Giggles burst around the table, and I smile, something warming the center of my chest when I do.

"Now…" I take advantage of the new camaraderie and lean forward. "Tell me about these rebels."

Ophelia's green eyes widen and Marisol shifts in her seat, fingers brushing over her blond hair.

*Interesting.*

"Did I say something inappropriate?" I ask. "Apologies if I did. I overheard talk and got curious, but from your reaction, I can see it's a sensitive subject." I pause, allowing my words to linger in the air before I continue. "You know… You should tell me anyway. I wouldn't want to embarrass myself in front of anyone, most of all the king." I place a hand on my chest, giggling. "Can you imagine?"

Ophelia hesitates before leaning in close. "They're the outliers."

"Outliers?"

She nods, and Marisol purses her lips before adding, "Filth is what they are. Disgusting creatures who think they have a right to live on our level."

My stomach tightens. "Do they not?"

Ophelia shakes her head. "They're criminals. People say they smoke and drink until they can't see straight and then sneak into the upper east side and snatch people right off the streets."

"For what purpose?" My brows draw in.

"To make a statement?" Ophelia bites on her lips.

"They're *jackals*," Marisol cuts in. "They've only become a problem recently, and now that they've thrown themselves at King Michael's feet?" She shrugs her shoulders, brushing her hands down her skirt. "They won't be around much longer."

Sheina's fingers pause from where she's pinning my hair. "That's rather harsh," she chastises.

Marisol's gray eyes cut to hers, her features drawing tight. "They hold human sacrifices in the middle of their dirty roads! Strip a person down until there's nothing left but their pride, and then they take that too, leaving only shame and whimpers for death in its wake."

"We don't know that for sure," Ophelia scolds. "No one's seen it happen."

I suck in a breath. "Surely not. Wouldn't they want the people on their side if they plan to go against the king? Wouldn't it be obvious people were missing?"

Ophelia shakes her head. "Sometimes, milady, there's no rhyme or reason to people's madness. And if they have someone leading them now…"

Her voice trembles and her eyes glaze over.

My heartbeat rages in the center of my chest. "They're that organized?"

I remember the unkempt woman from the party and the way she spoke. But I had filed that away as the ramblings of a deranged woman, driven mad by the famine running rampant in the city streets. King Michael didn't seem to be bothered, so I assumed there was no reason to take it seriously.

Marisol's spine stiffens, and she clears her throat. "Yes, well, we shouldn't speak of these things. It's forbidden."

I stare at Marisol, taking in her words and slotting them away to dissect further when I'm alone.

"Regardless," Ophelia says, "they're not the type of people you should consort with. Ever. It's enough to be tried for treason."

"Of course not." Reaching out, I lay a hand on top

of Ophelia's, smiling. "Thank you for telling me." My eyes flick to Marisol, then back. "We ladies need to stick together, after all."

———

It's long after everyone has turned in for the night, but I can't sleep. My mind fills with questions and my stomach floods with tension.

*Rebels.*

I've never heard of them before.

But Xander clearly knows.

Unease burns through me.

I had thought I was ready when I arrived, yet here I am, less than a fortnight, and already there's a wrecking ball thrown in my plans. A sound from outside the door makes me shoot upright in bed, my heart stuttering.

*Is someone here?*

I throw back the heavy duvet and swing my legs to the side, my feet meeting the rich fabric of the Persian rug.

Walking to my vanity, I slip on my deep-red nightdress, the long silk sleeves flaring out at the wrist and the hem kissing the floor. I cinch it tight at the waist and grab one of the blades I keep hidden in the top drawer before making my way to the door to see what caused the noise.

Twisting the handle, I throw open the wood door, glancing both ways but meeting only silence. The area is dark, lit only by the small iron wall sconces that decorate the halls.

Blowing out a deep breath, I tuck a loose black curl behind my ear and take a step out of my room, closing the door behind me, my nerves buzzing beneath my skin.

I only make it two steps before a body moves out of the shadows and stands in front of me.

"Oh!" I yelp, my stomach rising to my throat and then plummeting to the ground.

Prince Tristan gazes at me, his hands in his pockets and his eyes like stone.

"You scared me." My mouth is dry and my tongue swipes out to wet my lips as I take a large step back against my closed door, placing the dagger behind me. "Wh-what are you doing here?"

He cocks his head and moves closer. "What are you hiding, little doe?"

Irritation winds its way through my middle and I stiffen my shoulders. "That's none of your business. Why are you in my wing?"

His dark brow rises. "*Your* wing?"

"Yes, my wing. Do you see any other ladies here?"

He glances around. "I don't see a single one."

The insult slices through my chest. *Insufferable.* "You're as horrendous as they say, aren't you?"

His posture changes then, his shoulders growing taut, almost as if his aura itself is mutating into something dark. Something dangerous.

It's transfixing, the way he can morph from an unaffected

stance to whatever this is, and it makes my hair stand on end, my gut screaming that I should watch my step.

"This may be your wing, but it's my castle. These are my halls," he hisses, moving in so close his breath ghosts across my face. "It would be incredibly stupid of you to assume just because I don't wear the title of king, you shouldn't bow before me."

My breathing stalls, but the next words still slip off my tongue before I can swallow them down. "I only bow for those who deserve it."

He smirks, his body pressing into me, making heat surge through my middle, and my heart slams against my ribs. His hand slides up the outside of my sleeve, the fabric creating a delicious sensation against my skin, despite the way my insides are stewing with a vile brew of hatred and panic, not wanting him to see what's hidden behind my back.

"I could always make you," he murmurs.

My nostrils flare, a small slice of fear winding its way around my spine like a rose vine, the thorns pricking me with warning.

I ignore it.

"You could try," I snark.

His palm skims over my shoulder until it meets flesh, my stomach jumping when he touches me, skin to skin.

"This is inappropriate," I rasp.

His fingers dust across my collarbone before moving up the front of my throat, curling around my esophagus. His thumb presses beneath my chin, the pressure causing my head to tilt back until I'm meeting the fierce green of his eyes.

My chest pulls tight, anxiety swirling through my middle, and something heavy settles deep in my belly.

"Hmm." His nose skims the side of my cheek, moving back until it brushes against my ear. "I think you'll find I care little for what's *appropriate*."

His other hand grabs at my waist, and my eyes flutter from the heat of his touch, searing through the thin silk of my nightdress. My fingers tighten around the sheath of my blade.

*I could do it.*

He's distracted, and the knife would cut through his skin, sinking into his veins in seconds.

But I didn't come this far to be messy, and I won't allow something as silly as emotion to cloud my judgment.

A blunt stab of pain hits my shin, causing my legs to buckle. Tristan's grip is firm as he catches my fall, his hand pressing down. Bitterness rages through me as my kneecaps smack against the shiny tiled floor, causing me to wince from the impact, and the dagger clatters to the ground beside me.

His eyes snap to the weapon, and he cocks his head. "Interesting."

My chest burns, teeth grinding as I glare at him.

"I prefer you this way," he coos from above me. "On your knees, chest heaving, and face flushed while you stare up at your betters." He reaches down, his fingers cupping my chin and jerking until the muscles in my neck strain. "Let this be a lesson, little doe. Don't forget your place."

"And where is that?" I force out through the tightness in my throat, my body shaking from the anger that's pouring through my veins.

He grins, and the sight of it is so sinister it makes dread crawl through my insides like a thousand spiders.

"Trembling at my feet."

# CHAPTER 9

## *Tristan*

SMOKE CURLS IN THE AIR, A ROLLED JOINT perched between my two fingers as I sit, staring at my brother's oversize desk.

Xander and Michael are talking of Sir Reginald's funeral; or more so whether there should even be one. And as much as these two imbeciles make my stomach turn with their ramblings, being here and hearing what they're planning is better than staying in the dark.

I wonder how they would react if they knew it was my hand that severed Reginald's flesh from bone. That it was me whom he begged, pleading for salvation as if I were a god capable of granting mercy. I wish I could tell them that dear old Reginald wasn't so brave when there wasn't a table of men surrounding him and that he pissed himself on the dirty cement floor while I lit match after match and burned pretty scars into his skin.

"Sire, we need to shift the focus," Xander implores.

Michael groans, slamming his fist down on top of his desk. "I don't want to shift the focus, Xander. I want to find the filthy whore who dared to come into my castle, drop a man's head on the ground, spit at my feet, and then somehow disappear from the dungeons."

Amusement trickles through my insides as I watch the fury rise to Michael's cheeks. My mind wanders to Lady Beatreaux, and I wonder how much fire it would take to see the heat beneath her flesh.

"If we continue to bring up the disturbance," Xander continues, "the people will become uneasy. We need to shift the narrative. Find a distraction."

A chuckle rolls out of me, my leg crossing over my opposite knee.

Michael spins to face me, running a hand through his hair. "Something funny, Brother?"

I shrug, flicking the ash of my cigarette onto the expensive rug beneath my feet. A lazy grin pulls at the corners of my mouth, and I lean back in my chair, allowing the cushions to mold to my muscles. I wave my hand through the air. "Far be it from me to interrupt."

"You're already interrupting," Michael snaps. "What are you even doing here? Suddenly caring about the state of the monarchy?"

His tone is sarcastic, and I smile, biting back the urge to prove him wrong. To show him that all I've *ever* cared about is the monarchy.

"Just providing moral support after what was no doubt a tumultuous past few evenings for you. Are you doing all right, Brother? You look a little pale." I sit forward, my brows hiking into my hairline. "That woman didn't *scare* you, did she?"

Xander bristles in my peripheral. "Get to the point, Tristan, if you have one."

I spin the ring on my finger, the lion's diamond eyes glinting with every turn. "Like I said, I'm just here for support."

"Tristan."

"Xander," I reply, elongating the vowels as they roll off my tongue.

"While I can appreciate your sudden need to be in the conversation, it's a little late to play the part of dutiful prince." His eyes trail down my form as if the mere sight of me is offensive.

Maybe it is.

My grin drops, something heavy twisting my stomach. "There is no part to play. I am His Royal Highness Tristan Faasa, second son to the late King Michael II, whether you want to admit that or not."

Standing up, I move across the room until I'm in front of him, my body towering over his short and gangly frame. He glares up at me with his ridiculous horn-rimmed glasses, and I stare down at him, bringing the joint to my mouth and inhaling, taking in each uncomfortable tic of his features and every pebble of sweat that beads on his brow. I exhale, blowing out the smoke so it coats his face, making him sputter.

"I know you're a very important man, Alexander," I whisper. "Standing here, having the ear of the new king and the one before him, thinking you're beyond reproach."

My hand grasps his shoulder, allowing the burning tip of the rolled paper to rest close to his neck. The urge to stick it on his skin and listen to it sizzle is strong, but I hold myself back.

"But I want you to remember two things. One, that my blood runs truer than yours, even if it is hidden beneath 'ghastly' ink and a blackened soul."

I pause, enjoying the way he fidgets under my stare.

"And the second?" he asks, his Adam's apple bobbing.

"The second is that I know what you did to my father. And I'll never forget those who left him alone to die." The burning edge of my cigarette grazes against his jugular, my stomach somersaulting in delight as he jerks in my grasp. "Oops." I smile. "Did that hurt?"

"You know much less about your father than you think," Xander hisses through clenched teeth.

Huffing out a laugh, I glance at the ground before meeting his gaze again. "And you don't know *me*."

"What about Sara?" Michael cuts in. "Let's announce our betrothal officially. That should be enough to shift the narrative."

I turn my attention to my brother. "Already on a first-name basis? My, you move fast."

Michael's eyes narrow. "She's my wife."

"Not yet," I reply, my stomach souring.

Grabbing Xander's hand, I wrench it toward me, laying the still-lit joint in his palm and closing his fingers around it. His face scrunches in obvious disgust.

"You'll get rid of this for me, won't you, Xander?"

"Leaving so soon?" Michael asks, sticking out his bottom lip. "Pity."

I lift a shoulder. "You two are dreadfully boring."

"Talking about important things isn't supposed to be entertaining." He rubs his chin, chuckling. "Although you've never been one to care about anything important."

The hole in my chest twists, making my teeth grind. "Yes, well, if we all cared about *importance*, Brother, who would care for you?"

His smile drops. "Go fetch Lady Beatreaux before you run off to whatever whorehouse you're planning to waste your night in."

I click my tongue and nod, spinning on my heel as I head for the door.

If I were to turn around and look back, I'm sure I would see their faces painted in surprise at how easily I agreed. I'm not known for how well I take orders. But surprisingly, I *want* to find her.

Arousal surges through my insides, pouring down my

middle and pooling in my groin as I remember the way she looked last night, on her knees, chest heaving, and hair mussed as she stared up at me like she wanted to knife me where I stood. Most likely with the one she was hiding behind her back.

No one else has treated me the way she does—with anger brimming so potently that it tries to bleed through their gaze and strike me down. It makes me want to shove my cock down her throat and see if she'd try to bite it off, just so I could punish her for using teeth.

So I'll go find my little doe.

If only to get off on her hate before I toss her to her king.

# CHAPTER 10

## *Sara*

THERE MUST BE A DOZEN DIFFERENT KITCH-
ens throughout the castle, but the one I'm in now is the
largest.

Before coming to Saxum, I'd always been free to roam
where I please—within reason—and then retreat to my
room and bask in the solitude. But now, the only time I get
to myself is in my bed at night.

I never realized how suffocated it makes me to be
surrounded by people.

It's now been four days since I've seen or heard from my
husband-to-be. And while my mind should be focused on
the future and everything I came here to accomplish, I'm
finding it...difficult. But not for the reasons it should be.

I can't even sleep without visions of Prince Tristan
making his way into my chambers and forcing me onto my
knees, except this time for a *different* reason.

It's disgusting. Not because I'm a stranger to the act—although if anyone knew of my dalliances, I most likely wouldn't be sitting here—but because out of all the people I've met in my entire life, I've decided Prince Tristan must be the worst.

Him invading my dreams is an unfortunate turn of events.

Earlier, while playing bridge in my sitting room, Ophelia recommended an afternoon nap, no doubt noting the deep circles beneath my eyes. I took her up on the offer, although I wouldn't be using the time to catch up on sleep.

Instead, I grabbed the opportunity and made my way here, hoping to find someone working in the kitchens. I want to meet the people who are the true eyes and ears of the castle. Ingrain myself in their loyalty, so when the time comes, I can depend on them. And that's how I ended up sitting at a large metal table in a room the size of a house, with Paul, one of the castle's cooks, banging on pots and pans while he makes me tea and an afternoon snack.

"Honestly." Paul wipes his brow, his auburn hair held back beneath a netted cap. "You're gorgeous, milady, but your pretty eyes make me nervous when you watch me like that."

I smile, tapping my nails on the table's top. "No need to be nervous, Paul. I like your company already."

"You do?" he asks, spinning around from the stove. "Of course you do. I mean—" He huffs before throwing his arm across his belly and bowing at the hips. "Thank you, milady."

Amusement bubbles in my chest. "You know, you don't have to be so proper when it's just the two of us."

"Forgive me." He smiles. "I'm not used to royals coming down here to socialize." He walks toward me, plopping a plate down on the table and gesturing toward the dish.

I grin back, leaning across the metal surface. "Well, I think you'll find I'm not quite like the other royals."

"Technically," a smooth voice cuts in, "you're not a royal at all."

My spine bristles, every single hair follicle standing on end as Prince Tristan appears out of nowhere, his lips tipped up in that infuriatingly lazy grin, his eyes zoned in on me.

Paul gasps, dropping to a knee. "Your Highness."

"Hello, Paul. Keeping our soon-to-be queen company?"

Surprise flickers through me. I hadn't expected him of all people to be on a first-name basis with the servants. Most people aren't.

"So what if he is?" I cut in.

He turns to me, his eyes flashing. I sit straighter in my chair.

"Then I suppose he's the lucky one today, isn't he?" My stomach flips as he steps in close. "Always in places I shouldn't find you, aren't you, little doe?"

My shoulders straighten. "There's nothing wrong with getting to know the people who breathe life into the castle walls."

His brows rise. "I agree."

A muffled thud from the opposite side of the room soars through the air, breaking our eye contact as I twist to face the wall. "What was that?"

No one answers me.

Scooting back from the table, I stand, grabbing the front of my skirts as I walk toward where the noise came from. Another thud, this time louder, and I'm sure it's coming from inside the walls. I spin around, my eyes locking on Tristan. "What's behind here?"

He doesn't respond, leaning against the corner of the table, crossing his feet and smirking.

My jaw tenses. "Paul?"

Paul wrings his hands together in front of his oversize belly. "I'm not sure I know what you mean."

I quirk a brow when another thud hits. "You don't hear that?"

"Maybe there's something wrong with your ears," Tristan suggests.

"My hearing is just fine, thank you." My eyes narrow. "Stop making me feel crazy."

He straightens off the table and moves closer until he's standing in front of me, his shadow dwarfing mine. "Do I have that much power over you already?"

"I haven't given you *any* power," I seethe, my hand itching to reach out and smack the grin off his face.

He tsks, shaking his head. "That's the thing about power, *ma petite menteuse*. It's never given freely. You have to take it."

"You speak French?" I don't know what he just called me, but the way it flowed off his tongue like silky chocolate makes my insides quake.

He smirks. "I'm a prince."

His arm rises, and my breath sticks in my lungs, waiting for the searing heat of his touch, but it never comes. Instead, he presses his hand next to my head. There's a loud creak and then the wall is moving, an entryway appearing as if it's formed out of thin air. My eyes grow wide as I twist to face it, staring into a darkened tunnel, its walls made of rock as if the castle has melded its insides within the mountain it sits on.

"Lady."

My hand moves to my chest, my mind whirling with questions. *Do the tunnels only exist within the buildings? Do they go underground to town? Who all knows of them?*

"Hey, lady, you're stepping on my sword."

I'm jolted into the present, my eyes swinging down into the light brownish-orange gaze of a child.

"Oh." I step back, my foot releasing the toy sword trapped beneath me. "I'm so sorry." My corset digs into my ribs as I lean down to pick it up, staying crouched as I hold it in my hands. "Are you a knight?" I ask.

His chest puffs out, a small smudge of what looks like black soot streaked across his brown skin. "I'm the king."

"Oh." My eyes widen, and I raise my hand to my head. "Of course, I should have known. You look the part of a mighty king." Bowing my head, I hold out his toy. "Forgive me, Your Majesty."

A smile tips the corners of his lips as he reaches out, taking the sword back from my hands. "Who are you?" he asks. "I've never seen you before, and my mama knows all the people who work here."

"This is Lady Beatreaux," Tristan says from behind me. "Milady, this is Simon."

Simon's head cocks, his eyes trailing up and down my form as if he's judging whether I'll get to live or die.

"Do we like her?" he asks.

Tristan chuckles, and the sound sends confusion tinkling through my insides, twisting up the narrative of him I've had painted in my head. He seems genuine with this child, as if he cares for him.

His stare burns through me as he places his hands in his pockets and rocks back on his heels. "We do."

My breath catches, butterflies erupting until my stomach soars.

Simon scrunches his nose as he looks at me. "You're still a girl though, so I can't like you *too* much."

I laugh, standing upright and running my palms down the front of my dress, trying to shake off the unsettled feeling brewing inside me. "Well, I'm sorry to disappoint, Your Majesty, but there's not much I can do to help that."

"Yeah. I guess not." His eyes glance over at me once more before turning to Paul. "I'm hungry. Got any grub?"

Twisting toward the prince, I place my hands on my hips, keeping my voice low. "Why are you always showing up everywhere I am? I was told you were a ghost in this castle, yet here you are. All the time."

"Have you been asking about me?" He grins.

Irritation clamps down on my middle. "Please. Don't flatter yourself."

"Does it bother you that I'm here?"

"*You* bother me in general," I reply.

He sighs. "My brother requests your presence. I'm simply the pony brought here to carry you back."

I laugh. "I find it hard to believe you'd ever allow yourself to be ridden like a horse." His eyes flash, and embarrassment bleeds through me, realizing what I just said and how it sounded. His mouth opens, but I throw my hand in the air. "Don't. Say. Anything."

"Tristan! You can't leave!" Simon squeals, pushing past me so fast I'm jerked to the side. For the third time today, I'm surprised as this small child throws himself around Tristan's legs in a tight hug, and my irritation melts away as Tristan kneels until he's level with the little boy's face, brushing the smudge of dirt from his cheek.

"Have you been in the tunnels all day?" he asks.

Simon nods. "Yeah, don't be mad. I just…" He leans in and lowers his voice. "When the other kids see me, they laugh. They're mean."

My heart twists violently as Simon's knuckles blanch

where he grips his toy sword. Moving my gaze from him, they land on Paul, whose expression mirrors the feelings swimming inside me, although when he sees me looking, he wipes the emotion from his face, spinning around to face the stove.

Tristan leans back, his nostrils flaring, his veiny hands and ringed fingers gripping the boy's shoulders tight. "You're a king. Aren't you?"

"Ye-yeah." Simon sniffles.

"That's right. And those kids? They're sheep. We never allow ourselves to care about the sheep, little tiger. Do you understand?"

Simon nods.

"You're better than they'll ever be," Tristan murmurs, tapping the boy's chin with his fingers.

A knot lodges in my throat, something heavy and warm settling in my chest and swirling outward, like smoke unfurling through my veins and heating every part of me.

Tristan stands, smoothing his hand over the top of Simon's head before looking over at me.

"Come on, little doe. Wouldn't want to keep your new husband waiting."

# CHAPTER 11

## *Tristan*

"SO WHAT DOES YOUR BROTHER WANT?"

I glance at Lady Beatreaux from my peripheral as we walk down the long corridor. It's an unusually bright day in Saxum, the clouds breaking just enough to send small rays of sunshine through the stained-glass windows and splay across her skin. My fingers flex, wanting to grab my pencils and sketch out the vision.

"He's the king. He doesn't have to want anything to get it."

She smirks. "You sound bitter."

"Do I?"

"A little." Her shoulders lift. "Are you?"

My chest twists as I slip a joint from behind my ear and place it in my mouth, my tongue flicking the edge as it rolls across my lips. My private tutors called it an oral fixation, right before they'd try to lash it out of me, saying it was uncouth for a prince to be seen with things in his mouth. I tried to explain it kept me calm, kept away the obsessive thoughts and the anxiety churning like a stew in my gut. But they didn't care how it made me feel, only what it made me look like.

"Are we friends now, little doe?" I ask.

"Stop calling me that."

She cuts me a glare and my heart pounds, excited to be riling her up. "You're very demanding. Has anyone ever told you that?"

"And you're rude," she retorts.

"It's not an outstanding quality for a queen consort," I continue. "You may want to work on that before your etiquette courses start and they beat it out of you."

Her footsteps falter and she stops, spinning to face me.

"Beat it out…" Her voice trails off as she watches me, and I sense the tension in the air growing thick even before her gaze snags on my scar. It tightens around me until my lungs compress, but I revel in the discomfort.

"Don't worry." My finger taps against the raised flesh on my brow. "This isn't a result of bad manners. Not *mine* anyway."

She nods but doesn't avert her eyes. "Thanks for the tip."

I move to walk again, but she reaches out, her fingers wrapping around my wrist to keep me in place. My gaze drops to where we're connected, heat flooding through my veins.

"Tell me about the rebels," she demands.

My gut jolts and I spin to face her, allowing her touch to linger on my skin. I trail my eyes along her form, starting at the tip of her black-as-night curls, over her deep-chocolate eyes, before sliding down to the cleavage peeking from the top of her bloodred dress.

My cock grows stiff as I imagine ripping the fabric from her chest and sliding my length between the swell of her breasts until I'm crazy with the need to come.

She drops my wrist and backs up a space, her chin lifting like it always does right before she becomes defiant. The move showcases the expanse of her neck, and my fingers twitch to leave prints on her like paint on a canvas.

Slowly, I take the unlit joint from my mouth, placing it behind my ear as I bring my eyes back to hers. "What would you like to know?"

"Everything. I want… Wait." Her brows draw in. "You're not going to fight me on it? Tell me I shouldn't speak of them or ask questions?"

I tilt my head. "Now, why would I do that?"

"Everyone else has. I just—" Her teeth sink into her bottom lip.

The sight of her marring her own flesh sends another spike of desire through me, and before I can stop, I'm moving toward her, excitement sparking my insides when she retreats. I continue until she's underneath the stone arches of the window, her body pressing against the greens and yellows of the stained glass.

Her eyes flick from my face to the hallway and back as if she's scared someone will walk by and see us.

I enjoy making her nervous.

The mask she wears for the world drops away when it's just the two of us.

"I'm not everyone else, little doe." I step in farther.

The yellow specks in her eyes make my stomach tighten. I bring a hand up, running the backs of my fingers along her cheek, liking the way she flinches, either from the touch itself or the cool metal of my rings.

"It would be such a shame to lose that inquisitive mind," I murmur. "I don't wish to stifle it. I wish to break it apart and see what other questions I can find."

Her hands move behind her until they're pushing against the window, the colors creating a beautiful halo around her body as if she's divinity in human form, brought to earth to tempt me from my violent deeds.

But I already know she's no angel.

My fingers continue down until I'm grazing against her neck. I expect her to pull away, but once again she surprises me, tilting her head as if she craves my touch.

"You put a lot of trust in me, asking about a rebel faction and thinking I won't throw you in the dungeons and chain you up."

Her pulse thrums beneath my thumb, and my muscles cramp in anticipation at the way her nerves show themselves to me, no matter how much she tries to hide them.

"You wouldn't," she breathes.

"You're so sure?" My grip tightens around her throat, wanting to feel her pulse flutter as I whisper dirty words into her ear. "I think you'd look lovely tied to a wall and begging for mercy."

Something wild is unleashed inside me as her pupils dilate, my balls jerking, making my length pulse against the fabric of my trousers. I drop my hand to her waist, moving us until she's pressed into the alcove of the window's archway, our bodies centimeters apart.

"You shouldn't be touching me," she whispers. "If someone sees…they could put us to death."

"What are you going to do, take out your cute little dagger and try to bleed me dry?" I ask, my hand pushing against her torso so she's flattened against the wall. "Would you like to keep pretending? I know you're not the good girl you claim to be." Her palms jump to my chest, fingers digging into my black tunic. I lean in, my nose skimming along her hairline, breathing in her soft floral scent. "I see what you try so hard to hide."

I feel out of control. Every single piece of me is raging to grab her, fuck her, brand her, and keep her, which is crazy because I don't even *want* her.

"You don't have to hide from me, little doe."

"I'm not hiding," she purrs, her lips brushing against mine. "I'm revolted."

Footsteps sound from down the hall, and we pull away

from each other, her fingers tangling in the thin chain of her necklace.

I spin away, cursing myself for being so idiotic. *Why would I touch her in the middle of the hallway?*

*Why would I touch her at all?*

She's right. If anyone knew, it would be disastrous. My brother would jump on the chance to arrest and put me to death. He wouldn't *actually* be able to kill me, of course. I'd be gone before he could announce the trial, but being outcast to the shadowed lands isn't helpful to my goals at the moment.

Anger whips through me like a windstorm, and I turn a glare on Lady Beatreaux. *Is she bewitching me on purpose?*

"Stop looking at me like that," she hisses.

"Such a smart mouth," I snap. "Watch how you speak to your prince."

Her lip curls. "You are *absolutely* insane, aren't you?"

My teeth grind, irritation slashing against my skin.

"Your Highness," a deep voice booms off the stone walls, a royal guard walking toward us. He stops a few paces away and bows.

"What?" I hiss, twisting toward him.

His gaze bounces between us. "Am I interrupting?"

Annoyance licks at my spine, but before I can reply, Lady Beatreaux steps forward, her energy having changed in the blink of an eye into something harsher. Something more regal.

Her head rises high, her back is straight, and she looks

every bit like the queen she's about to become. "Who are you to question him?"

My cock throbs so violently I have to bite back the groan.

The guard's eyes narrow and he points to his chest. "I'm a commander in the king's army."

"And she is your new queen," I snap, moving so she's behind me.

The guard's gaze widens as he looks back and forth between us, and it's only then I realize he may have seen more than I thought.

I brush my hand down the sleeve of my black tunic, annoyed that I have to take time out of my day to solve this issue. "What's your name?"

"Antony," he replies.

"*Antony*." I smile. "Is anyone expecting you?"

He shakes his head, caution waving like yellow flags in his eyes.

"Wonderful. You'll come with me then. I was just on my way to collect a guard about a pressing security matter." I tip my head toward Lady Beatreaux. "Milady, I trust you can find your own way to my brother?"

She stares at me for so long, I become convinced she knows what I'm about to do, and I expect her to step in and put a stop to it, the way anyone else would.

But instead, she drops into the slightest curtsy, her eyes never leaving mine. "Your Highness."

And then she walks away.

# CHAPTER 12

## *Tristan*

IT CONTINUALLY SURPRISES ME HOW EASY IT is to end a person's life. Even as a boy, I never felt the type of attachment others do, and there's only been one death that's affected me.

Everyone else can rot.

Still, I've always known that I'm just a bit different. Smarter than most? Unspeakably. More fit to rule? Undoubtedly.

When you're forced on the fringes of society yet required to be there, you notice things that go missed when you're paraded in the middle of the stage like a puppet.

And most people, I find, are imbeciles.

Face value is the only truth, and blind trust is something often found in spades. Which, I suppose, explains the popularity of my brother. He isn't particularly charming, and he doesn't have the brains to be clever or witty. But he's conventionally attractive and spent his life being the crown prince, and for the masses, that's enough.

Even though Michael excelled in nothing but pushing down others in order to feel strong, people often want to believe the ones placed on pedestals deserve to be there.

But you don't need to have brawn to subdue and exert power.

True power lies in the ability to harness energy and wield it like a sword, becoming the puppeteer who masters all the strings instead of the marionette being forced to dance. Years of being tortured under Michael's hands taught me that, he and his pack of friends, laughing as they pushed my face into the dirt and told me I wasn't worth the mud being caked in my cuts.

They stole my power every day.

It wasn't until many years later that I learned to take it back, and it wasn't until my father's death that I craved taking theirs too.

Something sharp pricks at my chest and I shake off the thought, placing my hand on the shoulder of the royal guard as we reach the entrance to the dungeons. He glances back at me, his nerves so potent I can taste them in the air. I wave my arm toward the narrow staircase.

"The security issue is down here, sir?" His voice pinches.

"Please, give me some credit." I chuckle. "Would I bring you here for any other reason?"

He shakes his head. "No, of course not. I just... This isn't really my area."

"Your area is wherever I tell you it is."

He swallows, his eyes growing large. "Of course."

I follow behind him as we move into the dungeons, our footsteps reverberating off the dark walls as we walk down the concrete steps. The air is moist, and it smells like mold and despair, although there are no prisoners rotting away in the cells. Drips of water splash in the background from the castle's plumbing, and the only other sound is the harsh breathing coming from the guard himself.

Excitement winds its way through my middle at his obvious unease.

He glances back at me, and I force a grin, nodding toward the last cell as I walk past him and over to the far wall with the large skeleton keys that open the iron doors.

"Last one here," I say as I make my way to the final one on the left and insert the key, feeling the click as the lock unlatches. It creaks as I open it and let him go in first.

The guard cocks his head. "I'm not a carpenter. I think that's who—"

I move to where he stands, the metal key pressing into my palm as I shove at his shoulders, prodding him forward like cattle being led to slaughter. And it's only once he's within the cell that I drop all pretense, spinning around and closing the door behind us.

The slam echoes off the bare concrete walls, and the

guard tries to go back toward the door. "Your Highness? I—"

Reaching up to my ear, I slip the joint from behind it, pulling the matches from my pocket, my stomach tightening as I strike the flame and bring it to my lips.

"Antony." I snuff out the fire and puff on the hash, my gaze taking him in from the tips of his toes up to the top of his blond head. He looks every part a commander, the black and gold of his uniform striking and the lion in the center of his chest showcasing Gloria Terra's coat of arms. "Antony," I repeat. "Do you think I'm stupid enough to confuse a carpenter with a member of the king's army?"

His lips turn down. "No, I just—"

"You *will* refer to me properly. Your Highness. Master." I pause. "Or my lord, if you feel so inclined."

His body stills, no doubt sensing the malice that has dropped into my tone. "M-my lord?" he questions.

"You don't think it's fitting?" I cock my head, blowing out a plume of smoke as I walk toward him. "I know it's usually reserved for lower-class nobility, however in this case, its sentiment lends to more of a 'savior' type of title."

I step in close now, forcing him back, his hand flying to his hip. He draws his weapon, but his movements are clunky and sharp, and before he can even point the gun, I wrap my fingers around his wrist, twisting his hand in directions not meant for bone. He screams, the pistol clanking as it drops to the concrete floor, and I keep applying pressure until the resistance snaps away and his fingers grow limp, his hand flopping like a useless slab of meat.

"As I was saying, I've realized most people pray to find their savior right before they die," I continue, lowering my voice to a murmur. "I'm willing to be that for you."

The lighting is dull in the dungeons, but the small lamps resting outside the cell filter through the iron-barred window of the door, the dull glow glistening off the tears tracking down his face.

"P-please, Your H-h-highness," he stutters.

"Ah, ah, ah," I tsk. I place pressure on his wrist again, and he groans in obvious pain. "Bow before me, Antony, commander of the king's army."

He drops like a sack of potatoes, his shoulders rising and falling with his whimpers.

I take him in as he cowers at my feet, bringing the hash to my mouth and inhaling again, enjoying the way it makes my head buzz. My foot kicks his weapon farther away, and I walk around his trembling frame. "Rather weak for a commander, aren't you?" I question. "You know, if you tell me what you saw in the hallway, I'll set you free."

"Nothing," he forces out between gritted teeth. "I saw nothing."

I chuckle, pausing at his back. "I don't believe you. Somebody *always* sees something."

"I swear it, I–I…"

"There's an abandoned cabin deep within our forests,

and when I was a boy, I used to sneak away to it often. Did you know that?"

The guard's breathing becomes choppier, but he grows silent.

I grip the back of his sandy-blond head, ripping it upward until his face is exposed to the ceiling, the smoke from my cigarette curling between my fingers and wrapping around his skull. "Answer me."

His jaw clenches. "No…"

"Of course you didn't," I snap. "No one does. No one cared enough about little Prince Tristan to give a damn what I did with my time."

I toss him to the ground so he's forced to catch his body with his broken wrist. He collapses, groaning as he brings the limp fingers to his chest.

"Our tunnels lead right to it. Isn't that something?"

Cocking my head, I wait for his reply, but other than his whimpers, he stays silent. Irritation coils around my muscles, squeezing them tight.

My voice lowers. "I thought we had already gone over how I expect an answer to my questions, Antony."

"Yes! It's something." His voice cracks, and the obvious fear weaving through the tone makes me smile.

"The point is, I spent hours there. Usually taking my sketchbook and drawing until my fingers went numb. It was the only place I could go where the people who hurt me wouldn't follow." I crouch, my hands sliding around his shoulders, pulling him upright into a sitting position. "And everyone let me disappear, even though they all saw what went on. Perhaps they never cared." I shrug. "Or maybe they thought alone time would help my 'fragile mental state.'"

My gut churns and I bring the joint to my lips, allowing the smoke to seep from the edges of my mouth as I speak.

"But some people are beyond saving. Are *you* beyond saving, Antony?"

He shakes his head.

"That's what they all say." My fingers rest on the dip above his collarbone, directly below his neck. "If I were to press right here, it would drop you down and cut off your breath, but only for a moment. Do you know what it feels like to choke repeatedly for hours?"

"No," he whimpers.

"I can show you if you'd like." I pause. "Or you can tell me the truth and hope that I'll be *your* savior."

His eyes narrow, and even through his pain, defiance swirls through his irises. "You're no savior. Just a disfigured *freak*."

Anger slams into me, and my hand whips out before I can control it, the sound of my rings smacking bone loud in the concrete room. He flies to the side, grunting as blood pours from his mouth. He spits and a tooth flies onto the floor. I ignore his whimpers, lifting up my foot and slamming it down on the side of his face, my abdomen tensing from the rise and fall of my leg as I stomp his cheek, feeling the bone fracture beneath my heel.

Red liquid pools around my feet and I back up a space, closing my eyes and panting through the torrential downpour of fire that's raining on my insides from his words.

"Everyone *always* underestimates me." I sigh, stepping forward again, this time to press my foot on his wrist above the snapped bone. "But you're wrong, Antony. Because right now? I'm your *god*."

I grind my boot down, and he grits his teeth, a long groan escaping from his clenched lips.

"Don't be shy, sweetheart." I chuckle. "You can scream as loud as you want. No one will hear."

His working hand flies to my shin, his fingernails trying to claw my flesh through the fabric of my pants.

Bending down close to his face, my voice drops to a whisper. "Just a few paltry words, Antony, and all this can be over. Tell me what you saw."

"Will you…will you let me go?" he cries.

Laughing, I flick the end of my joint, pinpricks of pleasure racing through me as the ashes rain down on his sweaty, snot-filled face. "I promise to let you free."

"I s-saw you and the lady." His words are deformed, the *s*'s sounding like *t*'s, and every few seconds, he spits more blood at my feet.

I lighten the pressure on his wrist.

"In the windowpane, it…it looked like you were being intimate. Pl-please, please, I beg of you…*my lord*."

A satisfied breath escapes me, a thrill rushing through my veins even as his words remind me of how stupid and reckless I was.

"I appreciate your honesty." Walking behind him, my hands slide around his neck and grip just beneath his ears. "And lucky for you, I *am* a merciful god."

I twist until bones crack and separate. His limp body drops to the ground beneath me, his eyes wide and vacant, a pool of blood forming from where it dribbles out of his mouth.

"Be free, Antony."

I bring the joint to my lips, puffing one last time before dropping it on his corpse, allowing the lit end to burn through the eye of the lion in the center of his chest, a strange sense of satisfaction weaving through me as I watch it turn to ash.

# CHAPTER 13

## *Sara*

"I'D LIKE TO SPEAK WITH UNCLE RAF," I SAY TO Xander, who sits across from me as Sheina pins my hair. She's idly gossiping with Ophelia, who's crocheting off to the side.

He pushes up his glasses, bringing a thick cigar to his mouth and puffing on the end. The smell of the tobacco is sweet and smoky as it hits my nostrils, and it reminds me of sitting in my father's study for hours on end while he worked. A pang of homesickness hits the center of my gut, making me long for the sunshine-filled days in Silva.

"I'll arrange it," Xander says.

I force a smile. My uncle told me that Xander was my confidant. The one who I could depend on, the ace in the castle. But the longer I'm here, the more distrust replaces the confidence I arrived with.

"Sheina, Ophelia. Leave us," I say.

Their chatter stops, both of them moving from the room without a word. Ophelia doesn't look back, but

Sheina does, her wide eyes glancing between Xander and me before she spins around and closes the door behind her.

She's been quieter than usual the past couple of days, and when I watch her retreat, I worry that she's unhappy here. That if given the chance, she'd flee back home and leave me surrounded by people I don't know. It wouldn't be the end of the world, but she's a comfort to me. A small slice of familiarity in an unknown place.

I cross my hands in my lap as I stare at Xander, allowing the silence to linger long after they're gone. I may be a woman, but I am not a fool, and I'll no longer allow him to treat me like I am.

"Cousin," he starts.

"Do not cousin me, Alexander."

He stiffens in his chair.

"I'm tired of sitting here as if nothing is happening," I continue. "Your father told me I could trust you. Can I truly?"

"Sara, please." He drums his fingers on the wooden arm of the chair. "You're here *because* of me. But these things take time. They're fragile. Delicate."

My chest tightens. "Time moves a lot slower when you're used as a prop."

He scoffs, shaking his head. "Do you have any idea what has gone into this? What it's taken to get you here?" The chair creaks as he leans forward, resting his elbows on his knees. "I know it's difficult to wait, but everything is falling into place. You just need patience."

"Nothing is happening." I flick a curl that's fallen from my face. "How long am I supposed to sit here and pretend I'm happy gossiping with the ladies of court? I want to avenge my father, Xander. Maybe you don't understand that because you've never felt the pain of losing the only one you loved."

He rolls the cigar between his fingers. "In an hour's time, you'll head into the town square with His Majesty, where he'll dine with you and propose in front of the people. We'll have an engagement ball." He pauses. "*Everyone* will be there."

My breath whooshes out of me, relief replacing the tension that's been knotting up my spine. "And then we'll make a move?"

Xander nods. "Then we'll make our move." He cocks his head. "Is there something else going on?"

Now it's *my* posture that straightens, flashes of yesterday afternoon flooding into my brain. "What else could be going on? I'm all alone in an enormous castle with nothing but my thoughts and my...*trust*."

Xander's lips purse. "Well, once your betrothal is announced, you'll be much busier. Etiquette courses and wedding planning, of course."

My nose scrunches.

"Don't forget why you're here, Cousin. What this is all for," he implores, lowering his voice and leaning in. "We must move with precision, not haste."

"I know." I let out a sigh. "But it doesn't make it any easier."

He runs his fingers beneath the frame of his glasses, pinching the bridge of his nose. "I'm sorry you've felt so alone and in the dark. That was never my intention. I'll do better from now on."

The tangles in my stomach loosen. "Thank you."

"The wedding will be within six months' time." He stands, buttoning the front of his black jacket, his hand slicking over the top of his hair.

"Six months?" My eyes widen.

He shrugs, his eyes growing serious as they peer into mine. "No one said you had to *take* six months. Use this time to play the part…so we can rip them out by the roots."

"I know what to do," I snap.

A small smirk tips his lips. "Good. No worries then."

"Absolutely none." I raise my hands in the air, grinning.

The conversation should put me at ease. After all, he's finally speaking to me as if I'm part of the plans. But there's something about the way the air thins that sends alarm tickling my skin, making my hair stand on end, and it hits me that maybe my cousin Xander isn't the person my uncle has led me to believe he is.

The nausea in my stomach strengthens, churning like a looming storm.

---

"Lady Beatreaux, you look stunning."

Michael's voice booms across the court as my

ladies-in-waiting and I make our way to the automobiles lined up at the gate.

There's a chill in the air, even though it's just past September, and as the clouds loom over the sky, I have another moment of missing the sunshine of Silva. I wonder how two places within the same country can be so vastly different yet coexist within the same borders.

I suppose it's because borders are man-made and Mother Nature doesn't confine herself to the rules of man.

*If only we all could be so lucky.*

"Thank you, Your Majesty." I drop into a curtsy as I reach him, the stiff bones of my corset making my breathing shallow. I'm sure that Ophelia cinched it too tight, but I ignore the discomfort.

"Where are you taking me today?" I ask, glancing at Timothy, who stands by the back door with his hand outstretched.

Michael waves his arm as Timothy helps me into the automobile. "Don't worry your pretty little head about that," he says once we're in the back seats. "Just enjoy the day and everything that comes along with being on my arm."

I bite back the scoff that's aching to roll off my tongue, my head tilting as I take him in. *How do people find him charming?* To me, he comes across as arrogant and self-absorbed.

"How could I not?" I peer at him from under the wide brim of my purple hat.

Timothy moves into the seat across from us, and my

eyes fall to the coat of arms on his chest, my mind thrown back to yesterday afternoon—to the guard who left with Tristan. I was stupid, allowing the prince to corner me the way he did; simple acts like that can have disastrous consequences. And who is he to me?

Nobody.

Worse than that.

*A Faasa.*

But that doesn't stop my stomach from somersaulting at the memory of him pushing against me in the darkened corner. Of his hands touching me in ways no one is allowed to touch.

And then I think of that guard—the one who did nothing except walk into the wrong place at the wrong time—and while I can't say for sure what happened when they left, deep in my gut, I know the truth. When Tristan's eyes met mine, there was more being said between us than what we spoke into the air.

I don't wish death on innocent souls. But sometimes, sacrifices must be made for the greater good.

The automobile rolls toward the front gates, and my eyes glance out across the courtyard, snagging on the large weeping willow in the distance.

I hate myself for the way my heart drops the slightest bit when I don't see jade-green eyes watching me from the shadows.

# CHAPTER 14

## *Tristan*

MY SOON-TO-BE SISTER-IN-LAW HAS BECOME a bit of an obsession.

A distraction, if you will. One I don't have time for.

I'm convinced the only reason she plagues my thoughts is because she's a puzzle I haven't been able to solve, and since reading people is my specialty, the fact that she's a challenge makes her unbearably interesting.

The wood floors creak as I pace across the second-story room at the Elephant Bones Tavern, glancing out the balcony door windows. There must be hundreds of people huddled on the empty land behind the building, waiting for me to address them.

Anticipation swirls through me like a gust of wind until every single nerve ending is lit up with excitement for the future. For *my* future.

The one that *should* have been mine from the beginning.

Violence has grown in the past two years, ever since

my father's death and my brother's subsequent rise to the throne. Everyone assumes it's random. No one knows it's me pulling the strings, fanning the flames of their anger. It's easy to exacerbate issues when people are starved and forgotten. And it's even easier to gain people's trust and place them strategically throughout the kingdom, waiting patiently for when I call.

I push through the rickety double doors to the patio and step onto the Juliet balcony. Cheers erupt and I stand straight, basking in their admiration. Blood heats in my veins, rushing to my groin until my cock hardens. It's exciting to have them all stare at me. I enjoy being revered the way I should have always been.

"Hello, friends." I project my voice. "You've heard the whispers, so let me be the first to confirm. King Michael will marry."

"Who?" someone yells.

"Who is not important. I'm sure you'll find out when they make the official announcement." A flash of my little doe's face tumbles through my mind, and my chest tightens. "What matters is that you know someone placed her very strategically for one reason, and that's gaining your trust. To make you think sunny days are on the horizon. Comrades, I'm here to tell you the only blaze on the horizon is the orange glow of fire when we burn their king at the stake."

Yells erupt, boots stomping on the ground until there's a vibration through the air, creating a low rumble.

"Burn the king's whore!" someone else shouts.

My eyes fly to where the voice is coming from, my muscles growing taut. "She is not to be touched."

The cheers grow quiet at my sharp words, confused faces staring up at me. My gaze lands on Edward, standing in the back corner with Belinda and her husband, Earl, waiting for my cue. When our eyes meet, I see the surprise flowing through them.

He hadn't expected me to say that.

I hadn't expected to say it.

But here we are.

"It's important to not show our hands too early, friends," I continue. "We must bide our time. Allow them to believe she is their beacon of hope."

"And we're just supposed to trust you?" a voice rings out. "You're one of them!"

Silence descends over the crowd, and my jaw ticks. I raise my hands out to the sides. "If you have an issue with my leadership, you're more than welcome to come up here and take it from me. I'm nothing if not fair." No one moves a muscle, and I let the quiet linger, my eyes scanning the crowd to see who dares to think they can question me. "Don't be a coward now, when your voice was just so loud."

I continue to gaze out, my stare locking on a young man with torn clothing and dusty-red hair, his jaw set as he looks up at the balcony.

"It's an admirable trait and an honest question." I wave

my hand toward him, annoyance pricking against my skin. "Come forward. Stand here, at the front where everyone can see you."

His body stiffens, but he ambles through the crowd until he's in front of them all, forced to crane his neck to maintain our eye contact.

I smile. "Have I not given enough to earn your trust? How many times do I need to prove my worth?"

"It's been two years," he implores, shaking his head.

"It's been far longer for me. And we're speaking of treason. Enough to kill us all with one wrong move." I raise my fingers in the air and snap. Edward moves through the throng of people, carrying the corpse of Antony Scarenbourg—commander of the king's army.

Excited murmurs roll through the air like thunder.

"Do not make the mistake of believing that when I'm not with you, I'm not fighting *for* you."

The redheaded man's eyes widen as Antony's body drops at his feet, his uniform burned and his skin blue from rigor mortis.

Edward moves again, and I stand still, waiting as he grabs a bucket of kerosene and walks back, preparing to dump it on the corpse.

"Let *him* do it," I say, pointing at the fool who questioned my authority.

Edward glances up at me before nodding and passing the bucket off.

The young man stares down for long moments, taking in the singed and nearly unrecognizable insignia on Antony's chest, his face growing angrier by the second. And then he tips the bucket, allowing the liquid to pour onto the body, splashing off the ground and puddling around his feet.

Hoots and hollers from the rebels accompany his actions.

My eyes meet Edward's, and unspoken words pass between us. This man will not live to see another sunset.

But for now, I'll allow him this moment. It's good for morale.

Pulling a matchbox from my cloak's pocket, I strike a flame against the side.

"Brute force can win a war," I start, heat dancing against my fingertips. "But our strength is in patience. In planning. *That* is what topples empires. Together we rule, divided we fall."

Antony's body explodes into flames when I drop the match, the smell of burning flesh potent as it curls in the air as smoke.

"Down with Michael Faasa!" someone yells.

"Death to the king!" others chime in.

"We move soon, friends." I smile. "Stay prepared."

# CHAPTER 15

## *Sara*

I'VE BEEN HERE FOR A WEEK, BUT THIS IS THE first time I've ventured outside the castle walls into the actual town of Saxum. A clock tower sits in the center of the square, and businesses line both sides of the cobblestone streets, brand-new shiny lampposts accenting the sidewalks. I've never seen a streetlight in person before, and my insides churn as I realize just how prosperous the main area of Saxum is while Silva struggles without.

Michael and I have been sitting inside the Chocolate Gorge, a patisserie known for making the best sweets in the region. Timothy, Xander, and my ladies perch at a table across the room from us, and a few royal guards line the entrance, but other than that, there's no one here.

"Is it always this empty?" I ask, pushing my dessert plate away.

Michael smirks, his slicked-back brown hair gleaming

under the lights. "Couldn't have the commoners interrupting when I'm trying to woo you."

My chest pinches as I peer out the front windows where half a dozen people line up around barricades, trying to glance inside to see their king.

"Do you come here often?"

He shrugs. "Not since I was a child. My father used to bring Tristan and me here once in a blue moon."

My blood heats when he mentions his brother, but I ignore it. I will not let him affect me when he's not even around.

Still, I can't help imagining Tristan and Michael as children, eating all the chocolates and candies with their father looking on. Everything I've heard of King Michael II's legacy is in all the ways he failed his country. It's difficult for me to picture him as a man who cared for his family, and curiosity brims inside me, wanting to learn more.

"That's very sweet," I say.

Michael scoffs, his eyes moving past mine before coming back. He smiles, but I see the flash of pain that haunts his features. "Sara Beatreaux, you *are* a bleeding heart, aren't you?"

I sit up straighter. "Isn't that something you should want in your queen?"

He tilts his head. "And you're so sure you'll be my queen?"

Blowing out a breath, I stare down at my lap before peeking at him from beneath my lashes. "I'm sure that I was bred specifically for you, Your Majesty. I think you'd be doing yourself a great disservice to not keep me at your side."

He hums, his fingers coming up to rub at his jaw. "Bred *for* me?"

I nod, reaching out to grasp my cup of tea and taking a sip before placing it back on the table. "My uncle turned many suitors down, hoping one day, I would belong to you."

It's a gamble telling him this, and it's a gross exaggeration, but I'm banking on the fact that Michael loves having his ego stroked and is possessive over his toys. I was told this long before coming here, and it's noticeable in the way he preens whenever he's paid a compliment and sulks when something isn't going his way.

Hopefully, learning I was meant for him all along will entice him to snatch me up and collect me like a treasure.

He leans across the table, his brows rising. "And what of *you*, Sara? I'll be honest, I'm not very interested in what your uncle wants."

My eyes lock on his, the weight of responsibility dropping into my gut and pushing the words from my mouth. "After meeting you? I want nothing more."

A slow smile creeps along his face and he settles back into his chair, a satisfied look coasting across his features.

"Sire," Xander interrupts, coming to stand next to the table. "There's a journalist set up outside, ready to take your photos, and then we need to head back to the castle for a meeting with the privy council."

Michael nods, glancing out the front windows. His face pinches, nose scrunching up in obvious disgust. "So many people outside."

"They're behind the barricades, sire. They won't get near you," Xander reassures.

Michael stands, placing a top hat on his head and holding out an arm to me. "Showtime, Sara Beatreaux. You want this? Make it look good."

I grin back at him, although it feels as though an elephant is sitting on my chest. My fingers wrap around his elbow as I rise, stomach tightening in anticipation.

Timothy goes first, holding open the door for us, and we make our way outside, the guards moving to flank our sides. Murmurs race through the people on the sidewalk, and there's a man in a tweed suit ahead, a large tripod with a camera sitting on top placed next to him. He bows when we approach. "Your Majesty. Milady."

Michael stares down his nose at the man, his jaw ticking. I glance between the two of them, irritation grating my nerves, annoyed he isn't even acknowledging him.

"Are you the reporter?" I ask.

The man looks at me, a small grin gracing his lips. "I am, ma'am."

"Very well," Michael cuts in. He turns to me, winking as if he's about to pull a prank before he reaches in his pocket and takes my hand in his. "Lady Beatreaux, it would be my greatest honor if you would accept my hand in marriage."

I stare up at him, my neck craning to meet his eyes from under the brim of my hat. He clears his throat, his eyes hardening more with every passing second.

His grip on my hand tightens. I jolt out of my daze, realizing *this* was his grand proposal. No bended knee, no heartfelt speech. Just a few rushed words and expectation. I'm not sure why I was standing here like a fool, waiting for anything else. I'm surprised he did it in public at all—I had waited the first couple of days to see if he would extend a formal proposal, and when it never happened, I figured it was just assumed.

Adopting a surprised expression, I lift my free hand to my chest. "It's beautiful," I say, staring at the massive diamond cushioned by a pearl on each side. "It would be my greatest honor to be your wife."

He takes the ring from its ornate box and slips it on my finger. "This was my mother's. I hope you appreciate the sentiment."

I keep the smile pasted on my face as he pulls me into his side, even though the thought of wearing anything that belonged to the dowager queen makes bile rise to the back of my throat. Michael turns us, adopting a beaming grin for the camera. Cheers go up from the people behind the barricades, words of congratulations soaring through the air.

But it's all muddled behind the sudden whooshing in my ears as my eyes lock on a tall, cloaked figure across the street, leaning against one of those shiny black lampposts.

My heart skips.

I can't see his face, but somehow, I just know it's him.

*Tristan.*

Michael turns us to wave at the people behind the barricades before leading us toward the automobile. I follow, the smile plastered on my face like papier-mâché, my heart pounding in my chest, although I'm not sure why it's racing.

The guards crowd around us as we head toward the automobile, hiding everything from view, and it isn't until I'm in the back seat that I'm able to search again.

But he's already gone.

---

I've attended Sunday service my entire life.

When I was young, the pews were always full. But as time wore on and resources dwindled, attendance grew sparse. Turns out people lose their faith when faced with never-ending adversity.

The church itself was plain, small wooden benches and beige walls that had browned due to lack of funds and lack of willpower. That's what happens when your source of livelihood is ripped out from the roots. When the men who are put in positions of power decide to withhold funds and forget that you're part of what makes them whole.

And as I sit in the beautiful cathedral attached to the Saxum castle, I can't help but feel bitter for all the ways the people here have *everything*, while all mine have gone without.

We're the same country, yet we're worlds apart.

The cathedral itself is beautiful. Dark woods and gray stone archways carved with intricate designs, laced in gold detail. Soaring ceilings are covered with colorful art, the type I'm sure took decades to complete, and the only light other than the flame of candles is from the muted sun bleeding through stained-glass windows, splashing on the beige and brownstone tile in kaleidoscopes of color.

The service has ended, and while everyone else has disappeared, including my betrothed, I'm still here, having told them I wanted some time to pray.

Truthfully, I'm waiting on Xander.

I fidget in my spot, the wood bench numbing my legs. When I glance around and ensure no one else is here, I stand, moving to the walkway between the pews. My pale-pink dress kisses the floor; my hands—covered in matching gloves—run down my sleeves first and then the front of my skirt, smoothing away the wrinkles. My steps clack on the tile, echoing off the walls as I make my way toward the altar.

The crucifix is front and center, and something pulls in my chest as I stare at the sculpture, a hollow type of sadness spinning webs through my heart.

I've never questioned my duty to my family or the justice that we seek. It's all I've ever known, even before my father's death, all they have conditioned me to want. But for the first time, I'm empathetic toward the plight of Jesus, although I'd never dare to speak it out loud.

How unfair that he had to sacrifice himself to cleanse our sins.

Finally, I tear my eyes away and move toward the shadows, realizing there's a large oil painting hanging on display near the darkened hallway at the front of the room.

The portrait is of a king.

Black hair peeks from beneath his bejeweled crown, piercing jade-green eyes that come to life through the picture, fierce and harsh. A shiver skates down my spine.

"That's my father."

My breath whooshes out of me, stomach jumping to my throat as I spin around, coming face-to-face with Tristan. My hand flies to my chest. "You scared me."

The corners of his lips tilt as he steps up next to me, his hands in his pockets as he glances at the portrait.

I side-eye him, wondering what his relationship was with his father. Michael piqued my curiosity, and while I don't expect Tristan to open up, I can't help the question from flowing off my tongue. "Do you miss him?"

Something dark coasts over his face, his jaw tensing. "Yes."

My mouth pops open, turning my head to study him. "I miss my father too."

It's all I can think of to say. *"I'm happy he's dead and I hope he rots in hell"* seems like it wouldn't be an appropriate response.

He stares up at the painting, so I follow suit, taking in

the angles of King Michael II's face and how similar they are to Tristan's.

"He looks like you," I note, glancing at him again from the corner of my eye.

His brow rises. "You mean unbearably attractive?"

I smile. "Terrifyingly so."

"Hmm." He nods, twisting toward me. "And are you one who runs from your fears, Sara Beatreaux? Or do you face them?"

My heart kicks against my ribs, and my mouth goes dry. "I don't believe in running."

"No? You might change your mind living here."

My stomach drops, the good feeling disappearing. "Is that a threat?"

"A warning," he replies.

"I saw you yesterday," I blurt. "In the town square. You were hiding your face like quite the little creeper. Is that because you didn't want to be seen?"

He steps closer until his frame towers over mine, strands of his disheveled black hair falling over his brow. "So many questions for someone who gives nothing in return."

My legs freeze in place, like I've stepped into wet cement and let it dry around my feet. "What do you want to know?"

"Everything."

"That could take a long time."

"You're about to marry into the family. We have nothing *but* time. Unless Michael tires of you before the wedding and chooses one of his other whores instead." He cocks his head, his eyes calculating as they blaze over my skin. "Or maybe…you have a secret agenda."

Irritation rushes through my chest, expanding like a heat wave. "I am *not* a whore." My fists clench at my sides. "And just because you have no propensity for morals doesn't mean it extends to others."

He reaches up and cups my chin, his thumb brushing over my lips. "Such a smart mouth. Pity my brother won't know how to tame it."

Fire blazes through my veins so fast my stomach cramps. "I don't *need* to be tamed."

"No?" He smirks.

"I stand on my own."

"Yet you'll come here every Sunday, pledging your life to a man in the sky."

I crane my neck to maintain eye contact as he presses against me, his breath hot as it coasts across my mouth, making tension twist down my spine.

"If you want a god to worship, *ma petite menteuse*, no need to look so far."

Scoffing, I reach up to push him away even as arousal floods through my center and pools between my legs. "You're disgusting."

He grabs my wrists, pulling me flush to his body until I can feel every hard inch of his cock straining against the fabric of his clothes. "I'd teach you to love begging at my feet."

My core contracts when his words hit my lips, and I suck them in as if his breath is my air. My fingers clench his shirt, but instead of pushing him away, I drag him closer. "I'm tired of you playing games with me," I hiss.

"Is that what I'm doing?" he questions.

"*Stop*." Anger snaps at my nerves. "Nothing will get in my way of being Michael's bride. Not even you."

He leans back, his eyes flaring as his grip tightens around my wrists.

And it's only then that I realize what I've said.

*Stupid girl.*

"I see." One of his hands drops from my arm and rises along my side, goose bumps sprouting in every place his fingers touch. "You thirst for power?" he rasps, his palm ghosting across my collarbone before wrapping around my throat. "I can fill you with it until you scream."

My stomach jolts so fast my legs tremble.

His stare drops to my mouth.

A loud bang echoes off the cathedral walls, and I jump, icy dread trickling through my insides.

"Leave me alone," I plead, pushing at his chest.

He brushes his thumb against the underside of my jaw before he releases me. My body grows cold as he backs away, but I don't drop his gaze, even as my heart slams against my chest when I hear footsteps making their way toward us.

Any second and someone will see.

Tristan keeps his eyes on me for a second longer before spinning around and disappearing down the hall, like one of the ghosts rumored to haunt the corridors.

But his touch has branded itself on my skin.

And when I turn around, Xander stands in front of me, his beady eyes narrowed and lips turned down.

# CHAPTER 16

*Tristan*

DISGUST AND DESIRE MIX IN MY GUT AND explode outward, a volatile poison flooding through my system.

And that's what I'm starting to believe my little doe is. Poison.

Every time I see her, there's this need to push her until she snaps, breaking apart that painted-on poise she uses to fool the world. And snap she did.

She thirsts for the crown.

Unfortunately, she won't find it at my brother's side. The only thing she's guaranteed for herself is death. But I can admit that beneath the annoyance and the uncomfortable situations I find myself in while I'm with her, there's a budding respect. Admiration for the way she's able to slip into her role so effortlessly, and because of that, I'll make sure her execution is quick.

She's a cunning little temptress. Far from the innocent, blushing girl she claims to be.

Gritting my teeth, I storm through the hallway off the cathedral into the main foyer. My fingers slide along the wood banister of the large princess staircase that sits beneath a sparkling crystal chandelier, splitting in two directions that lead to opposite wings of the castle. My boots click on the gleaming cream tile as I make my way up the left side to where my private quarters are. Oversize portraits line the ornate walls, and their eyes burn into me, centuries of royalty judging me through the paint, as if they're as disgusted as I am from the way I allow this woman to twist me up and avert my focus.

I pass by people in the halls, a guard and a few maids, but they don't look my way, knowing better than to bother me. Other than Lady Beatreaux, everyone gives me a wide berth. I haven't decided yet if the reason she doesn't is that she's drawn to my power and unable to help herself or she's simply stupid.

Once I reach my chambers, I fling open the door, the echo of the slam reverberating in my ears as it closes behind me. I make my way to the table beneath the large bay window and grab the glass container placed in the center. Sitting down, I open the jar and take out the rice papers and a few buds of hash, knots tangling in my stomach and my cock straining, begging for relief that I won't allow.

*I will not make things worse than they already are by coming to thoughts of her.*

My fingers tighten around the paper's edges as I pour

my focus into the task, hoping that if I do, the leftover feelings surging through my body will fade.

I bring the joint to my lips and grab a match, striking it against the box until I hear the sizzle of fire. The first inhale swirls down my throat and into my lungs, the tension in my stomach easing.

The heat warms my fingertips as it chars the small wood stick, and an image of my little doe spread out on the table, submissive and pliant while the flame licks against her skin, flashes through my mind. I groan as my balls tense, my length growing rigid.

My hand glides into my lap, fingers wrapping around my shaft through the fabric, but instead of readjusting, I stroke to the thought of her pretty pink lips and how stunning they would look stretched around my cock while I cut off her air by sliding it down her throat.

My teeth bite into the end of my joint to keep it trapped between my lips and I widen my legs, slinking down in my chair as I unbutton my trousers, my abs tensing as I imagine fucking the insolence out of her, of showing her what domination *feels* like as it splits her from the inside out.

Her ass would be red and tender from me forcing the apologies out of her little lying mouth by pummeling her with my palm.

Lust clouds my reason as smoke curls around my face, and suddenly, gripping it through the fabric isn't enough. I need *more*. Need to feel the rough friction of my calloused palm as I close my eyes and pretend it's her tight cunt, sucking me in and pumping me until I explode.

Pleasure tiptoes from the tops of my thighs and into my abdomen as I run my hand up the shaft, squeezing the tip until a bead of cum drips out. My balls tighten when I think of her tongue running along the underside of my length, tracing the throbbing vein, and the tension coils even tighter when I picture my dick stuffing her so full she can't even *breathe* as she swallows every drop I give her.

The joint falls from my mouth, the end singeing the skin of my stomach, but I let it stay, throwing my head back and groaning through the pain.

And then, right before I'm about to explode, I remember that she's marrying my brother. That *he* gets to experience every curve of her body and every lick of her tongue.

My hands jolt back like someone has electrocuted them, and I stare down at my lap, my erection angry and throbbing as it begs for relief.

I won't allow a woman to interfere with my plans. Especially not one who doesn't belong to me.

She wants power?

She'll have to kill me to take it.

———

"You look spooked, sire." Xander's voice trickles through the door, and I press myself farther into the hallway wall, not wanting them to know I'm here.

It's a rare moment. There are no guards around, and I shouldn't be here. But I couldn't sleep, and while I was preparing to slip through the tunnels and go roam the forest, I saw Xander slinking through the darkened halls and followed him instead.

And now we're here, outside Michael's private quarters, in the middle of the night.

Xander rushed through the door, not even bothering to close it fully. But his mistake is my good fortune.

I lean against the jamb, straining my ears to hear.

"Would you like some dreamless sleep potion?" Xander asks.

"No," Michael scoffs. "That stuff makes my mind fuzzy for hours."

Xander sighs. "That's the opium, sire. If it would help keep the nightmares away…"

"Don't speak to me like a child," Michael snaps. "If you want to help, figure out how to talk to spirits and make my dead father stay *dead* instead of tormenting me."

My stomach flips. *Michael has nightmares of our father?*

The resounding silence is thick.

"What?" Michael hisses. "I see that pathetic look in your eyes, Xander. Either say something useful or get the fuck out of my room."

There's a vile undercurrent to his tone, one I've heard whispered in my ear since I was born.

In public, Michael has a charming—if not

overbearing—personality. But it's in these private moments that the snake sheds his skin and comes out to play.

Perhaps Lady Beatreaux and he are better suited than I thought.

My chest twists at the realization.

"Have you…"

"Spit it out," Michael snaps.

"Have you seen him again while you were awake?"

The resounding silence is thick. Shock punches through my middle, my mouth dropping open as I eavesdrop.

"Have you given any more thought to what I've suggested? To speaking with someone?"

"I'm speaking to you."

"Yes, but…I mean someone more equipped to help you with them. To figure out the root cause."

Another long pause, so heavy with tension that it bleeds through the walls.

"They would call me mad," Michael whispers.

A grin sneaks its way onto my face, satisfaction bubbling in my chest as I straighten off the wall and make my way toward the tunnels.

My brother isn't as infallible as he would have everyone believe.

And the people deserve to know when they're being ruled by a *mad* king.

# CHAPTER 17

## *Sara*

NEWS OF MICHAEL'S PROPOSAL HAS SPREAD, and things are happening in the castle. Almost everyone in the king's inner circle already knew why I was here, but now their heads bow a little deeper, their spines notch a little straighter. Respect that I have done nothing to earn is handed to me on a silver platter, simply because a man with the "right" blood in his veins asked for my hand.

Marisol came barging in at the crack of dawn, whipping open curtains and laying out color swatches, droning on about the engagement ball and how it was my duty to plan it.

*She knows nothing of duty.*

Her blond hair is coiffed and her gray eyes spear through me as she shows me the thirtieth shade of purple and asks me to compare it to the last twenty-nine, as if I've been paying attention.

"Marisol, I hate the color purple."

"What?" She half chuckles. "It's the color of royalty, my lady."

"Great. Pick *your* favorite and we'll go with that." I groan, standing up from my place on the couch. "I need some air."

Marisol's eyes narrow as she stares at the two fabric swatches in her hands, but my words make her look my way. "How come?"

My chest burns at her question. "Do I need to have a reason other than it's something I wish?"

Pursing her lips, she shakes her head. "You have a very busy schedule coming up. You won't always be able to run off and do as you wish. Especially once you're queen."

The bite in her tone doesn't go unnoticed, and my nerves bristle. "More of a reason to take advantage now then. Besides…" I pull my lips back into a thin smile. "I have every faith that you and Ophelia can handle the rest of the ball arrangements. Am I mistaken?"

Marisol's shoulders draw back. "Of course not, milady. It would be our pleasure."

"Fantastic." I stretch my neck to the side, the resounding crack unraveling all my pent-up tension. "Have you seen Sheina?"

Marisol averts her eyes. "I haven't."

My stomach twists. We've been here for days, and ever since my new ladies showed up, it seems like Sheina has disappeared completely. I'm curious to know what she's doing, but more than that, I miss my friend.

"I think I'll go try to find her." I move toward the door.

"Wait!" Marisol screeches. "You can't just go running around the castle on your own."

Tension knots up my spine and I turn, taking calculated steps until I'm standing in front of her. We lock eyes and she sucks in a breath, holding my stare, but I don't say a word.

Her fingers clench the swatches she's still holding, and she drops her gaze.

I lean in close, my voice quiet and sharp. "I wasn't asking permission, Marisol. You are not my keeper, and I will do as I please."

"I—apologies, milady."

Anger works its way through my middle and up my throat, but I push it back, allowing the uncomfortable air to sit stagnant for long moments.

Eventually, I step away, smiling. "It's settled then. I'm going for some air, and you'll stay here and plan the ball." I reach out, placing my hand on her shoulder and squeezing, my nails digging ever so slightly into her shoulder. "I trust you'll do an incredible job representing me. After all, it's not every day a king chooses you to be his wife, and I need a *stellar* reputation."

Her shoulders stiffen, and affirmation of what I suspected trickles through my insides. She's envious.

Spinning around, I make my way to the door and turn the handle, stepping into the dimly lit hall. Someone appears in front of me, making my heart slap against my ribs.

"Oh," I gasp, my hand rising to my chest. "Timothy. I didn't expect you here."

He doesn't respond, just stands there, his dark eyes watching me.

"Still not allowed to speak?" Sighing, I rest a hand on my hip. "If you're always here, who's with His Majesty?"

This time, he reacts, but only barely, lifting his brows as he takes a step closer.

"So you're my guard dog now, I take it?" I run a hand down the sleeve of my dress. "Very well. Let's go for a walk."

I turn away and move forward, hearing the clank of his footsteps behind me.

It must be five or ten minutes before I try to speak to him again. I'm sure I'm lost inside the maze that is the castle halls, but if Timothy isn't willing to step in and help a girl out, then I won't ask him to steer me in the right direction.

"Have you seen Sheina?" I ask, trying for the thousandth time to get him to crack.

I'm not surprised when there isn't a response.

"Who's Sheina?" A loud voice booms from around the corner. My footsteps stutter at the voice and I stop walking when Paul appears, dressed down in tan corduroys and a light shirt, a monstrous grin on his face.

"Paul, I was hoping I'd see you again." I smile.

His gaze falls behind me, landing on Timothy before they come back. "Were you?"

"Do you know Timothy?"

"Better than anyone." Paul's grin widens, his auburn hair bouncing as he places his hands in his pockets. "Timmy's my best mate."

Genuine shock ripples through my chest, and I twist to look at the guard behind me. "Oh?" I turn back around, bringing a hand up to cup my mouth as I speak to Paul. "He doesn't like to talk to me, you know? I think he's intimidated."

Paul smirks. "Of that, I have no doubt."

Amusement floats through my chest, light and airy, and I grasp on to the feeling, hoping if I hold tight enough, it will stick. "We're going for a walk. Would you like to join us?"

Paul hesitates, rocking back on his heels. "I'm not sure it's wise to be seen with me around the castle, milady."

I raise a brow, irritation bleeding into my skin. "Why don't you let me worry about that."

A beautiful grin takes over his face, teeth gleaming as he nods and walks right up to me, stretching out his arm. "Well, in that case."

I hook my hand in the crook of his elbow and allow him to escort me down the hallway, expecting him to lead me in the right direction, since clearly Timothy is content to allow me to walk around in circles. But he doesn't take us to the front of the castle like I expect. Instead, he leads us through narrow hallways and past countless rooms before we reach a small enclave with a dark wooden door.

"Is this a secret room?" I glance at him.

Paul smiles as he walks to the door and pushes it open. "Better."

The cool September air whips across my face as I walk toward him and into the open space, clouds looming over the skies and hiding the sun, as usual in Saxum. Waves crash in the distance, letting me know we're close to where the Vita Ocean meets the cliff's edge near the back of the castle.

But in front of us is a gorgeous garden, full of deep purples and stunning whites, small droplets of water beading on the petals, leftover from the early afternoon rain. Gargoyles and sculptures are scattered throughout, dark-green moss spreading across their sides and blending in with the gray of their structure, and a stunning three-tiered fountain sits in the center, two black benches with gold trim on either side.

"What *is* this place?" I ask.

"The queen's garden," Paul says.

I quirk a brow.

"The queen mother spent many days out here when she was pregnant with His Majesty and then again with His Royal Highness." Grass crunches beneath Paul's feet as he moves to stand beside me. "No one really comes here anymore. But it's a nice place to relax."

"It's beautiful." I walk away from him and closer to the fountain, my chest warming with every step. And then I look past it to the forest that surrounds us. Dense trees. A thousand different shades of green towering in the distance, reminding me of just how secluded the Saxum castle is.

Spinning around, I open my mouth, about to ask if it's safe to walk through, but the words stick on my tongue when I see Paul and Timothy huddled close together, my mute guard throwing his head back in laughter, his hand coming up to rest on Paul's shoulder.

It's a shocking sight. I was convinced he didn't know how to laugh at all. A hollow ache spreads through the center of my chest as I take them in, envious of the ease with which they enjoy each other's company. I'm not sure I've ever experienced that. I rack my brain, trying to come up with a single, solitary memory of letting my guard down and just being with another person, but I come up blank.

The ache grows, wrapping itself around the chambers of my heart and squeezing.

A muffled laugh soars through the trees, but it's enough to call my attention away and pique my curiosity. It's coming from the edges of the forest, and without thinking it through, I follow the noise, walking straight into the pines.

Twigs break beneath my feet, and I fist the fabric of my skirts, hiking them up as I make my way through the trees, searching for the laughter. And then two figures at the base of a thick evergreen appear, and my footsteps stutter as I grasp at the trunk in front of me, shrouding myself in the shadows of its leaves.

Simon sits cross-legged, his eyes wide and his mouth

spread in a giant smile. But it's the man he faces that steals my breath. Prince Tristan sits on the dirt ground, mirroring Simon's position, his back hunched and his disheveled black hair falling over his forehead as his brows furrow in concentration. He holds Simon's arm steady in one hand, his other one moving back and forth, the tip of a fountain pen pressed against Simon's limb.

He's the most casual I've ever seen him, wearing black trousers with matching suspenders over a cream tunic, rolled up at the sleeves. My core spasms, heat rushing through every vein.

They haven't noticed me yet, so I take the opportunity of being invisible, my eyes glossing over Tristan's body, the drawings on his forearms coming to life with his movements, as if they're living, breathing things instead of artwork inked into his skin.

He looks unguarded, his features softer than normal as he leans over, the corners of his mouth tilting up while Simon continues to giggle next to him.

"Stay still, little tiger." His voice is low and raspy, and the memory of his whispered words in the cathedral sends goose bumps sprouting along my neck.

"It tickles," Simon says back.

I blow out a heavy breath, trying to control the ridiculous way my body is reacting to a simple thought, and I shift on my feet. A twig breaks and Simon's head snaps up, his eyes squinting as they land on mine.

Tristan doesn't even falter from his movements, ignoring the fact that there was any noise at all.

"Hi, lady." Simon beams. "What are you doing here?"

My heart pounds in my chest, making my hands clammy, and I clear my throat as I make my way closer, my eyes flickering between the two of them.

"Exploring," I reply, smiling. "What are you doing?"

Simon's grin widens, his toy sword lying at his side.

As I look closer, I notice one of his eyes has a dark hue marring the light brown of his skin and making it look welted and purple.

I inhale a deep breath but don't allow my gaze to linger, not wanting to make him uncomfortable, even though the thought of something or someone striking this boy makes my blood boil like a volcano about to burst.

Glancing down, I realize Tristan is, in fact, drawing on Simon. And he hasn't acknowledged me at all, which makes my insides itch. I move even closer and my foot snags on yet another branch. A slight twinge radiates through my ankle, and I hiss at the pain.

"Perhaps next time you decide to traipse through forests, you should dress for the occasion," Tristan says, his voice soothing my skin like a soft caress.

I scoff and narrow my eyes. But he still isn't looking at me, keeping his focus on Simon's arm.

"I'm not *traipsing*. I heard a laugh and came to investigate."

Now he stops, glancing up at me. "You're out here all alone?"

"Yes." I lift my chin. "Well, technically, Timothy and Paul are back in the garden." I twist around to glance behind me. "They're probably searching for me."

Simon snickers. "I bet they're happy you left."

"That's not very nice." My hands drop to my hips. "I'll have you know I'm fantastic company."

"Well, yeah, but Timmy and Paul love each other."

My brows draw in. "What do you…"

"Simon." Tristan's voice is sharp.

My eyes bounce between them, but I let it go, filing away the information for later. Instead, I drop down, ignoring the way my corset digs into the very tops of my thighs from the maneuver. I don't want Tristan to know that he's right, that it *is* uncomfortable to be here with what I'm wearing.

"What are you drawing?"

Simon chews on his lip. "I wanted a tattoo, but he said no."

"So it's a temporary one then?" I lean in closer to look.

And when I do, my lungs compress as if someone reached inside my chest and stole my very breath. I've seen artwork before. Hundreds of paintings hang in the castle, and dozens more at my home in Silva. But I've never seen art like this. My eyes widen, heart thudding as I scoot forward to get a better look.

It's *stunning*, and a knot lodges its way into my throat, the simple act of looking at it causing emotion to surge through my middle and lock itself into the cracks of my soul. The way Tristan's hand glides across his skin like a boat on top of water sends tingles trickling through me, as if he's touching *me* with every stroke. It's incredible, the way he commands the pen, producing intricate lines and shading from a device I can't even get to bleed right onto paper.

The drawing itself looks as though Simon's skin has torn—like shredded fabric marred with gashes and holes. And behind it, the face of a tiger, with such depth in its features that part of me is convinced it will tear through his arm and leap out to devour me whole.

My mouth gapes as Tristan continues to draw, mind blown at his talent. He glances at me again, and I snap my jaw closed so fast my teeth smash together. A grin ticks the corner of his lips as he looks back down.

"What made you want tattoos, Simon?" I ask, ignoring the way my stomach feels like a thousand butterflies are taking flight. It's an unwelcome feeling. I'd much rather stay here on the ground.

Simon shrugs, chewing on his bottom lip as he stares at Tristan's face. "*He* has them."

My eyes flick to Tristan, whose jaw clenches as he continues to work.

"And they're too scared to hurt him," Simon continues. "I thought maybe if I had some...they'd fear me too."

My mouth dries, a balloon expanding in my throat.

Tristan leans back, flicking the hair from his face. "You're all done."

Simon's gaze widens. "I love it. You think it will work?"

He blows out a breath. "This is for *you*, not for them. Forget about them."

"I don't know how." Simon sniffles, moving his arm back and forth, the eyes of the tiger following the motion. "What happens when it washes away?"

"Then I'll draw it again."

"Lady Beatreaux?" A loud voice rings out from behind us, and I snap my head up, locking eyes with Tristan, so many unsaid words floating in the space between us.

I have despised no one more than I do him. He's vile, crude, and everything they warned me he would be. And yet right now, I don't hate him at all.

Timothy appears through the foliage, his brows drawn down and a scowl marring his face.

I sigh, standing. "Hi, Timothy. What took you so long?"

"You should not run off."

A smile breaks across my face. "I would have done it sooner if I knew that's all it took to hear your voice. Besides…" I lift a shoulder. "I'm not a child, and I don't appreciate everyone pretending I am."

His jaw tenses before his gaze moves to Simon and Tristan, his back straightening. "Your Royal Highness." He bows.

Tristan's features harden into stone as he stands, and I swear the air grows cold as he morphs from the man he just was into what everyone else gets to see.

*The scarred prince.*

He doesn't speak, but as he moves to walk by me, his hand brushes against mine, our fingers tangling for the smallest moment. And the way it makes my heart stutter out of rhythm should be the biggest warning I've ever had.

But like I've done with almost every emotion that concerns the prince, I ignore it.

# CHAPTER 18

### *Tristan*

THE UPSTAIRS OF THE ELEPHANT BONES Tavern has a narrow hallway with a small bathroom and two bedrooms flanking either side, one of which is kept clean for whenever I choose to stay. Which, I'll admit, has been sparse as of late. I've been spending more of my time at the castle, both because Lady Beatreaux fascinates me and because I like to be available when Simon needs to slip away.

But Edward tells me that morale is down since I haven't been making as many appearances, so tonight, I'm here to remedy that. Apparently, burning the body of the king's commander wasn't enough to prove I'm still focused on the cause.

I walk up the stairs and down the hall to the room, confusion lancing through me when I hear muffled noises from behind the door.

My brows draw in and I twist the handle, the air

whipping across my face as the door swings open, smacking against the wall. It cracks as if it might shatter from the impact, and it's enough to startle the two people naked and in the bed.

They jump up, scrambling. The woman squeals when the man moves off her, and she grapples for the sheets, drawing them up around her chest, her eyes growing wide as she takes me in.

I tilt my head, cataloging her features, rage burning through me when I note her frizzy blond hair and freckles.

Little doe's lady-in-waiting. Rosy-cheeked and freshly fucked by my most trusted soldier.

Edward.

How dare he bring her here.

My fists clench at my sides, my gaze swinging to him as he pulls on his garments. "Your Highness, I—"

I raise a hand, cutting him off midsentence, my eyes trailing along the form of the girl as she curls in on herself. "Did you bring me a gift, Edward?"

He swallows as he finishes buttoning up his trousers, running his hand through his disheveled hair.

"So thoughtful of you," I continue.

The girl scoots farther back on the bed, presumably to put more distance between us. I walk toward her until I'm standing at the side of the small mattress, and I reach out, grasping her naked arm, pulling her from the spot before shoving her onto the wood floor.

She makes a screeching noise, and the sound of her fear sends adrenaline coursing through my veins. This seems to snap Edward out of whatever daze he was in, and he moves forward, grabbing the woman's clothes and walking to stand next to me as he thrusts them at her.

I chuckle. "A bit late for modesty, don't you think?" Her cheeks heat, and I wave my hand in a placating motion through the air. "By all means, sweetheart. Get dressed."

She pulls her garments closer to her chest, but she doesn't make another move.

Irritation vibrates through my bones. "I don't like to repeat myself."

"Sheina, please," Edward pleads. "Do as he says."

"I don't want him to see me," she whispers at the ground.

"I tell you what. You take a few minutes, Sheina. Get yourself together." Stepping in closer, I reach down, running my hand over her tousled hair. "And then come downstairs where we can figure out just what to do about this...*situation*."

"She knows nothing," Edward whispers.

Anger makes my tongue sharp. "She knows enough."

He presses his lips together, and for the slightest moment, I think maybe he'll fight for her. But he simply drops his head and nods.

"Ten minutes," I say, turning to the door and heading to the staircase.

My shoulders tighten, my mind racing, warring between disbelief and disappointment. I've never once questioned Edward's loyalty. But then again, he's never given me reason to.

I don't want to make an example out of him, but sometimes, these things are unavoidable.

The stairs creak as I storm down them, and when I make it to the bottom, I head straight across the room until I reach Belinda, who's sitting on the lap of Earl, running her hand through his straggly beard and cackling in laughter.

They both straighten as I approach and she jumps up, dropping to the ground. "Sire," she whispers.

"There's a woman upstairs with Edward. Make sure they don't leave."

"Of course." She reaches out, grasping my hand and kissing my rings, and a rush of satisfaction flows through my veins at her subservience.

Out of all my followers, she is undoubtedly the most loyal.

"If they try to run, kill her. And bring Edward to me."

She straightens, her eyes maniacal as they gleam.

I make my way to the raised platform where a singular black velvet, high-back chair sits, a throne for me to watch over my people. It's nothing close to the real thing—to the one I *deserve*—but for the moment, it works.

My boots clunk against the wood as I plop down,

spreading my legs wide and drumming my fingertips on the arm of the chair, gazing out over the room. Everyone is busy slurping up soup and bread I had Paul send from the castle, and the tabletops are piled high with fur-lined coats to prepare for the winter months. A gift for their loyalty.

A handful of minutes pass until I hear the heavy thud of footsteps. My eyes flicker to the corner of the room, past the long picnic-style tables, to where the edge of the bar meets the staircase. Edward and his new love step down, their heads close together as they make their way toward me, Belinda prodding at their backs.

I rest my chin on my knuckles, watching while they weave through the tables and benches until they reach the edge of the platform. The noise around us quiets as people take note of something happening, and it pleases me that I don't have to call their attention.

"Kneel before greatness, girl," Belinda hisses, shoving at the girl's shoulders until she drops to her knees.

Edward cuts Belinda a strong glare, stepping forward until he's placed himself between them.

I smirk at his obvious attachment and wait for him to follow suit. He doesn't, and my grin drops, my insides seething. "Do you no longer bow before me, Edward?"

His eyes lock on mine as he drops to his knees.

Unease trickles through me at his hesitancy.

"Friends." My fingers grip the edge of my throne as I lean forward and look out into the crowd. "It would appear we have a new comrade in our midst. And from the *castle*, no less."

Grumbles spread through the crowd.

"Tell me, are you here to join our cause?" My fingers scratch against my jaw.

Sheina doesn't respond, her shoulders trembling as she stares at the ground.

Her disobedience makes my blood crackle, aching to string her up and make her scream, use her as an example to show what happens when you displease me.

"Or maybe you were only here to get fucked by the king's commander," I spit.

She gasps, her head snapping to mine, her cheeks growing ruddy.

Edward moves forward. "Stop."

That word.

That simple, *silly* word is the knife that severs my control, and I surge from my seat, flying down the platform until I'm in front of him, the back of my hand striking out across his face. His head whips to the side, blood splattering on the ground from where my rings cut into his flesh, and he stumbles, catching himself before he falls.

I wait until he rises before snatching his arm and twisting until the ligaments pop beneath my fingers. He drops to his knees, a small groan escaping from his gritted teeth.

"You do not tell me to *stop*," I hiss.

He winces. "I...I brought her here for you."

My brows jump, surprise filtering through me. I hadn't expected him to say this.

"Oh?" I ask, my eyes glancing at her, wondering if he's simply trying to save her from death. "So you *are* a gift."

I release Edward and move toward her instead.

"Tell everyone your name," I command.

"Sheina," she whispers, tears streaking down her face.

"Sheina." I let the syllables roll off my tongue, debating whether to announce that I know exactly who she is. But at the last moment, I decide against it. "And who are you to the king?"

"No one."

My nostrils flare as I stare down at her. "Speak louder so everyone can hear."

She sits up straighter, her chest heaving with heavy breaths. "I said...I'm no one."

"And his new queen?" I quirk a brow.

Her breathing falters, and even *I* can feel the eyes of the people as their stares burn through her back.

"No answer for that one, is there?" I murmur, crouching down and lifting her chin. "And who are you to *me*?"

Her tongue swipes across her lips and she swallows, glancing at Edward. He nods at her, his hand rubbing up and down his arm.

She turns back, her dull gaze locking on mine. "I'm whoever you need me to be."

I huff out a small breath, pinching her jaw before

dropping my hand and standing upright. She's not loyal to the cause, and even if she was, it doesn't change the fact that Edward brought an outsider—a *dangerous* outsider—into our home base and into our operation without telling me. But she's a new tool in my arsenal, one that I can find use for.

Crossing my arms, I stare down at her. "You may rise."

She puts her hands in front of her, pushing off the dirty wood floor as she stands, brushing her fingers down the front of her dress.

Stepping in close, I palm the back of her head, leaning in so no one can hear. "You will be loyal to me, or I will make you watch as I disembowel everyone you love."

Her body shakes beneath my touch.

"And then I'll chain you up like a broodmare and let the jackals stick their cocks wherever they please until you're gaping and broken. I will keep you alive solely for their savage pleasures." I pull back to look into her glossy, terrified eyes, and my free hand cups her cheek. "I'll continue even when you're begging for death. Do you understand?"

She nods and then hiccups, her cheeks wet with tears.

I step back, smiling as I face the rest of the room with my arms out wide.

"Everyone, welcome our newest warrior. She's here to join the fight."

# CHAPTER 19

## *Sara*

"I'M NOT AN IDIOT, MARISOL. I KNOW HOW to dance."

She purses her lips—her favorite thing to do these days—and places a hand on her hip. "This will be your first dance with His Majesty."

Walking to the edge of the ballroom, I grab a glass of water and sip from it, wishing this dreadful "class" would be over with. I've been taking dancing lessons since I was a small child. I know what to do.

"It's just awkward when your partner is another woman, that's all." I lift my shoulders.

She huffs. "Milady, I'm just trying to keep you from embarrassing yourself and the king."

My eyes narrow, her thinly veiled insult sliding across my skin like needles. "No, of course we wouldn't want to do that."

She steps over to the cylinder phonograph, its large bell end sticking out like a brass instrument, and moves the narrow edge down until music plays. Breathing in deep, I crack my neck just as the door to the ballroom on the far side of the eastern wall opens.

"Did I miss anything fun?" Sheina's voice flows across the room, and I spin, a smile breaking across my face.

"Sheina! Where have you been? I've missed you." I throw out my arms and drag her into a hug, my chest warming as I do.

"I'm dreadful for disappearing, aren't I?" She tightens her hold on me. "I have so much to tell you," she whispers in my ear.

Nodding, I break our hug, my hands trailing down her arms until I can squeeze her fingers with mine. Curiosity prods at the corners of my mind, wondering what it is she has to say and where it is she's been.

"Anything I can help with?" she asks, glancing around.

"Not unless you can find me a better dancer." I turn to Marisol, scrunching my nose. "No offense."

Marisol sighs, her blond brows furrowing. "This is pointless."

A laugh escapes me. "Oh, come on, Marisol. Lighten up!" I walk toward her, reaching out and gripping her shoulder. "Everything will be just fine. You're doing an incredible job managing everything, and I'm sorry I'm making things difficult for you. But I *do* know how to dance, I promise."

Her eyes soften, the corners of her lips tilting up, and she nods, exhaling a heavy breath. "I'm sorry for being so…well, you know." She shrugs. "Planning a ball is a lot of pressure."

I smile. "Which is why I tasked you with the responsibility. I know you can handle it better than anyone else."

Her features lighten as she nods.

"Why don't you go take a break and allow Sheina and I to catch up." I squeeze her shoulder, hoping that she won't argue with me. I know she doesn't wish to be here any more than I do.

"Thank you, milady." She curtsies before she walks across the polished ballroom floor, disappearing into the castle halls.

It isn't until the door shuts behind her, echoing off the arched ceiling and stone pillars, that I drop my shoulders and relax, turning to look at my closest friend. The one who's felt like a stranger since arriving here.

A smile breaks across my face and she mirrors it, both of us bursting into giggles.

"I don't think she likes me," I say through the laughter.

Sheina's blue eyes sparkle. "I don't think she likes anyone."

My hands rest on my hips, my head cocking to the side. "I'm pretty confident she likes my soon-to-be husband fairly well."

Her brows shoot to her hairline. "No, do you think? Is she one of his mistresses?"

I lift a shoulder. "Who's to say? I'm sure he has several. For all I know, *you* could be one."

She shoves at my shoulder. "Please, Sara. Be realistic."

"Well, what do I know? I brought you along to be my lady-in-waiting, and yet you've been like one of the ghosts you claim haunt the castle."

Her smile drops, fingers tangling in front of her. "I'm sorry. Don't be mad. I just…" Looking to the side, her cheeks grow rosy.

My chest pulls tight. "What is it?"

"I've met someone," she whispers. "He's a general in the king's military, and he's…*everything*."

My eyes widen, surprise dropping like a lead weight in my gut. "Already?"

"He's very handsome. And very good at…other things." The pink on her cheeks turns splotchy.

I lift my brows, unable to stop the grin from spreading across my cheeks. "And you call *me* the wicked girl."

Her hands shoot up to cover her face and she groans into them. "I'm foolish." Looking up, she reaches out to grab my palm with hers. "But I won't disappear on you again. I'm sorry I did."

The middle of my stomach burns in warning, just like it always does when my intuition is pricking at me, screaming to pay attention. "Well, do I get to meet the mystery man?"

Her features stiffen, and the change in her energy spikes through me like an arrow.

*Something is off.*

"I'd love that," she says.

But her smile doesn't reach her eyes.

------

"I want to go back to the queen's garden. Will you remind me how to get there?"

I peer up at Timothy from behind the top of my poetry book. He sits in the chaise by the fireplace in my sitting room, his body the most relaxed I've seen. Ever since he was forced to speak to me in the forest, he's loosened up, and as long as we're in my private quarters—which he actually steps into now as long as other people are present—he graces me with his beautiful voice.

Turns out he's not such a dead fish after all.

"Why?" he questions.

My brows rise and I set down my book. "Well, I'd rather leave the castle entirely, but I'm sure you won't allow that, since apparently becoming engaged is akin to regressing into an adolescent who needs a nanny."

His forehead scrunches. "Are you calling me your nanny?"

I shrug. "What else would you call it?"

He purses his lips. "I requested to be your guard."

"You did?" My stomach flips. "I don't know if I should be offended you think I need one or honored that it's you."

He tilts his head. "You're going to be the queen. If anyone needs protection, milady, it's you."

The way he says it sends a chill racing down my spine, as if he knows something—something that he isn't letting on.

"From whom?" I prod.

His eyes move from where they were settled on me to Ophelia, who is peeking at us from over her needlework. When I twist to face her, she drops her eyes back down, pretending as though she isn't paying us any mind.

"Never mind," I say, standing up. "If you don't know how to get to the garden, just say that."

He scoffs, rising from his seat. "I know every corridor in this castle."

"Oh?" My brows rise. "*All* of them?" Anticipation lights up my insides. "Ophelia, we're going for a walk. Would you like to come?" I ask to be polite, but everything within me is hoping she says no.

"No, milady, Marisol is supposed to meet here to go over the dinner menu for the ball."

I crinkle my nose. "That sounds awful."

She smiles. "That's why you're having us do it instead."

Walking over to Timothy, I link my arm in his. His jaw ticks as he stares at where we're connected, and I grin up at him, moving us toward the door. The second it opens, he drops my arm, adopting a glacial look, the man from moments earlier disappearing into the air.

I'm silent the entire way, memorizing our steps so I can sneak away and come back alone, but once we're at the garden's door, I spin around, pointing my finger at his chest. "You said you know *every* corridor."

"I do."

"Even the hidden ones?"

His dark eyes peer down at me as if he's deliberating on how to answer, and that alone is enough to send excitement sparking through my insides. *He knows what I'm talking about.*

"Will you show me?" I press.

He's silent for long, strained moments, the muscle in his jaw tensing over and over. Finally, he nods.

A smile creeps on my face, satisfaction worming its way through my veins.

He reaches to his side, placing his hand on a wall sconce. I watch his movements, fascinated, my heart pumping in my ears.

I wonder if when I look back, I'll think of this moment as the one when I realized everything hides in plain sight. Because the wall I was just staring at disappears, revealing a dark and narrow passage in its place.

# CHAPTER 20

## *Tristan*

WHEN MICHAEL AND I WERE CHILDREN, MY father was often too busy to spend time with us, and my mother didn't care. Even if she had, that's not how it works in the monarchy. Queens aren't meant to raise their offspring; they're only meant to birth them.

As a result—and as was expected—nannies were the ones who brought us up. The other kids who roamed the halls were families of the servants, ones who either we weren't allowed to play with or they weren't allowed to play with us. But Michael somehow always had his group of friends, and they would never miss an opportunity to come find me and rain down terror.

I was easy prey. I had no interest in being the center of attention and much preferred staying on the sidelines with my sketchbook, watching how everyone else interacted.

You can learn a lot about human nature when you observe from the outside looking in.

For some reason, my brother didn't enjoy that about me. He's enjoyed *nothing* about me, nor I him. We're connected only by blood, and even as a child, I would imagine chaining him up by his limbs and draining him of every drop, if only to sever our connection.

Back then, of course, I didn't have the wherewithal.

And it only takes so many times of being thrown in the dirt and told you're a freak for you to believe it. That because you're a little different, you're somehow less than.

It was beat into me by angry fists and brushed off as "kids will be kids." And the fact that when it came down to family, I was unseen and unimportant compounded the feeling. Being the second-born son gave me freedom, yet they forced me to live it in Michael's shadow.

But at least for a time, my father cared.

He would take me to the cliff's edge, showing me the constellations and how even in the darkest of nights, they light the way home. I treasured the quiet evenings with him because it was the only time I felt like I belonged. He *saw* me, and he *loved* me.

But as I aged, the late-night meetings grew further and further apart, his time for me replaced with preparing Michael to be king.

Just like with everyone else, eventually, I was forgotten.

And the stars don't shine as brightly when you stare at them alone.

Michael was the crown prince, and I was just…me.

So I never understood why, when he had everything, he always made sure I had less than nothing.

I thought maybe as we grew older, things would get better, but the opposite turned out to be true. The shoves turned to prolonged torture, and bruised ribs turned into fractured bones. I slunk away into the secret tunnels of the castle just to get away.

It was then I realized they led through the mountains and into the middle of the forest. And it was *also* there I first decided to stop being Michael's victim, spending hours visualizing the day I would take everything from him and everyone else who wronged me or stood by silently and watched.

That's the thing about resentment. It grows and wraps around every piece of you like ivy, feeding off the anger until it's so enmeshed that it becomes you. A living, breathing, *pulsating* incarnation of hatred.

And for me, the boy who was tossed to the side like garbage, I had nothing but time to pour water on the weeds. Let them fester and grow until they blotted out everything else.

Michael has always been stronger physically.

But I'm vastly more intelligent.

And he doesn't deserve to sit on the throne.

The scar on my face twinges, and I shake it off, gritting my teeth as I focus back on the dark wood of the chest that I keep beneath my bed. My insides dance as I close the metal lock on the front and place it back in its hideaway spot before grabbing a lit candle and making my way out of my room and into the hallway.

I move through the corridors until I make it into the tunnels. It's the only way I can get to my brother's office without being detected, and since it's the middle of the night, no one will be around. The tunnels are dark and narrow, the chill from the stone seeping through the walls and settling in my bones. I pick up my pace, unadulterated joy trickling through my veins as I imagine his face when he sees what I've left for him.

Something makes a noise from around the corner, and I slow my footsteps, cocking my head to listen for it again.

*Who would be in the tunnels at this time of night?*

Few people even know of them.

A deep sigh reverberates off the walls, and as soon as I hear it, I relax, grabbing the rolled joint from behind my ear and leaning against the cold stone, bringing the candle to my lips to light it.

I blow a cloud of smoke into the air, one foot crossing over the other as I wait, sparks biting at the lining of my gut. Suddenly the footsteps stop, and besides the choppy sound of breathing, silence presses in around me.

"Very brave for a little doe to sneak into the tunnels at night."

She doesn't reply, and the sound of her exhales disappears, like she's trying to keep herself a secret.

*As if she can hide from me.*

"If you don't come out, I'll assume you wish for me to chase you. And between the two of us, you're at a severe disadvantage." I wait a few more moments before dropping the hash to the ground and stomping it out with the corner of my boot. "Very well."

"Wait!"

My stomach jumps as she appears from around the corner, a small oil lamp in front of her face, making her look almost ethereal in the dark.

I take my time soaking her in, my gaze traveling from the tips of her boots, over her black trousers and dark cloak, up to her hair that's pulled into a bun at the nape of her neck.

A slow grin creeps along my face. "You look like you're up to absolutely no good."

She cocks a brow. "One could say the same about you."

"Who ever said *I* was good?"

She fidgets, biting her lower lip. The movement is a straight shot to my groin, aching to feel her flesh between *my* teeth instead, wondering what it would taste like to have her blood on my tongue.

She sighs, running a hand over her face. "You won't… you won't tell anyone I was here, will you?"

"That depends." I move closer. "What's in it for me?"

Her mouth pops open. "I…what do you want?"

I take another step, and then another, until the tips of my boots touch hers. I'm so close I see the muscles in her neck work as she swallows, and my fingers tense against the urge to reach out and feel her pulse, just to see how quickly I can make it beat.

"Tell me a secret, *ma petite menteuse*," I whisper.

The flame of my candle flashes in her eyes, and she cranes her neck to meet my stare. "I don't have any secrets."

I chuckle. "We all have secrets."

"So what's one of yours?" Her head tilts.

"Mine are a burden I wouldn't wish on anyone, even you."

She scoffs. "So tell me what you're calling me then."

I lift a brow.

"The French," she presses. "What is it?"

Tsking, I shake my head. "Always so many questions."

"And never any answers," she bites back. "At least tell me what you're doing here at three in the morning."

Now, I do lift my hand, unable to stifle the urge, resting my fingers around the side of her throat until I feel the steady rhythm of her heart. She sucks in a breath, and it races under my touch.

"Maybe I'm following you."

"Are you?"

"Would you like me to?"

She groans. "Do you answer everything with another question? It's infuriating."

Something warm expands in my chest, and it hits me that here in the tunnels, we're completely alone.

I could take her, fuck her, and *break* her, and no one would be the wiser.

The temptation is so strong, my fingers twitch, my cock jerking wildly as I imagine her naked and flush against the cold stone of the wall, her body shivering as I thrust inside her until she screams. I press my body to hers, wanting her to feel what she's done.

Her eyes widen at my movement, her fingers gripping the small lamp tighter.

"Do you react this way to *him*?" I ask, my stomach churning at the thought.

"What?"

"When my brother touches you." I skim my hand from her neck up to her jaw, coasting across the sharp angles until I'm tracing the lines of her face. "Does your breathing grow shallow and your skin blush pink?"

"That's none of your business," she breathes.

I bring my fingertips down the front of her throat in a soft caress, grazing against the pebbled goose bumps of her skin. "Does your sweet cunt drip from just the thought of him, the way I know it does for me?"

"I don't—" She jerks and gasps, her lamp clattering onto the ground and her hand grabbing at my shirt. "*Oh.*"

Glancing down, I realize my candle has dripped, falling onto the skin above her collarbone. My thumb moves to press against the cooling wax, desire shooting through me until my legs threaten to buckle when I notice it tingeing her flesh red.

I want to pour it on the rest of her and tear it off piece by piece.

Her mouth parts, tongue sweeping out across her bottom lip, and *damn* if I don't wish to lean down and steal her breath for my own.

There are a few seconds of silence, tension wringing the air tight as we gaze into each other's eyes, not knowing how—or maybe unwilling—to admit there's something more than animosity between us.

I bring the candle higher, the flame dancing as I tilt it, my cock leaking when a drop of wax falls to the creamy expanse of her throat and pools in the juncture of her neck, gliding down her exposed skin, creating a path I wish my fingers could follow.

Her eyes flutter and she tilts her head, giving me more access.

My hand moves to the front of her torso, pushing her as I walk us back into the stone wall.

"Tristan," she murmurs.

My stomach flips, an inferno of lust raging through my middle and scorching up my throat.

"Say it again."

"Say what?" she asks.

"My name, little doe," I rasp. "Say my name."

She blows out a heavy breath and I suck it in, desperate to taste her on my tongue.

"Tristan." Her fingers tangle in the strands of my hair.

I lean my forehead against hers, lust ripping through me until I can't see straight from how badly I want to strip her bare and fuck her raw. "I should kill you for making me feel this way."

"So kill me then," she whispers, rising on her tiptoes and tugging on my roots, her nose grazing against mine.

"Death would be a gift." My hips press into hers. "I'd rather see you suffer."

Bending down, I breathe in her scent, biting back the groan that begs to escape. My lips graze over the top of the hardened wax on her neck, my body coiling tight with the need to latch on to her skin and mark her for myself, so that even if she isn't *mine*, she's ruined for anyone else.

But I won't allow it.

I hate her for making me feel like this, for making me covet yet another thing that my brother gets. She *bewitches* me, and I would rather rid her from the face of the earth than exist in a world where she tempts me but leaves me with empty arms.

Wrenching myself away, I back up to the opposite side of the narrow tunnel, the resentment that's had twenty-six years to marinate against my brother overflowing until it pours through my veins.

"So you're a witch on top of being my brother's whore?" I spit.

Her features drop, her gaze narrowing into slits. "I—"

But before she can finish, I spin around and walk away, refusing to acknowledge the way my chest twists when she doesn't choose to follow.

# CHAPTER 21

## *Sara*

GOING TO THE TUNNELS WAS FOOLISH, BUT clearly, since coming to the castle, I've yet to learn from my mistakes. I thought I would be safe. But I should have known I would meet the prince there. He seems to love lurking in dark and shady corners, and he loves dragging me there with him even more, either to threaten my life or speak filthy words in my ear.

I don't know how to tame my reaction to either.

And I *loathe* him.

But there are moments. Ones where he doesn't seem so terrible. Like when his talented hands draw courage on Simon's arm or when he keeps my secrets safe. And whether I want to admit it, there's no one else I'd prefer to be caught by when I'm sneaking through the castle halls. There's a level of trust there—one I've never found with anyone outside my father—and I haven't quite figured out how to correlate the two mismatched emotions.

His brother, however, is an easier one to navigate.

"Thank you for inviting me to lunch today," I say across the small oval table to Michael.

I dressed for the occasion, assuming that meant we'd be making a public appearance, but I was brought to his office instead, where he had a light snack of sandwiches and tea for us to eat.

He smiles as he wipes a crumb off his mouth with his white cloth napkin. "My pleasure. So tell me about you, Sara."

"What would you like to know?" I tilt my head. I'm not stupid enough to believe that he's curious to get to know me. No man ever is.

He shrugs, a sly grin spreading across his face. "Anything you think is of importance."

I return his smile. "I'm a simple girl with simple needs."

He laughs, a hearty booming sound that echoes off the walls, his handsome face thrown back toward the ceiling.

The sound itself is overwhelming in its candor, and I find amusement bubbling in my chest.

"I find that very hard to believe," he says.

I lift a shoulder. "I'd much rather talk about you."

"Don't you read the papers, Sara?" His brow quirks. "What is there to know of me other than what the people have already said?"

His smile widens as he speaks, but there's a sadness that whips across his features so fast you can barely see it. A pang hits the center of my chest, but I brush it off, reminding myself that I don't care how he suffers. He deserves to suffer for the pain his family has caused.

"Well," I whisper, "we don't get the papers in Silva."

He laughs. "No? I thought everyone got the papers."

Disbelief coats my insides. Is he really so obtuse?

I blow out a heavy breath, gritting my teeth to temper the anger that's simmering at the base of my gut. "There's no place to print them. No business that can distribute."

"In Silva?" His forehead scrunches. "I don't believe it."

"Well, I think I would know," I snap. "I've lived there my whole life."

"I was there once as a boy, and it was a lovely town."

My heart twists at his words, memories of when I was a young child and Silva was still thriving floating through my head. Of times when my father was alive and people were happy and whole.

"It's incredible, isn't it?" I intone. "How quickly things can shift. One minute, you're on top of the world, and the next…"

His amber eyes grow dark. "I suppose it is." He takes a sip of his tea before grinning. "Well then, what do you wish to know about me?"

*I wish to know that you're dead.*

Tapping my nails on the table, I lean in. "I want to know what will make you a great king."

His smile drops, and anxiety plugs in the center of my chest until it feels as though my air has run stale.

"Are you insinuating I am not already great, Lady Beatreaux?" His voice is deeper, a sharp edge lining the tone.

I shake my head. "I'm simply asking what the people will remember you for. As your wife, it's my duty to highlight those features, to accent them. I must know your plans if I'm to be a suitable complement at your side."

His head cocks, his thick fingers rubbing against his jaw.

My heart thrums against my ribs and I lean in closer. "What makes you *great*, King Michael Faasa III?"

His eyes flare, but before he can continue, a knock sounds on the door and my cousin Xander walks in, a thin smile spreading across his face.

"You two look cozy."

Michael breaks our stare and sits back in his chair, his gaze flashing to me one more time before he grins at my cousin. "She is to be my wife, Xander. Did you think we wouldn't enjoy each other's company?"

"One can never be too sure, sire. Marriages aren't always about compatibility."

Michael stands, walking over to his oversize oak desk and flipping open the container of his cigar case that sits on the edge. "Well, lucky for us, my bride is beautiful and pleasant at conversation. We're more than—"

He stops in the middle of his sentence, his face draining of all its blood until it's a ghastly white, his eyes growing as large as cylinders.

"Sire?" Xander says, his face pulling tight with tension.

"What is it?" I ask, standing up from my chair, alarm circling through my veins. "Are you all right?"

Michael's jaw tenses, his hand wrapping around something in the box before he drops it and backs away, shaking his head.

"Your Majesty," Xander tries again.

Michael's face pinches as he turns to me, his eyes narrowed and panic swirling through their depths. "Did you do this?"

The sudden shift in his personality throws me off guard, my defenses rising.

"Do what?" I move toward the desk and peer in the case.

There are half a dozen cigars arranged perfectly, and right on top is a black handkerchief with gold lining, the initials MFII engraved in the corner.

Realizing they're his father's, I reach out to touch, but Michael flies forward, smacking my hand back. "Don't touch it, stupid woman."

I gasp, bringing my palm to my chest.

"Sire, *please*." Xander moves up next to me, his brows drawn as he reaches out to touch my arm. "Are you all right?"

I nod, my mind racing a thousand miles a minute as I watch Michael pace back and forth behind the desk, his fingers pulling at the strands of his hair.

"Xander, look at this." He throws his arm toward the open case. "What are we going to do about this? I'm not crazy. I *told* you I wasn't crazy."

My stomach tightens as I watch the scene unfold. Xander walks forward, peeking into the box, his glasses slipping down the bridge of his nose. His shoulders stiffen the slightest amount, and his head snaps up, staring at me just like Michael did. As if *I'm* the one who somehow put his father's handkerchief in the case.

He sighs, looking over at Michael. "There's an easy explanation for this, I'm sure."

"Then explain it," Michael snaps, his fist slamming on the desktop, making the foundation tremble.

Xander's eyes flick between us, his voice coming out controlled and slow, as if he's trying to tame the beast before it leaps from its cage and tears us to shreds. "Your Majesty, perhaps it's time we sent Lady Beatreaux back to her quarters before continuing this conversation?"

My jaw stiffens. I don't want to leave. I want to know what's happening. "I think if there's an issue that's worrying to His Majesty, it's imperative I stay, if only to provide support."

Michael takes large, quick steps over, his hand coming up to cup my cheek. His energy is manic; it winds through the air and wraps around me, vibrating until it sinks into my bones. And while his touch is warm, there's no comfort there.

No spark.

There is, however, a slight tremble.

"You *are* a treasure," he says, his eyes flicking from me to the wall and then back. "And I've overreacted. That handkerchief is…important to me. I thought I had lost it forever." His thumb tips up my chin. "Maybe you're my good luck charm."

I force a smile. "I hope to be more than that."

He grabs my hand then, pulling it to his chest. I let him and notice how quickly his heart is racing beneath his clothes. If I were a naive girl, I'd think it had to do with me.

But I know the truth.

Something has spooked him.

And it's something to do with his dead father.

# CHAPTER 22

## *Tristan*

WHEN I MENTIONED THE ABANDONED CABIN to Antony before I snapped his neck, I wasn't lying.

I found it one day after escaping from my brother and his pack. I'm not sure who originally owned the place, and I know even less about who inhabited the inside, but I *do* know in the ten years since I found it, there hasn't been another living soul that's known of its existence or been inside the shoddy, crumbling walls.

Over the years, I've cleaned it up. There's no running water, and electricity is too new for it to exist here, but despite all that, it's comfortable.

It's also in such a condensed area of the woods that nobody can hear the screams.

"I don't want to continue hurting you," I say, walking around Edward. I anchored his arms with thick chains to a long wooden table that's declined enough for his head to be beneath his body. "I *want* to trust you."

His breathing is choppy; I can tell from the way the dirty white cloth that's over his face morphs with each of his heavy breaths, being sucked into his mouth and blowing back out.

"You were foolish," I continue. "And as a result, everything could be ruined. Do you *know* what you've done?"

He shakes his head, the chains clanking from where his arms pull. "I'm sorry," he says, the words muffled behind the fabric.

My stomach burns from what he's forcing me to do, and I exhale a breath, clicking my tongue. "It's too late for apologies, Edward. We must repent for our mistakes and learn from them."

I dip the large metal jug into the bucket of water at my feet, bringing it over his head and tilting until the liquid pours in a steady stream onto his face, soaking the cloth and dribbling into his mouth until it fills his airways.

The tendons in his neck bulge as he thrashes against the table.

"I'm sure you know this is nothing compared to what will happen if your lover gossips and we're arrested for treason," I note. "After all, you've been the one doling out the punishment for years now."

His breathing garbles, his body rising and falling in jerky movements as he chokes on the water, unable to do anything except experience the sensation of drowning and pray that I let him live.

I snap the jug upright again and sigh, my insides curdling at the thought of having to resort to such extremes. The large bottle thumps against the rotting wood floor as I set it down before leaning over Edward and removing the cloth from his face.

His skin is sopping wet, broken blood vessels spinning spiderwebs around his eyes, his lips cracked and bleeding from where he's bitten into them in his panic.

I adjust the table until he's lying flat. "If you were anyone else, I would kill you."

His head lolls to the side, his chest heaving. "I know," he says, his voice broken and hoarse.

"Are you going to thank me for my mercy?"

His eyes find mine, his mouth parted and panting.

"I don't want to break your spirit, Edward. You must know it pains me as much as it does you." I place my hand on my chest. "But bringing someone in without my approval was dangerous at best and a suicide attempt at worst."

He blinks, his tongue swiping against the chapped flesh. "Thank...you."

"For?" My brows rise.

"For your mercy."

I nod, satisfied with his punishment, leaning down to move the water bucket to the edge of the room and extinguishing the candles that light the space. But I don't unbind him. He'll stay the night and I'll fetch him in the morning after I ensure he understands his loyalty and silence are of the utmost importance.

"Are you leaving me here?" he asks, his tone shaky.

Reaching out, I grip the rusty metal doorknob. "Think on your actions, Edward, and tomorrow morning, we can start again." I swing open the door, stepping outside into the crisp nighttime air. Pausing, I twist back to face him. "If something happens… If *anything* goes awry, it will be you who takes the fall. Do you understand?"

His eyes are hazy as he stares at me from where he's bound, bobbing his head against the wood.

And even though I've lost all my trust in Edward, for now, it's enough.

Slamming the door shut behind me, I take out the skeleton key and turn it in the lock before spinning to walk away. Tilting my head to the side, I crack my neck, grabbing my matchbox from my pocket, retrieving a rolled joint from inside.

Perhaps it was stupid of me to let Edward live, and if it were anyone else, I wouldn't. But Edward is a critical piece in the rebellion. Losing him would be akin to losing an arm, and that's a risk I'm not prepared to take.

Lighting the hash, I inhale deep and start the trek back to the castle.

The moon is high and bright tonight, the usual clouds that grace the Saxum skies missing, creating a haunting glow on the darkened ground. There's no clear-cut path to the cabin; I've taken different ways over the years to ensure the grass doesn't wear from my footsteps, but the easiest route heads straight to my mother's garden, and tonight, that's the one I take.

Torture can be *so* tiresome.

I come out of the trees and stop short when I see a shadowy figure sitting at one of the black benches surrounding the fountain. As I make my way closer, I realize that it's Lady Beatreaux.

Something unsettling jolts through me at the fact that my little doe is, once again, out when she should be safely away and tucked in bed.

"Insomnia is a serious health issue," I say, stepping up behind her.

She twists around, the moonlight splashing across her high cheekbones, a small smile gracing her lips. "You would know."

I walk around the bench and sit next to her, splaying my legs out wide as I tip the joint to my lips and inhale again.

She watches me, a curious sheen coasting across her face. It's innocent, I'm sure, but her gaze sears through me anyway, blazing a path beneath my skin until she's burned her way to the deepest parts of me. I lean my head against the back of the bench, the wooden slabs pressing against my skull, and reach out, offering her the burning paper.

Honestly, I don't expect her to take it, but she surprises me—as she's prone to do—when she grabs it from my fingers with her dainty hands. I roll my head to the side, watching as she brings it to her mouth, wrapping her lips around the end, her cheeks hollowing as she sucks.

My cock stiffens.

Her eyes grow large, a plume of smoke billowing as she coughs and sputters, her fist coming up to smash at her chest.

"That's—" She coughs again. "That's *horrid*. Why would you do that? It's torturous."

Smirking, I take the hash back, scooting closer to her on the bench. "And what do you know of torture, little doe?"

Her coughing dies down, her eyes glazed from where they've watered.

"It burns," she whines.

"You just have to learn how to inhale." I move in even closer, my stomach tensing as I bring the joint to her lips, wondering if she'll allow me or if she'll slap my hand away.

Both options excite me, and I can't decide which one I crave more: her submission or her fight.

Her fingers wrap around my wrist, the touch sending sparks racing up my arm, and I push the edge against her mouth. "Suck it slow."

My cock hardens until it's painfully swollen and pressing against my leg as her lips wrap around the paper.

I reach out, stroking two fingers down the front of her esophagus, because right now, when it's just the two of us, I can't *not* touch her. "Now swallow," I rasp.

Her eyes flash, but her muscles bob as the smoke swirls down her throat and bleeds into her lungs.

Our eyes catch.

"Exhale."

She listens, and a cloud curls around her face, obscuring her from my view. My insides preen from her obedience.

"Good girl." My fingers tap her neck before I take the joint away and bring it to my own lips, the end wet from her saliva.

Her dark eyes gleam when they lock on mine and then drop.

She clears her throat and scoots away on the bench. "I still don't think I like it."

I lean back until I'm staring at the sky, ignoring the way every nerve in my body is sparking like a cannon, urging me to let loose and either fuck her or kill her, just so I can regain the blessed type of numb I'm used to. "It's not for everyone, I suppose."

"Why do *you* do it?"

"Why not?" I shrug my shoulders.

She doesn't reply, choosing to mirror my body, stretching out her legs and tangling her fingers as they rest on her stomach, her head leaned against the back of the bench.

It's silent, the sounds of cicadas in the trees and the occasional hoot of an owl the only things that accompanies us.

"It calms me," I finally say.

Immediately, I want to take the words back, expecting her to jump on the chance to cut me down. But she doesn't. She just hums and closes her eyes.

"Do you ever feel like you can't turn it off?" I continue. "Your thoughts, I mean."

"Always."

"When the whispers won't quiet, my body revolts, turning into knots and tangles until I can't sit still. Until my lungs seize up and I can barely breathe through the panic…" I lift the burning paper. "This helps."

Her head turns toward me, her brows rising. "Did the mighty Prince Tristan just admit to me that something can best him?"

"Anxiety is something that bests everyone it touches. Even me." I suck in another hit before offering it to her again.

Surprisingly, she takes it, holding it between her fingers.

"I get it," she says. "Before my father died, I was like any other girl." She hesitates, glancing at me from her peripheral. "And then right before my twentieth birthday, he went out of town to do what he did best."

"Which was?"

"Be a good man." Her lower lip trembles. "He promised he'd be home in time, and every day leading up to my birthday, I'd sit at my bay window, staring out at the dirt road, waiting to see him come down the drive, this *sick* feeling swirling around my gut, making my nerves jump beneath my skin." She shakes her head. "Turns out I was right, and sometimes when you try to be good, you end up a martyr."

My chest pulls, wondering why she's telling me this and wondering why I care.

"Anyway." She laughs. "Ever since then, that feeling's never left. It just stews like acid, dissolving everything in its path. I'm always just…*waiting* for the next knock on my door, telling me that a person I love is never coming home."

I swallow around the unexpected emotion her words cause, my mind flashing to the moment I found out *my* father had died.

She brings the joint to her lips, rolling her head back to the sky, her throat bobbing as she inhales. Her silhouette is gorgeous in the moonlight, and before I can stop myself, I'm reaching out to brush a curl from her face, unable to temper the urge. "You'd make a stunning portrait."

Her nose scrunches, but she doesn't turn my way. "What?"

"I'd like to draw you," I rephrase, moving in closer, my fingers dancing across her skin. "Just like this, with your face kissing the stars… I think it's the most beautiful thing I've ever seen."

Her body stiffens, and my heart feels as though it's going to explode out of my chest. I'm not sure what loosens my tongue, and I don't know if I even mean the things I say. All I know is that in this moment, it feels like I might die if I don't say them.

"Are you calling me beautiful?" she whispers, her eyes wide as she looks my way.

My tongue swipes across my lips, and I lean in, my mouth brushing the edge of her ear. "I'm saying you could drive a man insane. Make him raze the world just to see you smile."

Her body shivers, and my cock leaks, every bone in my body screaming for me to grab her and pull her flush against me. To claim her beneath the constellations she outshines.

But then I think of how in a few nights' time, it's my brother's arm she'll be latching on to.

It's he who will take her to his bed.

And it's *he* who will have her ruling at his side.

Which means I must kill her, just like all the others.

So I pull back, dusting my fingers down her hair, and I stand up and walk away, wondering what the hollow ache is in my chest and why it's choosing now to appear.

# CHAPTER 23

## *Sara*

IT'S BEEN ALMOST A MONTH SINCE I'VE SEEN or heard from anyone in Silva, and while I expected it, that doesn't stop the longing from weaving through my chest, wrapping around memories of familiar faces.

And familiar lands.

I've always been a wanderer. But it's different from exploring unfamiliar terrain, not knowing what will happen when you turn a corner. I could traipse through every square mile of Silva with my eyes closed and my hands tied behind my back. Here, though, I still haven't been able to grasp on to anything concrete; the map in my head is blank with a few dots of knowledge sprinkled throughout. It's an incomplete picture, and every time I try to fill in the pages, something gets in my way.

Or rather, *someone*.

My stomach flips when I admit to myself that perhaps

that's why I spend my nights sneaking out instead of doing what I should. Or maybe it's the last vestiges of me hanging on to my freedom, knowing that soon I'll be stripped of even that. I'm not naive enough to think that after everything is said and done, I'll be the same girl I am now.

Death inevitably changes you.

Tomorrow evening, I'll parade around on the king's arm like a jewel he's captured and wishes to keep in his treasure chest.

"Tomorrow is important, Cousin," Xander says as we walk through the front courtyard.

Nodding, I swallow around the heaviness lining my stomach.

"You've been antsy," he continues. "I know. Like a sitting duck."

I quirk a brow as I glance at him. "Is it that obvious?"

"Other than you having told me?" He chuckles. "There will be reporters there."

"I'm not inept, Alexander. I can handle a few questions."

He stops walking, the gravel of loose stones crunching beneath his feet as he turns to face me. "After tomorrow, Sara, everything will change."

I know that he's right. The engagement ball is the first of many important moments that will plot out my future. I feel its truth deep down inside me, but for the first time, there's something else there too. It's heavy, and it throbs in the center of my chest, making it feel like I'm on a slow march toward death. Closing my eyes, I push down the selfish thoughts, locking them away in a corner of my heart, hoping they'll stay lost forever.

I walk again, and Xander follows, scrambling to catch up. "In other news, I have a gift for you."

"Do you?" I grin at him. "And what need do I have for a gift?"

He smiles back, pushing the glass frames up his nose. "I think you'll enjoy this one."

"Do I get to know what it is?"

"Soon."

Simon races out of a side door at the east end of the courtyard, drawing my attention away as he runs across the grass, his toy sword drawn out in front of him.

"Little shit."

I twist toward Xander so fast, my eyes cross. "*Excuse me?*"

He waves his hand toward Simon. "I don't know how many times we have to tell his mother to keep him out of sight and where he belongs."

My stomach sours, twisting until bile burns my throat. "And where does he belong?"

"Out of sight and out of mind." He scowls.

"He's a child," I snap, anger percolating in my gut.

"He's a *scullery maid's* child."

My brows rise, and I step away from Xander. "You believe his circumstance makes him less than?"

"Please, Cousin, don't be so naive. Everything is about stature in this world. Some belong, and some don't."

"Because of his skin?" My blood boils.

His face pinches as he glances at me and then back at the boy. "Because he's an abomination."

I laugh in disbelief, the blades strapped beneath my dress calling me, making me itch to stamp out his ignorance forever. "Oh, Alexander. I think it's *you* who's the abomination."

Spinning around, I storm away, my insides seething.

*How dare he.*

Simon stands beneath the large weeping willow in the back corner of the court, his front leg stomping forward as he thrusts out his arm. "En garde!"

Warmth spreads through my chest and extends through my limbs as I make my way toward him, and I wonder, not for the first time, how anyone can be so cruel to such an innocent soul.

Stopping a few meters away, I watch him sword fighting with the air. My heart squeezes when I remember the bruising of his eye and the tears in his voice, and I wonder if he's by himself because he doesn't have anyone else to play with.

"Keep your wrist straight," I call out.

He spins around, his eyes squinting as he zones in on me.

"Hey, lady." He beams. "What d'you know about fighting?"

"More than you think." I smirk. "Come here. Let me show you what to do."

I wave at him, and he skips over, gracing me with a beautiful, toothy grin. I spin him around by his shoulders, placing his hands in front of me and straightening out his form. Then I brush my fingers along the tops of his arms, jostling him just a little. "You can't be so tense, Simon. Your body will never obey you if you're stiff like a board."

His tiny muscles relax, and I move my hand down to cover his as he grips the base of his sword.

"Be like water. Fluid and quick."

"Water?" He scrunches his nose, and I move his arm, showing him what my father taught me when *I* was his age.

I step away, allowing him to continue the movements on his own.

"That's right," I say. "Water is the most powerful element in the world. Calm when needed and ferocious when tried. Never assume you know something's power because of how it appears."

He nods, his eyes wide. "How'd you get so smart?"

I brush off invisible lint from the sleeve of my arm. "You'd be surprised what a lady knows, Simon."

"That's right. You should never underestimate a woman. Especially this one," someone booms from behind me.

The voice makes my heart dive into my stomach, and I spin around, coming face-to-face with a broad chest and a sparkling smile.

"Uncle Raf," I gasp. "What are you doing here?"

His icy blue eyes gleam as they trail me from head to toe, his weight leaning heavily on a dark wooden cane. "Hello, sweet niece."

"And who are you?" Simon interrupts, having walked forward to stand in front of me, his sword pointing at Uncle Raf's chest.

My uncle glances down, his smile withering away as he takes in who's questioning him. My eyes narrow, the need to protect Simon surging through my blood like a fire.

"This is my uncle, Rafael Beatreaux." I place my hand on Simon's shoulder. "And this is His Majesty," I say to Uncle Raf, my eyes widening.

Simon glances up at me, his amber eyes sparkling. My breath whooshes from me as I look at him, realizing for the first time that his eyes bear a striking resemblance to Michael's.

My chest caves in on itself.

*No. Is he?*

Uncle Raf laughs. "Surely, you jest."

I shake my head. "No, he's the king. Don't you know how to greet royalty with respect?"

Simon's chest puffs out. "Yeah. I'm the king." He shoves the tip of his sword into my uncle's leg, and I stifle the laugh that wants to burst from me. "Bow before me."

Uncle Raf glances between us, and with every second he doesn't play along, my ire grows.

"Little tiger."

Two words and my insides flare to life.

My spine stiffens, hating the way my body reacts to the simple sound of his voice.

Simon spins on his heels, dropping his sword and tripping over himself to run and greet Tristan, and I can't help it when my heart squeezes, seeing the genuine affection in Simon's gaze.

He loves him.

And he might be the only one who does.

I glance up from Simon, meeting Tristan's eyes. Butterflies explode in the pit of my stomach, and dread follows, wishing that I could force them away. I don't want them.

"Is that…" Uncle Raf's hand reaches out to grip my forearm, but his touch is cold compared to the heat from the prince's gaze.

"It is." I step away, removing myself from his grasp.

"The scarred prince," he whispers.

My chest twists.

"Don't call him that," I snap, turning to glare at him.

"Why is he staring at you like that?" he asks.

I blow out a breath and force a smile. "Probably wondering why I still exist. He isn't my biggest fan."

"Good," he spits. "Keep it that way."

He places out his arm, and I slip my hand through the crook, trying to ignore the way Tristan's stare is burning a hole through my back.

# CHAPTER 24

## *Sara*

MARISOL FLITS AROUND ME, MAKING SURE my gown flares in the appropriate spots and cinches where it's supposed to. This is the last fitting before I wear it tomorrow night to the ball. And it's stunning. Black lace overlay on cream silk with ruffled fabric that pulls in the waist and a slight train trailing behind. The quartered sleeves are accented by black gloves that rest just over my elbows, and I've never felt more beautiful.

It's what I would choose for myself if I had ever scrounged together the funds for such an ostentatious dress. But until recently, that hasn't been my life. I have plenty of gorgeous gowns, but they're all hand-me-downs from my mother, from a time when we had the type of money to thrive. The ones I came here with have all been provided handily by my cousin, so we don't alert people that despite being the daughter of a duke, I'm actually quite broke. King Michael wouldn't take kindly to finding out the only regality left is in name.

Even more, he'd refuse to believe it's his fault.

"Milady, you look gorgeous," Ophelia swoons, her hands resting over her chest as she takes me in.

"Thank you, Ophelia." I smile at her.

Her innocence is something I long for. She's only three years younger than me, a fresh-faced eighteen, but it feels as though we're worlds apart.

I suppose that's what happens when you experience the harsh cruelties that this world and the people within it offer. And as I stare at Ophelia, her soft features looking up at me in awe, I send up a quick prayer, hoping she's able to hold on to that innocence for as long as possible. Once it leaves, you can never call it back. It just dangles as a memory you long to reach but that's always out of your grasp.

"Do you have family here, Ophelia?" I ask.

She smiles, nodding. "I do. Mama, Papa, and an older brother."

I grin at the love that seeps through her tone. "And what do they do?"

"Papa works with your cousin on the privy council. And Mama spends her time keeping the house."

"Everyone lives here in the castle?"

Her eyes widen. "Oh, no, milady. My parents live in Saxum, but not here in the castle. And my brother is in France."

Sheina sashays into the room with a tray of tea and stops short as she looks at me.

"Sheina, stop it." I laugh. "You're staring at me like you've never seen a nice dress before."

She shakes her head, the ornate metal tea tray clanking as she places it on a side table. "You just…" Her eyes gloss from the hem of the lace up to the risqué neckline. "You look fit to be a queen."

Nerves tighten beneath my skin.

I'm very anxious about tomorrow night—and all the nights that will follow—though I'd never admit it. To play in the realm of men, you have to stuff emotions down until you can barely find them, and there's a lot riding on my future here. Specifically, at the engagement ball itself. Everyone who's anyone will be there, including the entire royal family and the queen mother.

I blow out a deep breath, trying to collect my racing thoughts and stem the slight tremble in my hands.

There's a knock, and Timothy pokes his head in, his brows rising to his hairline, doing a double take when he sees me in my gown. All three ladies turn to face him as he opens the door, stepping to the side to allow for my uncle to move into the room.

The ladies twist back toward me, and after they do, Timothy shakes his head, winking as he rests a hand over his heart. Warmth trickles through my chest at his display, and a smile breaks across my face. He may not speak it out loud, but whether he wants to admit it, we're becoming friends.

"Sara, sweetheart. You look beautiful," Uncle Raf croons, his fingers tight around his cane as he makes his way across the room.

My gaze leaves the door where Timothy just was and I focus on Uncle Raf, a comfortable blanket of familiarity coasting over me as I take in his blue eyes and dark hair with thick streaks of white, more prominent than they were a few years back.

"Thank you, Uncle."

He stops when he's in front of me, his gaze moving over the faces of my ladies. "How much longer will you be? I came here to have tea and catch up."

I glance down at Marisol. "Boss?"

She scoffs at the nickname, a slight smirk lifting her lips as she stands up. "We can be done now, milady."

My hands clap together, eager to have alone time with my uncle. He's the most important man in my life, and while I may not trust his son, Uncle Raf I trust implicitly.

———

"It's time."

Uncle Raf's voice is serious, his fingernails creating a steady tapping rhythm against the top of his cane.

My stomach churns as though a thousand bees have

swarmed and stung my insides, and I swallow around the swelling.

I nod. "I know."

His brow rises. "Have you gained the ear of the king?"

I lift a shoulder, my teeth scraping the inside of my cheek until it bleeds. "As much as I can, but he's not always around." I glance down at my fingers where they tangle together on my lap. "And your son is...not as helpful as I had expected."

Uncle Raf's bushy brows draw in, his lips twisting. "That boy is always doing something." He leans forward. "But you can trust *him*. Change is on the horizon, sweet niece, but that doesn't mean it's easy."

I don't speak the questions that are heavy on the tip of my tongue. Like asking him to explain what on earth he means. I've learned long ago that Uncle Raf's riddles and nonsensical statements are best left as they are.

He hums. "You've always been the smartest child in our family."

"I'm not a child anymore, Uncle."

He chuckles. "To me, little Sara, you'll always be a child."

Smiling at him, I pick up my tea, letting the hot water scald my tongue as I sip from the cup, wondering how smart he'd think I was if he knew I spent my time dreaming of dark corners and dangerous princes.

Uncle Raf's grin drops, his eyes sparking as he leans

forward. "Your father would be very proud of you. And every single person with Faasa blood running through their veins deserves to pay for what they've done."

I nod. A heavy ball of sorrow surges into my throat until I can hardly breathe around the ache, and the weight of responsibility bears down on me in a way I haven't felt since before arriving in Saxum.

I let myself get distracted.

It won't happen again.

# CHAPTER 25

## *Tristan*

"MOST OF YOU ALREADY KNOW THAT TOMOR-
row evening is the engagement ball for my brother and his
bride."

Boos ring out from the sneering faces inside the tavern,
and someone spits on the ground in obvious disgust.

I bring up my hand, picking at a fingernail as I sigh.
"They will most likely not expect me to show. But we all
know how much I enjoy doing the unexpected."

Laughs trickle through the room.

"We're on the cusp of a new dawn, one where you aren't
limited based on circumstance. Where you aren't thrown to
the lions because you're a little *different*."

I pause, my gaze meeting the eyes in the crowd, feeling
the blaze burn through them as surely as if it was licking
against my skin.

"The king has gone mad, although he wishes for no

one to know." My lips pull back from my teeth. "But *I* know."

"Why can't we just storm the castle now?" a young woman in the front screeches, her stringy hair falling in her sunken face. "We have the numbers!"

Rumbles spread through the crowd. I raise a hand in the air, silencing them. "I understand the plight. But instant gratification rarely satisfies the need, and my desire, with your help, is to ensure freedom for us all. Ending Michael's reign is not enough."

"But if he dies, the crown belongs to you!" she presses, her fist smacking her other hand. "Where it belongs."

"That's true, and it will look *extraordinary* upon my head." I smile. "But our end goal is much greater than *just* me."

I reach down, lifting up the hem of my tunic until it exposes my chest, showcasing the fresh tattoo, still tender from where the ink pushed into my skin. It's of a jackal, teeth bared and spit dropping from its mouth, perched on top of bones, with flames reflected in its dark eyes.

*Together we rule, divided we fall* is scrawled underneath.

"I know most of you despise the name jackal. And who could blame you? Filthy, they say. Disgusting. Uncouth."

The faces in the crowd grow dark, scowls marring their features, and heavy energy wafts through the room from their tangible anger.

"But power only lies in the hands of those who *we* let have it," I continue, dropping my shirt and walking back and forth across the raised platform. "It's time for us to take our power back."

I meet the stare of the woman with her idiotic questions, shocks of pleasure surging through my veins when I see the admiration in her eyes. She shoots to her feet before dropping to both knees, bowing before me. Just the way I like it.

"They call us feral?" I stop pacing, a grin creeping along my face. "We'll give them so much worse."

Mugs slam on tables, a steady cheer growing like a tidal wave.

"For now, feast on the provisions I've brought. Go home with full bellies and kiss your families good night, knowing you've chosen to be on the right side of history."

Plates of food are carried from the back area of the tavern and placed on the tables, people scrambling to grab their share.

I step off the platform, weaving my way through the benches until I reach the back corner where Edward stands, his jaw set and his eyes wild, most likely still recovering from the psychological ramifications of the punishment he received. His new woman leans against his front, his arms wrapped around her waist.

"You've done well, Sheina, bringing food from the castle," I say when I reach them.

She inclines her head. "Thank you, sire."

"Did Paul give you any issues?"

"Not at all." She smiles, her eyes leaving mine and scanning over the tables of everyone surrounding us, no doubt taking in the rail-thin frames of people shoveling bread and beans into their mouths. "They eat like it's their first meal in days," she says.

I place my hands in my pockets, my thumb brushing against the rough edge of my matchbox. "For most of them, it is."

"What you're doing here…" Her eyes grow glassy as she meets my stare. "You're very different from what they say."

Edward's arms stiffen around her waist. It's subtle, but I catch the movement, filing it away for later.

I smirk down at the girl, unable to decide if she's too naive or stupid—or maybe she's already forgotten that I threatened to let the town rape her while I killed everyone she loved.

Either way, her words strike a chord. One that sits in the center of my gut, its reverberation vibrating through every part of me until the echoes make me ill. I lean in. "I am *everything* they say and many things they don't."

Her fingers tighten where they're wrapped around Edward's arms. "If Sara knew what you were doing, she would help," she whispers.

"Do not speak her name to me," I snap, my chest pulling tight.

"I just—"

"Shh." Stepping forward, I press my hand against

her mouth, smashing her lips until they mold around my fingers. "Do you remember what I told you? About what would happen if you were to betray me?"

Her eyes shutter and she nods.

"Good." I smile, although nausea burns in the pit of my gut. "Don't speak of her again in my presence."

I step back, spinning toward the crowd.

———

"Have you met her then?" my mother asks, her hands running down the front of her deep-purple gown, her gray hair strung up so tightly it pulls back her face.

The dowager queen never looks anything less than perfect, after all, regardless of the fact that she just spent hours traveling here from our country estate.

"I have," I reply, a cloud of smoke puffing from my mouth and swirling into the air from where I lie on the couch.

"And?" she continues, leaning forward in her chair.

"What would you like me to say, Mother?" I sigh, running a hand through my hair and sitting up to meet her gaze. "That she's everything you're not? She is."

She scowls and my insides tingle with glee, happy that I'm wedging a grudge before they've even met. I can't wait to see how my little doe fares against her.

"I wish you'd stop smoking that hashish," my mother quips. "It's a disgusting habit. You don't need anything else to mar your reputation."

A chuckle works its way through my throat, the scabbed-up wounds from when I was a child and still yearning for my mother's love throbbing as if they're new.

"I'm having a hard time caring about your wishes, Mother, considering you never took the time to care for mine."

"That's not fair," she huffs. There's a tense pause in the air, and just when I've decided she's actually going to shut up and allow me silence, she speaks again. "I know you're sad about your father. We all grieve, and if anyone understands, it's me. But it's been two years. It's time to move on, and—"

I stand from the couch and move toward her, my jaw clenching so tight my teeth crack. "Do *not* pretend to know about my grief." Crouching down once I'm in front of her chair, I flick the ash from the end of my joint and rest my hands on her knees, staring up at her. "Where were you the night of his death?"

She lifts her chin. "That's none of your concern."

Bile burns the back of my throat, my anger so palpable I can taste it in the air. "You surely weren't sharing his bed, since that's where he was found—his skin tinged blue and all alone."

Her spine straightens just as a knock sounds.

One of her ladies moves into the room and walks toward the door before opening it. Timothy walks in, clearing his throat and bowing deep. "Your Majesty, may I present Lady Beatreaux. She's here for tea."

My chest pulls tight at her name, and there's a sudden urge to stay, if only to protect her from my mother's sharp tongue and claws. Ridiculous, considering I was just fanning the flames, wanting to create the destruction myself.

My mother pats my hands. "Tristan, darling, I'll speak with you later."

I grab her palm and kiss the back. "We'll continue this *conversation* later, Mother."

Spinning around, I meet the eyes of Lady Beatreaux, looking beautiful as always and strong-willed as ever.

Good.

She'll need it.

# CHAPTER 26

## *Sara*

I HADN'T EXPECTED TO MEET WITH THE dowager queen in private, but she sent for me as if I were a pathetic servant just waiting for her to come and call. Truth be told, I don't wish to see her, but my uncle urged me to go, stating how important it is to stay in her good graces until I'm in a position of power.

So I strapped my blades to my thigh, dressed in the most expensive day gown I have, allowed Sheina to cinch up my corset extra tight, and here I am, taking in shallow sips of breath while I follow Timothy down the hall.

"Do you know the queen mother?" I ask him.

"I do," he replies.

"And?"

He quirks a brow. "And what?"

"Well, what am I walking into here, Timothy? Is she the rose or is she the thorns?"

"Milady, she's no rose." He chuckles as we approach

her door, turning to face me. "But neither are you. I think you'll handle yourself just fine."

Maybe I should be offended by his words, but instead, there's a comfort that spreads through my chest, because he's right—I am no rose, and I like that he sees me enough to know that.

The door swings open, a young lady in a simple pale-blue dress smiling and stepping to the side, allowing us to move into the room. My hands are clammy, making my pink lace gloves stick to my palms, but I breathe in as deep as my corset allows and straighten my shoulders to fake the confidence I'm not feeling inside. We're in her personal quarters, a place I've never been, and I'm struck at how similar to mine the sitting room is.

Deep brown woods accent the red-and-cream wallpaper, and a fire crackles in the center of the room. There are two burgundy couches facing each other, and at the head are two brown leather chairs surrounding a small round table, already set with a tray of tea and white china with blue birds and gold trim.

None of that, however, is what catches my attention. Because from the second I walked into the room, I could feel him. A hum that weaves through the air and dances on my skin, wrapping around my middle like rope.

I try to resist glancing his way, I do, but I give in, acknowledging—perhaps for the first time—that my self-control with the prince is severely lacking.

My father's pendant weighs heavily around my neck.

Our eyes lock. Tristan's gaze peers like I'm an animal at a circus, and even though he's across the room, it feels as though I'm on display just for him. My already shallow breathing stutters as he flicks his stare down to my décolletage, my thighs tensing to stem the ache flaring between them.

Timothy clears his throat, his hand grazing my elbow, and it's only then that I snap out of it, tearing my eyes away and focusing on the woman I'm here to see.

Queen Gertrude Faasa: the woman who stood by while her son killed my father, watching him hang for daring to question the crown.

Rage burns bright in my gut.

I step forward, dropping into a curtsy, the pale-pink hem of my dress fluttering on the ground at my feet. "Your Majesty."

"Come here, girl," she snaps. "Stand up straight and let me get a good look at you."

Her words slice through the air like a knife, demanding and almost cruel in their tone. I move forward, and when I come to a stop before her—her eyes squinting and jaw setting as she catalogs every piece of me—I've never wanted to revolt more.

"So you're the girl here to marry my son." Her eyes trail up my form. "Do none of your ladies know how to tame those wild curls?"

My back stiffens at her shallow insult, but my confidence surges, realizing that she's resorting to petty remarks instead of bone-deep jabs.

I let out a small laugh. "Curls like mine are difficult to tame, ma'am. My ladies do what they can with what God gave me." I tilt my head. "Perhaps you could do my hair one day and show them how it's done."

Her lips purse. "And what makes you worthy to wear a crown, Miss Beatreaux?" She smiles and I move without waiting for her invitation, sitting down on the couch next to her. "Please, make yourself at home," she quips.

I smile so wide my cheeks ache. "Thank you."

"Tell me." She nods toward one of her ladies. "Do you come from nobility?"

"My father was a duke."

The same girl who opened the door steps forward, pouring tea into the fine china before moving back to her place against the far wall.

"And what does he do now?" the queen mother continues.

The pit in my stomach gapes wider. "Rots in the ground, unfortunately."

A sharp laugh from behind us catches my attention, the sound making my stomach flutter. I twist my head, glancing at Tristan who's leaning against the door, his black boots crossed at the ankle. I'm not sure why he's still here, but oddly, I find his presence comforting. Almost as if he's standing at my back instead of hers.

"So he's dead then?" she asks.

I turn my attention to her, the butterflies in my belly dissipating as soon as she speaks.

"He is, ma'am," I confirm, although the conversation is sending a wave of anger through my veins.

She doesn't remember him. She knows my name, knows where I'm from, but doesn't even remember.

There have been many moments when life has smacked me upside the face and opened my eyes to the realities that drain your innocence away, but this is the first time that I realize how one experience can be so vastly different for two people.

To me, my father's murder was life altering. But to her, it was just another day.

I vow right here to never take death for granted, that even if people's lives end, I'll pray for them and the families of those who loved them. Everyone deserves to be remembered, even if it's to imagine their soul burning in the pits of hell.

"Hmm, pity." She picks up her tea, swirling a spoon through the liquid for long moments before tapping it against the side of the cup, the clinking sound sharp. "Both of my boys lost their father too." She shakes her head. "But of course, you'd have known about that already."

I nod, tangling my fingers together on my lap. "It was a momentous day indeed to learn of King Michael's passing."

"We still mourn," she sighs.

"Yes," Tristan cuts in. "*Tragic*. If you'd like to fixate on your husband again, Mother, by all means, let's continue our earlier conversation."

My heart skips at the sound of his voice, and curiosity winds its way through my heart as I glance back and forth between them. He speaks to her as if he can't stand the sight of her, which is so different from everything I've learned of them over the years.

I've always thought the Faasa family was a cohesive unit, loyal to only each other until the bitter end. And even though I realized that the king and his brother don't get along, I never imagined that would extend out to the dowager queen as well.

Not that it makes a difference. In order to end the Faasa reign, I must eradicate them all.

"Tristan, you may leave," his mother states.

Twisting toward him again, I smile. "Yes, there's no need for you *at all*."

He smirks as he straightens off the wall and walks toward us. He's wearing all black, as he usually is, his jacket covering the tattoos I ache to see, even though I convince myself it's to admire his art.

"How can I, when the conversation just became so interesting?" he asks, dropping next to me on the couch. "I think I'd much rather stay."

"Please, don't," I retort, although there isn't much conviction behind my words.

He tsks, the sound skipping through the air and tapping against my skin as surely as if he touched me with his hands. His legs splay wide and he flings his arm across the back of the couch, the tips of his fingers dancing perilously close to my shoulder.

My body coils tight, muscles stretching thin as I lean to the side to ensure that not a single piece of me touches him.

He's making it hard to focus, although maybe that's his goal. I'm convinced he loves to watch me squirm.

*Infuriating.*

"And tell me, Miss Beatreaux," the dowager queen continues. "How is it that a lady without a father can hold herself so well in polite society?"

My chest cracks at her words, but I keep the reaction from showing on my face. "The same way a widowed queen does, I suppose. With a heavy heart and a strong sense of self."

"Hmm." Her eyes flick down my body before meeting my gaze again. "A queen's duties are far superior to that of an orphaned child."

The urge to reach out and strangle her grows so strong I have to tangle my fingers together on my lap.

"I look forward to becoming queen then." I run my palms down my skirt. "Is it nice?"

She tilts her head.

"Oh." I laugh. "I'm curious if you enjoy not having

those duties anymore? I'm sure you're grateful that you can live your days at a cottage in the middle of nowhere, with no responsibilities left to your name."

She stiffens, her gaze narrowing.

"It sounds very relaxing," I continue. "Maybe one day, after I wed your son, we'll be able to visit, and I can reassure your doubts by showing you all the ways I've improved on the foundation you *tried* to build."

She sets down her teacup, the liquid sloshing over the sides as she turns to glance at her lady in the corner.

Tingles race along my spine when I feel a delicate brush at the nape of my neck, and I suck in a breath, my insides tangling tighter than they were before.

Tristan is touching me, his fingertips ghosting across my skin, making goose bumps pebble down the length of my body. Panic at his mother seeing mixes with the thrill of being touched, and instead of leaning away, I press back, my stomach flipping and surging until it settles next to my racing heart.

I don't dare look his way, but I can feel him staring.

And I shouldn't enjoy it as I do.

# CHAPTER 27

*Tristan*

IT TAKES SKILL AND PRECISION TO WEAVE magic with your words, and it's something I discovered at a young age I had a knack for. Even as a child, I could trick people into thinking that my ideas were theirs, so I spent years fine-tuning the craft until I was able to tell people to go to hell in a way that they enjoyed the trip.

Which is why seeing Lady Beatreaux hold her own against my mother by using those same tactics was intoxicating.

She's strong-willed. She's fire.

She's the devil parading as a snake, convincing people to eat the apple.

*Ma petite menteuse…* My little liar.

It's what's needed in a queen. You can't have a fresh-faced, innocent girl ruling kingdoms.

But the thought of my brother having her at his side

when it turns out she's so valuable makes bile tease the back of my throat. Violence thrums in my veins, urging me to kill him now and steal her for my own.

Within a fortnight's time, my brother and all who aid him will fall and I will step into place as the rightful heir to the throne. But having a queen was never in my plans.

"Ready?" I ask Edward, glancing at him as we walk to the banquet hall. The murmurs grow louder with every step, bleeding through the walls, and I smile, an excited energy humming beneath my skin.

"Everything will work out in the end." He smiles.

"Of course it will," I drawl. "Failure does not run in my blood."

He smirks. "Technically, your brother has that blood too."

"Unfortunately, that's true." I grimace. "I suppose I'll have to drain him of every drop."

Edward chuckles as we approach the dark wood doors, the deep-gray metal hinges creaking as he pushes them open and we step inside.

People's attention coasts across my skin, infusing me with strength as I feed off their energy.

The banquet hall is drenched in black and gold, our family flag flying high above our heads, long tables covered in white linens running next to the walls. The largest of them is perpendicular to the rest on a raised dais, overlooking the room, and my brother sits dead center, flanked by his bride-to-be and our mother, his advisers filling the other seats.

My stomach pulls tight as I glance over the faces of all the people who have stood in my way. People who have never shown me the respect they give Michael, when he's done nothing to earn it.

Heads turn as I make my way down the stone aisles, my boots clacking on the floor and echoing off the sky-high ceilings.

"The scarred prince," someone murmurs.

Once upon a time, that phrase cut deep, but now, I use it as fuel knowing that soon anyone who dares speak against me will have to beg for repentance at my feet.

My brother hasn't noticed me yet, deep in conversation with my mother and Xander, but my little doe is a different story. A dangerous heat crawls up my insides, knowing that while it's she and Michael everyone is celebrating, it's me who has her eyes.

Edward makes his way to one of the side tables, taking his spot next to other higher-ranking military and immersing himself in conversation. It's important to have plenty of eyewitnesses to attest that we were here.

I stop walking when I reach the platform, rocking back on my heels, my gaze never leaving Lady Beatreaux's. Her head tilts, brows furrowing, and I smirk, my tongue swiping across my bottom lip.

She fidgets in her seat.

"Tristan," Michael says, the deep bass of his voice bouncing off the walls. "What a lovely surprise."

Slowly, I move my eyes from his betrothed's to him. "Did you think I wouldn't show, Brother?"

"One can never be sure with you," he chuckles, waving his arm at a servant. "Bring him a seat."

"Lady Beatreaux." I let her name slide off my tongue, my attention falling back on her. "You look *devastating*. My brother is a lucky man."

A few gasps sound from behind me, no doubt surprised that I would be so bold. Excitement flutters in my stomach, wondering how she'll react—how my brother will react.

She smiles, tipping her head, but I see the flash of irritation swirling through the deep brown of her irises. "Thank you, Your Highness. That's very kind."

"I know your manners are rusty," Michael cuts in, his eyes blazing. "But be careful how you speak of my soon-to-be wife."

His hand reaches out and grabs hers, and she turns toward him, her features softening as she tangles their fingers together on top of the table.

Green gusts whip through my middle, and my jaw clenches so tight it cracks. I tear my eyes away, worried that if I don't, I'll storm the dais and rip his fingers clean off his body, making sure he can never touch her again.

I make my way up onto the raised platform and walk behind the backs of every chair until I come to stand behind my cousin, Lord Takan, who sits next to my little doe. *The treacherous witch.*

Bending down, I press a hand on his shoulder, the diamonds of my rings glinting as I squeeze. "Cousin, it's been a long time."

His body stiffens, wine goblet freezing halfway to his mouth. "Tristan, what a delightful surprise."

I lift a brow. "Is it? When was the last time I saw you?" I ask. "At my father's funeral?"

He clears his throat, placing his cup on the table, his fingers tapping a nervous rhythm on the top. "I believe so."

"Wow." I whistle. "Two years. Incredible." A servant interrupts, a large chair being hoisted between their arms, and amusement dances through my middle when Takan is forced to move out of the way to make room for me.

Once my chair is in place, I sit down, my legs stretching underneath the long white linen tablecloth that covers my lap. I turn my body toward my cousin, but I reach out with my right arm, placing my hand on Lady Beatreaux's thigh. Her entire body stiffens, her fork clattering when it falls on the plate.

"Are you all right?" Michael asks her.

My palm grips her tighter.

"What?" She laughs. "Oh, I'm just fine. Thought I saw something is all."

"Tell me, Cousin." I grin at Takan. "What have you been up to since I saw you last?"

My fingertips create small figure eights against the

fabric of her dress, crawling up her leg, pausing when I feel something bulky.

Her muscles tense, and I realize she has what feels like a dagger strapped to her. Smirking, I glance at her from my peripheral.

*Such a devious little minx.*

The vision I create in my head makes me harden, imagining her bound and naked, nothing touching her skin except the silver of her blade and the heat of my lips. My palm skims upward until I press into the crease of her inner thigh, my knuckles hitting the bottom of her corset as I force the fabric of her dress to meld to her skin.

I can feel the heat of her cunt, and I bite back a groan, my hand kneading her flesh.

My stomach flips when her fingers slam down on top of mine.

Takan wipes his mouth with a napkin, but his movements are jerky, beads of sweat forming on his brow, his jaw grinding back and forth. "Your brother has made me the viceroy of Campestria."

"A *viceroy*." I raise my brows. "How…quaint."

I tighten my grip, the tops of my rings pressing against my little doe's palm. Her hand moves off mine, and I dip my fingers in farther, leaning back in my chair and grabbing the wineglass from the table to bring to my lips.

She skims across my thigh, fingertips brushing against the edge of my erection. A cough whips through me, the wine burning as it races down my throat. My cock throbs, desperate for her touch. I'm half tempted to pick her up and throw her on top of this table, pushing up her dress and planting my tongue in her pussy, just to hear what her moans sound like in the *beautiful* acoustics of the hall.

I surge forward, my lips parting as she teases the side of my length with the back of her palm, the fabric jostling and creating a friction that has me close to coming without her even fully touching me.

Liquid oozes from my tip and my fingers grip the meat of her thigh so tight, I'm sure I'll leave a bruise.

"Sara, sweetheart." Michael's voice cuts through the fog, and her hand disappears as quickly as it came. "I'd like to have some time with you, alone, before the ball begins."

She blushes as she gazes at him. I clench the edge of the table, my knuckles lancing white from the harsh grip.

"Of course, Your Majesty," she croons.

She places her palm in his, and they rise, but before they can move, a large crash clatters through the hall.

I turn to my left, shock spiraling through me when I see my cousin collapsed on top of the table, grasping at his neck. His body spasms as if he has no control over his muscles. Red capillaries burst in his eyes, and I'm frozen in place, transfixed at the sight of him.

A scream sounds from somewhere beneath the dais,

and someone rushes forward, pushing me out of the way as they aid him. I allow them to move me, a sense of dread winding through my middle, recognizing that my cousin is poisoned, and not by me.

# CHAPTER 28

## *Sara*

STRYCHNINE.

Not the most subtle of poisons, but I didn't need subtlety. I needed something that had no known remedy and would work quickly.

Lord Takan is harmless—a sacrifice for the greater good—but somewhere in the deepest part of me, I could feel a piece of my soul wither and chip when I slipped the powder in his drink and watched it dissolve, knowing I was serving him nothing but death.

Lord Takan is a first cousin of the king, which makes him a Faasa, and although not high in line to assume the throne, he is *in* the line. And my thirst for revenge won't be quenched until I've eradicated every drop of Faasa blood from the earth.

Michael's hand trembles as he grips my forearm, beads of sweat forming on his brow as we're escorted by a corral of guards, led by Timothy and another man in uniform with shaggy blond hair. I can't remember his name, but I know he was the one who restrained that woman with Lord Reginald's head. Xander stomps in front of us, running a hand through his hair as if he can't calm his thoughts.

We file into Michael's office, and Timothy grips my elbow, his eyes scanning me from head to foot as if he's worried I too ingested poison that will paralyze my airways and have me seize until I die.

"I want to know"—Michael's voice shakes the walls—"what the *fuck* that was."

Xander paces back and forth in front of the desk.

He's a talented actor, I've decided.

After all, it was he who slipped me the poison in the first place.

"The ball must go on," Xander chirps. "This is the perfect time for you both to come together and reassure the people. Show them that in adversity, we find strength"—he points between Michael and me—"in each other."

I scoff. "Do you ever think of anything besides politics?"

His lips turn down, a sinister glaze coasting through his eyes.

The door flies open and Prince Tristan storms through, a dark energy swirling around him, making it feel like the temperature drops just from his presence.

I shiver, my heart thumping in my chest.

He does not look happy.

"Tristan," Xander snips. "It's always death that brings you around, isn't it?"

Tristan's footsteps are heavy, his long black jacket floating out behind him as he cuts across the room. Xander's eyes widen and he backs away until he bumps into the lip of the desk.

Quick as a flash, Tristan's hand shoots out, gripping Xander by the face until his cheeks smoosh, his glasses pushed until they're crooked and bent on his forehead.

"Tristan, please," Michael sighs, rubbing his hands over his face.

Tristan's jaw tenses as he lifts Xander up until his toes are kissing the ground.

There's a tendril of worry for my cousin, but I'm so surprised by the sheer energy radiating from the prince that I'm frozen in place, a heady sensation flooding through me as he dominates every other man in the room just by choosing to be in it.

My eyes track along the rings on his fingers, moving over the thick veins in his hand. My thighs press together when I remember that same hand dipping between my legs while dozens of people watched, none the wiser.

I regret not taking the opportunity of feeling how much I affected him when I had the chance.

"A family member has just been poisoned in our home, yet you still speak to me as if I won't slice up your body and feed it to the mutts for dinner," Tristan spits.

Nausea rolls through me at the visual his words create.

"I wouldn't recommend it, Your Highness," Xander stutters out, wincing when Tristan's grip tightens. "I'd be so chewy."

The prince sneers, dropping Xander to the ground, and I rush over, crouching beside him and helping him to stand.

"Be civilized," I snap, glaring up at Tristan.

His eyes rage like a wild storm, all his playful banter gone as if I made it up in my head. My heart stutters against my ribs as I hold his stare, and for the first time, I get why they fear him. My uncle's warnings blare through my brain.

*"The scarred prince is unhinged, Sara. Stay away from him until necessary, do you understand?"*

"How do you know it was poison?" Michael questions.

"Because I'm not an idiot." Tristan breaks our connection and spins toward his brother. "Did you not see the convulsions? The struggle to breathe? The quick and torturous death?"

Michael sucks in a breath. "He's dead?"

Tristan chuckles, the sound rumbling deep in his chest.

"*Jackals*," Xander hisses.

My brows rise to my hairline, irritation at the disgusting name bleeding through my pores. I get what he's doing, pinning the murder on the rebels. It wasn't the plan, but I see the appeal of using them as scapegoats to help us hide in plain sight. Still, the thought of innocent people being hurt drops in the center of my chest, weighing me down until my legs tremble. Hopefully, I can finish the job before it comes to that.

Michael huffs. "Here? In the castle?"

"They've made it in the castle before," I speak up. "Is it so far-fetched to believe they could again?"

Tristan leans against the wall, the muscle in his jaw tensing and releasing. He pulls a joint from behind his ear and rolls it over the cupid's bow of his lips before slipping it in his mouth, and even though it isn't an appropriate time or an appropriate reaction, my stomach tightens, desire pooling between my legs.

After our night under the stars, I don't know that I'll ever look at smoking the same.

He grabs a match from his pocket, a few wayward strands of his jet-black hair falling over his scar as he leans forward to light the end, the flame making his features glow a warm shade of orange. His eyes flash when they flick to me, and he straightens, allowing the fire to burn down the wooden stick until I'm sure it's grazing against his skin.

But he doesn't even flinch. Doesn't even move.

I swallow, stuck in his gaze like quicksand.

He smirks, smoke seeping out of his mouth and curling into the air.

"Regardless, there's nothing to be done for it now," Xander says, snapping me out of my daze.

My chest twists as I turn my attention away.

Michael paces back and forth, his eyes bouncing from one wall to the next, and I bite the inside of my cheek as I take him in, wondering why he seems so uneasy when a few short weeks ago, a decapitated head rolled at his feet and he couldn't be bothered to care.

"Don't worry," Xander continues. "I'll take care of everything."

# CHAPTER 29

## *Tristan*

"DO YOU THINK IT'S A REBEL?" EDWARD SAYS, adjusting the cuff on the edge of his uniform. "Someone who's grown restless and took matters into their own hands?"

A shot of rage fires through my chest at the thought of a rebel disobeying me, and I glance at Edward, distrust weaving through my mind.

"Why would somebody wish themselves a torturous death by my hands?" I ask. "They have to know that's what would await them."

He nods, rubbing at the scruff on his jaw. "Do you think it's Alexander? That pathetic little bird?"

"I think everyone is suspect at this point." I rise from my seat, making my way to the corner of Edward's room and staring into the mirror perched on top of his chest of drawers.

"Even Lady Beatreaux?"

Defensiveness slams down like a concrete wall, cracking my foundation with its force. I spin to face him, tilting my head. "If you have something to ask me, Edward, do it. I cannot stand guessing games."

He swallows, lifting a shoulder. "I mean nothing by it…but she *is* an attractive woman."

I clench my jaw, tamping down the urge to cut out his tongue for speaking of her as if he has any right. As if he has any clue of how *devastating* she truly is.

"She's my brother's."

He glances at me from his peripheral as he comes to stand next to me in the mirror. "Yet you warned the rebels not to touch her."

I sigh, tiring of his line of questioning. "I will be the one to kill her, Edward. Preferably while Michael watches."

My mind flashes back to the dinner, when she brushed against my cock, then placed the same fingers in Michael's hand, smiling up at him like he was her world.

A sudden thought strikes me like a sharp slap to the face.

*What if she was responsible for Takan's death?*

She's always sneaking around in places she doesn't belong, has knives attached to her thigh, and plays the part of a doting royal when I know for a fact she's a silver-tongued snake.

She was also sitting next to Lord Takan at the banquet.

A huff of air escapes me as the puzzle pieces slot

together, a cool trickle of relaxation sliding down my insides at the realization.

Of course it would be her.

*My little liar.*

I expect to feel anger, but instead I grow aroused, delighted that if it *is* her, she's far more nefarious than I thought. It makes me want to push her, see how far she'll go until she breaks.

My cock rises to half-mast from her devious deeds, and I sink my teeth into my bottom lip, biting back a groan, recognizing that this makes her even more attractive to me than she already was.

I straighten my black vest, then walk to where my black tailcoat is thrown across the chair, picking it up and easing my arms through the sleeves.

"This changes nothing with our plans," I say to Edward, a sly grin creeping along my face. "Might as well make tonight a two-for-one special."

———

The last ball held in the Saxum castle was when Michael assumed the throne, throwing the most lavish event since the turn of the century ten years prior.

I didn't attend.

Must have slipped my mind.

Still, I knew that by presenting Lady Beatreaux to the court, she would be the center of attention.

However, I didn't expect for it to affect me the way it is.

I watch her from the shadows of the ballroom, my blood bubbling like a vat of acid as I watch her paraded around on the arms of a dozen different men, all clamoring for a chance to dance with their future queen.

My brother sits next to my mother in a blocked-off area meant for the royal family, underneath a shimmering black-and-gold awning made of the finest drapery.

"She's quite the beauty, isn't she?" a slurred voice murmurs behind me.

I glance over, annoyance lancing through my bones that someone thinks they can speak of her. That irritation only grows when I see a short and stocky man with far too many jewels and red hair as bright as the sun swaying in place, his wine sloshing over his glass.

Lord Claudius, the Baron of Sulta, which is a town across the plains of Campestria near the southern border. He used to spend summers with our family at the country estate and has always been quite envious of my brother, almost to the point of obsession.

"Hello, Claudius," I sigh. "Good to see you're still quite the little creeper."

He grins, tipping up his glass and draining the wine. "And you, Your Highness, still lurking in the shadows. Still hiding from your brother like you did when we were kids?"

Chuckling, I spin around to face him, dwarfing him with my shadow. "Were you even invited tonight, little man? Or did you sneak your way in to be close to Michael?" I reach out, gripping his shoulder. "Maybe if you put on a dress, you can trick him into thinking you're a whore, and he'll let you slurp on his cock the way you've dreamed of for years."

His face drops into a furious scowl and he rips himself from under my hand, storming away without another word. My eyes follow him as he walks to the center of the ballroom, tapping the shoulder of the young man dancing with Lady Beatreaux and replacing him, his grubby fingers gripping her waist and pulling her into him.

Anger eats through my skin from the inside out when he touches her, her smile becoming forced, eyes flashing with unease.

Normally, I'd enjoy her discomfort. But only when it's at *my* hands.

He dances them around in a simple waltz, his palm moving farther down her waist until he's skimming just above the curve of her ass.

I'm two seconds from shoving my way through the ballroom and flaying every single one of his fingers, but before I can, she extricates herself from his grip.

He bows as she moves away, heading across the shiny tiled floor and out into the hallway.

Anticipation tightens my muscles as his beady eyes stalk her, and I see the moment he makes the decision. He stumbles his way across the floor, following her out the ballroom doors.

I glance at my brother, expecting him to be seething with rage, but instead, he's busy looking off to the side of the room, making eyes with one of the servant girls standing against the far wall.

Disgusting.

Cracking my neck, I weigh my options. I could follow them or I could ignore it.

Sara Beatreaux is not my problem.

Normally, I wouldn't care.

I *shouldn't* care.

But I do.

# CHAPTER 30

## *Sara*

I FEEL HIM BEHIND ME BEFORE I SEE HIM.

I've barely made it to the door of the ladies' washroom when I'm spun around and pulled into a dark corner off the main hall, pressed against the stone.

"Get your hands off me," I hiss, glaring at the ruddy face of Lord Claudius. His wine-soaked breath is putrid, even more volatile now than it was when we were dancing.

This is the last straw of my sanity, after having been paraded around on the arms of several men, dancing until my feet went numb. When Marisol had me practice, I had assumed it was to dance with my husband-to-be, not with everyone else attending.

But Michael has barely spared me a glance all night. He gave a half-hearted speech about how his cousin had been ill long before this evening and how he was lucky to have me at his side through the sorrow of his loss, but since then, he's been a ghost, pawning me off as if I'm an obligation he can't wait to be rid of.

"You'll regret this when you're sober," I try again, pushing against the lapels of Lord Claudius's tuxedo.

"You're a beautiful woman, milady," he slurs. "No one would blame me for sampling the goods."

"His Majesty would blame you," I reply, panic creeping through my muscles. "You'd be put to death."

His fat fingers slide down the front of my ball gown, scrunching the satin and lace, his forearm pressing against my windpipe, increasing pressure until my airway starts to close.

"No one would believe you." He chuckles. "You're practically begging for it."

Sharp razors slice down my throat as I struggle to breathe. I glance down the hallway as best I can, hoping to see anyone around to calm the situation.

But no one is here.

His hips press against me, the thick ridge of his erection prodding my stomach as his palm grips my side. I attempt to move my arms, hoping that I can get to the daggers on my thigh, but his body weight is bearing down and I have no control of my limbs.

My father taught me to be proficient in swords and daggers, and my aim with a pistol is almost perfect.

But he didn't train me well enough for this.

I allow my body to go lax against him, hoping that if I

stop fighting, maybe he'll loosen his grip. He grunts, thrusting himself into my belly, grinning as spittle flies from his mouth onto the side of my neck. He pulls at my skirts, the sound of the fabric tearing like an arrow to my chest, fear bleeding in to mix with the beats of my heart. He continues his trek until my stockings are exposed, running his hand underneath my chemise, his meaty fingers slipping to the inside of my thigh, bypassing the lace frill of my drawers until he meets my skin.

I'm thankful he either didn't feel the cool metal of my daggers or he's too drunk to notice, and bile crawls up my throat, nausea churning so sharply, I pray I vomit all over him, if only to get him away.

"Fucking heavy dresses," he mumbles, his arm pushing harder against my throat. He moves back to adjust, his hand centimeters away from brushing the soft curls between my legs, and I take the opportunity, my heart slamming against my chest as I reach next to his palm and remove one of the blades from my leather garter.

I snap it up to his throat, pressing the sharp edge against his jugular.

He drops my dress and stumbles back, tripping over himself, his eyes growing wide.

"Be careful who you corner in dark hallways," I hiss, liquid heat surging through my veins. "You never know which one of us has hidden claws."

Now it's me who moves into him, walking us backward

until he slams against the opposite wall, his hands flying up in surrender.

"Should I end your life here?" I ask, running my hand down the front of his person, disgust and rage mixing until I'm gagging from the taste. I bypass the waistline of his pants and grip his testicles in my palm, twisting through the fabric until he cries out. "After all," I continue, bringing my lips close to his ear. "You're practically *begging* for it."

I squeeze tighter, my wrist rotating so his skin stretches even more, and I can feel his Adam's apple bob beneath my knife, my hand jostling with the movement.

A thin cut appears when I push the edge of the blade in farther, blood trickling down the front of his esophagus and over his bow tie until it stains the crisp white of his shirt.

It would be so easy to slit his throat, and my body vibrates with the need. I grit my teeth, forcing the blade deeper, his labored breathing stinging my nostrils with its stench.

There's a loud clack of shoes echoing from down the hall, and I step back, hiding the blade behind my back, not wanting anyone to see that I have one or that I know how to use it.

Both of us stand, stunned and in silence, Claudius swaying in his spot.

Eventually, the footsteps disappear.

My body flies forward as I'm jostled from his stocky frame shoving by me, running down the hall until he too disappears from my view.

I consider chasing him for a few moments, but the adrenaline has already worn off, being replaced by a heavy sick feeling that weighs me down from the tips of my toes to the top of my head. Sinking against the stone wall, I raise my hand to my mouth, muffling the sob that breaks free. My eyes slam shut, trying to stem the tears, afraid to let them fall; not wanting to give that pathetic excuse of a man any more power than he's already had.

But a few escape anyway.

They're hot as they trail down my cheeks, and they feel a lot like failure.

*You're okay. You stopped him. You're strong.*

I stand back up on shaky legs, making my way into the washroom, my body jumping with every single creak of noise, my nerves nothing but frayed edges unraveling at the seam.

He didn't get far, yet somehow, I still feel like he stripped something of mine away.

My dagger trembles in my hand as I reach out and turn on the faucet, running the blade beneath the water to wash away the small drops of blood, hoping that maybe by doing so, it will also cleanse the scratches he's caused on my soul.

Because while he didn't take my innocence, he took something far worse.

My dignity.

And I'm not sure how to gain it back.

# CHAPTER 31

## *Tristan*

I FOLLOW THEM.

*Of course* I follow. How could I not?

But by the time I find them, it's already too late, and I'm greeted with the sight of Claudius's filthy hands ripping at her dress and his disgusting hips pressing into hers. My logic flies out the window, chest tightening until my lungs shrivel, charred from the blaze of fury racing through my insides.

I can't move.

I can't hear.

I can't speak.

I can only think one thing.

*Mine.*

The word shakes through me like an earthquake, cracking my foundation and all the defenses I've built up with it, creating a chasm so deep there's no way to dig myself out.

Lady Beatreaux—*Sara*—is mine.

I see our future laid out before us clear as day: me sitting on the throne and her at my side. Because why not? Why *shouldn't* she be at my side?

"Fucking dress."

Claudius's mumble snaps me out of my frozen state, and I move forward, my sole focus on reaching him and murdering him, bathing in his blood while I stake my claim on her body and soul.

My limbs tremble from the violence brimming inside me, its talons scratching beneath the surface of my skin until it cracks and bleeds.

*How dare he touch something that belongs to me.*

She shifts then, and the energy changes as she holds a blade to Claudius's throat, and my heart stutters, my cock growing stiff when passionate words pass her pretty little lips, threatening to kill a man where he stands.

I make it two steps before I freeze again, watching this *fierce*, incredible woman who can twist and turn into whatever she needs to survive, take care of the threat herself. A sudden shot of arousal mixes in with the anger, creating a sensation I've never felt.

It's not an unwelcome feeling. Not anymore.

With acceptance comes clarity.

My little doe is no doe at all.

She's a hunter, pretending that she's prey.

I lean against the wall, my hand coming to rest over my

heart, pressing firmly to keep it from bursting through my rib cage and exploding on the floor.

She's a fucking vision. The kind that should hang in galleries and be revered by the masses.

The perfect type of art.

*Mine.*

Footsteps sound from the distance and I move quickly to avoid being seen, not stopping until I'm standing at the end of the hallway, next to the portrait of my great-grandfather.

Eventually they fade, and then only thick silence surrounds me. I strain my ears but don't hear a peep. I wonder if she killed him. Disappointment settles in my chest, wishing I could have seen her do it, that I could have gone along for the ride.

But then another set of footsteps sounds, and a gift is given when I see Claudius's grimacing face as he runs down the hall toward me.

My hand snakes out before my mind can even process it's happened, my rings cutting into the skin of my fingers as I grip his neck, dragging him into me, his back slamming into my front.

He gurgles from my grasp, but my palm slaps his mouth, my hand pinching his windpipe, feeling the muscle crunch beneath my touch.

"Shh, don't be afraid," I murmur.

I move my palm away from his lips and reach up,

tilting my great-grandfather's portrait to the side, the wall disappearing from behind me. I sink into the entrance of the tunnels, pulling a squirming Claudius with me.

Once the wall slots back into place, I spin us around, tossing him to the ground, reveling in the sound of his skull cracking on the hard stone floor. Blood splatters from the impact, and he groans, rolling onto his back, his hands coming up to grasp at his head.

Anger percolates in the base of my stomach, and I try to tamp it down, closing my eyes and breathing deep. He moves to stand, his arm shaking as he pushes himself off the ground, and I step forward until I'm hovering over his torso, the thick base of my boot pressing into his chest and shoving him back down.

"Oh, Claudius," I tsk, bringing a joint from behind my ear and biting the end with my teeth while I dig in my pocket for a match. I fish one out of the box and strike it against the side, the sound loud in the cramped space. Crouching down as I inhale, I let the sweet tang of hash sit on my tongue. "What shall I do with you?"

He groans, his eyes hazy and unfocused.

I strike him against the face so hard my hand tingles. "No passing out. Stand up and come with me."

His brows draw in. "No."

Reaching out, I grip his arm and pull him to a stand, bending it at a ninety-degree angle. His knees buckle, but I hold him upright. "It wasn't a choice."

Adrenaline pumps through my veins, fueling my strength as I half carry him through the tunnels and into the dark forest until we reach my cabin in the woods.

There's no light on the path, but I've traversed it so many times I know it by heart, so the trip is quick. I kick open the door, leaving a dusty imprint from the bottom of my boot, and toss Claudius inside, his body slamming against the worn wood of the floor. I pull another joint from my pocket and light it, inhaling deep as I twist to face him, narrowing my gaze.

"You've always been a very naughty boy, Claudius, but I don't think I can let this one go."

I pluck the hash from my mouth and place it in the ashtray on the small oval table that sits to my right before walking over to him. He's pushing himself to a sitting position, blood dripping down the back of his head and onto his neck, the thin gash from where Sara cut into his throat already having scabbed over and dried.

"Your...your brother will...hear about this," he mumbles, his words slow and slurred.

I sigh, blowing out a breath until my cheeks puff. "You've always underestimated me."

He scoffs.

"It's fine." I wave my hand, walking toward the cupboards where I keep all the tools used for maintenance on the cabin. "I'm used to it. The *world* underestimates me, and it will be their downfall, as surely as it will be yours."

I grab what I need before twisting back around and taking slow and steady steps toward him. His head lolls to the side and his body sinks, falling from where he was leaning on his elbows and dropping back down to the floor.

"Oh no," I tsk, twirling the hammer around in my hand. "Don't tell me you're about to lose consciousness. We're just about to get to the fun part."

Smiling, I stop when I'm next to his head, bending and smacking him again, irritation squeezing my center at the fact that he thinks he can pass out and not experience every single iota of pain that I'm going to cause him.

His eyes snap open, and once again, he tries to jerk upright.

"I wouldn't do that if I were you." I walk around his body and crouch down to hover above his kneecaps, one leg on either side of his body. "Do you know why you're here with me, Claudius?"

"Because you're insane?" He lifts his head and spits at my feet. "I am the Baron of Sulta and your brother's friend. You cannot *do* this and get away with it," he forces out.

"Ooh." I grin. "I'm *shaking*."

"You're unhinged!" he screeches.

"So they say." My smile drops and I lift the hammer. "But I am also your prince, and I do as I please."

I bring the mallet down, his loud scream piercing through the air, drowning out the sound of his kneecap shattering.

"Yeah." I scrunch my nose, satisfaction collecting in the base of my spine and trickling outward. "I bet that hurt." Sighing, I allow the sharp edge on the back of the hammer to skim across the top of his intact bones. "You're *here* because you touched something that wasn't meant for you."

"You're insane."

Lifting the hammer, I use it to scratch the corner of my forehead. "Speaking of my mental health, I cannot *stand* leaving things uneven."

His head droops to the side.

"It drives me mad." I rest the blunt edge of the metal against his knee. "Makes me itch. Are you ever like that?"

His screams are even more delicious with the second blow, tears running down his face and mixing with his snot, every piece of the man he was draining away as he suffocates in his pain.

I throw the hammer to the side, leaning forward and running my fingertip along the gash in his throat, the one left behind by Sara, pride shooting through my chest like fireworks.

Standing up, I walk around his mangled legs until I'm by his head and grip him by the shoulders. His screams turn to whimpers as I drag him across the floor to the back of the cabin where two large pieces of wood are affixed to the wall.

A cross, with leather cuffs attached to the bottom piece and both of the sides.

Grunting as I hoist up Claudius's limp frame, I push him against the beams, leaning my body weight into his to hold him in place as I grab one of his arms and lock him in the leather restraint.

He sucks in a breath, blood trickling down his forehead. "Tristan," he whispers, hiccupping around his words. "Please."

I smile at his pleading, working on attaching his other wrist. "Do you not want to play anymore?"

"No," he whispers, his voice hoarse.

I squat down, wrenching his legs together, causing him to scream out again as I bind his ankles to the bottom of the cross.

Standing back up, I look him in the eyes, revulsion bleeding from my gaze. "I didn't want *you* to play with Lady Beatreaux either. Yet here we are, with you having done it."

"I don't—"

"Shh." I press my fingers against his mouth. "No more speaking, or I'll chop off your cock and make you choke on it." I step back, looking over my handiwork, ensuring that he's bound tightly. "I have to admit, I prefer fire." Moving across the small room to the cupboards, I rummage around the shelves until I find a carving knife, holding it in front of my face to inspect the sharp edge. "But the punishment *must* fit the crime."

"I've committed no crime," he rasps, his voice weak and pathetic.

"You've touched something that isn't yours to touch. In fact, I've recently concluded that she's *mine* to touch." Making my way back toward him, I skim the blade up his arm until I reach the forefinger of his left hand. "So the fact that you know what her skin feels like? Well, that's *unacceptable* to me."

I press the curved part of the knife into the tip of his finger and drag it down the underside, feeling his flesh peel away from his bone like the skin of an apple. He screams, his body thrashing against the tight leather bindings.

"Does it hurt already?" I ask, tilting my head. Once the thin sliver is to his palm, I tear it from his hand, dangling it in front of his face. "Rather ghastly looking, isn't it?"

Claudius's body shakes so hard, the wood of the cross trembles.

"One down, nine to go!" I drop my voice. "You know, this is *so* much fun. Reminds me of when we were kids… when you'd help my brother as he beat me black and blue."

Rage curdles my stomach and billows through my chest, and I drop the piece of skin, moving even closer to his arm.

"Please, God," he cries.

Chuckling, I grip his second finger. "*I'm* your god now. And I don't hear your pleas."

# CHAPTER 32

## *Sara*

MY EYES SCAN THE BALLROOM. OVER AND over, they flick from one corner to the next, waiting for the stumpy frame of Lord Claudius, but he's nowhere to be found. It doesn't ease my anxiety or calm the embers of anger glowing in my chest.

Regret is already settling in thick that I didn't kill him when I had the chance, fear whispering that maybe he's found someone else to prey on, someone who isn't hiding daggers on their thigh.

Michael sits next to me as we stare out at the dance floor, his mother and my uncle both having retired for the night. The shiny tile reflects people's smiling faces as they drink and dance the night away, and I can't help but feel like I'm watching a show. Hundreds of people who live in an alternate reality, so different from what I know to be the truth.

But isn't that the case with almost everything? We spin

tales and weave stories, creating a narrative that dictates how we're perceived. Or in some cases, how others live.

"Are you having a good time?" Michael asks, engaging me in conversation for the first time all night.

I grin. "It's lovely."

He stands, reaching out a hand. "Shall we dance?"

My brows rise, nausea teasing my esophagus, but I place my palm in his and let him lead me to the dance floor, hoping that nobody can see the slight tearing near the hem of my dress.

The ballroom clears, people moving to the outskirts to make room for us, and I feel sick.

I feel *sick* when his arm wraps around my waist, pulling me in close.

I feel *sick* when his hand grips mine.

And I feel *sick* when he smiles.

"You are quite the prize, Lady Beatreaux."

Bile climbs up my throat.

I'm *no one's* prize.

The musicians end the song, immediately starting up another, and I groan at the thought of having to continue this dance. My feet are aching, and my soul is sore.

"Your Majesty." Xander's voice breaks through the fog. "May I cut in?"

Michael nods, and it doesn't escape my notice that I never get a say. No one asks if *I'd* like to continue. They just pass me around like an object, here for everyone's viewing pleasure.

Xander steps in close, and I smile as he takes my hand, but he doesn't return the gesture.

The next song starts, and he jerks me across the room, my feet stumbling as I try to keep up with his steps. I wince when his palm tightens around mine, crushing my fingers together until my knuckles crunch.

"What do you think it is you're doing?" he hisses.

His tone catches me off guard, and I jerk back. "Excuse me? I have done nothing."

"Don't play innocent with me, Cousin," he sneers. "I *saw* you."

My heart deep dives to the ground. "I—"

"I won't have everything we've done—everything we've worked for—thrown in the trash because you can't keep your legs closed."

Shock rips through me, a knot of emotion expanding in my throat until it seems like it will burst. "I have done *everything* that you've asked. And yet you accuse me like this?"

"I *saw* you," he repeats. "With Lord Claudius."

"You saw nothing, clearly."

"If it had been someone else?" His brows rise to his peppery hairline. "If it had been the king?"

I clench my jaw, shaking my head, because while his accusation is wrong, everything he's saying still rings true. Michael wouldn't have cared how it was happening or whether I had a say. He'd only care how it looks.

My face burns, and I nod, trying to stem the rush of

tears begging to escape. "You're right," I choke out. "So let me finish the job now, and I'll die happily. What are you making me *wait* for?"

"Quiet," he snaps. "People can hear."

"You're the one speaking of it!" My voice grows louder, unable to temper the emotion pushing against the wounded walls of my chest.

"I believe you owe me a dance."

Xander stumbles to a stop at the sound of the silky voice, and my heart spins on its axis as I meet Tristan's gaze.

His eyes are tumultuous—*wild*—as he stares down at my cousin.

"You're dismissed, Alexander." There's no room for argument in his tone, and even if there was, Xander couldn't refuse. Not here, not in front of people.

As I glance around the room, it's no surprise that people have stopped to stare.

They always do when Tristan is near. I don't blame them. I can't *ever* force myself to look away.

Clearing his throat, Xander gives a thin smile and releases me, waving his arm and tilting his head in a pathetic attempt at a bow. "Of course, Your Highness."

The disrespect is clear.

But Tristan doesn't even flinch, instead moving toward me.

My heart sputters, the butterflies in my stomach taking flight. Normally, I'd despise them for showing up, but compared to all the other emotions I've been having tonight, they're a welcome distraction. His eyes meet mine as he swoops in, his arm wrapping around my waist and pulling me close. My breath whooshes from my lungs when our hands tangle, and my heart dives into my stomach, wanting to rip off my black satin gloves just to feel what it's like to have his fingers pressed to mine. He lifts our palms out to the side, and then we're waltzing.

He commands my body the same way he commands a room: effortlessly. I sink into his hold, allowing my mind to shut off for the first time all night.

For some reason, the way he's holding me, the way he's pulling me just a *little* too tight and a *little* too close, makes tears crop up behind my eyes.

He makes me feel safe. Important. And I haven't known that since my father.

If I dig a little deeper, it's easy to see that Tristan and I, we're cut from the same cloth, and that's part of the reason I can't stand the sight of him. Because looking at Tristan is like looking in a mirror and seeing the pieces of myself I try so hard to hide.

But he *doesn't* hide them, and I'm not quite sure how to handle that.

My jaw stiffens as my vision blurs, and I try harder to hold back the sadness, not wanting to show weakness in a roomful of people.

Tristan's face softens, his fingers tightening around

my waist before he pushes me outward, spinning my body around and drawing me back in, closer than we were before. Too close to be appropriate. My stomach flutters like it has wings, and wetness seeps between my thighs.

His lips brush my ear. "No, little doe, not here. They don't get your tears."

I nod against him, my nostrils flaring as I breathe in deep to stem the angst that's rolling around my insides like a wrecking ball.

I'm sure people are staring.

But I revel in his touch.

His fingers dig into me, like he never wants to let me go before he steps back, his hand slipping into his pocket as he bends at the waist and grips my fingers, bringing them up to his mouth.

Arousal pulses through my core when his lips touch my skin, my forehead scrunching when something crinkles between the pads of our fingers. I tighten my grip so whatever it is doesn't drop from my grasp.

"Thank you for the dance." And then he spins around and storms away, his black tailcoat whipping behind him.

My fist closes around the piece of paper, my heart beating wildly in my chest.

I smile at the few lingering eyes, and as casually as possible, I walk to the side of the room, nodding at people as I pass them by, anticipation winding tighter with every step I take.

It isn't until I make it to the far wall that I turn away and unfold the note with trembling fingers.

*Meet me where you kiss the stars.*

# CHAPTER 33

## *Tristan*

JEALOUSY IS QUITE THE EMOTION.

I would be a liar if I said I've never had it sear against my insides and singe wicked thoughts into my brain. The first time was when my father missed our evening talk, choosing instead to meet with Michael and go over a privy council meeting that was happening the next day. For hours, I sat at the edge of the cliff, trying to convince myself that he would show while knowing deep down he wouldn't.

But I worked through the envy years ago, knowing I was destined for greatness, that I would rise and take everything in the end. As for my father...well, things don't hurt as bad when you learn to numb yourself to the pain.

The scar on my face twinges, and my fingertips graze across the rough edges, trying to come to terms with the fact that once again, the bitter tang of jealousy is carving itself into my psyche, creating emotions I haven't felt since I was young.

Seeing Sara get manhandled by Claudius sent a rage unfurling within me, disgusted he thought he was worthy of speaking her name, let alone touching her skin.

But seeing her with my brother? The jealousy is a *sickness*, mutating every cell and infecting every organ, until it coats my insides and settles into the marrow of my bones. It makes me feel, once again, that I'm nothing but a lost little boy, stuck in the shadows and watching him hold everything I wish to have.

But Michael would rather kill her first than allow the embarrassment to his name of letting her go. So until I give the jackals their revolution and assume the throne, all I can hope for is stolen moments in the shadowy nights.

The grounds are darker than normal, thick clouds looming over the city and hiding the sky from view. I have no clue if the ball rages on, but now I don't care. Edward's already told me we've accomplished what we set out to do, and out here, in my mother's garden, no one is around.

Leaves crunch on the ground behind me, and I tilt my head back, blowing rings of smoke in the air.

"Technically, there *are* no stars out tonight for me to kiss."

I smile at Sara's voice. "Maybe they were waiting for you to arrive."

She scoffs, walking around the bench with her hands

on her hips. Gone is the woman in the lace ball gown, and in her place is a simple girl in a black dress with a skirt that stops above the ankle.

Earlier, she was beautiful, but it's in these moments that she takes my breath away.

Smirking, she walks up to me, her floral scent wafting into my nostrils as she bends down and takes the joint from my mouth, bringing it to her lips and inhaling, her gaze holding mine.

My fingers tense with the need to pull her into my lap.

"So…" She straightens, glancing around. "This is different."

I quirk a brow. "Is it?"

She sighs, pursing her lips as she stares down at me. "I've decided you're incapable of having an actual conversation. All you do is ask question after question."

My legs stretch out until they surround her, caging her in. "Do you think so?" I ask, my hands reaching for her hips.

Her eyes widen when I grab her, pulling her forward until her shins kiss the bench, my boots skimming the tops of her ankles.

"You've forgotten your place," she gasps.

"No." Lifting my hand, I pluck the hash back from her mouth, allowing the tips of my fingers to graze against the pout of her lips. "I've simply figured out yours."

Her breathing stutters.

"You asked me once to tell you a secret," I continue. "Do you still wish for one?"

She moves, sitting down next to me, her head tilting as she watches me with a curious gaze. "This feels like a trick."

Chuckling, I lean back against the bench.

A crack sounds from the forest, and her eyes fly to the sound before she whips her head around from side to side. "I should go," she says.

I wave my arm toward the door. "So go."

She doesn't move, although her eyes scan the perimeter.

"*Ma petite menteuse*, we both know the risk excites you." I slide closer to her on the bench. "Doesn't it?"

She blows out a breath. "Stop doing that."

"Doing what?"

"That," she snaps. "You're infuriating. I'm not sure why I even came here. I'd rather drink a gallon of bleach than listen to you answer everything with a question for the rest of the night."

My lips tip up in the corners. "So ask me one instead then, little doe."

"Stop calling me pet names," she gripes. "It's not appropriate."

I smirk, puffing on the end of my joint.

"Fine." She leans her upper body in close, and my stomach flips, my eyes dropping to the swell of her breasts and wondering what her nipples look like. How they feel.

If they're dying to be sucked the way I'm desperate to taste them.

Her hand moves from her lap, rising until she's dusting her fingertips along the edge of my face.

My nerves sizzle beneath her touch.

"How did you get your scar?"

The question snaps me out of the haze as quick as lightning, and I straighten, my mind getting lost in the memory.

*"What's that?" Michael's voice creeps along the back of my neck like a spider.*

*I stiffen in my spot next to the fireplace, my fingers tightening around my charcoal as I work on the finishing touches to my latest piece. It's of my father and I, his arm around my shoulders as we stand at the cliff's edge. Shifting, I hunch my shoulders, turning my body as I smudge the edges on one of the trees, trying to ignore my brother's presence.*

*The paper slices against my skin as the book is ripped from my hands. Anger pummels through my chest and I grit my teeth, nostrils flaring. "Give it back," I whisper.*

*He looks down at the drawing, his brows morphing into sharp angles as he narrows his gaze, and when he raises his eyes, there's a hatred swimming through them so potent it wraps around my neck like a noose.*

*"How cute," he mocks, his knuckles turning white where he's gripping the edge of the drawing.*

*My stomach churns. "Give it back, Michael."*

He cocks his head to the side. "Is this what it was like? Back when he used to pay you attention?"

"Michael," I start, standing up, my stomach tensing into knots. "I'm not kidding. Give. It. Back."

"What are you gonna do, little tiger?" He singsongs the nickname, elongating the vowels. "Father isn't here to save you. He's busy preparing for a luncheon, one that I will attend at his side."

My fists clench, his words slicing through me like a knife, nicking my bruised, abandoned heart.

"Why are you even still here?" he continues, stepping closer, a haughty look coasting across his face.

I stumble as I move away, the heat of the flames licking across my back as I press against the fireplace mantle.

"You're worthless. A waste of space, Tristan. The sooner you realize that and disappear, the better." He taps his chin. "Maybe you should run away. Go rut with jackals in the shadowed lands or die from starvation in the plains of Campestria." He shrugs. "See how much our father really loves you when you're wishing for him to hunt you down and bring you back home."

My chest aches, every insult hitting their mark. Because the truth is, my father hasn't spent time with me in months. Not since Michael turned fifteen and started showing an interest in his title.

"The only reason Father even talks to you is because you were born first," I hiss. "At least when he gave me attention, it was because he enjoyed my company."

Michael's face turns to stone, his voice dropping to a deadly whisper. "Tell yourself whatever you need, Brother. But I've heard him say he wishes you'd never been born."

My heart falters. "You lie."

"We all wish for it." He moves closer again. "You're a stain on our name, Tristan. That's why no one cares when you disappear for days. We all hope you'll stay gone, but for some reason, you don't get the hint, and you keep. Coming. Back."

I swallow around the thick knot in my throat, breaking eye contact as I try to shove down the gaping wound that's being torn through the center of my chest. "Give me back my drawings, Michael," I whisper, my voice breaking on his name.

"You know what?" He clicks his tongue. "Why don't you go...catch it."

He tosses the sketchbook into the fire.

"No!" I surge forward, reaching out, but the flames shoot higher, crackling as they eat the paper like fuel.

Something snaps inside me, and I spin, all my pent-up rage propelling my limbs as I charge at him. I'm three years younger and far less capable when it comes to physical strength, but I still knock him off his feet, both of us tumbling to the ground.

"I'm going to kill you," I seethe, my hands wrapping around his neck and squeezing. Black fury races through every piece of me. Envy from him getting my father's time mixes with the sorrow of him destroying the only other thing that matters. My sketches.

They're all I had to keep me company. My only friends.

*He overpowers me, throwing me across the room, my back smacking against the wood floor. Groaning, I roll over, squeezing my eyes shut at the sting in my spine. And then, a sharp pain slices up the side of my face, agony spearing through me, making a scream scratch my throat raw as it pours from my mouth.*

*Liquid gushes into my eye as I try to blink, my vision going red and dark, before gushing down my cheek and slipping through my lips, a metallic flavor settling on my tongue and making me retch.*

*My head grows dizzy, woozy from the pain, and I throw my hand over my face, my fingers becoming slippery as they're coated in blood.*

*The blurry form of Michael hovers over me, a fire poker gripped in his hand. "Now you don't even look like him," he sneers, spitting on my broken body. "See how much he loves you when you're nothing but a disfigured freak."*

*He walks away and I curl into a ball, consciousness weaving in and out while I wish for someone to come and find me. To hold me. Heal me. Love me.*

*The way they would if it were him.*

*But no one ever comes.*

"Tristan."

Sara's voice snaps me back to the present, and I force a smile, my chest aching from the memory.

She shakes her head, removing her hands from my face. "You don't have to tell me. I shouldn't have asked."

Snapping my arms out, I grip her palms in mine, bringing them back until they cup my jaw. "My brother was never a fan of the way I resembled our father. I suppose this was his way of settling the score."

Her eyes flicker down the length of the jagged mark. "Michael did this?"

"Michael has done many things, little doe. This is just one of them."

Something dark coasts across her face, her jaw tensing as her fingers grip tighter on my face. "I know."

I bring the joint to my lips one last time, the paper having burned to where it touches just above my fingers, and I inhale before tossing the end on the ground and stomping it out with my boot.

My hand slides behind her, grasping the nape of her neck and dragging her into me until mere centimeters separate us, energy weaving between our bodies and spinning electricity through my chest, making my heart beat a staccato rhythm and nerves dance beneath my skin. I tilt my head, my thumb pressing into the bottom of her chin, forcing her perfect, pouty lips to part and ghost across the edges of mine.

The tension of being so close yet so far almost kills me, and I swear to God I would give it all up, *right now*, if she would promise to be mine.

I exhale, the smoke billowing from my mouth into hers.

My cock is *painfully* hard.

Her eyes widen in surprise, and my fingers tighten on the back of her neck, holding her in place, my other hand moving to her throat, two fingers stroking down the front as she swallows, the smoke that was inside *my* body escaping from *her* lips.

"I'm going to kiss you now," I tell her.

"Why?" she whispers.

"Because, *ma petite menteuse*, the thought of *not* kissing you makes me want to die."

Our lips collide, and with just one touch—one single moment—I know I'll never let her go.

# CHAPTER 34

## *Sara*

AS USUAL WHEN I'M WITH TRISTAN, EVERY-thing around me mutes, dulls like it wasn't there to begin with. I don't worry about the ball that's likely still going strong at the other end of the castle. I don't think of how we're in the open, and while I've been assured no one comes to this garden, technically, we could be found at any time. And I definitely don't focus on how I'm somehow supposed to kill this man.

His kiss overwhelms every single one of my senses, and I sink into it, drowning in his essence, hoping the burn of his touch can blaze away the imprint of the ones before.

He groans, his palm tightening on the back of my neck, his other hand sliding down my side. His touch soaks through the thin material of my slip dress and the chemise underneath, sending goose bumps sprouting along my arms. He reaches the outer part of my thigh, bunching the fabric in his fingers as his lips break away, skimming down the expanse of my throat.

I tilt my head, allowing him easier access, even though somewhere in the deep recesses of my mind, I know I shouldn't.

But I like the way his lips feel pressed against my skin.

"We shouldn't be doing this here," I force out.

"I disagree." His teeth nip my collarbone, his fingers slipping beneath the shoulder strap of my garment, tingles sprinkling through my middle and pooling between my legs.

"Someone could—"

He bites my shoulder this time.

"S-someone could see," I stutter.

"I'll kill anyone who does."

The words he just said so casually should give me pause, but they don't. They excite me more.

It's intoxicating to have a man willing to do *anything* just so he can keep touching you.

Still, the risks outweigh any momentary reward, so I push against his chest and scoot away, reaching up to smooth the flyaways of my hair. "And your brother will kill *me* if he finds out."

Tristan exhales a deep breath, his jaw grinding. He hops up from the bench, grabbing my hand and pulling me behind him before I can even process the fact that we're moving.

"Wait," I say as he drags us toward the forest. "Tristan,

*wait!* What are you doing?" I try to rip my fingers from his grip, but he just smirks back at me and picks up the pace.

I should put a stop to whatever this is. There's no way it will end well.

But I let him lead me anyway.

He doesn't stop until we're in the middle of thick trees, the leaves covering us in darkness that even the moon can't shine through. "Where are we going, Tristan? You cannot just traipse into the forest and manhandle me however you...*oh*—"

He jerks me forward, my body twirling around him and slamming into the thick trunk of a tree. The bark scratches my upper back, creating a sharp sting that radiates down my spine, and the sleeve of my dress falls off my shoulder, revealing the white lace of my chemise underneath.

He presses into me, the hard planes of his body molding to my soft curves, his arms coming to rest on either side of my head until I'm blocked in, surrounded by temptation and bad decisions.

"Do you *ever* stop talking?" he quips.

Irritation winds through my middle and I open my mouth to reply, but before I can, he sweeps in, claiming my lips in a bruising kiss. My hands fly to the back of his head as I pull him closer, inhaling the hint of smoke on his breath and trying to implant the taste on my tongue. He groans, his hips pushing harder against me, the thick length of his cock gliding along my belly.

His teeth sink into my lip, piercing my flesh. A moan pours from my throat, and he swallows the sound, licking along the wound and sucking, his tongue swiping over the bubbling liquid.

I jerk back. "Did you just *lick* my blood?"

One of his hands grips my waist and drags me until we're plastered together, his other palm grabbing the back of my head, fingers digging into my bun and pulling the strands until my neck bends.

"I will lick and suck and cut any part of you I wish, as *often* as I wish, until you're begging me to slice you open and do it some more."

My stomach flips at his words, shock mixing in with the sharp rush of desire that splices down my middle.

"I want to consume you, Sara, until I feel you thrumming in my veins."

"That's *sick*," I say. "I thought you hated me."

He pauses at this, his hand releasing my hair and moving to cup my jaw, his thumb wiping the remnants of blood from my mouth. "What is hate but obsession tinged with fear?"

"I—"

His palm slaps over my mouth, the rings on his fingers cold against my flesh. "Stop. Talking."

He grips the skirt of my dress and moves it slowly up my leg, the fabric tickling my skin. My abdomen tightens, a warm sensation spinning like a cyclone in my stomach.

My leather garter is exposed, and his fingertips trace over the daggers, his stiff cock pulsing against my torso as he traces along their sharp edges.

"*Ma petite menteuse*, pretending to be so pure." He drops to his knees, leaning in and kissing the spaces between my blades. "So innocent."

My chest heaves as my heart slams against my ribs. He works his way inward, his lips peppering kisses across my flesh until he reaches the lace edge of my drawers. Quick as a flash, he's removed one of the blades, twirling it in his fingers. My stomach jumps, wondering if I've made a mistake. *How stupid a woman must I be for giving my enemy a blade and trusting he won't slit my throat?*

Still, I don't move from my spot.

If this is where death finds me, at least it will be my choice.

With one of his hands holding up my dress, the other drags the dagger up my thigh, creating pinpricks of sensation as a shallow red line appears. He hasn't cut the skin, but he's dangerously close, and the anticipation has my senses heightening, wetness seeping from my center. He slips the tip of the blade beneath the lace and glances up at me, his green eyes blazing with heat so fierce I swear I can taste it in my soul.

"Do you trust me, little doe?" he asks.

My heart stalls. "No."

He smirks. "Good."

And then he flicks the knife, splicing open the fabric until cool air whips across my bare skin, making me gasp from the sudden chill. But I needn't worry, because soon enough, his mouth is on me, his nose pressing into my soft curls and his tongue lavishing attention on my sensitive bud, making it pulse and swell with every swipe.

I moan, my body collapsing into the tree, fingers tangling in his disheveled locks as I push my hips against his face, letting him suck my cunt like he's a desperate man.

"I—" I pant out, the sensations almost too much to bear.

He alternates between licking me in long strokes and pulling me into his mouth, his cheeks hollowing as he does.

"I can't..." My fingers tug at his head, torn between trying to wrench him away or smothering him whole, the pressure coiling inside me too much, too fast. When everything squeezes until I black out from the pleasure, I force him away, ripping his hair at the root as I pull him off my throbbing pussy.

I heave deep and unsteady breaths, my mind whirling and my muscles tight, begging for release. He drops the dagger on the ground and slides up my body, his eyes dark and his mouth glistening. I can smell my arousal and it makes my nerves pulse. I want to lean in and lick away the wetness from his lips, just to see how I taste when I'm fresh off his tongue.

His hands grip my wrists and move them above my head, the trunk of the tree chapping my overheated skin as he locks them in one of his palms.

"Do *not* keep me from you," he demands.

His other hand glides back up the inside of my thigh, finding my core drenched and needy, and he slides two fingers in to the hilt, curling them forward to rub against my inner walls.

"Oh, God," I cry, my legs buckling as pleasure cascades through me in fierce waves.

"Such a filthy little liar, pretending you don't want to come for me," he whispers in my ear, his hold tightening.

I arch my back, heat collecting deep in my core and spreading outward until I can't see straight.

"So *naive*, assuming I would stop if you told me no." His thumb presses against my swollen clitoris before releasing it, causing my pussy to clench around his thick fingers, my insides winding so tight it steals my breath.

"Please," I beg, growing delirious from his teasing.

"Please what, little doe?"

"Make me come. I need to come."

"Do you deserve it?" he asks.

"I will *kill* you," I snap, frustration overflowing like a bubbling pot.

He chuckles, drifting his fingers in and out, a torturous pace that's keeping me riding the edge, so close to exploding yet never enough to make me burst.

"Tell me you're mine, *ma petite menteuse*. That no other man has had you."

The anger explodes like a gunshot inside me, irritated he thinks he can control me the way he is. Annoyed that it seems to be *working*. Snapping my eyes open, I meet his stare. "But then I'd be a liar."

His entire frame stiffens, his movements freezing. "Who?"

"None of your business."

"Tell me his name," he croons. "So I can hunt him down and cut him to pieces."

I arch my back until my chest grazes against his torso. "No."

He grins, letting out a controlled breath as he releases me so fast I drop to the ground. "Then you don't deserve to come."

"You're *disturbed*, Tristan!" I yell after him. But he's already walking away, leaving me a panting, infuriated mess.

# CHAPTER 35

## *Sara*

"I DO NOT CARE FOR THIS. LET ME SPEAK TO my brother!"

Michael's voice is high-pitched and strained, so loud that I shrink back against the wall. My uncle stands on the other side of his desk, his body rigid as he leans on his dark wood cane. He glances to me, his icy eyes dark and raging as if this is somehow *my* fault.

I'm not even sure what's going on. I woke up to Ophelia throwing open my door, saying the king demanded to see me. I barely had time to let her dress me, and as a result, I'm nowhere near being presentable. My hair is still in its natural curly, frizzy state, brushing against the middle of my back, and I only had time to grab a simple day dress— sans the corset. I feel naked and like I've walked into a room with a loaded gun.

"What's happened?" I ask.

My uncle turns to glare at me. Again, I'm taken aback by his obvious anger. I've seen it several times, especially when he's passionately speaking about vengeance for my father, but this is the first it's ever been directed at me.

My stomach drops to the floor, my face heating as if a thousand suns have exploded inside it.

*Did they find out about last night?*

Impossible. I'd be thrown in the dungeons, not standing here without shackles and chains.

"What's *happened*," my uncle starts, "is that your cousin—*my son*—has been kidnapped."

My lungs collapse. "What?"

"Stop, stop, stop!" Michael screeches, his hands coming up to tug on his hair. My eyes widen as I stare at him, noticing the pallid skin and deep bluish-purple bags welting under his eyes.

He looks ill.

"They know," he mutters to himself. "He must be telling them."

I step forward, my insides churning with his ramblings. I'm not sure what has him so out of sorts, but something tells me to tread carefully. "Your Majesty, *who* knows?"

His eyes snap to mine and he shoves forward a square wooden box with dusted black metal hinges and an image carved into the wood on top. As I move closer, I realize it's a jackal standing on a dead lion—its teeth bared and its black eyes reflecting flames.

The detail is immaculate, and before I can think twice, my fingers are smoothing over the indents, mesmerized by the intricate design.

"Open it," Michael whispers.

I do, and my stomach revolts at the sight, nausea whipping through my middle and up into my throat. It's a hand, severed at the wrist with dried blood caked on every inch of skin until it looks as though it's been gnawed on. And right beside it is a pair of horn-rimmed glasses.

"Is that...?" I ask, my eyes flicking from Michael to my uncle.

Uncle Raf nods, his nostrils flaring as he slams the base of his cane on the floor.

"There's a note," Michael whispers, his voice cracking.

He slides a piece of paper to me, but before I can see what it says, the door swings open and Tristan waltzes inside as if he owns the room and everyone in it. His piercing jade eyes land on me, his gaze flicking up and down my frame, flaring as they coast over my unpinned hair.

"Tristan, *finally*." Michael blows out a breath.

"You rang, Brother?" Tristan smiles, walking farther into the room. "You look dreadful. Bad sleep?"

"This is no time to be joking," Uncle Raf cuts in. "I demand we call a meeting with the privy council."

Confusion drops through me like a falling piece of paper. My uncle hates the privy council and everything they stand for. They're partly why my father had to beg for aid in the first place, filled with selfish men who forgot about our country and became about greed.

"Uncle, honestly, what do you think the privy council could do?"

Again, he slams his cane on the ground. "Silence, girl. We don't have time for stupid questions."

His words smack across my face as surely as if it were his hand.

Tristan's head snaps to him, his gaze narrowing.

Michael's fist beats down on his desk, the strands of his usually slicked-back hair falling on his forehead. "You do not make demands of *me*, Rafael. I am the king, and you are no one."

"With all due respect, you are only as strong as your weakest link, Your Majesty, and clearly there are a lot of weak links if my son is so easily taken." Uncle Raf steps closer, jabbing his finger in the air. "Your father would have *never* allowed this to happen."

Silence. Tense, heavy silence.

"Not to interrupt this fascinating show," Tristan drawls, "but why am I here?"

"Yes," Michael snaps, turning to Uncle Raf. "Leave. Before I take out a pistol and shoot you where you stand."

"Your Highness, I—"

"I said leave!" His voice booms off the furniture and echoes around the walls so loud it vibrates my eardrums.

My eyes fly back and forth between them, my stomach tangling in knots.

Uncle Raf bows at the waist before standing upright and making his way toward me. He grips my arm, jostling me along with him as he pulls us to the door. I flinch at his tight hold but allow him to drag me forward, not wanting to start a scene in front of the people we're trying to rise against.

It's important to look united in front of others.

Just as we reach the door, the pressure leaves my arm, relief flowing through the muscles as the ache disappears. I twist around, my heart faltering when I take in the way Tristan has my uncle's hand in his grasp, bent at an awkward angle.

"Tristan!" I gasp, reaching out to separate them.

"Do you always handle women in such a way?" Tristan asks, ignoring my efforts.

My uncle grits his teeth. "She is my niece and my responsibility, Your Highness."

"Then I suggest you take better care of your family." He dips his head, eyes staring into mine as he whispers in my uncle's ear. "Do not put your hands on her again."

My chest pulls, wanting to calm the situation down. The last thing I need is my uncle becoming suspicious of why the prince cares. But beneath all that, there's another feeling blooming like a spring flower, casting a warm glow from the middle of my chest.

It's nice to be protected. To realize that someone has your back. Even if that someone is the very person who shouldn't.

Tristan releases him then, barely sparing me another glance before making his way back over to his panicked brother.

My uncle's eyes narrow as he shakes out his hand, aggressively waving toward the door. "Well…"

I blow out a shaky breath, nodding as I walk through. We're greeted by at least five royal guards, and my brows draw in as we pass them, wondering why there are so many of them suddenly guarding the king's private office.

Timothy steps out from the line and trails behind us. Silent as a mouse.

"Uncle, I know it's difficult," I start, keeping my voice low, "but try to keep the faith."

His lips purse, and even though words aren't said, the energy between us seems off.

The tension continues all the way back to my quarters, and when we reach the doors, I spin around, expecting Uncle Raf to take his leave. Instead, he pushes open the door and storms inside, whirling on me the second we're alone.

"It's the rebels."

My brows rise. "Do you think?"

He scoffs, walking past the foyer and into the sitting room, collapsing down on one of the two dark-green couches. "You saw the emblem? A *jackal*. They're mocking us. And now they've killed my son. My chance."

I tilt my head. "What do you mean, *your* chance?"

His back straightens, fingers tapping the top of his cane like they do every time he's in deep thought.

"Uncle," I sigh, tucking a curl behind my ear and walking over to sit down next to him. I reach out, grasping his hand in mine, trying to provide support. "Not that it helps, but I don't think Xander is dead."

"No?" he asks, glancing at me from the corner of his eyes.

"Well." I chew on my lip, thinking through everything I saw this morning and everything I *didn't*. "They left a note, right?"

"They sent his severed hand, Sara."

"But it wasn't his head." I grimace, knowing that what I'm saying isn't coming out right. "I'm just saying, what if they're using him as bait? Or to send a message? They'd want him alive for that."

At this, my uncle twists to face me, his features drawn and filled with obvious sorrow.

"And if he's alive," I continue, hope flaring in my chest, "we can save him."

His hand tightens around mine, but he shakes his head. "It's too dangerous."

I scoff, my insides flipping from him dismissing me. "Everything we're trying to accomplish is dangerous."

"Nobody goes to the shadowed lands," he snaps. "Your father did and look what happened to him."

His eyes widen after he says the words, but it's too late. I've already heard.

Everything inside me freezes, and I snatch my palm back, my breath pushed from my lungs as they fold in on themselves. Confusion blankets my mind, and I try to wrap my head around what he just said.

"What?" I ask.

He grabs my hands, squeezing my fingers. "Listen, Sara, if you think you can get there—to the shadowed lands…"

My stomach jolts, anxiety slithering through my muscles until it squeezes tight. "What? I—"

"You're right," he presses. "We can *save* Alexander."

I shake my head, brows pulling in until my forehead creases. "Wait. Tell me what you meant about my father."

He lifts a shoulder. "I meant…look what happened to him. He was murdered."

My teeth grind, sharp pain radiating up my jaw. "Don't treat me like I'm inept. If there's something you're not telling me, then *tell* me." My stomach rolls like waves of the ocean in a looming storm. "I deserve to know."

He swallows, dropping my hands and bringing his up to run through his hair. "It wasn't the king who killed your father."

Disbelief slams into me, ripping through my skin like he shoved the words straight into my chest. "I don't understand."

"It was the rebels. They captured him on his journey

home and tried to use him as a bartering tool, the same way they are with your cousin. Only last time…"

His voice shakes as it trails off, and my body freezes, shock spreading through every limb until it grows numb from the icy chill. "But you said… You *told* me—you *lied* to me? All this time?"

"Your father was a duke, sweet niece, gifted the title by King Michael II himself. The rebels saw an opportunity, wrongly assuming the new king would find him too important to lose."

I shoot to my feet, betrayal slicing through my insides like a heated blade, grief for my father and the realization that everything I've been told is a lie pouring through my middle like lava. "So what was the point of all this?"

"The point?" He glances up at me, his eyes glossy. "The point is the same as it always has been. They captured your father. Tortured him. And the crown did nothing but stand by and watch. They're just as responsible. Don't let this distract you from what we came here to do."

"No." I shake my head, the omissions of my family sitting heavy on my tongue until my mouth tastes sour. "No, you don't get to do that. You don't get to stand there and tell me how to feel or how to act. Not when you've been lying to me." A burn scorches up my throat and settles between my eyes, tears threatening to blur my vision. "You *lied* to me!"

*Not here, ma petite menteuse. They don't get your tears.*

Tristan's voice rings through my head as if he's standing behind me and coaching me through the pain—through the absolute devastation of everything I thought I knew being demolished from the inside out. I stiffen my jaw, forcing the emotion back down.

"I was trying to save you!" my uncle shouts. His hand turns white as he presses down on his cane to help him stand. "Your father trained you very well, Sara, but going to the shadowed lands is too dangerous." He walks closer, his eyes trying to capture mine, but I glance away, unable to even look him in the face. "I'm sorry," he whispers. "I'm so sorry we kept this from you. I've tried to do right by you my entire life, and when he died—" His voice cracks. "I was terrified to lose you too."

"Yet you'll send me here for no reason."

"No." His hand cups my jaw, tilting up my head. "The Faasas are still guilty. They still deserve to rot. But the rebels are uncivilized, their leader a ghost. It's a different game to play. I couldn't bear for something to happen to you too."

My teeth grit together, a new fire burning in the pit of my stomach, one that blazes brighter with every word he speaks, snuffing out everything in its path.

"I welcome death, as long as I take the ones responsible down with me," I hiss through my clenched jaw.

Uncle Raf blows out a shaky breath, nodding his head. "Then you'll need to kill the rebel king."

# CHAPTER 36

## *Tristan*

*THE GUILTY MUST PAY FOR THEIR SINS.*

I stare at the scrawled note—the one that was written by me—before placing it down on Michael's desk and looking up at him.

"And what have you done to be guilty of, Brother?" I ask. "What has Xander done?"

Michael's eyes shift from left to right. "Nothing, of course."

My boot presses on the wood floor, causing it to creak, and his body jumps. Amusement rains down my insides and I remind myself to smother the grin wanting to spread across my face.

"Do you ever think about our father?" he asks, his fingers white-knuckling the back of his chair.

The question makes my stomach twist, like it does any time I think of our father.

"Did Mother put you up to this line of questioning?" I glance around, half expecting her to be in the room. Truthfully, I'm not sure if she's even still in the *castle*, but I can't be bothered enough to care either way.

He shakes his head.

I place a joint in my mouth and walk to the sitting area, bending over the coffee table to light the end on a candelabra, puffing a few times as I make my way back toward Michael and offer it to him.

He stares at the burning paper as though he doesn't trust it not to be poisoned.

"If I were to kill you, Brother, I would make sure you knew it was coming." I nod at him. "Take it. It will ease your conscience. At least for a while."

He swallows, reaching out and gripping it between his fingers, bringing it to his lips and scrunching his face as the smoke cascades like a waterfall from his nose.

"Do you believe in God?" he mutters, staring down at the hash.

I place my hands in my pockets, tilting my head. "I do."

"You hardly attend mass." He peers at me from under his brows.

"There's a difference in beliefs and blind worship, Michael. One builds a sense of self, and the other strips it away." I move back to the sitting area, settling into the chaise longue and leaning back. As I gaze at the ceiling, anticipation flies around my stomach like buzzing bees, opportunity staring me in the face. "However, if you're speaking of life after death, I think there must be. How else could I see our father's ghost?"

I snap upright to a sitting position, slapping my hand over my mouth.

Michael's eyes widen and he stomps around his desk, the joint burning in his fingers as he fumbles his way across the room, plopping in a chair across from me. "Say that again."

Shaking my head, I scoot back, running a hand through my hair. "No, I…I don't know why I said that. Ignore me."

"Tristan." He leans in. "Do you see our father?"

I rest my elbows on my knees, drawing down my brows and making my breathing stutter. "I think I might be going crazy."

Michael laughs; a light, tinkling sound. One that bleeds with relief.

*Imbecile.*

"It's when I'm sleeping mostly," I lie, raising my head to stare into Michael's eyes. "He warns me of things to come. At first, I…I thought they were just dreams. But lately…"

Michael nods, his eyes wild, their amber sheen hazy and unfocused. "Lately?"

"Lately, the things he says…they've been coming true." I scoff, pushing myself to a stand. "You must think I'm mad. Forget I said anything. *Please.*"

I rush toward the door, but before I can even make it halfway across the room, I'm stopped by the sound of his voice.

"I see him too."

This time, a smile does creep along my face.

---

I find Sara in the servants' kitchen, sitting at the small wood table, her head thrown back in laughter. My heart clenches at the sight.

Simon, Paul, Timothy, and one of the ladies-in-waiting surround her, beaming as if she's the center of their world. My muscles tighten, a sick feeling swimming in my gut at the thought of other people getting to enjoy her, of them getting the pieces she only ever shows me.

"Tristan!" Simon squeals, jumping up from his stool and racing over, grabbing on to my legs in a tight hug.

"Hello, little tiger." My eyes scan across the table. "What do we have here?"

"Just enjoying some tea, Your Highness," Sara says. "Care to join us?"

Paul scrambles to a stand, rushing to the kettle sitting on top of one of the stove's burners. "Yes, yes, let me get you something."

"I'm not thirsty."

He pauses, dropping his arms to the sides. "Oh."

I walk over, Simon hot on my heels, and take up the

spot that Paul just vacated, my gaze never leaving my little doe's. "How's your uncle's hand?"

Her shoulders stiffen. "Just fine, thank you. How's His Majesty?"

"Depends on who you ask." I tilt my head.

"Did you know lady could fight?" Simon says to me as he plops down at my side.

My blood heats as I trail my gaze along her body. "Can she?"

"Good to see your annoying habit of answering questions with questions extends beyond just me," she cuts in, grinning.

Smirking, I turn my attention to Simon. "Let me guess, she taught you to be valiant and brave? Honorable and strong?"

Simon scrunches up his nose. "No, she said to drink water."

"I said to *be* water." She laughs.

She picks up her tea, bringing it to her lips. My eyes zone in on her throat as she swallows the liquid, my cock springing to life when I notice the tiny cut on her bottom lip.

The memory of her flavor teases my taste buds, and I find it almost impossible to look away from the mark, aching to split it open again, just to hear her moan as I soothe her pain with my tongue.

"Being honorable only works when both sides play by

the rules." She glances to Simon, leaning across the table. "Enemies *never* stick to the rules."

Simon nods, gazing at her with adoration, a look that, until this moment, I thought was reserved only for me.

I don't blame him for falling under her spell when even I can't outrun it.

"That's right." I nod. "The trick is, little tiger, to be *smarter*, not stronger."

"Oh?" Sara answers instead, her lips lifting in the corner. "Is that the trick?"

My fingers tap on the table, the tip of my thumb rubbing the underside of my father's ring. "One of many I could show you."

Her eyes flare, lips parting.

"Milady," the young girl at her side interrupts. "Don't forget, we have an outing in less than an hour. Should we head back to get dressed?"

Sara's cheeks flush as she breaks our stare, smiling over at her. "I'm ready whenever you are, Ophelia." She turns toward Timothy. "Are you ready?"

"An outing?" Simon asks. "Can I come?"

Paul walks back from the stove, placing a plate in front of Simon, his gaze briefly locking on Timothy's before turning away. "Simon, your mama will whoop you black and blue. You know you can't go into town."

His face drops. "I'm never allowed to go anywhere."

"Never?" Sara grins down at him, cupping her hands

over her mouth and whispering loudly. "One day, I'll take you."

Paul and I share a look, but we say nothing.

The royal bastard of Gloria Terra is the castle's best-kept secret.

I don't tell her the reason he doesn't go anywhere is because no one can know he exists. That whether we want to admit it or not, if word got out about a brown boy with the same striking eyes as the king, chaos would follow.

Or how, if my brother simply acknowledged him, Simon would be the rightful heir to the throne.

# CHAPTER 37

## *Sara*

THIS HAS BEEN MY FIRST OFFICIAL EVENT—besides the ball—as the king's betrothed, and I've been instructed that there's certain decorum I'm expected to maintain.

Do not stop and talk to people.

Do not leave the guards.

Do nothing other than smile and wave, cut the ribbon for the grand opening of the new medical center, allow photos to be taken, and then straight back to the castle.

And I do all that. I follow the rules spectacularly. It isn't until later, Timothy and all three of my ladies surrounding me, that my good intentions turn to dust. Because there's a boy standing at the edge of the street, in torn and dirt-ridden clothes, his hair buzzed close to his head as he stares directly at me.

There's something off about his face, although from

this distance, it's difficult to see. But either way, his gaze slams into the center of my gut, and I'm turning before I can help myself.

"Timothy," I say, keeping my eyes on the child. "Do you see that boy?"

He moves to stand next to me, looking to where I point and nodding.

"Bring him here."

"No," Marisol cuts in. "In and out, milady."

My insides spit fire like a dragon, and I pull my shoulders back, walking over to her until we're nose to nose. "You are not my master. And you do *not* get to tell me what I may or may not do. I've been very nice to you up to this point, Marisol. Don't make me show you how cruel I can be."

"Milady." Ophelia steps next to us. "What Marisol means is we need to tread carefully. That boy...he...well, he doesn't look like one of us."

Sheina snaps her head to Ophelia at the same time as I do. "And what does he look like, Ophelia?" I hiss.

Her cheeks blossom a deep red, and she turns her face toward the ground until the brim of her hat hides her eyes from my view.

"He's deformed," one of the guards spits. "It's easy to see from here. Most of them are—if not physically then mentally."

I close my eyes to calm the raging storm brewing in my gut. "Most of *who* are?"

He waves his arm toward the child. "The jackals, of course. Rebels. Whatever you want to call them."

"He's most likely a trap, milady," Marisol adds, her eyes squinting as she stares at the boy.

"I'd like to speak with him."

Nobody moves, and the longer they stand stagnant, the heavier the disappointment gets, like bricks being dropped in the center of my chest.

My heart twists. *How can they be so callous?*

"Fine." I force a smile, my eyes meeting Sheina's. A small grin breaks across her face, her gaze sparkling with mischief. It reminds me of when we were girls, figuring out ways to break the rules so we could sneak out past our bedtime. She moves until she's standing between Timothy and me, allowing easier access for me to escape down the road.

I spin, racing down the street, the material of my shoes rubbing the sides of my feet raw.

"Milady!"

"Sara!"

Glancing behind me as I run, I laugh at Sheina trying to block their paths. She won't be successful for long, seconds at most, but it fuels me, allowing me to ignore the burn of my legs or the way my lungs ache for deeper breaths of air.

Finally, I reach him. He hasn't moved this entire time, and as I kneel, my knees dusting along the dirt road, I admit to myself that maybe this wasn't the smartest choice. He looks to be in need, but it's odd for him to stand and stare the way he is, especially with the spectacle I just put on.

"Hi," I say, staring up at him.

This close, I can confirm the guard was correct. He has a cleft lip, the center of his mouth missing. His dark eyes are big and round, and bones protrude from his skin.

The injustice of it all makes me want to scream. It isn't fair that he stands here on a road lined with thriving businesses and groundbreaking technology, yet this is how he lives. And everyone ignores him, cringing away when they see him, assuming that because he's different, he's somehow less than.

Anger bubbles like a cauldron deep in my chest, reigniting the fire that burned while I was in Silva, when my father and I used to sneak rations of food and any money we could find to the people. How I used to sneak money even after his death, stealing it from my uncle's safe and slipping it into Daria's hands.

"What's your name?" I try again.

The boy's gaze shifts behind me. "A royal guard," he whispers.

A grin pulls at his face, stretching from ear to ear, and it makes every single hair stand on end, a shiver racing through me.

And then he runs.

"Wait!" I yell, standing up.

"Sara!" Timothy's voice is loud, and the sound of it is

so jarring—so different from what I'm used to—that I stop in place, my palm shooting to my chest as I spin around to meet his stare.

"I'm fine, Timothy. Everything is—" A blast sounds, and my ears ring with a high-pitched noise, dulling everything around me. I curl in on myself, bending over as my hands fly to cover my ears.

I glance up. Timothy's eyes are wide, his mouth dropped open as he stares at me, less than two feet away, his hand cupping his chest.

All three of my ladies stand shell-shocked behind him, many people running outside to line the streets.

Timothy falls to his knees.

"No!" I cry out, my chest seizing as I rush forward, feet stumbling as tears burst from my eyes and streak down my face. "No," I plead again, dropping to the ground in front of him.

His eyes are frantic as they watch me break apart, my heart shattering, the sharp edges splicing through my middle until my insides spill onto the ground.

My hands fly to his chest, my jaw tensing as I push down with my body, applying as much pressure as possible, digging my fingertips into the wound to try and plug the bleeding.

But it's too much.

It's too fast.

His palm wraps around my wrist loosely, and it's

enough to give me hope. Random curls fall from my updo, sticking to the wet trail of tears that stain my cheeks, and I whip my head around, looking at the dozens of people who stand by—their hands covering their mouths in horror—and do nothing.

*Dozens.*

"Do something!" I scream, all of them gawking as if they don't have feet and hands to help. "Don't just stand there!" My voice breaks, my breathing coming in small pants until I feel as though I'll suffocate from the lack of air. "Hold on, Timothy." I focus on him, but his gaze is growing milky and I can feel his presence slipping away. "You are *not* allowed to die," I demand, my teeth gritting. "Do you hear me? We're supposed to become best friends."

The corner of his mouth twitches, his blinks growing further apart.

"Long talks by the fire, you know?" I hiccup, trying to ignore the way my fingers are slipping from all the blood. "Your favorite thing to do."

His hand falls from my wrist, splashing as it lands on the puddle growing beneath him.

"Please," I murmur, my mind screaming and my chest caving in. "I'm sorry. I'm so sorry."

But it's too late, and no one hears my pleas.

I feel the moment his soul leaves his body. A giant exhale, and then he's just gone.

Sobs rack through me until my entire body shakes,

and I collapse on top of him, my arms stained red and my fingers drenched. I drop my head in my hands anyway.

"I tried to tell you," Marisol whispers, wiping a tear from her cheek. "It was *you* they were after."

My stomach rolls, an icy chill skating through me until my entire body feels numb. I snap my face up and meet her gaze. "Then I will make sure they pay."

# CHAPTER 38

## *Sara*

THE SILK SHEETS ARE SOFT AGAINST MY SKIN, the blanket heavy as it warms my body, but I'm numb to the comfort.

I am *sick*.

Timothy's blood has long since been washed away, yet somehow, I feel as though I'll never be clean again. The sins of my decisions have always been heavy, but tonight, they're crushing me beneath their weight.

*If only I had listened.*

If only I hadn't been so stuck in my ways. Then maybe Timothy would still be here.

He'd be living. Breathing. *Existing.*

My eyes are puffy and swollen, the corners of my lids tender, but my tears dried long ago, drummed out by the pulsing beat of anger.

The rebel king sent his people to kill me.

But they missed, and now I will make him wish for death.

No one has spoken to me since we arrived back through the castle gates. No additional guard has been sent to stand outside my bedroom. No consoling touches or reassuring words.

Not that I deserve them.

My heart squeezes tight. I had thought maybe my uncle would show, but he's been a ghost along with everyone else.

A low rumbling sound vibrates across the walls, but I don't turn to see. Not even when footsteps creep behind me and the mattress dips beneath a person's weight.

I'm too drained to move, too broken to care.

"*Ma petite menteuse.* What am I going to do with you?" Tristan's voice caresses my body like a kiss, creating a chasm in the center of my chest. I glance down when his tattooed arm encases my waist, pulling me flush against the hard planes of his body and hugging me tight.

It's a simple act, but it pricks at the wound in my heart, the one I've bandaged and tried to pretend isn't there.

A tear drips down my cheek, hot and salty, as it cascades over my lips and seeps into my mouth. My simple white cloth nightgown is the only barrier between us, and his fingers stroke over my stomach, petting me—*comforting me*—as if I deserve consoling.

His breath whispers against the juncture of my neck,

warm kisses peppered along my skin. They're tender and so different from everything I've known Tristan to be, but I welcome them all the same.

In a world of people who don't see me, sometimes it feels as if he's the only one who does.

Another tear escapes, dripping off my chin.

His arm moves, hands pressing against my hips as he turns my body until I'm flat on my back, his green eyes sharp as he hovers, scanning the length of me.

"Are you hurt?" he asks, his fingers coming up to wipe away the wet from my cheeks.

I shake my head, a stuttered breath escaping from deep in my lungs, my heart splinting as it tries to break the icy hold my guilt has encased it in.

He nods, his features relaxing. He strokes along the planes of my face. Beneath my eyes, over the cupid's bow of my lips, down the bridge of my nose. Over and over, he repeats the motion, and slowly, the weight of my grief becomes a little less to bear, as if he's lifting it from me and keeping it for himself.

"Tell me what you need," he says.

My chin quivers and I turn my head to the side, not wanting to let him see me be so weak.

His hand cups my jaw, turning my face back to his. "Tell me what you need, Sara. And I will give it to you."

I think about my answer, a thousand different emotions mixing in my gut, but the one closest to the surface wins.

Rage.

It presses against my skin, trying to burst through and spread through the entire city, obliterating everything in its path.

"I want you to find who did this." My voice cracks. "And I want them dead."

The words feel bitter on my tongue, but I don't take them back.

His eyes flash and he leans down, pressing his forehead against mine, our lips so close we're breathing the same air. "Done."

He says it with such conviction, such surety, that I don't doubt him for a moment. And the way he stares, as though he's diving into my soul and seeing every part, makes me feel like I could ask him for the world, and he'd tear it to pieces just to fit it in my hands.

Being so cared for breaks something apart in the center of my chest, like concrete boulders slamming against stone walls. Every single reason I've had for denying myself, for trying to keep him at arm's length, shatters with each swipe of his fingers.

Maybe that makes me selfish. Maybe I don't deserve it.

But in a world full of pain, he's my only respite.

My fingers reach up to tangle in his hair.

"Kiss me," I breathe.

He does. Without question. With no hesitation. He drops, melding his lips to mine, his soft touch turning to a firm hold, keeping me together while my pieces break apart.

My mouth opens wider as his tongue sinks inside, and arousal curls its way around my body. It's heavier than usual, tinged with sorrow, but somehow despite that— maybe even because of it—everything feels like *more*.

He groans when I suck on his bottom lip, his hips driving into the space between my legs until his thick cock is pressing against my center. My back arches, fingers tearing at his strands as I mold myself to his body, needing to get closer. To feel deeper.

Maybe if I drown myself in him, I won't suffocate from the pain.

His palm cups my breast, his fingers teasing the nipple through the thin fabric of my gown. He breaks his lips away from mine, moving to skim the corner of my jaw and then farther down, latching on to my neck. His teeth nip the skin until it stings, making goose bumps sprout along every inch of my body.

I moan, wetness dripping from my core and sticking to the insides of my legs, wishing he would touch me where I need him.

He hesitates, pulling back and gazing into my eyes, and for a slight moment, I worry that he'll change his mind.

But with Tristan, I should know better.

Another tear trickles down the length of my face, and I reach to wipe it away, but he grips my hand tight and then moves to grab the other, placing them above my head and tangling our fingers. He leans in, his lips moving from the base of my jaw to the corner of my mouth, his tongue swiping against my skin as he kisses the evidence of my pain away.

"Sara," he murmurs.

Our lips meet again, and my desire ratchets higher, heat making my insides throb. I press my hips into his, wrapping my legs around his waist to pull him in deeper. He groans, the sound vibrating through my mouth and sinking into my bones, and I shudder from the feeling. It's intoxicating, seeing someone like him get lost in passion and knowing I'm the cause.

His fingers tighten around mine, and he presses our hands deeper into the pillows as he pulls back to gaze into my eyes. "You're mine."

It isn't a question.

I nod anyway, lifting so I can speak it into his lips. "Yours."

Maybe I should feel embarrassed—weak—as if I need a man to claim me. But when he lets go of my hand and brings his down to the neckline of my gown, pulling until it tears, all I feel is power.

And I'm desperate for him to fill me with it until I scream.

Just like he promised.

# CHAPTER 39

## *Tristan*

ONE WORD AND I'M FERAL.

My hands grip and grope and grab, needing to feel with my fingertips that her perfect skin is unmarred. I'm enraged somebody thought to take matters into their own hands after I explicitly stated not to touch her. When Edward told me, a blinding fury overwhelmed me, but it was also mixed with a new emotion.

*Fear.*

There's only been one thing I've longed for in this world, and it's at my fingertips, the crown so close I can almost reach out and place it on my head.

But now there's her.

And everything else pales in comparison. There is nothing I wouldn't do to keep her by my side. She is *everything*. And if she's hurting, I will torture the people who caused it until they beg me to let them die.

I cup one of her breasts in the palm of my hand, feeling her soft skin mold beneath my grip. Her nipples are hard, pebbling beneath the thin material of her torn nightgown, and my mouth waters, demanding that I lean down and have a taste for myself. So I do.

"Tristan," she moans, her fingers tugging at the strands of my hair until the roots sting.

My teeth sink into her skin and she yelps, her hips lifting until she's pressed against my groin, making my cock jerk from the friction. I release her nipple with a pop and move off her, smirking.

"Where are you going?" she complains. "Come back."

I ignore her pleas and walk to the nightstand, grabbing a thick candle off its base and heading back toward the bed. She's watching me, her forehead scrunched and her cheeks flushed red as she sprawls out against cream silk sheets, her black hair splayed wildly around her.

My footsteps falter as I take her in, nude and aroused, her body high and sensitive from the roller coaster of emotions she's no doubt already gone through today. A lesser woman would have broken. Yet here she is, acknowledging her pain and letting it mold her instead.

She's *breathtaking*. I want to fuck her until she breaks, breed her until my cum oozes from her pores and every person knows who it is she belongs to.

I reach for her ankle, dragging her down to the edge of the bed, placing the candle on the ground next to my side.

She shrieks, her long legs kicking at my chest, and I smirk, delight filling my veins that my smart-mouthed witch is still alive and well. My grasp tightens and I tsk at her, fingers dancing along the front of her shin, over the top of her knee, and to the inside of her thigh.

And then I pinch.

Her eyes flutter and her mouth parts.

"I think you like pain with your pleasure, don't you, little doe?" I tilt my head, trying to keep myself from pouncing on top of her and burying my face in her pussy.

"You don't know what I like," she bites back, her eyes flashing.

I let out a soft laugh, my hand smoothing over the reddened area from where I smarted her skin. "We both know you'll take whatever I give you, *ma petite menteuse*."

Grabbing the hem of my shirt, I lift it over my head, the air hitting my skin and causing a slight chill. Or maybe that's her eyes soaking up my body like it's water, flicking from the artwork detailed along my upper arms to where tattoos cover the front of my chest.

*Together we rule, divided we fall.* She mouths the phrase as she reads my tattoo, and it sends a shot straight to my dick, wanting to know what it would feel like if she spelled the words out with her tongue.

I roll my tunic in my hands, folding it over. "And when you're on the edge of oblivion..." Her eyes close when I lay the fabric on top of them, my fingers slipping behind her curls to wrap it around her skull until she's blind. I bend until our lips brush, reaching down with my hand and grabbing the candle, a shot of desire flying through me when the flame grazes my skin. "It's *my* name that will be screaming from those pretty little lips."

I raise the candle above her forearm, tilting my hand until the melted wax trickles from where it pools beneath the flame, drizzling onto the perfect cream of her skin.

"Oh," she gasps. Her mouth parts as she jerks her arm back, but I grab her wrist, bringing it up to my mouth and blowing, watching as it hardens to a cast on her skin.

"Tristan," she whispers.

"Do you like how it feels?" I ask, running my fingers through the cooling liquid. "I *know* you do. I bet, if I reached down right now, your perfect little snatch would be crying for me. Begging for something to fill it. Wouldn't it, filthy girl?" Moving to the top of her arm now, I repeat the action, the white wax pouring onto her skin as my other hand slips from her collarbone, down the length of her torso, until I'm brushing against soft curls. "Do you know how badly I've ached to touch you?"

I lean down, no longer able to resist the urge to have her taste in my mouth, and lave kisses along the middle of her belly, tilting the candle as I do, pouring a long line of paraffin to trace the places I've just marked with my lips.

She moans, her back arching off the bed as her legs clench together, her thighs pressing my hand between them. I force them back apart, my fingers gripping her inner thigh. "Keep them open. I want to see your pretty cunt as it swells and begs me to let it come."

Her breathing falters, but her body relaxes, and her legs fall open wider than they were before. The sight of her pussy glistening and ripe makes my balls tighten and heat coil around my spine.

She's surprisingly noncombative in this setting, and it pleases me. My hand slips from her thigh, running over the hardened wax and up to her throat, squeezing until I feel her heartbeat beneath my fingers. "Such a good girl."

She licks her lips, and I move the candle to her collarbone, watching her reaction as I dribble the hot liquid onto her skin, moving my hand so it creates lines of wax along her chest, over the pink of her nipples, and down the line of her stomach, pooling in her belly button.

I blow out the candle and drop it on the floor. My hand on her neck tightens as I lift her by the throat until our lips graze. "So quiet, little doe. What happened to that smart mouth of yours?"

Her tongue peeks out to swipe across her lips again, and I take the opportunity, sucking it into my mouth and groaning at her taste. I release her neck and push the blindfold from her face, desperate to have her eyes on me, to know I'm affecting her the same way she is me.

Because she *wrecks* me. Destroys me from the inside out.

Her eyes are dark, swollen and puffy from her earlier

tears, and I step back, enjoying the way her gaze heats my skin as I undo my slacks and step out of them, my cock springing free, hard and angry, drops of cum creating a string of wetness that drips from the tip.

She watches me grip myself and stroke, and I love having her eyes on me. It turns me on, my head falling back from the sensation as I jerk off just for her. *Because* of her.

"Do you see what you've done?" I rasp, stepping closer to the end of the bed. "You've made me insane." I move onto the bed, spreading her legs wider as I crawl into the space between them. "I can't eat. I can't sleep. I can't fucking *breathe* without thinking of you."

Leaning down until our chests graze, I slap my cock against her swollen cunt, heat spiking through me when I can feel her nerves tense and pulse beneath my shaft.

"Do you deserve to come yet, *ma petite menteuse?*" I ask, thrusting my hips so my length slides along her soaking folds.

She moans, her breasts pressing into me as she arches.

"I *always* deserve to come." She smirks.

My tongue traces along the seam of her lips, and I glance down, watching my dick slip along her pussy, my head engorged and purple as the skin pulls back with every forward thrust.

"I could tease you all night like this." Rising, my hands grip her thighs, spreading them wider. "It's a thing of beauty, making you wanton and flushed beneath me."

"Tristan," she mewls. "*Please.*"

"Are you a virgin, Sara?" My movements halt, muscles tensing as pinpricks of pleasure skitter through the tops of my legs and up my abdomen. Another man has touched her. She's already told me as much. But I can't imagine she would come to the castle without her purity intact, knowing she was planning to bed the king.

The thought of her with my brother is a serrated knife slicing through my middle, allowing jealousy to pour into the gaping wound like salt.

"Yes," she whispers.

One word and my edges fray and snap, delirious with the need to be the one who claims her. Unable to bear the *thought* of it being any other way. My hand squeezes my throbbing cock and I slide it down her wet slit until it's pressing against her tight little hole. I lean forward again, my chest grazing hers and my mouth skimming against her ear. "And if I were to take you?"

Her legs wrap around my hips, pressing me farther into her. "Then I'm yours for the taking."

Heat shoots through my core, and my muscles tense with restraint.

I press in, the tip spreading apart her lips until they stretch around me, making my mind crazy with the need to thrust. *To pump. To fuck.* "And tell me, *ma petite menteuse.* Do you trust me?"

She hesitates, her eyes flaring with a dark emotion. "No," she whispers.

I smirk. "Good."

And then I slide inside her, all the way to the hilt, my eyes rolling back as her tight cunt swallows me whole. There's resistance, but it breaks, and my self-discipline disintegrates when I picture her blood coating the length of my dick, proving she's mine and no one else's.

The feeling of having her after trying to resist so long is a drug. It flows through every vein and tantalizes every nerve, making warmth spread through my body until euphoria fills me.

She cries out, her legs tightening around my waist. I run my hand along the top of her hair and over her cheek until I'm cupping her face. "So *fucking* perfect."

My chest pulls and my cock pulses against her walls, her tight virgin hole squeezing against me with every breath.

I lean down and kiss her because I *need* to kiss her. Want to feel her lips on mine and her breath against my mouth as I make her come apart around me.

Her arms fly to my shoulders when I start a slow and steady rhythm, pulling almost all the way out before sliding back in, relishing in the way her body molds to mine like the missing piece of a puzzle.

"Are you okay?" I whisper against her mouth.

"You're right." She sinks her teeth into my lip, biting down until skin breaks, my balls drawing up so tight, a little cum leaks out. "I like the pain."

I groan, throwing my head back. I'll be damned if this woman wasn't molded in the heavens and plucked from the sky just for me.

"Harder," she demands, her legs tightening around my waist.

Heat collects at the base of my spine as I pull my cock out to the tip, glancing down to see her wetness coating along the shaft. I slam back in. She cries out, her fingernails digging into my back.

I hiss at the sting and increase my pace, unable to hold back, an animalistic need blinding me to everything except the need to claim her. Sweat collects on my brow as I drive inside her, over and over, from root to tip, her walls fluttering around me and squeezing tight.

"You try to be so difficult," I rasp. "But you're such a perfect filthy girl when I'm breaking apart your cunt."

Her eyes flare, mouth parting on a silent scream.

"Does it hurt?"

"Yes," she whispers.

"Good." I rise up, my hands gripping beneath her legs as I lift them, spreading them apart so I can watch her swollen and abused center take my cock. The sight is incredibly erotic, and a sense of rightness spreads through my chest. *Nothing* has ever felt like this.

Her walls flutter, and I drop her, chasing the high that only she can provide. My fingers slip to where she needs me most, rubbing until her head thrashes back and forth.

She's close. I can feel it in the way her muscles tense, arousal dripping from her and making a mess of me. Lifting my hand, I bring it down on her swollen nerves, a sharp smack resounding through the air.

She gasps, crying out as her legs tremble at my sides.

My muscles tighten as pleasure threatens to consume me. "Such a *filthy* girl, drenching my dick like you're my whore."

I do it again, sharp slaps that make her skin puffy and red, her inner walls milking me until my vision blurs.

And then she explodes, the top half of her body flying from the bed, her arms and legs wrapping around me, her chest pressing against mine. My hands move to her hips, holding her to me as I thrust up into her, chasing my high as she shatters around me.

"Tristan!" she cries.

She bites the juncture of my neck, whimpering as she holds on.

My balls tense, and for just a moment, I consider coming inside her. Everything in me screams to do it. To coat her walls, ensure that no one else can claim her as theirs. But a bit of logic floats in, knowing if she were to become pregnant before I ascend the throne, there would be nothing but death in her future.

So at the last second, I push her back down onto the bed, slipping out of her with a pop, and I pull at my length, her wetness making my hand glide along the shaft effortlessly. Groaning, I throw my head back, my muscles seizing tight. "Tell me you want it."

"I want it." There's no hesitation in her tone now.

"Beg for it," I demand.

She moves from where she's lying, flipping around until she's on all fours, that perfect ass high in the air as she crawls toward me until she's beneath my rigid length. She looks up at me from beneath her lashes, her hands gliding up the insides of my thighs.

My abdomen clenches in pleasure, the coil winding tighter inside me. It's an incredible sight, her slinking toward me like an animal, her virginity smeared along my cock as she prepares to beg me for my cum.

"Tristan," she whispers. "*Please.*"

My muscles tense, my shaft jerking in my hand.

"Paint it on my skin so everyone knows who I belong to."

And that's all it takes for me to explode, stars dotting my vision as my cock spurts shot after shot all over her face, dripping down her cheeks and splashing onto the swell of her breasts.

My chest heaves and my ears ring from the blinding pleasure.

I look down at her, my mouth parted, aftershocks vibrating through my veins.

She smirks, her tongue peeking out to lick the cum from her lips, her fingers swiping through the mess on her collarbone and rubbing it into her skin.

"Yours," she purrs.

Reaching down, I smooth my hand over her face, my thumb pressing into the wetness on her cheek and smearing it before moving it to her mouth.

She sucks, her tongue swirling around the tip of my finger, and my cock twitches again, something I've never felt before bursting like fireworks in my chest.

# CHAPTER 40

## *Sara*

BY MORNING, HE'S GONE.

He has to be, of course. Nevertheless, my heart aches as though it's been abandoned.

Holding on to my virginity was never something I did because it was expected. I don't prescribe to the belief that it's a gift to be given. I had just never found someone who I cared to experience it with. It's vulnerable. Intimate. And while I've fooled around with boys in the past, there's been no one I've considered my equal.

Until him.

A sharp knock raps on the door, and I stretch beneath the covers, my insides twinging in pain. Before I can say a word, it swings open, all three of my ladies waltzing in as if privacy is something I don't deserve.

Marisol heads straight to the large windows on the far side of my room and whips open the heavy curtains, allowing the dim light from the gloomy Saxum skies to pour into the space.

"Rise and shine," Sheina singsongs as she moves past me, her eyes as bright as her blond hair.

Frowning, I move to sit up on the bed, the sharp ache between my legs cutting through me like a sword, making me gasp from the feeling. Ophelia clears her throat and moves toward me until she's pressed against the edge of the mattress.

"Milady," she whispers, her eyes glancing to Marisol's back and then to me again. "Are you all right?"

I tilt my head, assuming she means from everything that's happened in the past twenty-four hours. The truth is, I'm not all right—the sticky fingers of grief don't let go easily—but I won't show it to everyone. Showing emotion is weak, and I cannot afford to look *weak*, especially now.

"Of course I am, Ophelia." I smile at her.

She leans closer, her brows drawing in. "There's blood on your sheets." Her voice is quiet, as though she's trying to keep from letting the others hear. Embarrassment slams into me, and I glance down, realizing the blankets have slipped, specks of red dotting the fabric, surrounded by crumbled, hardened wax.

My cheeks flush, and my fingers grapple for the comforter, pulling it over the mess as I clear my throat. "Thank you, Ophelia."

She grins and tips her head.

"What is it we're doing today?" I ask, trying to remain calm even though my heart is beating out of my chest. Stupid to fall asleep like this.

Marisol spins around, her eyes narrowing on me. "Your uncle and His Majesty wish to dine with you."

Her words are sharp and they sting as they whip across my face. I'm not sure if it's from the tone of her voice or the thought of having to put on an act with the king when I've just been stripped of my innocence by his brother, but either way it smarts.

She slaps her hands together and walks my way. My insides tighten and I grip the comforter higher up, realizing that I'm naked beneath the sheets.

"Get out of bed, milady, so we can get you dressed and ready."

Ophelia moves over to Marisol and links their arms together, pulling her to the washroom. "We'll draw you a bath. I'm sure you could use the relaxation after yesterday."

The reminder of yesterday twists my chest, but I smile, grateful that she seems to be in my corner. Once they disappear, I blow out a slow exhale, turning to find Sheina smirking at me from the other side of the room, a robe in one hand, the other on her hip.

"Don't look at me that way, Sheina. Get over here and help me," I hiss.

She lets out a small laugh before walking over and holding it out to me.

"Marisol must be blind as a bat," she chides. "Your hair is an absolute rat's nest, and you're clearly not wearing any clothes." Her eyes sparkle.

Scoffing, I grab the silk robe from her hands, shielding myself as best as possible when I toss off the comforter and stand to slip it on. My muscles groan in protest and again, a sharp stab careens through my center, making me jolt from the pain.

I like the way it feels.

Strangely, the ache is a comfort, a reminder that Tristan cares. That out of everyone in my life—Sheina and my uncle included—he's the only one who showed up and held me through the night. Who distracted my mind and let me break in his arms, giving me his strength when he knew I had none.

"Quiet," I snap, although I can't keep the grin from curling in the corners of my mouth.

She giggles. "Well, at least wipe the freshly fucked look off your face."

I gasp, shoving at her shoulder, allowing the smile to break free. "Watch your mouth, Sheina! Lord, what happened to my friend? I've never heard you speak so crudely."

Tying the sash of the robe together, I glance around, cringing when I see the bed is in such disarray.

"Don't worry," she says. "I'll take care of it."

Sighing in relief, the tension eases from my shoulders

and I reach out, grasping her forearm in my hand. "Can we spend some time this evening after dinner, just the two of us?"

Hope blossoms in my chest, wanting to feel some sense of normalcy, knowing I've had none since before coming to Saxum and embarking on this long, torturous journey.

Her eyes shutter and she glances away. "Of course."

My chest twists, the smile dropping from my face at her lack of enthusiasm. "If you're busy…"

"For you, milady? Never." She grins, squeezing my arm. "Your bath is probably ready."

Unease sifts through the air and settles on me like a blanket as I watch her move to my bed and strip the sheets, and the feeling stays through the rest of the morning, as my corset is cinched tight, my hair scrunched and pinned, and fresh rouge put on my cheeks.

The only thing that distracts me is in the evening when we're on our way to the dining hall, and we run into Paul.

My heart stutters at the sight of him.

"Paul." I stumble to a stop in the middle of the dimly lit hall, Marisol—who decided it was her responsibility to escort me here—jerks to a halt behind me.

"Milady," she says. "We don't have—"

I spin on her, my eyes narrowing and jaw clenching. "Marisol, the dining room is right there." I point to the doors at the end of the hall. "You've been an excellent guard dog, and I appreciate you leading me here. But you're dismissed."

A slight grin tips the corner of Paul's face, although it's easy to see the sorrow that fills his eyes.

"Now," I hiss when she doesn't move.

She huffs. "You can't be alone with a man in the hallway, milady. It's untoward."

"Let me worry about that." I step into her, and she stiffens her shoulders. "I'm tired of you always putting up a fight. I can tell that being in charge is important to you, and while I respect that, I'm kindly reminding you that you will *never* be in charge of me."

Her lips thin, but she bends into a curtsy before traipsing down the hall, most likely to tattle on me like I'm a child. I spin back around to give Paul my attention, my chest pulling tight when I take in the deep frown lines marring his face.

"Paul, there's—"

He shakes his head, nose scrunching as he glances down. "They're not even going to have a proper burial for him." He grits his teeth, his eyes flashing. "Can you believe that?"

"What?" My hand flies to my chest. "They have to. They...he's a royal guard."

Water lines his lower lids, and my chest cracks as I step closer, grabbing his hands in mine and squeezing.

"Paul." Emotion clogs my throat. "I'm so sorry. It was my fault, and I—"

"No worries, milady." He breaks one of his hands away and tips my chin. "He died doing what he wanted to do."

I huff out a disbelieving breath, rolling my eyes to stem the tears. "What, being a martyr?"

He smiles. "Protecting you."

My stomach cramps and I inhale, my face scrunching from how heavy those words hit.

"You know," he whispers, his grip tightening on my fingers. "I'm not sure who's worse, the people who killed him or the ones who won't honor his memory." He hesitates, dropping my other hand to wipe away a stray tear that drips down his cheek. "At least the rebels take care of their own."

My nerve endings stand to attention, and I tilt my head. "How do you know that?"

Paul jerks back, running a hand through his auburn hair, avoiding my eyes.

"Sara." The deep voice cuts through the tension, and I glance over to see Uncle Raf standing in the hallway, one hand in his pocket as he leans on his cane.

I smile. "Uncle, I was just on my way to see you."

"Milady," Paul mutters, rushing down the hall. He doesn't turn and give proper notice to my uncle, and the slight doesn't go missed, Uncle Raf glaring at Paul's back as he retreats down the hall.

"Were you planning on keeping the king waiting all night?" he asks.

My insides roll with disgust, but I push on, knowing that now more than ever, it's important I tread carefully. If he knew what I was doing last night, I'm not sure how he would react.

At best, he'd call me a traitor and disown me from the family.

At worst? I'm not even sure.

Anxiety swirls in my gut as I make my way over to him, afraid that when I get too close, he'll smell Tristan on my skin. Notice the difference in my walk or the new cadence of my heart, screaming that a Faasa prince owns me, body and soul.

I ache to find him, even now, and the guilt from that notches its way up my throat until it swells.

When I reach him, I wait…although for what, I'm not sure. Maybe realization that someone tried to end my life just the day before. Maybe acknowledgment that I'm not okay.

It never comes.

And when we walk into the dining hall and he escorts me all the way down the long table with no less than twenty seats, ornate crystal chandeliers sparkling from above us, I just feel hollow.

Michael sits at the head of the table, dressed in expensive evening wear and a smile on his face, and disgust rolls through my center, the strongest it's ever been.

"Lady Beatreaux, you're looking lovely," Michael says as a servant pulls out my chair, allowing me to sit.

I glance back and smile, thanking them, and Michael grimaces at the action.

"Your Majesty, it's good to see you looking so well."

Uncle Raf starts in on him almost immediately about calling a meeting with the privy council, and as I sit and listen, taking small sips of water from my glass, I realize that he's stepped into the role his son had, advising the king. Which means he doesn't plan on going back home soon. I wonder how my mother fares all alone, although I doubt she's spared me a second thought since I left.

The first course is brought to the table, and my gut grumbles, unable to stomach eating when my insides feel so torn and tossed. I fidget in my chair so the ache between my legs will spear through me and remind me that Tristan was there. That he cares, even when it feels as though no one else does. It's odd how just the memory of him is enough to bring me comfort, but I welcome it, wanting something to keep me from breaking down and ruining everything I came to Saxum to accomplish.

I clear my throat. "Is it true you aren't having a proper service for Timothy?"

The words fly from my mouth before I can bite them back, and my uncle shoots me a sharp glare, his fork pausing halfway to his mouth.

Michael, who was taking a drink from his glass, places it back on the table and looks at my uncle and then back to me. "That's correct. We don't think it would be best."

Anger sludges through my veins like mud. "He deserves to be honored for his service."

"The rebels would see it as a victory," my uncle cuts in. "We cannot give them that satisfaction."

I huff out a breath, my spine straightening. "They already *have* a victory. They've murdered someone who was doing his job in protecting me."

"Sara, that's enough," my uncle says.

I lean forward until my ribs bump against the edge of the table. "When he was lying on the dirty ground, grasping my wrists and struggling for air, it was *me* who had their hands elbow deep in his chest, trying to keep his heart beating. It was *me* who prayed to God that he would spare him, begging him to take it back—" My voice cracks, and my fist slams on the table. "To take me instead."

"He was not even supposed to *speak* with you," Michael says.

I turn toward him, my jaw clenching. "No worries, Your Majesty. Now he never will again."

Michael's eyes are wide at my outburst, his jaw muscle tensing.

I cover my mouth with a trembling hand, nausea surging through my throat. "I'm sorry, if you'll excuse me. I'm feeling rather ill. I think I need to go lie down."

"Sara," Uncle Raf starts again.

I put a hand out to stop him. "I'm fine, Uncle. Nothing a rest can't fix."

Shoving from my chair, the wood legs scraping against the floor, I toss my napkin on the ground and flee from the room, worried that if I stay even a moment longer, I'll say things I can't take back. And that's the last thing I want.

But I needn't worry, because no one follows.

———

The fire has long since been put out and I'm sitting in front of it, yet another layer of sadness dropping in my chest.

Sheina never came.

I'm angry. And honestly a little afraid that the girl I thought I knew is actually a woman I know nothing of. Serves me right, I suppose, considering she doesn't know much of me.

Glancing at the brown floor clock as it ticks against the far wall, I sigh, deciding to focus on something I can control—learning more of the tunnels.

The couch cushions groan as I stand, walking from the sitting area over to my freshly made bed. Dropping to my knees, I peek beneath the mattress's frame, my arm stretching until I grasp the corner of a small chest. I pull it toward me and open the top, breathing a deep sigh as I pull out the black ensemble I used to wear when sneaking out at night in Silva to take the stolen money from my uncle's safe and put it in Daria's hands.

I strip out of my nightgown, slipping on the black pantaloons and the long-sleeved black tunic before sitting down on the edge of the bed and lacing up the boots. When I move to the mirror to place my curls back into a bun at the nape of my neck, a sense of calm cascades over my shoulders, finally feeling like myself.

Not all women are meant for frilly dresses and fancy crowns that sparkle in the light.

Some of us prefer the anonymity that comes along with shadows.

Slipping my arms in the black cloak, I put the hood over my head, gripping the edges with my fingers and pulling until it hides my face from view. And then I'm out the door, already knowing there won't be a new guard there to keep watch. With Xander gone, I'm nothing but an afterthought.

My stomach tightens as I make my way to the nearest secret door, and my stomach jolts when voices filter around the corner, sounding as though they're heading in the same direction. I spin around and run as quietly as I can to the end of the hall, hiding behind the far wall so they don't see me.

*Sheina*. My heart falters. *And Paul*.

My brows draw down, and my insides curdle with confusion, wondering what it is they're doing together and why they're lurking through the hallways late at night.

When they open the secret passageway and step into the castle's tunnels, my stomach drops to the floor. I follow behind them, trailing far enough away where they won't notice I'm there. It takes ten minutes to reach the end of the tunnels, a small stone staircase leading to a small door that opens to the outside, and they exit, whispering words too low for me to hear.

Again, I follow, stepping into the chill of the cloudy night and realizing we're in the middle of the forest. And I have no idea where they're about to go.

# CHAPTER 41

## *Tristan*

IT'S A VERY INTERESTING TURN OF EVENTS TO have my brother listening to my words as though they're gospel, and it's just more proof that he's truly lost his mind.

If I wasn't so fixated on the memory of how my little doe felt wrapped around my cock, maybe I'd find some humor in the irony of the boy who spent his life telling me I wasn't worth the dirt on his shoe asking me what he should do.

Granted, all this is from my careful manipulation of his hallucinations. I saw a weakness, and I pounced. The rebels are many and growing every day. I have many factions hidden in plain sight. We're *everywhere*, even in the spots you wouldn't suspect. But I'm not an idiot, and if there's opportunity to strengthen our odds, I will always take it.

Which is why I lightly suggested last night that Timothy not have a proper burial—something that Edward could use to sway opinions of the king. People don't do well when one of their own isn't treated with respect.

"Brother, I'm sorry to bother you, but I didn't know where else to turn." I shake my head, pacing as though the thoughts are plaguing my mind.

"Out with it, Tristan. I'm busy," he snaps, leaning back in his chair and puffing on a cigar.

"It's about Father," I whisper, glancing around the room as though someone will overhear.

This gets his attention, and he sits forward, his brows rising. "Has he told you something else? Come to you in a dream again?"

I hesitate for a few long moments. "He has. But...I don't know."

"Tell me," he hisses.

"In my dream...the king of Andalaysia was sending troops to our southern border."

Michael grips the roots of his hair. "What? You think they mean to wage a war?"

Blowing out a deep breath, I shake my head. "I don't know, Michael. It's probably nothing. *Fuck!*" I kick the wooden chair leg. "I feel like I'm going crazy."

"No." He shoots to his feet, walking around the desk until he's in front of me. He grips my shoulder tight. "You're not crazy. *We* are not crazy."

I nod, running my palm over my mouth.

"Did he say when?"

Shrugging, I glance up at him from under my brows. "I can't be sure."

Michael chews on the inside of his lip. "We can't tell the council of this. They won't believe it."

"Michael, you're the *king*. This is an absolute monarchy, not a democracy," I say. "Don't let others make decisions as if Faasa blood runs through their veins. It doesn't."

His eyes flare, his chest puffing out as my words sink into his psyche. "We'll send troops to the southern border. Just to be safe."

"Brother, I think that's the right choice."

———

Edward stares at me as I lean against the tavern's bar top, lighting a joint and bringing it to my lips, saddened that I can't still smell Sara on my fingertips.

Every cell in my body is craving hunting her down and chaining her to my side. It's unhealthy, this obsession, but it's here all the same, and I've never been known for my solid state of mental health.

"You seem different," Edward states, sipping from a pint of ale.

"Do I?" I smirk. "Must be because we're on the verge of everything I've ever wanted. My brother has gone mad, Edward. He believes I see the ghost of our father, who whispers warnings in my ear. And this time tomorrow, much of the king's military will be on their way to the southern border to guard against a fictitious threat of war."

Edward's grin stretches across his face. "And in the end?"

I smile. "In the end, I shall wear the crown either way. Preferably with a brand-new council, not filled with people who disrespected me as sport my entire life."

"Victory is ours, Your Highness. I can feel it. Several of my men are already teetering on the edge. They aren't happy with how things are." He claps his hands together before taking another sip of his drink. "And the boys in the basement who attempted to kill Lady Beatreaux? What would you have me do with them?"

My blood boils as I think of the rebels who took it upon themselves to stage an assassination. "Keep them locked up. I plan to give them as a gift."

"To whom?"

I smile. "To Sara, of course."

His eyes alight in recognition, but before he can say anything else, the door to the tavern bursts open and Sheina walks in, her eyes skimming the area until they land on us. A smile breaks across her face when she sees Edward, and he straightens from where he was leaning against the bar. And then, just as I instructed, Paul Wartheg follows behind her, his gaze growing wide as he takes in the three dozen people eating and drinking at the tables and his mouth dropping open when they snag on the iron cage constructed in the far corner with an unconscious Xander chained to the wall and on display.

I stub out the end of my joint and saunter over to them, adopting a warm grin on my face.

"Welcome, Paul." I clasp my hand on his back. "I'm so happy to see Sheina convinced you to come."

"It's *you*," he whispers. "You're the rebel king?"

My grin widens. "I am many things, but right now, I'm just a friend."

I prod him forward, and Sheina breaks away, moving to where Edward is and sinking into his arms, their lips locking in a long kiss.

"I'm glad you're here," I say to Paul. "If only to see what your months of hard work, providing the food that makes its way here, has done." My hand waves over the tables, pointing to the random faces. "If it wasn't so late, you'd see small children getting their first meal in days. You'd see mothers holding babes to their chest while they cry in relief from what you've given them when the monarchy has failed to provide." Turning toward him, I lock him in my stare. "I want you to know how incredibly sorry I am about Timothy."

His eyes narrow, shoulders stiffening as he meets my gaze.

It isn't spoken about—not out loud—but I *know* of him and Timothy. Of stolen moments and secret nights. Of love that would have ended in a much worse fate than a gunshot to the chest had anyone found out.

And while I don't mourn Timothy's passing, for one

of the first times in my life, I can empathize with the thought of his death. I understand the pain of having to love in secret, and I do not wish to ever endure the agony of reuniting with the other half of your soul only to have it unjustly ripped away.

It's hard enough being told they aren't meant for you when they're the only thing that's ever felt like yours.

I place my hand on his shoulder. "I promise you, Paul, the ones responsible will pay."

"They won't give him a funeral," he hisses, his voice low and tortured.

I nod, drawing my brows down. "Then we will have one for him here."

A single tear drips down his face and he wipes it away. I pretend I don't see.

"I didn't give them this order, but I bear responsibility all the same."

"I believe you." He clears his throat, speaking the next part in a whisper. "I don't think for one second that you would allow any harm to come to Lady Beatreaux."

My chest cramps, hoping we aren't as obvious as he's making it seem, but I smile. "And you would be correct."

"I never came here before because I refused to pick a side," he says. "But I can no longer stand by and watch as a corrupt monarchy destroys our people. Gloria Terra is a proud country, and we deserve a king who will bring us glory. Not shame."

Satisfaction, heavy and thick, rolls through my blood like molasses. "Do I have your loyalty, Paul Wartheg?"

His eyes flash, and he drops on bended knee.

I hold out my hand, and he grips my fingers, kissing the top of my lion's head ring. "I swear it."

"Together we rule, divided we fall," I whisper. "It's my honor to welcome you to the rebellion."

# CHAPTER 42

## *Sara*

ICY COLD SHOCK POURS THROUGH MY VEINS as I watch a roomful of people fall on bended knee, one right after the other, spurred on by Paul, who was just kissing Tristan's hand in subservience, and I'm...numb.

Tristan is the rebel king.

*Of course he is.*

How could I have been so blind?

I followed Sheina and Paul here, all the way to the shadowed lands, where the lights disappear from street corners and sleek roads turn into broken pavement, potholes so big they could fit a small house. The buildings all have dirty windows or boards in place of glass, and while Silva has been impoverished for years, this is beyond anything I've ever seen.

I'm not sure what I expected when I peered through the crack in the door of the Elephant Bones Tavern, but it wasn't this.

*Anything* but this.

My eyes scan over the people, my heart screaming and spitting in the center of my chest, but I ignore the pain, refusing to admit to myself that the man I've fallen for is the one who murdered my father.

The tavern itself is dingy and dark, worn wood panels and a strong scent of mothballs and mold, but the atmosphere is upbeat. As if they know they're on the cusp of something great. Something more.

They set a large iron-barred cage up in the far corner, and I squint my eyes, confusion running through me at the sight. *Why on earth is that there?* I try to get a better view, but I can't open the door any farther without the risk of being seen, and Tristan's tall frame blocks me.

But then he moves, and I see the hunched figure of my cousin, bloodied and chained, unconscious against the wall.

My stomach somersaults. *He's alive.*

Caged like a bird and missing a hand, but still...alive.

My stomach rolls, the vengeance in my heart growing brighter.

Tristan turns then, walking away from Paul and moving toward the front of the room with a shoddy raised platform and a single high-back chair sitting in the center. He walks straight to the middle, a god among his men, and speaks.

"Friends." His arms rise to the side. "The time is near. You've all put incredible faith in me, and it's time to return the favor. A new dawn is on the horizon!"

Cheers ring out across the tables.

"No longer will we be cast to the shadowed lands while the rich and perfect get to live in the light. It is *our* time to shine."

More yells and hollers, a few people throwing bits of trash into the iron cage that houses Xander.

My stomach cramps, aching to turn away—to make this nightmare disappear—yet I'm glued to the spot, unable to do anything other than watch. His charisma is astounding, and the more his words flow from his mouth to the rest of the room, you can feel the energy shift, as if he's molding it into whatever shape he desires and feeding it back to them like it was always theirs. It's the most incredible sight I've witnessed, and I have no doubt that if he desires the crown, it will end up on his head.

He speaks so eloquently, so mesmerizing, that even I fall under his spell. My heart beats faster, my breathing comes harsher, and excitement wells up in the center of my stomach, expanding through my limbs until I picture what it would be like to stand at his side.

But then I remember where I am and who *he* is. And the feeling disappears, replaced with bile that turns my stomach from the inside out.

I skim the surroundings again, moving over the people until my eyes land on Sheina, her arms around the neck of a rebel in the king's uniform. I rack my brain, trying to remember his name, but come up blank.

She's a fool. The same kind I have been. Losing myself in the arms of a man.

A lying, pathetic excuse of a man.

My legs ache from my crouched position, and I shift on the balls of my feet, that ever-present ache flaring to life between my legs, only this time it doesn't bring comfort.

I can hardly stand to look at him, but I force my eyes there anyway, maybe to prove that I can live through the worst kind of betrayal, or maybe the masochist in me wants to live in the pain as I try to come to terms with the fact that despite everything, the one person I thought I could trust turned out to be my worst enemy.

He licked my tears and told me I was his, right after he sent men to kill me.

My chest squeezes until it feels like the blood vessels burst, exploding in a fury until all I can taste are the sour notes of betrayal.

The rebel king. *The scarred prince.*

My hand flies to my mouth to stifle the scream.

I let him see the darkest parts of me. Allowed him to mark me and hurt me, and I *begged* for it while I rubbed his cum into my skin and prayed to God it would brand my soul.

My teeth grit as hatred, black and true, burns through me until I shake, violence pounding in my ears.

I've done many things that will keep me from the gates of heaven. I've come to terms with my sins, giving up my faith long ago in order to seek vengeance. But right now, I feel as though I've truly betrayed my father's memory for the first time.

I slept with a Faasa. But worse than that, I fell for the man responsible for his death.

My heart trembles and cracks, the jagged edges slicing through tendons as they fall to my feet until nothing remains but a blackened hole that *almost* knew what it felt like to fall in love.

Tristan's head snaps to where I am, green eyes piercing as his head tilts.

Jumping to my feet, I turn and flee, adrenaline pumping like acid through my muscles as I run back the way I came, promising my father's ghost I won't forget why I came. Not again.

I will eradicate the Faasa family and kill the rebel king...no matter how much it may break me.

# CHAPTER 43

## *Tristan*

MY BROTHER ASKED IF I WAS A MAN OF FAITH.

I'm a man of many things, but faith is something that is best suited when it's placed within yourself instead of seeking it in other people.

Other people disappoint.

I saw her. It was quick, just a flash, but I'd know those dark eyes anywhere.

Everything in me demanded that I follow, that I hunt her down and sneak into her room like I did the other night. But something is telling me I shouldn't. Not yet.

So I went to her cousin instead.

Xander has been with us since the night of the engagement ball, naturally. And in the time since, he's been on display, beaten and abused, the open wounds growing infected and causing what I'm sure is an immeasurable amount of pain. I imagine sepsis will set in soon, eating him from the inside out.

I splash a bucket of water on his face, rousing him. He looks around, but I've tied him to a wooden slab in the tavern's backyard. I secured both of his legs with rope, and his good hand as well.

He jerks but realizes quickly he isn't going anywhere. Even if he was free to move, he's far too weak to escape.

"Good morning, Alexander." I smile.

"I've told you," he mumbles, his tongue peeking out of his dry mouth to wipe over his cracked and bleeding lips. He coughs before he continues. "Everything…I know."

Tsking, I shake my head. "Come now, Xander. We both know that's not true. You haven't told me anything."

"Just kill me," he whispers. "*Please.*"

I place the empty bucket at my feet, moving to where a gallon of kerosene sits at the end of the table. "You believe you've paid your penance?"

He nods.

"And what were your crimes?"

He presses his lips together, turning his face away. Everything he does is in slow motion, as if he doesn't have the strength to exert the proper amount of energy.

I step up next to him, staring down at his beaten and bloodied face. "I tell you what. I'll be honest with you first. That way, it's more of a tit for tat." Blowing out a breath, I crack my neck. "*Honestly*…you're going to die today. Phew, it feels good to get that off my chest. Now you go."

His eyes flare, but he stays silent.

"All right then." I raise the kerosene above his torso, tilting the bottle until it pours onto his skin, dousing his flesh and pooling into the wood at his sides.

He shivers when it hits.

"This isn't for me, you know," I say, moving my way around his body until I cover every single inch of him in the liquid. "This is your chance to confess and hope that God will grant mercy on your soul."

He scoffs, but it turns into a cough, the sound wheezy and wet, as if sickness has already taken his lungs. "You're no priest."

I lean in close. "But I can be your savior."

"Are you going to kill her as well?" he asks.

My chest cinches up tight. There's only one *her* I imagine he'd be speaking of, and she isn't someone I have any intention of harming. "I'm afraid you'll need to be more specific."

"My cousin."

I clench my jaw and he doesn't miss the movement, a slight smirk breaking through his fatigue.

"You don't hide it well, you know? Your sick fascination with her." He coughs again. "You're lucky your brother is a complete imbecile."

Irritation bleeds through me. "Do not speak of her to me," I spit.

He laughs. "I brought her here to *kill* you, fool."

Something dark settles in my chest at his words,

although I don't doubt that he's telling the truth. I've always known there was something hiding just beneath her surface, nefarious acts by an innocent face. It explains the daggers on her thigh, the fire in her breath, and the eyes that stare through cracked doors and starless nights.

But until last night, I'm certain she hadn't known I was the rebel king.

I wonder if that makes her want to kill me more or less.

My cock hardens at the thought of her ire.

"That doesn't surprise me at all," I laugh. "Be honest, though, Xander. Who put her up to it?" Reaching into my pocket, I grab the Lucifer matches, picking one out and holding it above his head. "Tell me quickly, or I will light this fire and burn every inch of your skin. And then I'll put it out so we can play this game over and over until the flames eat your muscle and char your nerves." I stare at the matchstick. "I hear it's the most dreadful of ways to go." He purses his lips, and I sneer, moving to light the flame. "You're *such* a bore."

"My father!" he yells, his voice sounding hoarse and painful. "She was supposed to rid the world of you and your pathetic excuse of a brother so the Beatreaux line could finally take their rightful place."

My head falls back with my laughter. "You would never be next in line for the throne."

"We have the support of the privy council," he rasps, his eyes swinging to the match in my hand.

Now this surprises me, my brows shooting to my hairline.

"A coup d'état then?" I click my tongue. "Color me impressed." Sighing, I bring the match to the box, the sound of it striking against the side like music to my ears. "One more confession, Xander." I lean in, the heat of the flame sending a tendril of excitement through my veins. "Was it you who poured poison down my father's throat?"

He swallows, resignation settling heavy in his eyes. "No. *That* was your brother," he says.

I'm not surprised, but the betrayal stings all the same.

"Your mother and I simply nudged him in the right direction."

Nodding, I raise my hand above him. "May God have mercy on your soul, Alexander. For I shall give you none."

The kerosene lights quickly as I drop the match, his skin catching fire and blazing high into the sky. I move back, closing my eyes and relishing in the tortured screams, rage swirling like a hurricane in the center of my gut.

# CHAPTER 44

## *Sara*

MY BLADES ARE SHARP.

I haven't changed my clothes since last night when my world flipped inside out.

Instead, I've been sitting in front of the fire, my mind replaying everything I know to be true. And the only conclusion I've come to is that I'm tired of the waiting game. Of waiting for direction from others whom I'm not sure I can trust. I no longer wish to play the perfect part of wanting to be queen. I just want them dead.

It's the only thing that pulses through my insides, pumping from the space where the beating organ should be, half convinced that my twisted need for vengeance is the only reason it still beats at all.

*Can you die of a broken heart?*

I do not care for politics or preserving the integrity of the crown—all things my uncle told me were necessary so the country wouldn't break apart at the seams when the Faasa dynasty fell. But I've had all night to replay his words in my brain, and things just aren't adding up.

If I wasn't already crushed into a thousand pieces, maybe I'd feel shame for how easily I've been manipulated. As it is, I only feel the emptiness that comes after accepting disappointment.

A thick fog rolls through the trees and blankets the cold ground, dew drops forming on the blades of grass as I make my way out of the main castle and across the court into the cathedral.

I'm sure today will be my last day on this earth. I have no delusion that it will end in anything other than death. I welcome it with open arms, as long as I take down the others who have wronged me.

Even so, I wish to pray.

Not for absolution; there is no remorse in my soul. But for clarity. Purpose.

My fingers wrap around the cool metal handles to the front of the church, and I wrench open the doors, stepping inside the expansive room, my gaze locking on a lone figure standing at the front of the altar, his hands in his pockets and his tattoos on full display as he stares up at the sculpture of Jesus on the cross.

Tears spring to my eyes, my chest squeezing so tight it feels like it will snap me in half. I swallow them back down, refusing to let them fall.

As quietly as possible, I slip a blade from the inside of my cloak, pressing it against my trembling palm.

My boots echo off the walls as I make my way down the center of the pews, and there's no way he doesn't hear me coming. I expect for him to turn, to say something. *Do* something.

But he doesn't.

I grip the dagger as I continue my trek toward him, and my stomach rolls, nausea teasing through my middle and surging up my throat when I stop a few paces behind.

*Do it*, my mind whispers. *Reach out your hand and plunge the blade into his skin.*

It would be so easy, letting him bleed on the cold church floor, as I stand over him and watch while the traitorous life leaves his body.

The thought of it makes my insides quake, and I feel weak for struggling with the decision. I raise my hand, swallowing the bile that rises along with it, the cavity in my chest cracking down the center as I bring the knife closer to his back.

"Somehow, I knew you'd find me here."

My hand freezes, heart shooting to my throat.

He spins around, those stupid, *perfect*, jade-green irises staring at me as though I'm the only thing he sees, and it sends rage careening through my body, hating that even now, he's so convincing with his lies.

"One of us is always finding the other," I say through clenched teeth. "I wonder why that is."

He smiles, although it doesn't reach his eyes. My fingers tighten around my knife, and his gaze swings to where it's held in my hand.

"Are you going to kill me, little doe?"

My stomach flips and I bring the dagger high, pointing it at his chest, the weapon shaking in my palm. I swallow and clench my jaw, my chest burning from the thought.

*Do it. Do it. Do it.*

But my hand stays still.

His Adam's apple bobs as he steps in close, the tip of the blade pressing into him. "I do not wish to see you fail," he whispers. "Even at this."

My broken heart stutters, emotion exploding through me until I can barely think through the turmoil. "You don't get to say that to me," I spit, pressing the weapon farther into his chest. "Don't pretend you care when all you've ever done is lie."

"*Ma petite menteuse*, the world is full of lies."

The nickname flows from his tongue and spears through my middle, the pain so intense it makes me want to die. His palm reaches out, slipping along my skin, his fingers wrapping around my wrist, causing heat to flare up the length of my arm.

"The truth is, I am yours. Wholly. Inexplicably. *Painfully*. Unconditionally." He moves my hand until the dagger presses against his throat. "And if you need to sacrifice my soul so you're able to live with yours, then do it."

I suck in a shaky breath, hot tears cascading down my cheeks as my mind wars with my heart, confusion muddling up my thoughts until my vision blurs and I can't see straight.

*Do it.*

"This is a trick," I hiss, pushing the blade until it nicks his skin.

He smiles, his fingers stroking along my arm, causing goose bumps to sprout in their wake. "No tricks, little doe. Not this time. Not with you."

My face scrunches up. "You killed my father," I cry out, the blade cutting into his flesh until blood trickles down the front of his throat.

Still, he doesn't move.

"You tried to have *me* killed. How can you stand there and profess the way you do when all you've ever done is cause me pain?" My voice breaks, and I heave a staggered breath.

My words are anguished. Like his hand has reached into the deepest pits of my being and wrought them forcibly from my soul. His palm glides up the length of my arm, over my chest, and to the front of my neck until he's cupping my face, his fingers rubbing against my cheek.

I close my eyes as I lean into the touch, sick as a dog that I'm unable to resist the comfort, even as my dagger is seconds away from ending his life.

"It isn't fair," I whisper, my free hand gripping at the

fabric of his shirt. "It isn't fair for you to do this to me. Why did it have to be you?"

He lets out a humorless laugh. "You think I wished for *you*?" His grip tightens against my jaw. "I would scourge the earth if I thought it would erase you from my brain."

My chest twists, agony pouring through my veins.

"The problem is, Sara, there *is* no erasing you. And now you're part of me. One that I can't snuff out, no matter how much I may try." He steps in closer, forcing more blood to seep from his throat. "And I'm part of you too. Even if you hate that it's so."

His other hand flies up, twisting my arm away until it moves from his neck, and I gasp, my stomach somersaulting, expecting him to attack.

But he drops to his knees instead, his arms splaying wide at his sides. "I am *nothing* if I'm not yours." His jaw tenses, water lining his lower lid until it spills over, a single tear tracing the raised flesh of his scar and dripping off his chin. "So do it. Kill me, Sara. Put me out of this constant purgatory of needing you without *having* you."

My throat swells until I can hardly breathe, indecision weaving through me as his words leak through the cracks of my shoddy foundation and bleed into the crevices of my soul.

"I will die happily if it's what will bring you peace," he rasps, thick emotion bleeding into his tone.

A sob breaks free from the deepest parts of my chest,

echoing around the cathedral chambers, mocking my pain as it reverberates against my ears.

*Weak, Sara. Do it.*

"Give me a reason," I say instead. "One good reason why I should let you live."

His eyes flare. "Because I love you."

I drop the knife.

The sound is loud as it clatters to the ground, but I barely hear the noise because the moment I let go, Tristan is reaching, his hands grabbing my body and dragging me into his lap, fisting the back of my hair as he consumes my mouth, my lips, my tongue, my soul.

I cry out against him, sinking into his hold, hating myself for being so weak but loving the way his touch soothes the pain.

# CHAPTER 45

## *Tristan*

HER TOUCH IS THE SWEETEST SURRENDER.

I decided long before ending up here that if she wished for me to die, I would lie down at her feet. I have no interest in fighting her. No interest in living if she doesn't wish for me to be.

No longer do I thirst for the throne. No more do I wish for vengeance on those who have wronged me.

It all pales in comparison to her.

Blood seeps down my neck from where her blade nicked my skin, and my cock pulses from her violence. She's an absolute vision in her rage, and when she drops the knife and falls into my arms, my chest implodes.

"Show me your pain, little doe. Give it to me so you don't bear it alone," I rasp against her mouth as I suck down her cries.

My hands claw at her clothing and she gives as good

as she gets until we end up bare, with her in my lap, fabrics tossed to the side, shredded and in forgotten piles. My dick slides between her pussy lips, desperate to sink inside her.

I fist her hair, pulling until her back bows like a pretzel, the ends of her curly strands grazing against the floor until her breasts are exposed, dark pink nipples begging to be sucked. I lean down like a ravenous animal and wrap my mouth around her pebbled flesh, growling when her taste explodes on my tongue, and she grinds her hot cunt along my shaft.

"Tristan," she pleads, her juices running down the length of me and pooling on the polished tiled floor of the cathedral. "Please, I—"

I release her nipple with a pop, sliding my tongue up her chest until I'm sucking on her neck, bringing the blood to the surface, not caring if I leave a mark, desperate to show the world that she belongs to no one else but me. To mark her skin like she's marked my soul.

Someone could walk in at any time, but I don't give a damn. Let them watch.

This isn't love. This is obsession. It's madness. It's salvation.

"Shh." I move my lips until they brush against hers. "I know what you need."

I let go of her hair, moving both my hands to grip her hips, and I raise her up, my cock angry and throbbing beneath her. And then her wet heat encases me from root to tip, her soft walls hugging every single ridge of my dick until my abs tense and I see stars just from the feel of being surrounded by her.

Her head flies back as she moans, rotating her hips in a figure eight, every motion making me leak.

She rides me so good, and this time it's *her* who rips me by the hair, the sting making me groan as her lips work their way down the front of my neck, sucking when they reach the thin cut on my throat.

I throb inside her.

"Yes," I hiss, bucking up and collapsing on my elbows, her body following as she continues to lick at the wound she made. "You filthy girl, riding my cock and licking up my blood like you're starved for me."

She moans again, the sound vibrating through me, and then she's moving until her back is straight, and her hands are cupping her breasts and tweaking the nipples until they stiffen into hard peaks. My abdomen clenches tight as I watch her throw her head back and squeeze her eyes shut, wondering how it's possible she exists—half convinced that I've gone mad and she's nothing more than a figment of my imagination.

Suddenly, the feeling is too much, and I shoot forward until our chests brush, her hips faltering in their rhythm. My fingers grip her cheeks. "Look at me."

Her perfect dark eyes spring open, and *Christ*, it makes me feel like the luckiest man to have her in my lap, on my cock, and in my goddamn veins. "Did you really think I would *ever* harm you?"

I punctuate my question with a sharp thrust into her slick heat, keeping myself pressed against her as she rotates her swollen core against my groin, her body shaking as her walls flutter around my dick.

A tear escapes the corner of her eye and trails down her cheek, and I lean in without thought, my tongue swiping out and licking it away.

Her sorrow is now my sorrow.

Her pain is now my pain.

"I will torture and maim any person who dares to even *think* your name," I say against her ear, holding her face against me while I continue to fuck her hard and slow.

She lets out a whimper, nodding her head as she leans in to claim my lips again in a bruising kiss, and my heart falters, needing to feel her deeper—wanting to somehow dig my way beneath her skin and stay there for eternity.

My hands leave her face and grab on to her hips instead, pushing her down until every single inch of my cock is buried deep inside her, but still, it's not enough.

I lift her off me, my shaft engorged and glistening with her arousal, raging as it escapes the warmth of her. Wrapping my arm around her waist, I spin her until she's bent over on all fours, her elbows on the edge of the raised dais. I sit back on my heels and soak in the vision, committing it to memory so I can tattoo it on my skin.

Her pretty little pussy is exposed, and she's leaned down as if she's bowing in prayer, the stained-glass windows sending sprinkles of colors across her perfect creamy skin and the deep wood of the crucifix looming heavily over our sins.

I move forward, slipping my fingers inside her needy cunt, curling them forward to find that soft, spongy spot that will make her come undone.

"Should I punish you for your lack of faith?" I ask, spreading my fingers apart before bringing them back together and curling them again.

She groans, her head dropping onto the backs of her hands, which push the cheeks of her ass out toward me. They're begging me to turn them red.

So I do.

I slip my fingers from inside her and use that same hand, slick with her juices, to whip across her skin, the crack resounding off the high arches of the church's ceilings. Heat collects at the base of my spine, and I have never been harder than I am right now, watching her skin ripple and turn pink from my hand.

Her fingers scrabble for purchase at the base of the altar, and her nails scratch against the floor.

"You've been a very bad girl, Sara." My hand rubs over my palm print, and she purrs, pushing herself farther into my hold.

*Crack.*

I smack her ass again, my cock leaking pre-ejaculate onto the floor.

It's filthy, and a thrill rushes through my veins as I imagine people kneeling right here as they take communion.

Groaning, my free hand grips the base of my shaft, holding back the urge to explode from the thought alone. I push forward until the purple head of my length slides along the outside of her core, hitting her sensitive bud. I bring my hand down a third time, and she yelps, wetness seeping from her hole and onto the skin of my dick.

My lips drag kisses up her spine as I lean over her, fisting her hair in my hand and wrenching her head back, forcing her body to rise until she's flush against me, my breath blowing in her ear.

"So pliable and submissive when you're on your knees and begging for my marks," I whisper.

Her body trembles, her thighs tightening as she pushes against me, jerking me off with her pussy lips. Back and forth she glides, rubbing herself on my straining erection, making my stomach tense with the need to bury myself as far inside her as I can go.

"Tell me you're mine," I demand. My hand moves from her hair around to grasp the front of her throat, her back rubbing against my chest and creating a delicious friction. I thrust my hips forward, my eager cock throbbing. "I'm a desperate man, Sara."

My fingers tighten around her throat, my other hand

wrapping around her waist and sliding down until I find her center, my thumb pressing against that perfect sweet, swollen bundle of nerves that's begging for me to rub against it until she blacks out from the pleasure.

"Tell me," I repeat. "And I'll make you come so hard you'll need me to piece you back together."

She sucks in a breath, and even the sound of her sigh sends arousal racing through me so fiercely that I bite my cheek until it bleeds.

"Yours," she whispers.

I slide inside her with one solid thrust.

Both of us groan, and I start a punishing pace, my balls slapping against her cunt and my hips clapping against the red and tender cheeks of her ass. My eyes drink her up, and heat coils around my entire body, making me wild with the need to come inside her, just a little, just to know what it's like.

My balls draw up until they're almost level with the base of my shaft, and I lean forward, rutting into her like an animal, my knees scraping against the stone floor until they bleed.

"Oh my god," she cries out, her body vibrating.

Is it possible to be jealous of God? Because when his name leaves her lips, I want to slit my wrists and fly up to his kingdom, just to burn it to the ground.

My hand cracks against the flesh again, harder this time, enraged that she would dare call his name when it's me breaking her apart. Angry that she would think to *kill* me before she gave me the pleasure of diving into her sweet cunt one last time. "You say *my* name when you're coming around my dick, *ma petite menteuse*. No one else's."

I wrap my arm around her waist, squeezing tightly and running the tips of my fingers down until they slip through her core, pinching her clitoris until she screams.

"Tristan!" she cries out again, her walls slicking with her cum as she tenses around my cock.

"That's right, little doe. It's *me* making you crazy. Only me. Only *ever* me."

And then she explodes, my name pouring from her lips, and that's all I can handle, my muscles coiling tight and my vision blanking out as thick jets of cum spew from my tip, pulsing as I coat the inside of her. My fingers dig into her hips, and I glance down, watching as thick white gobs seep out of her pussy and glide back down the shaft of my dick.

It's the most beautiful sight I've ever seen.

Panting and spent, I collapse on top of her back, leaving lazy kisses along her spine and knowing, without a doubt, that she's the only thing that's ever mattered and the only thing that ever will.

# CHAPTER 46

## *Sara*

TRISTAN'S FINGERS TRAIL UP MY ARMS, HIS front pressed against my naked back as we lie in his bed. It's the first time I've been in his room, but it's exactly as I imagined it would be; rich burgundy furniture and black silk sheets. Remnants of his cum stick to the insides of my thighs, but I'm too exhausted to clean it up, my mind and body waging a war inside me, collecting the last particles of my energy and grinding them to dust. My ass is raw and my emotions are spread thin. And I still feel unsettled.

But I won't lie to myself. I can't kill him, even though I know I should.

Whether that makes me a selfish woman or a weak one, I'm not sure.

Maybe it makes me both.

"What happened to Timothy…" he blurts.

My lungs cramp up tight.

"I didn't send them there," he continues. "I expressly forbade them to touch you."

His words trickle through me and root around in my chest, trying to find a place to settle. I believe him, and that probably makes me the stupidest woman to ever live, but if he feels even a fraction of what I feel for him, then I don't doubt for a moment he never meant to harm me.

I held a blade to his jugular and still couldn't follow through.

"My father was my best friend," I blurt out, rolling on my back until I'm caged between his arms. "He taught me from a young age that just because I was a girl, that didn't mean I needed to be meek and mild."

Tristan smirks. "He taught you well."

I narrow my eyes, swallowing around the sickness that talking about my father causes in the depths of my gut.

"Yeah, well, he was a duke. Did you know that?"

"I did." He nods, his fingertips tracing along the edge of my hairline.

"He loved our people. So when the funds stopped coming, the businesses shut down, and the people lost their homes...he was sick over it." I swallow. "He used to hand me bits of money he could scrounge together and warm wool clothes and send me out in the thick of night to take them to people in need."

"Sounds like a great man."

"He was." The knot swells in my throat. "When he

died, the grief overwhelmed me, but more than that, I remember drowning in anger."

"I know that feeling well," he replies.

"All he wanted was to ask for help." My teeth clench. "He traveled here to Saxum and bent the knee, all to beg for your brother to just *see* us, because for so many years, we'd been brushed aside and forgotten."

My hand reaches up to cup Tristan's face, trailing over the raised edges of his scar, feeling the ridges and marred flesh beneath the pads of my fingers. He flinches, but he doesn't pull away. Instead, he leans into it. I flick my gaze to the tattoo on his chest. The jackal on top of bones with a phrase scrawled underneath. *I should have known from that alone.* I was so enamored with the words, I didn't take in the rest.

"Coming here was supposed to be vengeance against those who took him from me."

I expect to see surprise filter through his eyes, but there isn't any to be found. Just warmth and understanding. It makes holding on to my anger incredibly difficult, and a bit chips away, falling to the ground and smashing into pieces.

"My cousin brought me in to marry your brother…but you know that already, of course."

His eyes harden, his grip tightening from where it rests on my waist. "He cannot have you."

"He never will," I respond, hesitating before I continue.

"I saw you when I followed Sheina and Paul last night to the shadowed lands."

He nods, again with no surprise lighting across his face. "I know."

Tears well in my eyes, even though I thought they had long since dried. "I *saw* you, Tristan."

"I know," he repeats, his gaze never leaving mine.

"You have my cousin caged."

His mouth parts then, blowing out a deep breath, his fingers pausing from where they flick against my skin. "Not anymore, little doe."

My heart stutters, but it's slight. "You killed him?"

"Would it help if I said he deserved it?"

Maybe I should be enraged, but I'm not. I barely feel anything at all. Truthfully, I was never close with Xander, only having met him once or twice when I was a child. The relationship between us was built on loyalty to family, but as I imagine Tristan ending his life, I can't find it in me to care.

Turns out some things bind thicker than blood.

"What did he do?" I ask.

"Killed my father." He says it with no hesitation, no inflection in his tone. It's just stated as fact.

The words tremble against the wall that still sits between us, keeping me from giving in to whatever this is. No matter how badly I may want to.

"And you killed mine."

His brows draw down, eyes flashing.

My hand cups his face. "So you see, Tristan, I *can't* love you. Because loving you means forgetting him."

"Little doe—"

"Nicknames and sweet words won't change the truth, okay?" My bottom lip quivers, my sutured-up heart tearing at the seams. I slide from under his grasp and push up on his bed until I'm sitting, slapping my hands down on the mattress. "What else do you want from me? What else can I give? You have taken *everything* from me, and yet you want my heart too?"

He pounces, his body looming over me, his aura pressing in and his face dark and drawn. "Yes," he says. "Yes. I want it all. I want everything. I demand it."

"Well, too bad," I spit, shoving at his chest.

He grips my wrists before I can move them away and pulls me into him. I kick out, my feet hitting the bone of his shin until he sucks in a hiss, and I flail, trying to break free from his grasp. Chuckling, he tugs me close, rolling us until I'm pinned beneath him, his body weight keeping me flush to the bed. His legs tangle around mine, and his hands push into my arms as he presses them above my head.

It's a precarious position, and one that has heat spreading through my core and pulsing in my center, whether I want it to or not.

"You are *mine*, Sara." He punctuates his words with a sharp thrust of his hips. "And if I have to sink my cock inside you every morning and spank your ass until it's bruised every night just so you feel me with every step, that's what I'll do."

I scoff. "Please. You don't *own* me."

He grins. "Now who's the liar, *ma petite menteuse*?" He thrusts himself against me again, and my traitorous legs fall open, giving him more room.

Leaning down, he sucks my bottom lip into his mouth, kissing me with teeth and tongue and spit. It's sloppy. Messy. Everything that I crave but nothing I can have.

"I've killed many men," he whispers against me. "And I remember the face of every single one, soaking their images into my brain as they pray to me for absolution."

"You have a complex," I sneer.

"Sara, I didn't kill your father."

I stop fighting against his hold, growing slack in his arms, confusion racing through me as my brows draw down. "No, you did. My uncle told me it was you. He—"

"Wants to take the crown," he cuts in.

I'd love to deny it, and for the next few moments, that's what I do. I search every single crevice of my memory, trying to drag up something that proves his innocence. That proves he would never. He was so *convincing* in his plan for me to kill the rebel king, and if even *that* wasn't genuine, then I wonder if I really have known him at all.

My uncle has been like a second father to me. But he's also been the one in my ear at every turn, fanning the flames of my fire and directing them on where to go. *Was everything manipulation for his end goal?*

"You were their scapegoat, little doe. The one who would take the fall for the murders of the monarch and blaze the path for them to steal the crown."

My chest cramps. "What?" I shake my head, disbelief pouring like icy rain through my body.

His fingers press against my lips, brushing over them in a soft caress. "You know I don't wish to hurt you."

"No, they wouldn't," I say again. "*He* wouldn't. I'm his family."

Even as I say the words, the truth sinks into my bones, making them ache, and I know.

I am such a foolish woman.

Sympathy coasts through his eyes. "*I'll* be your family now, little doe."

My chest feels heavy, and my soul feels worn, but there's also a sense of relief that lifts a burden from my shoulders, the chains tying me to the Beatreaux name breaking away and smashing as they fall to the ground.

"Swear it," I plead. "Swear to me, on your father's grave, that you speak the truth."

He cups my cheek. "I swear it on my father's grave, Sara. I will only *ever* tell you the truth."

My gaze moves back to his, my heart swelling as I stare into his perfect face. "Did you mean it when you said you love me?" I ask.

He sighs, moving my arm from above my head and resting it over his racing heart. "I've only ever wanted one thing in my entire life: the throne. I've been plotting and planning for so long, I can't remember what life was like before. And I'm so close, Sara. *So close* to victory."

My stomach tightens.

"But you…" He licks his lips. "You could burn down the entire kingdom until it's nothing but charred rubble, and I would crawl over the embers with glee, so long as I could worship at your feet."

My insides quake from the magnitude of his words.

"If that's love, then yes, I love you." He lifts a shoulder. "I can't feel anything *but* loving you."

I bite back the emotion that's stampeding through my chest, lifting my hand to push the stray hair off his forehead. My breathing stutters, and I know that with my next words, everything will change. "I love you too."

His eyes darken, and his cock pulses against my center.

"And it would be such a shame not to see you wear the crown."

# CHAPTER 47

## *Tristan*

"WHAT ARE YOU DRAWING?" SIMON'S VOICE cuts through my concentration, and on instinct I jerk away, trying to hide the work in progress from his view.

He grins at me, his gap-toothed smile making something loosen in my chest, and I lean back against the bark of the weeping willow, watching as he plops down next to me, laying his toy sword at his side and peering over my arm again, trying to get a good view.

"Is that lady?" he asks when I don't respond fast enough.

I hesitate for many reasons, the foremost being that Simon is ten years old. He has loose lips without meaning to, and I'm unsure what will happen if he runs and tells his mother that the prince was drawing pictures of the king's fiancée. I have no clue whether she's still warming Michael's bed, but there are many people in this kingdom who will take information and use it to give themselves an advantage, no matter how trustworthy they seem. And I don't trust Simon's mother as far as I can throw her. Anyone who allows their child to be beaten and bullied or doesn't mind if they run through tunnels all day long doesn't deserve to *have* a child.

My chest pulls with anger, memories from years ago resurfacing when I think of similarities between how he's treated and what I went through back then.

"It is," I reply, hoping I haven't made a mistake.

Because as much as I've claimed Sara—as much as I know that she's mine—we still need to hide away in secret until my carefully laid plans come to fruition.

Michael has sent troops to the southern border, just as I suggested. The privy council is up in arms, but at the end of the day, they aren't king. He is.

For now.

My stomach cramps in excitement and anticipation, feeling like I can almost breathe for the first time in years. I was willing to give it all up, to let it all go, run away with Sara, and never look back. But then she said those words. Those perfect, magical, beautiful words: how she wanted me to wear the crown. My soul exploded as I slid my cock deep inside her and fucked her silly while she called me her king.

After we were sated, she placed her head on my chest and asked about the rebels, and I told her of my goals. We planned and plotted until the early morning hours, my heart straining against its cage with every whispered word, not realizing how much I ached to have her this way. As my equal. As my *queen*.

"She's pretty when you draw her, but she's prettier in person," Simon notes.

"She is," I confirm again.

He's quiet for a few moments, and then he glances out at the gates as they open up, a set of three automobiles driving through into the front courtyard and rolling to a stop, my heart pulling tight in my chest, knowing that Sara is in one of them, most likely on the arm of my brother, so close yet so far away.

My jaw clenches at the thought of them.

"Do you think that one day, maybe *I'll* be able to have a lady?" Simon asks.

I break my stare away from the cars, looking to him instead, my brows rising. "You can have anything you dare to dream of, little tiger."

He nods before his eyes shutter. "Well…then…do you think maybe one day, I can have a dad?"

My stomach rolls and I lean my head back against the trunk of the tree, tapping my fingers on my knee as I stare at him, having no clue what to say. "Having a father is overrated. Trust me, I speak from experience."

He chews on his lip, his enormous amber eyes wide and trusting. "Do you think maybe you could do it?"

My heart squeezes.

"No one would have to know," he rushes out, his tone hopeful. "It'd just be pretend anyway. And it could be fun! Like...like now, only you tell me you love me and teach me how to be a man."

"I don't think your mother would approve." I chuckle through the ache that's digging its way through my chest as I reach out to ruffle the top of his head.

He scoffs, his eyes going to the ground, disappointment drooping his shoulders. "Mama wouldn't even notice."

"I tell you what." I sigh, closing the sketchbook and placing it to my side before turning to face him. "I can't be your father, but I'll always be your friend."

"Yeah, okay," he mumbles, his toe kicking the blades of grass.

"There's a secret place my father used to take me at the cliff's edge at the back of the castle. One day soon, I'll take you there. And I'll teach you everything I know."

His eyes light up, that gap-toothed grin coming back full force. "Promise?"

Laughter from across the courtyard draws my attention away before I respond, and even though I know what I'll witness, even though I expected it, white fiery rage surges through my body regardless.

Michael and Sara pose for a cameraman, his arm wrapped around her waist and his fingers gripping her tight to his side.

My teeth grind until they threaten to break in half, and

I have to restrain myself from standing up and going over to rip his fingers off her. But I breathe deep, reaching in my pocket and pulling out a joint instead, allowing the hash to buzz through my veins and do its best attempt at keeping the jealousy at bay. It doesn't work, the feeling slamming into my chest and spreading like a poison until everything I see is tinged in green.

She twists her head, glancing around the courtyard as if she can sense that I'm near, and then she locks her gaze on me. I hold her stare, my dick straining and my insides seething with the need to stake my claim.

I want to grab her from his hold and bend her over the hood of my brother's favorite automobile, flipping up her skirts and impaling her deep on my cock until she screams out my name and gives everyone else a show.

Maybe then he'd know better than to put his mangy hands on her.

I've come on her and *in* her and told her she was mine. Yet he's the one who gets to parade her around to the world.

And when he leans in, his arm tightening around her waist and bending her backward to kiss her on the lips, I lose it, shooting to a stand so fast that Simon jolts from the movement, my vision blurring to everything except the murderous rage that's pouring through my insides.

# CHAPTER 48

## *Sara*

I'VE BEEN WAITING FOR HIM. I KNEW IT WAS only a matter of time after Michael bent me backward and pressed his thin lips to mine.

But what I didn't expect was for him to not show up for hours, until the dead of the night, and then storm into my quarters without even knocking.

"Tristan." My hand shoots to my chest, the other tightening around my water cup as he rushes across the room with fire in his eyes. "What are you—"

He walks into me, the glass in my hand dropping to the ground and shattering as he shoves me against the wall, his lips claiming mine in a brutal kiss. I moan, my arms flying up to wrap around his shoulders as he consumes me, his body pressing against mine as he licks inside my mouth, his hands roaming over my sides like he can't bear the thought of not touching me.

"You let him put his hands on you," he rasps, his voice tortured and low.

"What would you have had me do?" I whisper back as he sucks and bites down the length of my neck. I tilt my head to give him better access, my core pulsing with need, his possessiveness spreading arousal through my insides, loving the way it feels to be wanted so desperately by someone with so much power.

"It makes me *crazy*, Sara." His grip turns bruising, and then he's ripping my red nightgown from my body until I'm naked and bared before him, goose bumps spreading along my skin. "I can't stand it."

My hand runs down the front of his chest, my heart pounding with sudden desperation to prove to him that no one else has me, that I *only* belong to him. His nostrils flare as he glares at me, the rings of his fingers glinting as I drop to my knees, reaching out to undo his slacks, my mouth watering at the thought of having his thickness in my hand and on my tongue.

"I'm yours, Tristan." I rub my palm up the length of his growing erection, excitement skipping through my chest when it hardens beneath my touch.

He fists my hair, the way I know he loves to do, his other hand reaching under my jaw and tipping up my chin until I'm staring him in the eyes.

"Take it out," he growls.

My center throbs and I slip my hand beneath the

waistline of his slacks, underneath his underwear, until I grip his shaft, feeling it hot and hard as a rock in my palm. I run my fingers along him, and he sucks in a deep breath, gripping the strands tight as I pull him from his pants. My stomach tenses as it bobs in front of me, and I lean forward, opening my mouth to devour him whole.

His grasp tightens on my hair and he pulls me back, his hand coming down to grip his own cock, stroking it from the root to the tip.

"You love being on your knees for me, don't you?" he asks, moving in sure motions up and down the length of himself. I nod, licking my lips as I watch his balls tense and release while he manipulates his flesh. He brings the head of it down and slaps it against the tops of my breasts, leaving behind a string of arousal from the tip of his cock. The act itself is so dirty that it makes my cunt drip down my legs, desperate to have him fill it.

He rubs the tip in the small puddle he left behind before dragging it up to my neck, repositioning it so it rests on my lips. I can't help but peek my tongue out and lick up his essence, moaning when the salty flavor hits my taste buds.

"Open your mouth." His fingers flex in my hair, drawing my head back more.

I obey. Not because I'm weak and not because I have no choice but because surrendering to him makes me happy. Powerful. It's intoxicating, owning the passion of a man like Tristan, so I'll worship him like a god because I know he does the same with me.

I'm his equal.

And right now, I'm his *whore*.

He slides his cock inside the open hole of my warm, waiting mouth, hissing as I leave it wide so he can see every inch as it slides inside. My insides flutter and my core tenses, wanting to watch from my knees as he comes apart down my throat.

I'm ravenous for it.

I don't think I'll survive if I can't have it.

His hips thrust forward, the tattoos on his forearms coming alive while his muscles tense. The vein on the underside of his shaft throbs as he slides it along my tongue, and I have to stop myself from closing my lips around him—from sucking him as deep as I can take.

Instead, I wait for him to give me direction, knowing he'll take what he needs.

His fingers tighten their grip, creating a delicious sting that strikes through my middle and pulses between my legs.

"Suck."

It's one word, but the second he says what to do, I'm there, running my tongue around his silky shaft, feeling him throb as I hollow out my cheeks, wanting to milk his dick until cum bursts in my mouth.

He groans, his other hand flying up to meet his first

on the back of my head, and he thrusts in and out. His eyes are half-lidded but they never leave mine, and I swear I'm close to coming apart without even being touched, just from watching him fuck my mouth.

I've done this act before, but it's never felt like this.

"Look at you," he whispers, his fingers caressing down my face until they grip the base of my chin. "So pretty on your knees while I choke you with my cock."

He surges forward as he says the word and hits the back of my throat. I *do* choke, only a little, but the discomfort ratchets my arousal higher, making my cunt squeeze against air, wishing it was wrapping around the length of him and feeling him paint my insides.

"You love it, don't you, filthy girl? I bet if I put my fingers in your pussy, it would drench my hand with how sopping and eager it is to take me." He thrusts again, and this time, I suck harder, swirling my tongue around the throbbing vein that runs on the underside of his sensitive length. Groaning, he pulls his hips out until his heavy erection bobs in the air, tensing and growing right in front of me.

He closes his eyes, breathing deep.

And then he grips himself with his hand and smacks me with it. It's nothing more than a light tap, but the act itself sends shock waves of tension rippling through my middle, and I lose control of my limbs, my fingers sliding down into my begging cunt, finding it sopping and wet, just the way he said it would be.

His eyes flare as he watches, his fingers stroking up and down his spit-soaked shaft, and he groans as I finger myself, my insides coiling tight until I'm on the edge of an explosion.

"That's it, my little liar. Fuck yourself on your fingers and imagine it's my cock." He bends down. "Spread your thighs and show me how bad you want it."

I'm not sure if it's his words, the sound of his voice, or the fact that it's just *him* telling me to do something, but when I do as he says, my body seizes up tight, pleasure skittering through my insides as my walls contract so intensely that it hurts. My vision blacks out and I fall forward on my knees, bliss exploding inside me and coating my every nerve.

He catches me by the face, my chin held in his grip as he continues to jerk himself off. I'm malleable beneath him, a willing servant begging for every drop.

His face scrunches up and I can see the moment his balls pump, the vein in his cock pulsing as the cum pushes up through his shaft and explodes from his tip, showering me with his orgasm. I moan, the hot liquid pouring onto my skin, and when he drops to his knees, I get on all fours and crawl toward him, remembering the fire in his eyes when I did it before, diving down and swallowing him whole, small spurts of his cum spraying down my throat.

He groans, his hands gripping my hair as he spasms against my tongue, and I continue to lick him clean until he's spent, softening in my mouth.

Finally, I slip him out of me, sitting back as I stare at him, warm and gooey love filling up my chest. He leans forward, tangling our mouths together so our breaths become one, and I lose sight of where he ends and I begin.

"Don't shower before you go to him tomorrow," he demands, pecking my lips between words. "I want him to smell me on your skin."

I nod. I've felt loyalty before; it runs through my veins deep. It used to beat for family, for duty. For my people.

But with Tristan? I would light myself on fire and revel in the burn if I knew it would please him. It's a scary feeling but one that I embrace, because he is my king and I am his queen and together we will rule the world.

He moves from beneath me and stands, grabbing his pants and stepping into them. I move also, walking over to the hook that has my night robe and grabbing it. Before I can put it on, he slaps it out of my hand, wrapping his arm around my waist and lifting me up as he walks us toward my bed and throws me down.

I bounce when I hit the mattress, and he smirks, crawling between my legs, his hands spreading them wide, tingles spreading up my body as he does. And it's only then I realize he has a pen in his hand. The ink is cool as it bleeds from the tip of the ballpoint onto my skin, and my heart spasms in my chest.

"What are you doing?" I whisper.

"Branding you," he replies.

His face is serious, his eyes focused and hands weaving magic, and I've never been more attracted to this man in my life as I am with him lying between my legs and drawing artwork on my thigh.

"Should we talk about tomorrow night?" I ask, my stomach jumbling from anxiety at the thought of the plans we've made.

His jaw tenses, his movement faltering before he resumes drawing lines on my skin. "I'd rather not. The thought of it makes me want to tie you to my bed and never let you leave."

My heart warms, knowing that he's just as nervous as I am over what we've talked about. "Everything will work out." I rub my hand over the top of his hair. "Tomorrow night, I'll go to your brother and convince him to take me to his quarters."

His grip grows tight enough to bruise.

"And then you will be there," I soothe. "Before anything can happen. And I will have slipped laudanum into his drink."

"It's too risky."

"There is no reward if you don't take a risk, my love." I reach down, my hand touching his cheek. "I trust you. I believe in you. Let me *help* you."

He continues drawing, although he leans into my touch. "I don't wish to use you this way."

"It's the easiest plan, Tristan. *Please.* I can do this. And before he can even blink, you'll gather the rebels and come find me." My heart kicks in anticipation, sick and twisted excitement bleeding through my pores. "You'll take what's yours. And your people will be behind you, ridding you of any person who wishes to keep you from the crown."

His eyes snap up. "*Our* people."

Emotion swells in my chest. "Our people," I correct.

He blows out a shaky breath and leans in, leaving a light kiss on my thigh, his fingers smoothing over it after, before he sits back, grinning at his art.

I push up on my elbows and stare down at what he drew.

It's a heart. Not the kind that you see kids draw or the type that you would expect in paintings that depict love. This one is of the organ, blood dripping off its edges and vessels running through the muscle. A thick chain wraps around its center and coils beneath it, a padlock on the end. I squint my eyes and look closer, realizing there's writing on the lock.

*Tristan's Property.*

I scoff, shoving at his shoulders. "Romantic."

He lets out a small laugh, sliding up my body and pressing a kiss to my lips, his hand gripping my face. "For you? I'm barbaric. And after tomorrow, when we kill Michael and seize the castle, I'm going to fuck you while his spirit is still in the room, just so he knows you never belonged to him." His other hand skims up the inside of my thigh, resting on top of the bleeding heart. "And then I'll tattoo this on your skin so you never forget I own you as much as you own me."

I lean in and press my lips to his again, passion surging through my center and exploding through my pores until it wraps around us both. It's intense and I'm not sure if it will lift us up or burn us down.

But either way, it consumes me.

# CHAPTER 49

## *Sara*

MY NERVES ARE AT AN ALL-TIME HIGH. Before, when I was planning on killing the king, it was personal. And while it still is, now it's mutated, tinged with devotion. As crazy as that sounds.

But it's *devotion* that makes me slip the laudanum in the small pocket sewn into the hem of my skirt, and its devotion that has me batting my eyelashes and whispering soft words into Michael's ear, asking if we can go somewhere private.

Tristan has proven time and time again that if I fall, he will catch me. That if I break, he will hold the pieces until I'm ready to stitch them back again. So I'll do the same for him and stand by his side, helping him claim the throne. Helping him seek his vengeance.

I ache with every move like he's still perched between my thighs, taste him on my lips as though he's resting on my tongue, feel him in my veins as if he's fed me all his blood.

We are intrinsic. Fated. Destined.

Or maybe we're simply mad.

But I'll gladly live insane if in the end, it gives me him.

"How was dinner?" Michael asks as he sits next to me on the couch in his private quarters. The fireplace crackles in front of us, and the sheepskin rug is soft beneath the pads of my feet. It's untoward for me to be here before the wedding, but Xander isn't here anymore to speak sense to the king, and Michael thinks with his cock and not with his head when it comes to women.

It was just as easy as I thought it would be.

I smile, lowering my lids to half-mast as I stare at him through my lashes. "It was delicious."

He smirks, his hand landing heavy on my thigh and rubbing over Tristan's mark.

"I hope you still have room for dessert?" he asks.

My stomach is in my throat as I continue, knowing that after this, there's no turning back. "Actually, I'd love some more wine."

"Of course." He twists around to grab the bottle on the table to his side and I take my chance, uncorking the laudanum and trickling it in his glass before he turns around, sweat beading on my brow and my heart slamming so fast against my ribs that I feel as though I may have a coronary.

He twists back, pouring the wine into my glass until

it's almost full. I watch it swirl around, splashing against the bottom of the crystal, imagining that it must be similar to how my insides look as they flip and churn, threatening to spill over with anxiety.

He sets down the bottle, and I lean forward, grabbing both glasses, handing his over before taking mine. "Thank you, sire."

He sits back, staring at me for long moments, his eyes intense, and for the first time all evening, a trickle of unease swims through my veins. Michael has never looked at me this way before.

"I tire of games," he says. "Are you here to give yourself to me, Sara?"

The thought alone sends bile surging through my throat, but I grin through the nausea, knowing that Tristan will be here in less than an hour, and he'll wash all the filthy feelings away.

I run my fingers along my collarbone, tangling in the thin chain of my father's pendant, while my eyes flick to the wine in his hand—the one that he still hasn't taken a sip from.

"I just thought we could get to know each other better." I smile, scooting closer to him on the couch. "We'll be married soon. Don't you think it's time?"

He smirks, setting down the glass, and I curse internally, frustration wrapping tight around my middle, squeezing until it feels as though I'll burst.

His arm reaches out, wrapping around my waist and dragging me into him. My hands fly out to gain purchase on his chest, and I grip the fabric, my ass practically sitting in his lap. I swallow around the disgust lodging itself in my sternum.

"What is it you'd like to know?" he murmurs, leaning his head down and skimming his lips across my skin.

I play my part—even though, God, it feels as though doing so is the worst type of betrayal—leaning into it, knowing I need to make it convincing. Tristan is depending on me. My hands move to Michael's face, pulling his eyes up to meet mine. I graze my nose against his. "Everything."

He pulls me flush on top of him now, and my mouth sours with vomit as he grinds his hips into me, his erection digging into my center. He groans as he does it, his fingers tightening from where they're wrapped around my waist, and I throw my head back, pretending as though what he's doing is exciting.

Suddenly, he stops, his eyes like two amber pits of fire, and he reaches out to the table, grabbing his glass of wine. Relief trickles through me. But then he pushes the glass against my lips, and panic spreads through my chest.

*A small sip should be fine. As long as he drinks the rest.*

I open my mouth, just a crack, but before I can stop him, he's gripping my chin and tipping the entire glass of liquid until it pours down my throat and I choke and sputter, my eyes growing wide and frantic as I attempt to spit it out.

His face drops into a sneer. I move to scramble off his chest, but he grips me by the hair, yanking it until it rips from my head as he stands, dragging me until my knees scrape across the floor, my fingers digging into the skin of his wrist as I flail, trying to break free.

"You stupid woman, did you think I wouldn't know?"

"I don't—"

He throws me to the ground, and I tumble, my arm screaming in pain as it slams against the wood. I flip onto my back, pushing myself up with my hands, but I don't get far, his palm swinging down and cracking across my face until my body flies, skidding across the ground. My hip throbs from the impact.

He leans over me. "I *always* know." He grabs me by the arm and pulls me to a stand, wincing from the deep ache blooming across my cheek, no doubt already swelling from where he backhanded me.

I reach down, attempting to lift my skirts and grab a blade, but he grips my hand, squeezing until my bones crunch.

"Don't do something you'll regret. I'd hate to punish you in front of your lover."

My heart drops. *Tristan.*

He pulls me into his front, fingers tracing along my hairline. I turn my head away, gritting my teeth. "Would you like to go see him? He's being kept comfortable, I assure you."

"You lie," I spit, not wanting to believe what I can feel in my stomach is true.

He smirks. "Out of the two of us, *I* am not the liar here." I try to flail from his grasp, but he grips my shoulders. "Come tie her hands," he demands.

My head grows woozy and my movements sluggish as the effects of the laudanum start to grab hold of my psyche, and my breathing stalls, wondering who he's speaking to. And then my hands are wrenched behind me and cuffed in metal before I can even blink.

Despair works its way through me. *This is not supposed to happen.*

Michael smiles, releasing me, before putting his arm out and dragging someone into his side. And when he does, my organs scream and curdle, withering as if they poured acid through my insides.

"Hello, milady."

I clench my jaw, tears of betrayal stinging the backs of my lids. "Ophelia."

"You know," Michael states, "the best decision I've made since your arrival was telling my sweet Ophelia to keep her eyes and ears open." He glances down at her, tipping up her chin as he presses a kiss to her lips. "You've done so well, sweetheart."

She beams at him, and my stomach folds in on itself, because of course. I should have known. Didn't I even think of them being at my side, hoping to secure favor with the king?

"You're a phenomenal actress," I tell her, hatred brewing deep in my gut.

She grins at me, tipping her head. "Thank you, milady. I learned from the best."

I smirk, even though the opium is creating a buzzing sort of calm, making me drowsy. I fight it with everything in me, not wanting to give in to the tincture until I'm sure Tristan is safe.

"Although, His Majesty and I," she continues, her hand rubbing at his chest as she stares up at him, "we're much better at being discreet than you and the scarred prince. Pity you didn't pay closer attention."

I huff out a laugh, because I can't disagree. Clearly, somewhere, somehow, we went terribly wrong.

"Most nights, I would hide in the darkened corners of the halls, waiting and watching. Usually it was boring. Sometimes, when I would follow you, I'd get a show." She giggles. "I thought it was going to be so easy to get rid of you when that idiot Claudius slipped his hand up your skirts."

"That was *you* I heard?" I gasp out, my heart rate slowing as the drug sloshes through me.

She nods. "But then the scarred prince had to ruin it. Stealing him away and doing God knows what to him."

My chest cramps. *Tristan was there?*

"And then it was back to watching. And waiting." She sighs, and Michael's hand strokes up and down her arm.

"But last night, I saw him storm into your room. Heard you both doing *treasonous* things."

Rage circles through me, that she was there, tarnishing our precious moments.

"It was so easy to press my head against your door and listen to the words you spoke." She smiles. "You really have yourself to thank."

*Stupid. I'm so stupid.*

Michael claps his hands together in glee, a smile stretching across his face from ear to ear. "Speaking of my brother, shall we go pay him a visit? I'm sure he's desperate to make sure you're okay."

# CHAPTER 50

## *Tristan*

SEARING PAIN SPREADS FROM MY SHOULDERS and extends through my entire body, the type of which I've never felt before. My arms are tied behind my back and slung over a wood beam that's been placed in the middle of the courtyard. Occasionally, a guard walks over and pulls, forcing my body to rise off the ground by mere inches.

But I won't give them the satisfaction of screaming.

I was woken in the rudest way. With a cloth full of chloroform and half a dozen guards.

And now they've taken to strappado. A form of torture that's Edward's personal favorite. It gives him a thrill to watch the agony spread across his victim's faces as their shoulders become dislocated and their limbs slowly tear from their bodies. Part of me wonders if this is his doing. If he's finally betrayed me and is seeking his revenge for the just punishment he reaped at my hands.

But he's nowhere to be found.

It doesn't matter. *Nothing* matters except for the fear that courses through my insides at the thought of Michael having Sara.

They can kill me. They can torture me for hours and I'll sacrifice myself gladly, so long as I know she's safe.

I'm not sure how long has passed, only that the sun has set, the full moon casting an eerie glow, the chilly night-time air sticking to my clammy, bruised skin and a bonfire raging only a few feet away.

It's cocky of Michael to place me here, but my brother loves to put on a good show.

My head is pounding and blood drips from cuts in my torso where I was kicked and dragged by the guards, but I have long since leaned into the pain, letting it become part of me until I'm numb. After a lifetime of being beaten black and blue, physical pain loses its edge.

"Surprise," my brother's voice booms, sparking an ember in the center of my gut.

"Brother," I force out through the dryness of my mouth and the throbbing ache in my shoulders. "So nice of you to show."

He laughs, a deep chuckle straight from his belly, and when I lift my head, the ember ignites into an inferno, scorching through every part of me. Sara is with him, her hands cuffed behind her and her dress torn on the side. *But she's alive.*

Her gaze is unfocused, and her cheek is red.

I have hated my brother for many things, but it isn't until right now, this moment, that pure and absolute loathing pours into my veins.

"Surprised?" Michael grins wide. "I thought you two would want to be reunited. One last time."

I grit my teeth, my eyes never leaving Sara's. Her movements are sluggish and stilted, but when her gaze locks on mine, energy wraps around the beating organ in my chest and shocks it into a faster rhythm. I'm sure I will meet my death, and I will welcome it with open arms, as soon as I make sure Sara won't have the same fate.

What good is a world without her in it?

"You've always been a gracious host," I snark.

His grin drops, turning into a sneer, his amber gaze narrowed as he drops Sara to the ground and walks toward me, not stopping until I can see the black specks in his eyes. "What am I going to do with you?"

I smile. "You could always kill me, maybe turn me into a trophy to place in your room."

He tsks, walking to the side and grabbing something from the guard's hands before walking back over. When he arrives, I realize it's a fire poker, the same type he used to give me the scar that became my namesake, only now, the end is bright orange from sitting in the open flame.

My insides tense.

"Maybe I'll flay the skin from your bones," Michael

spits, holding up the poker and watching as it glows. "Use you as a rug in my bedroom so even in death you never forget your place."

"Oh, Brother." I grin. "We both know that even *in death*, I'll haunt you. Just like our father does."

His eyes rage and his hand jabs forward, the hot brand searing into my chest, directly over the jackal tattoo, the smell of burning flesh curling into the air as I bite down on my tongue so hard that blood floods my mouth.

"Tristan!" Sara cries out from where she's still sprawled on the ground, although her voice is muddled.

"I should have known it was you. Running to gather the rest of the freaks to band behind you." Michael laughs. "What did you think, that you would rule Gloria Terra? That you would kill *me*?!" His voice rises, manic in its high pitch and tone.

Finally, he removes the metal from my skin, the burn so powerful it makes my eyes blur from the pain.

He steps in close, the fire poker hanging at his side. Leaning in, he rests his forehead against mine. "Blood of my blood, you have done *so* much to bring shame to our name. When I rid you from this earth, the angels will sing in heaven, and our ancestors will cheer with joy."

My chest pulls tight, knowing that he's won, and there's nothing to be done for it.

It's over.

"I'm going to leave you here to think about what you've

done," he whispers. "And I want you to know that while my guards are prodding and poking until the rest of your skin is as scarred as your face, I'll be ripping your lying slut of a woman apart piece by piece."

"When I am free of this," I say, swallowing around the scratch in my throat, "I will kill you for touching her."

Michael cackles, throwing his head back, his hand resting on his chest. "Oh, Brother. I'm not going to *touch* her. I'm going to fill every hole until it gapes and tears, until my seed seeps from the bleeding wounds I've created in her tight little body. I'm going to erase your existence within her and replace it with my own, right before I cut out her heart and feed it to you for dinner." He presses the poker against my other side now.

And this time, I *do* let out a scream. A guttural roar, promising violence and reeking of pain, my chest exploding until the rage floods through my body like water rushing from a broken dam.

"And then I'll kill you too, and we'll go on here in Gloria Terra as if you never existed at all." He blows the tips of his fingers and pops them open. "*Poof.* Just like that."

My eyes roam the grass until they fall on Sara's form. She's unconscious now, and my heart falters. "Sara," I rasp, although my entire body burns from the word. "Sara!" I yell louder, desperate for her to move, for her to show me she still breathes. But she doesn't.

She lies there instead.

"Maybe if you pray hard enough, Brother, they'll reunite you two in the afterlife." Michael smiles and then passes the poker off to a guard on his right. "Stick him every hour until he begs for death."

# CHAPTER 51

## *Sara*

THIS IS MY FIRST TIME IN THE DUNGEONS, and they're exactly as I expected them to be. Dark and dreary and smelling of must.

My head pounds from the remnants of the laudanum, and I clank my chained-up wrists against the dank stone wall, knowing they're much too strong for me to break.

I have no clue how long it's been. I'm not sure if Tristan is still alive, although as insane as it sounds, I think I'd know if he was no longer in the land of the living.

Despite everything, there's still a small ember of hope flickering in my chest, and that keeps me holding on.

All is not lost until it is *lost*.

A door slams open and small cracks of light filter through the iron-barred window of the concrete door. My stomach cramps, icy tendrils of fear worming through my psyche as I wonder if it's the king coming to claim retribution for my sins against him. Or maybe it's a guard wanting to take advantage of a chained-up girl with no way to escape.

Turns out, it's neither.

The cell door swings open, and Marisol, wide-eyed and wild-haired, rushes in, her hand covering her mouth as a muffled sob breaks free. She runs over and scans me from head to toe.

"Marisol," I croak, my voice shaky and strained.

"Milady," she whispers. There's a key in her hand, and relief pours through me until I shake. "Quiet. We have little time." She looks behind her as she unlocks my chains, blood rushing through my limbs as they drop to the ground. I wince as the feeling comes back into my extremities and I heave myself forward onto my knees, gritting my teeth through the ache of my muscles as I push myself to a stand.

"How?" I ask, rubbing my wrists to help the blood flow.

Marisol smiles. "Together we rule, divided we fall."

Shock freezes me in place. "You're a *rebel*? But you spoke of them so cruelly, I don't—"

"Once upon a time, I was young and foolish and desperately in love." She pushes me forward, out of the cell, lowering her voice to a whisper as she leads us to the back corner of the dungeons until we're facing what looks like a solid stone wall. "He was a penniless man with no title to his name." She shakes her head. "But I loved him more than anything." She turns toward me then, gripping my shoulders tight. "You asked Ophelia about her family, but you never cared to ask of mine. If you had, you would have learned that my father is a social climber. So…"Tears spring to her eyes. "It should be no surprise he threatened to kill my child in order to keep glory to our name."

My heart clamps down, somersaulting with pain for what she's saying.

"But someone came to my aid and took my precious baby, hiding him deep in the shadows along with the man I loved. He fed them, clothed them, and promised safety as long as I helped usher in a new dawn."

My breathing stutters, hope flaring to life in my chest. "Tristan."

"The scarred prince." She nods. "The rebel king. He saved my family. It was imperative no one knew of our connection. So yes, I said despicable things. But only because my son's life depends on us succeeding. I could not trust you, and therefore, I could not speak."

I open my mouth, my brain trying to catch up and slot the pieces of the puzzle into fresh places. "I—"

She shakes her head. "There is no time for this, milady. You must go. Edward is waiting for you in the black forest. He will take you to the shadowed lands, and you can lead the rebels here to save our king."

"He's alive?" Tears burst from my eyes, and relief drums through my veins until my legs threaten to collapse. "Tristan's alive?"

"He is." She nods, her hand pressing against the stone until a secret passage opens wide. "Now go, before they catch us both."

———

Edward's not alone. Sheina stands next to him, holding my boots, trousers, and black cloak, my daggers lying on top. Emotion swells like a balloon at the sight of her, and I fall into her arms, the clothes dropping into a heap at her feet.

"Shh, milady. Everything will be okay."

"Sheina, I can't—I don't…" My body trembles as I hold her against me.

She strokes my hair, rocking us back and forth, tears streaming down her face as fully as they pour down mine.

"Don't worry, Sara." She pulls my face up to hers. "We will save him."

"Why didn't you tell me?" I whisper. "You could have trusted me."

She smiles. "I could say the same, *best friend.*"

I smirk and move my gaze to Edward, who bows. "Milady."

Stepping in close, I grab his hands. "Tristan trusts you. Can I?"

His jaw ticks, eyes blazing as he bows and kisses the back of my palm. "I swear it."

Nodding, I step back, turning to grab the clothes on the ground, grateful that I can get out of this soiled and torn dress. "Sheina, help me out of this." I twist back to Edward. "And then take me to the rebels."

It's a thirty-minute trek through the forests and back alleys into the shadowed lands, but we make it in one piece. And now I'm in the second story of the Elephant Bones Tavern, staring out the double doors leading to the Juliet balcony, anxiety filling me to the brim as I stare at the hundreds of people standing outside, spread so far, I wonder how many acres they must cover.

"Morale is low," Belinda—the woman I've only seen once before when she rolled a severed head to my feet—hisses as I strap blades to my thigh and take the pistol from Edward's hands and place it in a holster on my side.

She watches me, her gaze wary.

"You don't trust me," I say.

She tilts her head. "You are the king's."

I reach out, placing my hand over hers. "I am *your* king's. And I will save him with or without his people."

Her grin spreads across her rotten teeth and she waves her arm at the door. "Well then, time to convince his people."

My stomach flips, nerves threatening to tear me apart from the inside out, but I swallow them down, closing my eyes and trying to reach through the ether to find Tristan's power and channel it until he infuses my every cell.

With a deep breath, I step through the doors and out onto the balcony.

The air grows still and tense.

I lick my lips as I look out over the rebels, the *jackals*, putting faces to the thought of them for the first time. There are small children staring up with wide eyes, women and men with sorrow in their eyes and exhaustion in their pores.

Ragged and worn but glorious.

These people are the lifeblood of Gloria Terra, just as we are in Silva, and they deserve to be able to live free.

"I am not your king," I start.

"No shit," someone yells out.

My chest tightens. "I'm terrified to be standing before you, so much so that every fiber of me wants to turn around and run away. But your *leader* is in trouble."

Closing my eyes, I picture Tristan, swallowing around the agony that strips me bare at the thought of never seeing him again, never feeling his lips brush against my skin or his love devour me whole. I think of all the whispered secrets he spoke into my soul, of how I was his filthy girl, and how he couldn't wait to see me in a crown and at his side. Of his vision for the future and the memories of his past.

My eyes pop open.

"I don't pretend to know what it is you've gone through, but I've seen struggle and I've known strife." I hesitate. "When I came to Saxum, it was to kill the Faasas, every last one, *including* the scarred prince."

Rumbles sound through the crowd.

"But then I got to know him—" My throat swells. "And he made me believe in a better way."

My eyes scan their faces, noticing Belinda has moved to the front of the crowd down below, Edward and Sheina standing at her side. My eyes lock on my friend, and she nods, giving me strength.

"It's over," a woman says. "They caught him. We've lost."

"You would give up so easily?" I argue. "How many times has he proven himself to you over and over? And yet at the first sign of struggle, you turn your back?"

I shake my head, praying that my words hit their mark. I don't *know* any of this for sure. I'm only going off what Tristan has said, trusting that he speaks the truth.

Belinda steps forward, turning toward the crowd. "He saved me when I went into the castle and was promised certain death."

The rumbles grow louder.

Then Sheina steps forward, and my heart pounds. "He brings you food. He clothes your babes."

Gratefulness wraps around my chest and tugs. "He's risked his life to give you yours," I cut in. "But this isn't just about him. I will get him back with or without your help. This is about standing up and seizing the moment. About vengeance for every time they've killed someone for simply speaking truth. For every curse, every name, every bruised and broken bone as they screamed you weren't worthy."

Faces change in the crowd, an electric feeling pulsing through the air, building higher with each second.

"I'm not great with words," I continue. "I can't wrap the atrocities of what has been and realities of what will come in a pretty bow and make it look like it's in your favor." I slam my fist against my chest. "But together we rule, and divided we fall. I am asking you—*begging* you—to stand with me. There is no one better to lead you than Tristan Faasa. And he deserves your fight, the same way he has *always* fought for you."

Belinda is the first to fall, her head bowed, a loud wail crying from her throat. And then, as if in slow motion, others follow.

One by one, they sink on bended knee, a chant starting slowly. At first, I don't understand what it is they say, but it grows and rolls over the air and hits my chest as surely as if they struck me in the heart.

*"Long live the queen! Long live the queen!"*

Tears spring in my eyes as I look over them, staring down at the people—*my people*—the lifeblood of Gloria Terra, trusting me to lead them to their king.

"We are warriors!" I raise my voice until it's soaring over their heads like arrows. "This is the revolution! And it's time for us to take back our home."

# CHAPTER 52

## *Tristan*

"PSST."

My eyes struggle to open, my head foggy as I come to. And once I do, I wish I hadn't, because there isn't a single piece of me that doesn't ache. My bones feel brittle, my muscles atrophied from lack of use, and I'm quite certain it's been days since I've had a drink of water.

"Tristan," a small voice chokes out, and when I register who it is, then I do force my lids open, staring down into the horrified face of Simon, his toy sword limp at his side and his face scrunched in terror. "What have they done to you?"

My tongue swipes over my chapped lips and my mouth pries itself apart, unsticking my dry tongue from the roof. "Little tiger," I rasp out. "You shouldn't be here."

His eyes glance around the courtyard, the sun setting behind the horizon and casting an orange glow on the ground. I flick my gaze to the guard standing at the side, his eyes looking at Simon and then to me but not moving from his spot.

"Leave, Simon." I try to infuse strength in my voice but come up short.

He hiccups, stepping closer, and when he does, the guard moves too, tightening his grip on the rifle at his side.

"Simon. Leave." Urgency spreads through me.

He shakes his head, big fat tears spilling from his eyes. "I can't... Where's lady? Why isn't she here?" His voice grows manic. "She could save you. Why d-did they do—"

"Simon." Pain tears through my side, the scabbed-over wounds reopening, and I grimace. "Go to your mother, okay? I'll be fine. This is just..."

The guard moves over now, stepping in front of me and blocking my view, and my chest splits open, realizing this is the last time I'll ever see Simon's face. The last time I'll get to hear his voice or tell him he's strong. The last moment that he'll see me and know that I'm *not*.

He doesn't even know we're family.

Simon rages, throwing his toy sword up at the guard. "Unhand him."

The guard chuckles. "Might want to work on that growl, kid. Get out of here. I don't want to hurt you."

Something cracks in the distance, and all our eyes turn toward the noise.

"What was that?" the guard asks.

Another sound, this time closer, and although I can't explain it, a feeling trickles down my spine, infusing me with a bit of strength.

Simon's gaze locks on mine. "I'm going to save you."

Panic wraps around my middle, not knowing what's about to happen but feeling in my gut that whatever it is, it's no place for him to be. "Someone already is," I lie. "Go wait for me in the tunnels, okay?" My voice is breathy and weak. "I'll meet you there."

His lower lip trembles. "Promise?"

"Promise."

---

Something tugs at my wrists, causing the worst physical pain of my life as my arms drop from where they've been hung. My eyes spring open, meeting the silent, pitch-black of the night, and my body drops to the ground.

Delicate hands grab at my face, and I try to shake the fog from my mind so I can focus on what's in front of me.

Something in the air has shifted.

Something has changed.

Water dribbles over me, and I tilt my head back, opening my mouth, gulping the liquid, allowing it to soothe my parched throat and sore muscles. Finally, logic filters back in and Sara's beautiful, perfect features come into my view, looking like an angel of death as she grins.

She's tied her hair in a bun, but curls fall out of the

edges, and there's a deep red line smeared across her cheek that looks a lot like blood.

"Are we in heaven?" I murmur. I try to lift my hand, but agony shoots through my limb.

She grimaces. "No, my love. Right now? We're in hell."

I cringe when she helps pull me to a sitting position, and I shake my head of the haze and glance around. The guard from earlier is dead, sprawled on the ground with a shiny dagger sticking from the front of his throat.

"How?"

"Shh," she whispers, her arms running down my naked chest and over my torn-up body. "I'll have to relocate your shoulders." Her eyes meet mine. "It will hurt."

I manage a soft smirk. "No more than thinking you were dead."

She smiles, leaning in to press a soft kiss against my lips, and with a sharp snap of her body weight, there's an acute, agonizing pain, followed by a dull throb.

Groaning, I sink my teeth into my bottom lip until I taste blood.

"One more time. Ready?"

"Ye—"

She snaps it back into place before I can finish the word, and I let out another groan of pain. Glancing around, she digs a small bottle out of her pocket.

Laudanum. "Are you going to drug me now?"

She lifts a brow. "Just take a little. For the pain."

I grab the bottle and allow the bitter liquid to slide down my throat, and then she helps me to a stand. My body is worn and tired, shaky and bruised. But I'm alive. *She's* alive.

"How is this possible?"

Shouts sound in the distance and she places her hand over mine, looking at me. Fear squeezes my chest. I just got her back; I'm not ready to lose her again.

"Can you run?" she whispers.

I nod, and she pulls me along with her, my muscles screaming in protest and my lungs burning as we sprint from the middle of the court to the far east side, hiding behind a wall that leads into the tunnels.

The courtyard lights flare to life, and dogs bark in the distance, and I know before anything is said that means the military will be flooding here soon. If I hadn't convinced Michael to send away most of his troops, she wouldn't have even made it to me.

"What did you do?" I ask, gripping her face.

"You left the rebellion," she says, smiling up at me. "So I brought the revolution to you."

My heart cracks wide open and I need to kiss her, even though I shouldn't, even though I'm beaten and worn, and I'm sure I smell like death. I bend down anyway, shoving my tongue in her mouth and dragging her into my newly formed scars, reveling in the pain it causes, because if we're going to die, I'll be damned if I don't get to taste her one more time.

Moaning, she gives as good as she gets, and then she breaks away. "I have them in the tunnels."

My stomach cramps. "The rebels?"

She nods. "I wasn't sure if Michael knew of them, but it was our best chance to break into the castle, to make our way here without being shot at and killed. Edward's with them, and they're ready to fight, Tristan. We can *do* this."

I bob my head, taking in her words, even as shouts sound closer now than they were before, and a gunshot rings from outside the castle walls. Any moment now, and we'll be caught.

And then a sick thought hits me and my heart ramps up in my chest, exploding through the cavity as I grip her arm. "Sara."

She looks up at me from where she was peering around the corner.

"Simon is in the tunnels."

Horror overcomes her features, her mouth parting wide and her eyes growing big. "Are you sure?"

"Positive."

"Tristan, you have to get him out."

I shake my head, my jaw tensing as my soul tears in two, fighting between what I know is right and what I refuse to do. "I'm not leaving you here."

She grins, although I see the turmoil brewing in her dark gaze. "Do you think you fell in love with a weak woman?"

My chest pulls, emotion wringing my bones.

"I can take care of myself," she promises, her words tasting like the most bitter type of lie. "Go save your nephew."

My breath whooshes from my lungs. She knows. *Of course she knows.*

Doors from the castle slam open, echoing through the nighttime air, and as I peer around the corner, I see at least two dozen uniforms with dogs pulling at their leashes.

"Sara." A loud voice rings out.

She falters from where she was just pushing at my chest, her eyes narrowing as she spins to face away from me.

"There's no escaping us, sweet niece. Come out and surrender, and we shall grant you mercy."

She moves forward, her anger so potent I can see it singeing off her skin.

"Are you fucking insane?" I snap, grabbing her arm. "Do not go out there."

"We've found all your friends," her uncle continues. "If you both surrender, we'll let them live."

"Go," she demands, prodding at me.

I shake my head back and forth, a ball of absolute terror expanding in my chest, making me hyperventilate as I struggle to breathe.

"Tristan, listen to me," she pleads. "You know the tunnels like the back of your hand. You're the *only* one who does." Her eyes well with tears. "I'll never forgive myself if something happens to him, and even though you won't admit it, neither will you. You have to save him. *Please.*"

Talons rip through my chest cavity and tear out my heart, throwing it on the ground at her feet. I don't bother picking it up, knowing it only beats for her anyway.

My nostrils flare as I grip her face in my hands, my eyes soaking up her features as I rest my forehead against hers. "You are not allowed to die. Do you hear me? I *will* come back for you."

Her lip trembles. "I know."

I pull her close when she tries to turn away, pressing her lips to mine one last time. "If something happens, know that I will find you in every lifetime, Sara Beatreaux. You are mine, and not even death can keep you from me."

She muffles a sob and shoves at my chest, and I turn and run, sprinting toward the tunnels.

# CHAPTER 53

## *Tristan*

IT HAD TO BE ME.

As much as I wanted to sacrifice myself and let her flee in my place, it had to be me. No one knows the tunnels as well as I do. No one else could have gotten Simon out in time.

The military pressed in on the rebels from all angles, and when they were pressured, they panicked, creating a human stampede. I felt the rumbles in the tunnel floors as I sprinted through them, fighting the fatigue and the unbearable pain of my tortured body. I heard the screams as they echoed off the stone walls, people crying as gunshots were fired and they pled for their lives.

But I found him, his arms wrapped around Paul, his leg bent and broken and tear tracks on his face, his mother lying trampled at their feet.

"You came," he whispered. "Just like you promised."

So how could I turn around then? Even if everything in me was screaming to go back to where I left my heart, I grabbed Simon and Paul instead, and I set them free, banishing them from Gloria Terra.

To keep them safe.

It's been three days since, and while my body is sore but healing, my mind is a gutter of a place to live. Michael is taunting me with Sara's captivity. But at least she's alive.

He has publicly stated if I give myself up, turn myself in, he'll let her go.

I'm now an official outlaw. And all the while, the people of Saxum are none the wiser to the truth of what happened. They have no clue people are lying dead in the underground tunnels, their bodies decomposing and their children crying as they search for their missing parents.

I could pretend if I tried, could put on a mask and weep for those we've lost. But I'm tired of playing games, and the only thing I care for is holding Sara in my arms. Until I have her back, nothing else matters.

Besides, out of the grief from those we've lost comes fury.

And my people are *furious*.

Edward heaves a deep sigh as he grabs the joint from my hand and puffs on the end, leaning against the brick wall behind the patisserie in downtown Saxum. "Are you sure you want to do this?"

I cut him a glare. "If I don't, then all your hard work over the past few days is for naught."

Where I've been healing with tinctures and potions to speed my recovery, Edward has been busy whispering words in his soldier's ears. Swaying them to our side. Making sure they know just who it is that they serve. Gathering our forces from every corner and laying out our plans.

"You should take Sheina and leave town," I say. "You've served me well, Edward. I don't wish to see you both perish."

He grits his teeth, shaking his head. "Our loyalty is to you."

"Loyalty means shit," I hiss. "I am trying to spare you, Edward. You're my only friend, and the only one who has stood by me through it all. Please, take this gift and let me do this on my own."

"With all due respect, Your Highness." He straightens. "I'm not leaving until you're either dead or wearing the crown."

Clenching my jaw, I nod, peeking around the corner and seeing there's about a dozen military men laughing and walking into the town's bar. Right on cue. "Are you ready then?" I turn toward him.

"Let's burn it down."

I smirk, grabbing the joint back from his fingers and slipping it in my mouth as I move to the bar across the street. I slam open the green double doors with my boot, the thick wood hitting the walls as I step inside. There's about a dozen people here, most of them the king's military, and all of them with fresh drinks in their hands.

I smile as they turn toward me, my insides feeling empty except for the burning flame of determination. "Hello."

A man at the front of the bar stands, his black stool spinning in place behind him. He creeps his arm toward his waist, reaching toward his weapon.

"Ah, ah, ah," I tsk, walking toward him. "I wouldn't do that if I were you." I grab his wrist and snap it back, the gun flipping from his grip and into my own. "Oops! Would you look at that?" I stare down at the pistol and then back to him.

Another man stands, his brown hair sticking up in random spots and his gray eyes narrowed in disgust. "Do you have a death wish?" He laughs, glancing around. "You must be as crazy as they say, walking into a bar filled with your brother's army."

Chuckles float through the room, and I suck on the end of my joint, letting the smoke unfurl through my nose as a few of them rise and point their guns at my chest. Chairs scrape and there's a flurry of activity, the sound of pistols cocking loud in the otherwise silent space. But instead of aiming them at me, they aim them at the ones who wish to harm me.

"Well, I *am* as crazy as they say. But I also brought reinforcements." Grinning, I throw my hands out to the sides, the pistol heavy as it dangles from my finger. "I suppose I should have led with that."

I point between the four men who are now being held at gunpoint.

"Now." I walk closer, taking the joint from between my lips. "Which one of you wants to be the one who lives?"

They're all silent, obviously afraid to move, to breathe, in fear they'll be shot on the spot. I don't blame them.

They would be.

"I'll tell you what." I clap my hands, ash falling like snowflakes on the floor. "I'll be outside while you decide who gets to be the lucky soldier to take a message back to my brother." I cock my head. "But I should probably warn you, I'm a little antsy. You see, he has something of mine, and I'm *desperate* to get it back."

The man in the very front lifts his chin. "What's the message?"

Sighing, I pinch the bridge of my nose, walking toward him and placing my arm around his shoulders. "Fine." I roll my eyes, dragging him with me to the door. "I pick you."

I wave my hand behind me, and gunshots ring out in tandem, the sound of bodies dropping to the floor following soon after. I don't bother turning to look, but I make a mental note to never torture Edward again after how effortlessly he set up our plans when I wasn't able.

Gripping the man to me tighter, I walk us through the front doors and outside, pointing at Edward, who's in front of the patisserie, then Sheina, who's at the building next to him, and then across the street to Belinda and Earl. "Do you see them?"

His body trembles, but he nods.

"*Good.* Do you know what my favorite part about an ethanol fire is?" I ask, glancing down at the glowing end of my joint.

The uniformed men who are now *my* loyal soldiers leave the bar, walk down the steps, and move to stand behind me.

"Your Highness..." the man says as I spin around to face him.

"It's extremely difficult to put out the blaze," I continue, cocking my head. "You might want to move."

He throws his body forward at the same time as I flick my joint, grinning as it hits the building and catches on fire. I watch the flames, satisfaction brewing in my gut, before twisting to make sure the others have started theirs as well.

They have.

The guy on the ground gapes, wide-eyed at the four burning buildings, smoke curling up in the air as people scream and run outside, trying to escape the fires.

I step closer to him, gazing down as he trembles at my feet. "Tell my brother that if he doesn't give me Sara, I will burn this entire city, this entire *country* to the ground until he has nothing left to rule."

# CHAPTER 54

## *Sara*

THIS TIME, ALTHOUGH I'M STILL IN CHAINS, AT least I'm in a room.

It's been days now. They haven't hurt me physically, in case they need to use me for photos in the press.

They're trying to lure Tristan in by using me as bait.

And through it all, the only thing I can think of is *he's alive*. He made it.

The door to my room opens, Michael and my uncle stepping inside, the way they do every day around this time, just to torment me.

"Sara," Uncle Raf starts. "We don't wish to keep you chained up forever."

"Then kill me," I hiss.

"You are my blood, child. Don't be absurd." He sighs, walking toward me and sitting on the edge of the bed. Hatred burns bright in my chest as he does. "Change is scary, I know. We've lost your cousin and your father, may they rest in peace."

My insides boil at the mention of my father.

"But change is also good," he finishes, leaning in to pat my hand, the chains clanking when he does.

I spit in his face.

Rage twists his features, and he slams his hand against my cheek, his rings cutting across my skin. Smirking, I fling the curls from my eyes and glare at him. "Finally, Uncle. Your true colors show after so many years."

Michael sighs from across the room. "I'm tired of you two bickering. I should kill you just to be rid of it."

"I wish you would," I quip. "If you think Tristan's angry now, just wait until he hears that I'm dead." I smile. "I think I'll come back and haunt the castle walls just to watch the show."

Heavy footsteps make their way down the hall and bang against the door.

"Enter," Michael spits.

A young soldier runs into the room, his brow sweaty and his face pale as if he's seen a ghost. "Your Majesty." He bows. "I have a message." His eyes flicker around the room, hesitating when they land on me. "From your brother."

My heart leaps in my chest.

Michael stands straighter, walking toward the man. "And?"

"He's crazy, sire. He...he's burning *everything*. He sent

me to tell you that he won't stop. Not until you give her back."

Michael's head tilts, growing still and calm. "What do you mean he's 'burning everything'?"

The man's eyes flick to me one more time, and I lean in, something eager swirling through my gut, thinking of Tristan coming to save me. Just like he said he would.

"I mean, the entire main strip of Saxum is gone, sire," he whispers. "And now they've moved on to the eastern end. And the fires…water isn't working. They're spreading fast."

Michael roars, flipping the table next to him, the lamp sliding off the top and smashing to porcelain pieces on the ground. He turns to face me, pointing his thick fingers at me. "This is all your fault."

I grin, my blood heating in my veins. "You reap what you sow, Michael Faasa. May God have mercy on your soul when Tristan gets his hands on you."

Yells sound from down the hall, and Uncle Raf stands from where he was still sitting against the bed. Marisol appears in the open doorway, her cheeks flushed. Hope springs alive in my chest. I wasn't sure if she had survived after freeing me.

She drops into a deep curtsy. "Your Majesty."

"Speak, woman." Michael paces back and forth, wearing a hole through the deep burgundy carpet.

"The castle is on fire."

418 | EMILY MCINTIRE

My arm jostles as Michael throws open the front doors to the courtyard, dragging me along with him.

I glance around, my nerves jittery, but I don't have to look for long.

Because there he is.

Standing like a god in the middle of the court, his hands in his pockets, suspenders hanging off his waist, black sleeves rolled up to his elbows, and a joint between his lips.

My beautiful, scarred prince.

His eyes lock on mine, and a calm takes over. *He came back.*

"Brother," Michael growls from next to me, his fingers tightening on my arm.

Tristan ignores him, his gaze sweeping up and down my body like he's checking for a single scratch. "Are you hurt?"

"No," I reply. "But I wish for you to kill them anyway."

He laughs—a genuine laugh—throwing his head back and cackling, smoke puffing out with his breaths.

"How did you get through the gates?" Uncle Raf steps forward, his cane slapping against the ground as he stops next to me, a few of the military guards following behind him.

"Well, we tried to use the tunnels last time, and that didn't work very well." Tristan smirks.

Uncle Raf's knuckles tighten around the top of his

cane, and he glances to the few guards scattered around the entrance. My eyes move past them, and I can see smoke clouds pluming behind the gates, licks of fire flickering with the wind.

"Call the guards, you imbeciles!" Uncle Raf spits at the soldiers who stand still.

"You could try," Tristan drawls. "But the dead don't often answer calls."

Michael slams me on the ground, and I roll forward, my face smacking against the concrete as my body flings down the cold stone steps until I'm splayed on the grass.

I cry out from the surprise, and when I breathe deep, a sharp pain splices through my side. I glance up and see Tristan's grin drop, his eyes turning feral.

"I warned you once what would happen if you touched her," he says. "I've come to collect."

Michael yells, "I am the *king*! Seize him!"

A few guards start to move but hesitate before stalling once again.

"They no longer answer to you." Tristan's voice is lethal, and as inappropriate as it is, my body heats, arousal curling through me at the power that bleeds through his tone. "And the few who do are smart enough to realize when they're fighting a losing battle. You see, Brother," he continues, moving closer toward us, as if he's taking a casual walk through the court. "While you've spent your years throwing parties and rubbing arms with the men in high places, while you've planned and plotted and *murdered* our father." He pauses, and Michael stiffens. "I was in towns, in people's homes, and in their ears. Showing them a better way. Showing them what would happen if they just pledged their loyalty to *me*."

Michael scoffs. "We killed your pathetic jackals. Their corpses rot in the tunnels as we speak."

Tristan chuckles, twisting as he looks behind him. "You've always underestimated me." And then he raises his hand in the air and flicks his wrist, and the heavy iron gates swing wide, dozens of people storming through them with fury on their faces and jackals patched onto their sleeves.

My chest swells with hope. *Rebels.*

Tristan moves forward, and I surge to my feet, ignoring the pain in my side. He takes giant steps, and he doesn't stop until he reaches me.

The second he touches me, my body comes alive, his arms smoothing up my sides and cupping my face, ignoring everyone. "Let me show you what a *true* revolution looks like," he whispers.

And then he kisses me.

Yells and hollers sound from behind, and chaos breaks out, although I couldn't tell you who was fighting whom. I'm too lost in Tristan's mouth to care.

He breaks away, and I turn just in time to see the castle doors fly off their hinges, Edward, Sheina, and Marisol carrying torches, flames crawling up the walls behind them.

My heart pounds in my chest when I see them, and I bite back a sob, knowing there will be time for emotion later. Because I can feel it even now—we will win.

Tristan runs a hand down my hair before breaking away and moving toward his brother. "Where is our mother? Is she still here? Will I be burning her alive, or do I get the pleasure of chasing her down and snapping her neck?"

Michael shakes his head back and forth, his eyes widening as he stares at the few dead guardsmen at his feet and then swinging his gaze to where Edward is kicking my uncle Raf to his knees, pointing a gun at his head.

"No!" I scream, running over to stand in front of them.

Uncle Raf coughs as he stares up at me. "You've *always* been the smartest child. Thank you."

"Did you kill my father?" I question, my voice low.

His face drops. "Sweet niece, you must understand. I—"

Throwing my palm in the air, I cut him off.

"*Tell* me!" I scream. "Admit it was you. It was you all along. You planned it from the start, didn't you? Killed my father, then sunk your claws into my grief, molding it to fit *your* goals."

His eyes widen. "I've always done *everything* out of love. For our family."

I huff out a laugh, sorrow and anger bludgeoning my insides. "You don't love me. You don't love anyone but yourself."

He coughs again. "*Please…*"

I don't allow him to finish, my fist snaking out and slamming into his face until blood spurts from his nose and he flies onto his back. Reaching over his head, I grab the torch out of Edward's hands, the weight of it comforting as it sits in my hand. And then I drop it on my uncle's chest, watching as the fabrics of his clothes are lit aflame. He screams, a piercing, high-pitched wail, and flies down the stairs, his bum knee making him stumble and fall as he rolls on the ground. But it's no use, and while I watch him burn alive, the blaze engulfing him the same way they're licking at the far castle walls, I feel…empty.

Because as it turns out, there is no happiness in vengeance.

"Milady, we must move!" Edward yells, grabbing my arm and running away from the fire that's now burning around the edges of the door. "Go!"

I glance around, my stomach surging into my chest as I look for Tristan, but he's nowhere to be seen. And neither is Michael.

"Where is he?" I cry, fighting against Edward's hold to find him.

"He's already out of the gates, going after his brother."

I give in then, choosing to believe him, choosing to trust that after everything, after all this, he wouldn't lead me astray.

So I turn, lifting my skirts and running for my life, trying to escape the heat of the burning castle as it rages at my back.

# CHAPTER 55

## *Tristan*

MICHAEL HAS ALWAYS BEEN A COWARD, SO IT isn't surprising when he flees, forcing my battered and still-healing body to chase him around the front of the castle and out to the cliffs. The ocean rages against the rocks below us, and I stalk toward him, feeling for the first time in my life as though he realizes just how powerful I am.

"They'll never let you rule," he sneers. "Not after this."

I chuckle, sauntering forward as he backs up to the cliff's edge. "After what? The fires *you* started as the mad king?"

His face darkens. "They won't believe you."

"I think you'll find that I can be *very* convincing." I step in closer.

His head swings around as he backs up another step, gravel flinging off the ledge and clacking as it bounces on the rocks on the way down.

"All these years." I throw my hands out to my sides. "All the times you could have taken me under your wing and made me someone who worshipped you, but instead, you only made me hate myself."

"You're so dramatic," he scoffs.

"You had *everything*," I hiss. "And all I wanted was a little bit of it too."

His eyes grow wide, his hand slamming against his chest. "I had everything?! You must be out of your mind. Father only ever saw *you*. No matter what I did, it was always *Tristan*. You were the one he loved. I was just an obligation."

I grit my teeth, my heart splitting in two. "You don't get to talk about him. Not when you're responsible for his death."

He scoffs again. "Oh, get over yourself, Brother. You're no different from me. I killed him for the crown, and here you are killing me."

I take another step forward, and he inches back, his foot slipping out from underneath him until he stumbles and falls, his body lying prone on the ground.

My heart lurches violently in my chest. and I rush forward, staring down at him, pathetic and weak. He looks up at me as though I'm in control of what happens next. *This is my chance. The moment I've been waiting for my entire life.*

He tries to move quickly, but I'm faster, my boot slamming down on his throat until he gurgles, pinning him to the dirt floor, his head dangling over the edge of the cliff.

Something explodes from the fire that rages behind me, growing closer every second to where we are. Time is of the essence, or else both of us will die in the flames. Despite that, I can't take my eyes off him. I press forward, my body weight cutting off his air supply, his face turning purple and garish.

"This is a very precarious position we're in, isn't it?" I say, frowning. "A little anticlimactic, but I'll make do with watching you suffocate under the boot of the one you tortured."

Finally, I tear my gaze away, but only when I hear Sara calling my name as she and Edward run out the castle gates. It's just a moment, but that's all it takes, Michael's hands flail, his fingernails digging harshly into my shin, trying to gouge my flesh while he throws me off balance.

Sara screams as I fall to the side, Michael scrambling on top of me. And now it's his hands that are around *my* neck, and my breath being wrought forcefully from my lungs.

I fight, I swear I fight. With everything in me, my arms reach up and I bash my fists into the side of his face. But I've never been stronger than Michael, at least not physically. As my vision starts to blur, the edges growing dark, and my head falls to the side, it's Sara's face that I see, running up behind Michael, her skirts raised high, as she pulls a dagger from her thigh.

"No!" she yells.

Then the pain is gone, and I'm able to suck in lungfuls of air, my eyes bulging and my chest heaving as though I've run across all of Gloria Terra. I roll over onto my hands and knees, coughing and spitting, trying to regain my senses.

I look over and Michael is on his knees, his hands trying to reach his back, blood dribbling from his mouth.

"Brother," he sputters.

Slowly, I stand, my eyes finding Sara immediately from where she's off to the side, a bloody dagger closed in her tight fist.

My lungs are still recovering from the lack of air, but I force myself to move, walking over to where Michael has grown pale, now lying on the ground, the life slowly leaving his eyes.

Part of me wants to let him bleed out, then be consumed by the fires raging just a few short paces behind us. But I won't be satisfied until I know he's gone for good.

I grip him tightly on the arm, dragging his dead weight until my muscles ache, and pull him to the edge of the cliff. He doesn't even fight, already half dead, and surely knowing what's to come.

It's a single kick, the toe of my boot shoving into his side, sending him careening off the edge. I watch his eyes grow wide with his last moment of awareness before he falls, his body crashing on the rocks at the base of the cliff.

When it's high tide, the water will rise and sweep away his remains, and we can go on, pretending as if he were never here.

I blow out a deep breath, searching inside myself for

something to feel. Expecting maybe happiness, relief, or some type of enlightenment. But all I feel is disappointment. I had hoped to torture him for what he did. But I suppose I'll settle for taking his crown.

I spin around, the heat of the fire getting much too close for comfort, Sara and Edward both staring with wide eyes. Moving away from the cliff, I jog over to my little doe, wrapping her in my arms and slamming my mouth to hers, sucking her tongue inside me, my hands groping anywhere they can reach, wanting to assure myself that she's here, and she's real, and she's mine.

"I should kill you for making me leave you here."

She grins against my mouth. "If we don't move, you probably will. What were you thinking, burning everything like this?"

I glance at the Saxum castle, my home for the last twenty-six years and my family's legacy for the last three centuries, and shrug. "They wouldn't give you back."

# CHAPTER 56

## *Sara*

AGAINST ALL ODDS, WE MADE IT.

It's been several weeks since Michael's death. The queen mother's execution is next week, and while normally that would be news, it's overshadowed by the Saxum fires.

They lasted for two weeks before we were able to put them out. The entire city is decimated, half the forest is burned, and the castle itself is destroyed. But the people are resilient and most of all desperate for a leader, someone to step in and rejuvenate their hope. Tristan slid in effortlessly after spinning a tale of his brother, the mad king, who framed him and burned down the city from insanity.

And when Tristan speaks, people listen. They *believe*.

Not that they'd have a choice. The throne defaults to him either way, now that Michael is dead.

None of them need to know it was he who started the flames.

Now, we're at the edge of town, ash still covering the streets, while Tristan holds on to my hand and weaves whispered words of promise to our people.

I look out over the crowd as he speaks and see a flash of red from the corner of my eye. Tilting my head, I squint, realizing there's a young girl standing in the back, a hood over her face and bright red hair peeking from the edges.

Ophelia.

Breaking away from Tristan, I make my way to the back, feeling his eyes on me the entire way, even as he continues to preach to the people. I follow her down a back alley and to the edge of the Fiki River. It runs along the border of Saxum and is used for fishing and leisurely swims, although right now, it's infested with soot, a black layer floating on top of the normally crystal-clear surface.

"Ophelia," I say. I search for my anger when she turns to face me, but I find only sadness. Sorrow that this young girl wasn't who I assumed and empathy for the way her face looks drawn and pale. "Are you all right?"

Tears burst over the lids of her eyes, streaming down her face, her fingers gripping a large boulder to her chest. "I was pregnant," she whispers.

Shock flows through me. "With Michael's child?"

She nods, hiccupping as she covers her mouth with her hand. "But he made me cut it out, s-said one bastard child was enough."

*Simon.* My heart aches, and I take a step toward her.

She glances up at me. "I'm sorry, for what it's worth."

And then she throws herself over the ledge and into the water, her body sinking to the bottom.

My heart jumps into my throat, and for just a moment, I think of trying to save her life. But then I remember all I went through because of her and I peer over the ledge, watching to make sure she drowns instead.

Eventually, the bubbles stop popping on the surface.

Spinning around, I jump when I run into Tristan's broad chest.

"Everything all right?" he asks, wrapping me in his arms.

I smile up at him. "Everything's perfect."

He leans down and kisses me before moving his lips to my ear. "Is she dead?"

Nodding against him, he thrusts his erection into me, and I scoff, shoving him in the chest.

He chuckles, his hand smoothing from my waist down until he grips my ass. "Such a bad girl, watching a woman drown while I'm steps away promising the people their future." He presses his lips to mine again, and I moan into his mouth, happiness suffusing through my every pore.

Through it all, we survived. Even though we've suffered substantial loss and even though our souls are stained in black, Tristan somehow makes me feel like the luckiest girl in the world.

And I guess, in a way, I am.

Because my heart belongs to the scarred prince.

The rebels' savior.

The crowned king of Gloria Terra.

And he made *me* queen of the ashes.

# EPILOGUE

*Tristan*

*Seven Years Later*

"TRISTAN," SARA MOANS. "THE PEOPLE ARE waiting."

"So let them wait," I whisper in her ear.

She's pushed up against the hallway wall, her skirt around her waist, my cock bobbing free as it slides between her creamy, pale thighs, making me crazy with the need to sink inside her. And I do. I drive myself deep into her warm, wet hole and start thrusting, desperate to fuck her harder.

Arousal spreads through my nerves until I can't see straight, love and lust exploding through my pores as my dick spears between her legs, glistening with *her* every time I pull out.

"Your pussy is a thirsty girl, isn't she?" I rasp against her, my hand wrapping around her throat and squeezing.

"When I don't have to rule this place anymore, I'm going to spend every single second of the day buried deep inside her, feeding her what she craves."

Sara moans again, her hands falling to the wall as she pushes back against me, grinding herself on my shaft as she works to get herself off.

"That's right, filthy girl." My hand cracks against her ass cheek, the sound reverberating off the high archways of the hall. "Work that pussy on my dick until you come."

Her walls flutter around my length, milking my every ridge until my orgasm tears through me, shooting deep inside her, and she—the *wretched* witch that she is—spins around midway through, my cock pulsing into the air as I groan at the loss of heat. But then she drops to her knees, her perfect little mouth opening wide and her warm hand wrapping around my thickness, stroking until she drains every drop onto the flat of her tongue.

She smiles and swallows, stuffing me back into my pants and righting her skirts.

Winking, she stands up, running her hand over the jeweled tiara on her head. "Come on, we're late. Marisol's going to murder you if my outfit is a mess."

She moves to walk in front of me, but I reach out, gripping her by her hair and pulling her back until her body slams into mine. I dive down, claiming her mouth, our tongues swirling together and my hands grabbing any part of her they can reach.

Years later, and it never changes. This need for her never goes away.

We've rebuilt Saxum from the ground up. New buildings and a new castle we've called home for the past three years. And we've spread the wealth throughout Gloria Terra, ensuring there aren't people struggling for food while others have feasts.

I'm proud of what we've accomplished.

But I would burn it all down again in a heartbeat at the first threat of losing her.

My need to prove my place in this world has shifted and changed over the years, but the one constant has *always* been her.

We walk down the hall of our home and open up the double-paned doors, stepping outside onto the large balcony and staring down at our people.

Cheers rise from the crowd, and Sara bounces on her toes, her smile lighting up with the biggest grin I've seen in months.

"Are you excited, little doe?"

"No." She shakes her head.

"*Ma petite menteuse.*" I grin. "You still think I don't know you?" I pull her to me, not caring that we're in front of thousands of eyes.

They all know their king is wild for his queen. Let them see just how much.

"I know what your every breath feels like as though

it is my own." Her eyes flutter, and I trail my fingertips down her collarbone. "I know what every heartbeat sounds like because I've caused them all under my hand." I slip my touch even farther down, pressing between her thighs, right against that tattoo I promised I would give her. *Tristan's Property* written on her for the rest of our days.

And when we die, I'll hunt her down in the afterlife and figure out a way to brand her soul.

"It's okay to be excited, little doe." I kiss her forehead and slip my hand into hers, tangling our fingers and turning to face our people.

The sun is shining bright today, and I glance around the balcony, Edward and Sheina off to the side, their three-year-old son beaming up at me from where he's locked in Edward's hold. And then to the other side, to two newcomers, ones who Sara goes to stand next to while I turn and speak.

Blowing out a deep breath, I stare out at all the faces, reminiscing once more about all the things we've accomplished the past several years and all the ways it turned out to be better than even my wildest dreams. A deep sense of contentment settles in my chest, and I glance behind me, soaking in Sara's gaze, letting her infuse me with the strength to say what needs to be said.

This is all for her anyway.

She is my past, present, and future. She's the only thing I see.

And this is what she wants, so I'll give it to her.

Because if I'm honest, it's what Gloria Terra deserves.

"Friends," I start, twisting back around to stare out at all the adoring faces beneath us. "It has been my greatest honor serving as your king. Rebuilding our home and fixing what has been broken for far too long."

Cheers surge through the crowd and whisk through my body, electrifying me from the inside out. I'll miss this part the most.

"But today is a joyous day!"

I wave my arm to the side, toward where Sara is beaming at the two newcomers as though they're her long-lost friends.

And I guess, technically, they are.

Paul Wartheg, aged and smiling, prods at the back of the person next to him, pushing him forward with tears in his eyes.

Simon walks toward me, only stopping once he reaches my side.

I take a long moment to soak him in. He matches me in height, his amber eyes far less innocent than they were when I sent him away all those years ago. But his smile is just as bright, and he draws me into a hug before I can stop him, his arms wrapping around my shoulders and gripping me tight.

"Hello, Uncle," he says, his voice a deep timbre similar to his father's.

Something warm expands through my chest as I pull back and smile. "Hello, little tiger."

I turn to Sara, and she twists to grab something from behind her, walking it over and curtsying as she holds it out toward him. It's a sword. A real one this time, sparkling with jewels and encrusted with diamonds. It belonged to my father and his father before him.

Simon reaches out to take it, every inch of his smooth brown skin covered in dark tattoos. Just the way he always wanted.

Glancing over at me, he smiles.

People in the crowd gasp, confused murmurs racing through the air.

I turn back toward the crowd. "I'd like to introduce you all to Simon Bartholomew Faasa. Son of King Michael III. Rightful heir to the throne of Gloria Terra."

Reaching up, I take the crown off my head and place it on top of his.

"And the one true king."

# EXTENDED EPILOGUE

## Tristan/Sara

*Tristan*

INTERVIEWS.

It's something I have no interest in doing, but Simon begged for Sara and me to make an appearance. *"Uncle, please. Come fully into the twentieth century with the rest of us."*

Still, I refused. I have no urge to speak with reporters. Nothing that could possibly be happening in my life that I feel is any of their or the people's business. I've done my part for Gloria Terra, more than I ever wanted to if we're being completely honest, and now that I've accomplished what I set out to do, I want to spend my time basking in everything that is my little doe.

But being here makes Simon happy, which makes Sara happy. And whatever Sara wishes for, she gets.

Simon knows it too. He only has to go to his *lady* for

me to give in. It's rare he'll ever come straight to me for anything these days, not that he needs to. Although I'll never admit it out loud, he's done a far better job of ruling the kingdom than I ever did.

Truth be told, I've never cared much for what happens to others, my goal was always to simply take the throne for myself because I deserved it. Because people should *revere* me instead of mocking me the way they did while I was growing up.

And Simon has qualities that I lack.

Empathy.

A moral goodness that skipped over my generation. He isn't sunshine and rainbows by any stretch of the imagination, but people manifest trauma in different ways, and while Simon has maintained his innate goodness, he's rough around the edges. Long gone is the little tiger I used to know, and a fierce king was born into his place. He's never talked about his time away—the time that I *sent* him away—but I know demons when I see them, and Simon has several to keep him warm through the cold winter nights.

He's a better man than I am.

He keeps his nightmares at bay. *Usually.*

I'm still around for whenever he has need of me, but as the years drag on, the calls to court have become less and less, until Sara and I have been perpetual ghosts, lingering in the dark. It's the way I prefer it.

Even though living life in the shadows is much different now than it was a decade ago.

The 1920s have changed the foundation of society to something it's never been before, and while I do enjoy the new developments and technological advances, I can't say I enjoy being thrust in the limelight.

Once upon a time that was my goal, but these days, I just want solitude and Sara.

"Your Royal Highness," the reporter bows before sitting down across from me in his tweed suit, twiddling a pen in his hand.

I lean back, enjoying his discomfort, lighting the end of my joint with the lighter Sara bought me as a birthday gift, before reaching over and tangling my fingers with hers, settling our hands nicely in the center of my lap.

The reporter is a scrawny fellow, his brown hair greased back and round spectacles on his face. They remind me of Xander. Disgust curdles through my middle.

He wades through the preapproved questions, Sara jumping in to reply far more than me, and with every question she answers, he grows a little more in tune with her. His eyes sparkle a little brighter. His smile deepens into something more.

Something I don't like.

My gaze narrows as his flicks down from her face, coasting over the swells of her breasts that peek out ever so subtly from her dress, after she raves to him of the new era and how Simon is ushering in great things for our people. Irritation bursts through my chest and spreads through my veins at the disrespect. I lean back farther in my chair, splaying my legs in front of me and bringing the joint to my lips, inhaling the smoke slowly. I move Sara's hand from mine, and then reach over, grasping the top of her thigh, squeezing until her body jolts the smallest bit.

Improper?

Undoubtedly.

But Sara is mine and if I have to claim her in front of a thousand people, let alone a nobody reporter, I'll do it.

"So tell me," the reporter clears his throat, his eyes following the movement of my hand. "What is it that the infamous Prince Tristan Faasa and Princess Sara Faasa do with their time?"

She glances over to me a small smile lining her perfect face. I tighten my grip, the insides of my fingers brushing back and forth against her thigh.

My cock twitches thinking about how I had her on every surface of our estate before making our way here— how my cum is still dripping down the inside of her leg, bleeding out from her cunt where I filled her up until she wouldn't be able to move without feeling me.

"Don't be shy, *ma petite menteuse*," I rumble, smirking at her. "Tell the man what we were doing before you dragged me here."

Her curly hair bounces as she shakes her head and

laughs. "Tristan and I find plenty of ways to pass the time. Mainly, we enjoy taking in how His Majesty has continued our work of ensuring Gloria Terra prospers, and *we* continue to help in that regard whenever and wherever we can."

The reporter's eyebrows lift. "Oh?"

She grins, and my hand tightens. "Yes, of course. If we aren't at home, we're traveling to regions on the outskirts, making sure their grievances are heard so we can bring them back to His Majesty and ensure *all* our people are taken care of." Sara turns toward me, her dark eyes flickering with pride. "Anything you'd like to add?"

Nodding, I agree with her. "I'm very proud to call the King family."

The reporter's face changes then, a wicked gleam coasting over his features, and he leans forward, his chair creaking from the movement. "But between us, he *isn't* your family...not fully anyway, is he?"

Sara stiffens and my teeth dig into the side of my cheek. I lean back, a smile gracing my face as I place the butt of the joint down on the ashtray to my left.

This pathetic excuse of a man was already treading on thin water with me from the way he thought he had the *right* to look at Sara, but now he's going to die.

Having Sara didn't soften me. Gaining a family did nothing to temper the blackness that oozes between the cracks of my stitched-up soul. And when someone deserves death for their disrespect, I feel giddy with the chance to give them their comeuppance.

"You'd do well to watch your mouth when it comes to speaking of His Majesty," Sara spits, her gaze soaring across the room and cutting into the man like razors. "You could be hung for treason…or worse."

I harden as I watch her. Her violence always has turned me on and made me ravenous. I think I'll fuck her in the automobile on the way home, let her take her aggression out as she rides my cock in the backseat.

My head leans to the side, and I run my fingers down the front of my suit and address the man. "I'm quite sure I don't know what you mean."

"Well, I mean…technically speaking, he's the basta—"

I shoot out of my seat quickly, my rings clacking as I grip his face between my fingers and squeeze until his lips mash together. Leaning in, I speak against his ear. "Think very carefully about your next words. My wife is correct. Not only is it treason, but on a *personal* level, I'll take offense."

His body trembles as I step back, loosening my grip slightly on his face. The room is quiet except for the rustle of Sara's skirts as she moves to stand beside me. She places her hand on my arm and I glance over at her, fire thrumming through my veins, *needing* to end this man's life.

"Tristan, not here," she whispers.

My jaw clenches and I squeeze the reporter's face tighter in my hands until I'm sure I'll leave bruises, and then begrudgingly I release him, allowing him to fall back into his chair with a plop. I turn and grab Sara by the back of her neck and drag her into me, melding our lips together and snaking out my tongue to tangle with hers.

Even after all these years, she tastes like everything good. She tastes like *mine*.

Breaking away, I close my eyes and rest my forehead against hers, keeping my hand clasped around her. Violence thrums through me to the heightened beat of my heart. "Be a good girl, *ma petite menteuse*, and go wait outside with Edward and your guards for me. I'd rather you not see what happens to the fools who dare to disrespect us."

She stares at me for long moments, and I keep her gaze. After a moment she nods, certainly realizing that she won't win if she fights me on this. She leans in and presses a chaste kiss to my lips before spinning around and letting her personal guards lead her out of the door.

A thin smile spreads across my face as I turn back to the pathetic man who dared to call my nephew a bastard and think he could stare at Sara with repercussions.

It's been a long time since I've had the outlet for my darker tendencies anyway. This will be a *treat*.

*Sara*

THERE'S SMALL SPLATTERS OF BLOOD ON the cuff of Tristan's suit, but my eyes are only on it for a moment before he's inside the automobile and reaching out to grasp me roughly again behind the neck. He drags me into him until our bodies are plastered together. Awkward in the small space but not the first time he's taken me in the back of our vehicle.

We're in a deserted area on the outskirts of Saxum, no one is around to see, but even if they were, I hardly think I'd be able to find it in me to care. My adrenaline is running too high, my need for him is too strong.

Like it always is.

I moan when his teeth bite into my lower lip.

Do I think that reporter deserved to die?

Not truly.

But over the years, I've found it increasingly difficult to care. People are quick to whisper behind Simon's back, regardless of the fact he's their king, and Tristan's steadfast loyalty to our nephew does nothing but make me love him more.

It's quite attractive.

I wrap my arms around Tristan's neck, letting my nails dig into his skin until I feel it break, and he slams me back until I'm flat against the seats.

"Let me inside of you, little doe. I want the world to hear you scream."

My stomach tightens in anticipation as I fumble with the buttons on his trousers until he's popping out, hard and ready, the tip of him leaking with excitement.

He pushes up my skirt and rips my underwear from between my legs and my fingers wrap around his thick shaft, pulling him closer, needing him to fill me up.

You'd think after so many years that the urge would die down, that this incessant need would cease to be so completely overwhelming, but it hasn't. If anything, it's the opposite.

Being with Tristan is like breathing.

It's intrinsic. Effortless. He's the other half of my soul, intertwined so tightly that his flawed parts fit my missing pieces. If I don't have him then I don't have myself. Nothing besides that matters.

He thrusts violently, aggressively, as if he can't stand the thought of *not* being inside of me for another second. I suck in a harsh breath at the way his cock hits every single inch of my insides so perfectly and I lift my hips when he pulls back, needing to feel him again. We start a punishing rhythm, a give and take, and I'm sure he's speaking terribly naughty things in my ear, but I'm so lost in the pleasure that it's difficult to focus on what they are. I'm wound so tightly that I know it will only take moments for me to come.

His hand wraps around the back of my curly strands of hair and tugs harshly. "That's right, filthy girl, drench my cock. Give it to me like a good little wife."

That's all I need, and before I can stop it, I'm falling, clenching around him while I fly apart into a thousand different pieces and hope he's there to put me back together again.

He follows soon after, the spasms of his bare cock sending me into another bout of ecstasy as he groans deeply in my ear and collapses on top of me.

Our tryst was quick and dirty, the way they often are, and just the way I like. I know he'll take his time with me once we're back home at the countryside estate. The same one his mother was in before he put her to death.

Slowly, he pulls himself out, tucking himself back into his trousers. But he doesn't clean me up, choosing to leave his cum dripping out of me the same way he did earlier before we went to the interview.

He isn't worried about getting me pregnant. It hasn't happened yet, and for all intents and purposes I don't think it will. Some things aren't in the cards for people, and I've never ached for a child the way other women do.

My love is reserved for my husband, and our nephew, and the people of Gloria Terra.

And one day, after we're both dead and gone, we'll get buried in the earth next to each other, and become the soil that nurtures the grass, which grows the crops that feed the people.

Even in death, we'll continue to prosper.

And that's enough for me.

# *Character Profiles*

## Tristan Faasa

**Name:** Tristan "the Scarred Prince" Faasa

**Age:** 26

**Place of birth:** Saxum, Gloria Terra

**Current location:** Saxum, Gloria Terra

**Education:** Well educated

**Occupation:** Prince

**Income:** Extreme wealth

**Eye color:** Jade-green eyes

**Hair style:** Black hair, slightly messy

**Body build:** Tall and lean

**Preferred style of outfit:** Fitting in the Edwardian era, always wearing suspenders

**Glasses?** No

**Any accessories they always have?** A rolled cigarette/joint

**Level of grooming:** Well groomed from circumstance but disheveled

**Health:** Healthy

**Handwriting style:** Small and perfect cursive

**How do they walk:** With confidence, a swagger

**How do they speak:** Charming and manipulative, cutting when angry

**Style of speech:** Proper

**Accent:** Posh accent, British (although this takes place in a fictional land)

**Posture:** Perfect

**Do they gesture?** Every movement is controlled, so only when he wishes to

**Eye contact:** Always

**Preferred curse word:** Cunt

**Catch phrase?** *Ma petite menteuse*

**Speech impediments?** No

**What's laugh like:** Deep and dangerous

**What do they find funny?** Making Sara angry

**Describe smile:** Perfect smile, charming

**How emotive:** Very guarded

**Type of childhood:** Lived in the shadow of his brother; never good enough, bullied mercilessly

**Involved in school?** He was privately tutored

**Jobs:** Was always a prince

**Dream job as a child:** Wanted to be king like his father

**Role models growing up:** His father

**Greatest regret:** Letting his father be murdered

**Hobbies growing up:** Drawing

**Favorite place as a child:** The edge of the cliff at the back of the castle where his father would take him

**Earliest memory:** He tries not to think about his childhood

**Saddest memory:** The memory of getting his scar

**Happiest memory:** Killing his brother and getting Sara back

**Any skeletons in the closet?** Secret leader of the rebellion against the king

**If they could change one thing from their past, what would it be?** Allowing his brother to torment him as often as he did

**Describe major turning points in their childhood:** His father stopping their one-on-one time to focus on raising Michael well enough to be king; the night he got his scar; all the bullying from his brother and friends

**Three adjectives to describe personality:** Manipulative, cunning, dangerous

**What advice would they give to their younger self?** Stand up for yourself instead of bottling emotions

**Criminal record?** No, he is above the law

**Father**

    **Age:** Deceased

    **Occupation:** King of Gloria Terra

    **What's their relationship with character like?** Was a great relationship when he was a boy, and as he grew older, it became strained; he felt like he was never good enough for his father's attention

**Mother**

>    **Age:** 45
>
>    **Occupation:** Queen Dowager
>
>    **What's their relationship with character like?** Strained, not a close relationship by any stretch of the imagination. She's never been there for him and he can't stand how she plays the games of the court

**Any siblings?** An older brother

**Closest friends:** Edward

**Enemies:** His brother and numerous others

**How are they perceived by strangers?** Intimidating and dangerous, a rebel, weird

**Any social media?** No, social media didn't exist

**Role in group dynamic:** Leader

**Who they depend on most:** Edward and the rebels, although he'd say nobody but himself

**Who they depend on for:**

>    **Practical advice:** Edward
>
>    **Mentoring:** His father and then no one
>
>    **Wingman:** Edward
>
>    **Emotional support:** No one
>
>    **Moral support:** No one

**What do they do on rainy days?** Draws

**Book smart or street smart?** Both

**Optimist, pessimist, realist:** Realist

**Introvert or extrovert:** Introvert with the ability to pretend he's an extrovert when necessary

**Favorite sound:** Charcoal on paper

**What do they want most?** The crown

**Biggest flaw:** His inability to let go of the trauma from his past, which causes him to hold on to grudges and blindly torture and kill anyone he thinks might cross him or disrespect him

**Biggest strength:** His ability to manipulate people

**Biggest accomplishment:** Becoming king

**What's their idea of perfect happiness?** Making Sara happy

**Do they want to be remembered?** Yes

**How do they approach:**

    **Power:** Demands it

    **Ambition:** Aggressively ambitious

    **Love:** Once he meets Sara, he's obsessed

    **Change:** Adapts to it

**Possession they would rescue from burning home:** His sketchbook

**What makes them angry?** Everything

**How is their moral compass, and what would it take to break it?** Nonexistent

**Pet peeves:** Disrespect

**What would they have written on their tombstone?**
Together we rule, divided we fall.

**Their story goal:** Tristan starts off as a severely neglected and bullied child who grows into a man set on revenge. He's an outcast, a loner, yet he knows just how to speak to get people to believe in whatever cause he's pushing. When he meets Sara, his world tilts on its axis. He will learn that sometimes love overpowers everything else, that revenge against those who wronged you and unmitigated power over everyone and everything isn't what will bring happiness or peace. In the end of the story, he will come full circle, maintaining his darkness and his persona, yet realizing that some things are more important than power, more than prestige. He will end the story by giving Simon (who he sees so much of himself in) the life he always longed for and the type of recognition he wished his father would have given him. Tristan's love for Sara overshadows everything he once ached for, and he will abdicate the throne after fulfilling what he believes was his prophecy. He's proven himself and now has nothing left to gain from something that doesn't matter to him as much as she does.

## Sara Beatreaux

**Name:** Sara Beatreaux

**Age:** 21

**Place of birth:** Silva, Gloria Terra

**Current location:** Saxum, Gloria Terra

**Education:** Regular schooling

**Occupation:** Daughter of a duke

**Income:** N/A

**Eye color:** Brown

**Hair style:** Long and curly

**Body build:** Petite

**Distinguishing features:** Her hair and her smile

**Preferred style of outfit:** Her dark trousers and hooded cloak

**Glasses?** No

**Any accessories they always have?** A thigh dagger

**Level of grooming:** High

**Health:** Healthy

**Handwriting style:** Slightly messy cursive

**How do they walk?** Regal and with purpose

**How do they speak?** Proper

**Style of speech:** Proper

**Accent:** British, although this takes place in a fictional land

**Posture:** Great

**Do they gesture?** Yes

**Eye contact:** Almost always

**Preferred curse word:** Doesn't have one

**Catch phrase?** N/A

**Speech impediments?** No

**What's laugh like?** Soft and melodic

**What do they find funny?** She likes banter and smart wit; she has a dry sense of humor

**Describe smile:** Wide smile that shows all her teeth and lights up her entire face

**How emotive:** Very but she's learned to control it

**Type of childhood:** Good childhood; loved by her father, her mother never cared

**Involved in school?** No

**Jobs:** Never worked

**Dream job as a child:** She didn't dream of having a job

**Role models growing up:** Her father

**Greatest regret:** Letting her father go to Saxum, where he was murdered

**Hobbies growing up:** She loved to learn how to fight and spar with the men in her family

**Favorite place as a child:** In the library with her father

**Earliest memory:** Her father reading with her in his study

**Saddest memory:** Learning that her father was dead

**Happiest memory:** When Tristan survived his torture and escaped

**Any skeletons in the closet?** Yes

**If they could change one thing from their past, what would it be?** Allowing herself to be manipulated by everyone around her

**Describe major turning points in their childhood:** Father's death

**Three adjectives to describe personality:** Charming, smart, cunning

**What advice would they give to their younger self?** Learn to think for yourself and look at every angle before blindly siding with something

**Criminal record?** No

**Father**

    **Age:** Deceased

    **Occupation:** Was a Duke

    **What's their relationship with character like:** Great relationship; they were very close.

**Mother**

    **Age:** 38

    **Occupation:** Doesn't work

    **What's their relationship with character like:** Nonexistent—she doesn't enjoy her daughter, so they never had a relationship growing up; Mother was the silent and stony type

**Any siblings?** No, only child

**Closest friends:** Sheina

**Enemies:** Faasa family

**How are they perceived by strangers?** Attractive, joyful, regal

**Any social media?** No, social media doesn't exist

**Role in group dynamic:** Follower (although she's only putting on an act)

**Who do they depend on for:**

    **Practical Advice:** Her uncle

    **Mentoring:** Her uncle

    **Wingman:** Sheina

    **Emotional Support:** Sheina

    **Moral Support:** Sheina

**What do they do on rainy days?** Read

**Book smart or street smart?** Street smart

**Optimist, pessimist, realist:** Realist

**Introvert or extrovert:** Extrovert

**Favorite sound:** The sound of her father's carriage coming home

**What do they want most?** Revenge for her father's death and justice for the people of Gloria Terra

**Biggest flaw:** Trusts blindly and allows herself to be manipulated

**Biggest strength:** Her loyalty

**Biggest accomplishment:** Becoming betrothed to the king

**What's their idea of perfect happiness:** Someone who puts her and what she wants first

**Do they want to be remembered?** No

**How do they approach:**

> **Power:** Attracted to it
>
> **Ambition:** Seeks it
>
> **Love:** No time for it
>
> **Change:** Isn't bothered by it

**Possession they would rescue from burning home:** Her dagger and her cloak

**What makes them angry?** Her people starving and wasting away

**How is their moral compass, and what would it take to break it?** Bendable—her loyalty to someone would break it

**Pet peeves:** Bullying people because they're different

**What would they have written on their tombstone?** Queen of the people.

**Story goal:** Sara starts out as a young woman who has been molded into the perfect weapon by her uncle. She is blood thirsty and aching for revenge, grief clouding her logic for both the death of her father and the absolute tatters that her people are in due to negligence from the Faasa family. She has no time for love, but she does have blind loyalty and is on a mission. When she meets Tristan, she will fall for the first time, and through her falling for someone she knows she shouldn't, she will open her eyes and start to question everything around her. She'll realize that not everything is black and white and that you can't always trust what and who people say they are, that people will use and discard you even when you thought their love was pure. She learns that blind loyalty gets you nowhere and that the only person you can truly depend on is yourself and your gut instinct. She will realize that every story has more than one side and in that will grow into the true queen who can temper a dark king with her love and help her people prosper.

# THANK YOU FOR READING!

Enjoy *Scarred*? Please consider taking a second to leave a review!
Come chat about what you read!
Join the McIncult (Facebook Group) at
facebook.com/groups/mcincult.

# JOIN THE MCINCULT!

EmilyMcIntire.com

**The McIncult (Facebook Group):** facebook.com/groups/
mcincult. Where you can chat all things Emily. First looks,
exclusive giveaways, and the best place to connect with
me!

**TikTok:** tiktok.com/@authoremilymcintire

**Instagram:** instagram.com/itsemilymcintire/

**Facebook:** facebook.com/authoremilymcintire

**Pinterest:** pinterest.com/itsemilymcintire/

**Goodreads:** goodreads.com/author/show/20245445.
Emily_McIntire

**BookBub:** bookbub.com/profile/emily-mcintire

# *Acknowledgments*

To my husband, Mike: The man who does everything behind the scenes. Stickers, merchandise, baby duty, dish duty, dinner duty, working out plots, and supporting me while I live my dream. I love you. Thank you for loving me too.

To my best friend, Sav R. Miller: You already know and I say the same thing in every book. Thank you for being my rock. Here's to the smokies. Love you and wouldn't want to do this without you.

To my team: You all make my books (and my life) pretty and ready for the masses. Thank you so much for everything you do.

To the McIncult: Thank you for being my biggest supporters and loving the words I write. All this is possible because of you.

To *all* my readers, new and the OGs: Thank you for

taking a chance and picking up my books. For reading until the end and making my dreams come true.

And last but certainly not least, to my daughter, Melody: You are now and always will be the reason for everything.

## *About the Author*

Emily McIntire is an international and Amazon top-15 bestselling author known for her Never After series, where she gives our favorite villains their happily ever afters. With books that range from small town to dark romance, she doesn't like to box herself into one type of story, but at the core of all her novels is soul-deep love. When she's not writing, you can find her waiting on her long-lost Hogwarts letter, enjoying her family, or lost between the pages of a good book.